WHAT BOOKS PRESS

AN IMPRINT OF

THE GLASS TABLE

COLLECTIVE

LOS ANGELES

ALSO BY A.W. DEANNUNTIS

Master Siger's Dream

THE MERMAID AT THE AMERICANA ARMS MOTEL

A NOVEL

A.W. DEANNUNTIS

LOS ANGELES

Throughout the composition of this novel, Tom Micchelli provided constant insight, unflagging encouragement and patient support, for which the author offers thanks.

A portion of this novel appeared in somewhat different form in the *Cimarron Review*, for which the author offers thanks.

A portion of this novel was completed while the author was in-residence at Mercyhurst College in Erie, Pennsylvania during the Summer Writer's Program held under the direction of Jack (W. S.) Kuniczak, a fine and good man, for which the author offers thanks.

A portion of this novel was completed with the inspiration of Bob Loy, for which the author offers thanks.

Publisher's Cataloging-In-Publication Data
DeAnnuntis, A. W.
  The mermaid at the Americana Arms Motel : a novel / A. W. Deannuntis.
    p. ; cm.
  ISBN-13: 978-0-9845782-3-8
  ISBN-10: 0-9845782-3-4
  1. Painters--Europe--20th century--Fiction. 2. Art and society--Europe--20th century--Fiction. 3. Art and business--21st century--Fiction. 4. Art--Philosophy--Fiction. 5. Europe--History--20th century--Fiction. 6. Art teachers--United States--Fiction. 7. Didactic fiction. I. Title.

PS3604.E16 M47 2011
813/.6   2011914294

What Books Press
10401 Venice Boulevard, no. 437
Los Angeles, California 90034

WHATBOOKSPRESS.COM

Distributed by Small Press Distribution, at spd.org

Cover art: Gronk, untitled, mixed media on paper, 2011
Book design by Ashlee Goodwin, Fleuron Press.

THE MERMAID AT THE AMERICANA ARMS MOTEL

A NOVEL

for Mary,
and for Bob Loy, with thanks

CHAPTER ONE

DONALD HAS NOT come here to tell me this story.

Beside us the blue swimming pool mirrors the infinite sky. The light is white, it dances like crystals, like stars, on razor thin ripples that race across the water, casting off silver sparks that pierce my eyes. It is late, the sun is low, but it burns.

Sheltered by his sunglasses, Donald has become gloomy. He seemed cheerful enough when he arrived. Perhaps it is his big, bony hands which are gloomy. The heat, perhaps, and the wine, perhaps, have made them gloomy.

This stainless afternoon I feel better than I have in several days. The wine and the sun take away pain. The pain in my shoulder and the throbbing of my leg, all of it evaporates with wine and sunshine. Yet it seems the lighter I feel, the more burdened Donald's hands become. As if the tendons of his fingers strain against my weight.

But that has nothing to do with Donald's story or why he tells it. And yet as I observe his gloom, the depression of his hands, I am grateful for it.

He volunteers his story and I am not certain why. An insect, some sort of beetle, crawls slowly across our white metal table. Draped in bright silence we have watched its small shell shimmer with iridescence. The sunlight, as if striking raw steel, leaves after-images of yellow and blue and white, bright as flaming phosphorus. The insect labors anciently, its tiny legs move slowly. Suncleansed and silent, Donald and I have continued to watch. The insect does not hear the passage of time, that minute tremble of a beating heart.

I suppose he tells his story from boredom. He is here because of what I can no longer do. He assists me in not painting and we are not painting again today. Sometimes he asks questions, occasionally he makes notes. Certainly he would rather be somewhere else. But he is here and time burdens his hands as a terrible weight. One day before I die I will paint a great canvas of Donald's large bony hands carrying a millstone shaped like a man.

Stories are our protection against solitude. He and I are alone, this concrete sundeck around the swimming pool is abandoned to our silence. Within the individual apartments of the building surrounding us like a bastion, life continues. We impinge upon no consciousness, attract no attention, deflect no purpose. The sunlight is entirely ours and we need share it with no one.

His folded hands sit firmly on the table. Even tainted by their gloom they radiate strength. His large hands are poised, elegant as toads. Above them his face looms. His sunglasses, insect-like, successfully disguise sentience, his broad, brown mustaches in place of mandibles. My pain has seeped slowly into him and he reacts without recognizing it. Even as it diseases his dreams and troubles his ease, its source is an annoying mystery. But the young are strong enough to carry even great burdens.

He leans back and sighs, a gust of frustration or resignation; perhaps those are the same to him. Tall, slim and broad-shouldered, scare-less and clear-eyed, straight white teeth and a laugh like a breeze at dawn, a smile as open as a pie, and he is not yet thirty. He is here, he thinks, and he will remain here for a long time. He cracks his knuckles with loud pops whose sound reverberates across the pool like that of breaking bones. My arthritic hands twitch with assumed pain. I want my bones to be soft enough so that I may casually crack my knuckles. Youth is enviable because it is undeserved.

Unprompted I refill his glass. My stupid hand trembles, some wine spills on the table. A puddle forms beside the insect, it turns, slow legs moving, poises over it.

"This is a funny story about my Dad. He dug a swimming pool." Donald points his thumb over his shoulder. "Not as big as this one, but big. Do you understand this? To build a swimming pool? No, you can't. On a quarter-acre lot. Before he started it was all nice and green with bushes and everything. One night he went into the yard and dug himself a swimming pool. Got this thing into his head; who knows where it came from. He wanted a damn pool and he didn't have any money for it. So he just got his shovel and dug. You can't understand this, really. Foreigners find this difficult to understand, no offense. I was maybe twelve years old. One night right after dinner he got up from the table, went into the garage, came out with a spade and just started digging. Big clumps of dirt flying everywhere. The whole neighborhood quiet except for a couple of kids playing. And the sound of the spade sinking into the warm earth, and my Dad grunting to lift. My mother came out into the yard drying her hands on a dishtowel. She came to stand next to me and she whispered, 'I'm very concerned about your father. You're old enough now and I'm going to confide in you. I'm very concerned about your father. He isn't well and I'm worried. What in heaven's name does he think he's doing'. "

"I said, 'He's digging a swimming pool.' But she wasn't listening to me. She just watched him, twisting and turning that dishtowel like she'd rip it apart. 'I'm very concerned about your father; really I am.' My Dad must have heard us talking. He didn't even bother to turn around. Between lifts he said, 'Goddamnit Donald, get that other shovel.' My father was a very blunt man. And now he was possessed. Out there steady digging, the air getting darker and darker and him just digging away."

"He scared me, really, but I felt sorry for the guy. I mean there I am, eleven years old or something, feeling sorry for my old man as the dirt piled up all around him. It wasn't right somehow. And him screaming, 'Jesus Christ; somebody turn on the goddamn porch light. I can't see shit out here.' He couldn't even see where he was throwing the dirt. He didn't even know where he was going to put it all. I asked him once but he didn't say anything. Because he had no idea. I said, 'I hate to say this, Dad, but where you going to put all this dirt?' In the dark I thought he'd take a swing at my head. 'How the hell do I know? What do I look like? Go tell your mother to turn on that goddamn light.' Then he went back to digging."

Donald shakes his head. The points of light from his sunglasses sweep across the dark glass, a smile curls around his lips. I remember then that I had intended to call Marla. I could leave him in the middle of his story, go up the stairs to my apartment and call her. But the sun and the wine have removed me from this moment, and I cannot. Shakily I refill Donald's glass and spill nothing. He does not look up, does not appear to notice. For a moment the sunlight softens, a small cloud drifts quickly across our absurdly blue sky.

"You couldn't stop him, he was unbelievable. Just stay out of his way. Don't help him, don't offer to help him, just get out of his way. Digging his goddamn hole, and all the piles of dirt. Two nights later they sat together at the dinner table, just him and my mother. Not a word between them. Mom looked like somebody had hit her hard, had just punched her really hard in the stomach. She was taking it all very hard, believe me. It was on her face. Her life was a pile of mangled rose bushes; she was demoralized. The whole backyard was dug up, it looked just awful. Like something in a war movie. Before, there had been this neat little patio with a flower border and a small vegetable garden. But he tore up those flowers, tore out all the vegetables, cement patio busted up, pieces of concrete and piles of dirt everywhere. The place just looked like shit."

"But every night he was out there. Work all day, home to dinner, then right out there again, banging away. And everybody else in the neighborhood sitting around getting blasted watching t.v. This is difficult for most foreigners to understand, no offense. Every night my mother stood beside me saying, 'I want to confide in you, Donald. You're old enough now. I want to confide in you.' I laugh now, but he built that pool. If my mother had left him alone he would have built the whole thing with his bare hands, and then dug the well for the water to fill it. He was that kind of guy. But Mom finally talked him into getting a guy with a back-hoe to dig it all out, and another guy to haul away the dirt. And my Dad didn't even want to do that. But he did all the rest himself. He built that pool. Put in the diving board and the sliding board, trimmed it all out himself. You know, you have to measure that stuff out to the precise inch. And he was out there every night and all day on weekends. Amazing. When I think about it now it amazes me. Hell of a man, really. Even Nulty said so."

Donald reaches, drinks his wine to the bottom, returns his glass to the table. He leans forward, face in hands, fingertips just under the edges of his sunglasses. He might be studying the insect which still has not moved. Partly from the pressure of his fingertips his smile broadens nearly to his ears.

"Nulty. I haven't thought about him in years. He had this wig. Just standing there and scratching his wig saying, 'Hell of a man'. And he had such a give-away wig. You felt like saying to him, 'Please take that thing off your head.' Like you could hardly take a word he said seriously with that stupid thing on his head. And he had this kid. I've got to tell you about his kid. Anyway, when my Dad finally finished the pool some township inspector stopped by to tell him that before anything else, he's got to have a fence built around the whole thing. My Mom hears this and she turns to me saying, 'Aw my God'. Really, she was taking the whole thing very hard. The inspector said the fence had to be six feet high because you can't have any of the neighborhood kids falling in and drowning. And my Dad didn't say anything. My Mom was near a heart-attack; she'd already had three. But my Dad just stood there waving as the inspector drove away. And the very next night he was putting up that fence. He wouldn't quit. Understand? They'd drop him and he'd just get right back up. Unbelievable. No brains, but tough."

"And he can't even swim! Never could. He couldn't swim to save his ass. I'll never forget my Mom turning to me saying 'Sweet Jesus, he can't even swim. Does it make any sense to you? Answer me. He can't even goddamn swim.' My Uncle Ed walks over from his own house down the street. He's a tall guy and he takes a long look at the backyard with all the piles of dirt and everything, and he yells to my Dad, 'Hey Art, I didn't know you could swim.' And my Mom yells, 'But he can't, Ed. Does it make any sense to you? He can't even goddamn swim.' My old man just had something come into his head."

Donald laughs silently. Just below his sunglasses tears sparkle on his cheeks capturing the light, flashing. I re-fill his glass. A warm breeze rises, ripples the surface of the water. The water filter at the end of the pool clicks on, then settles into a quiet hum.

"But he gets in there now. Every summer he gets in two or three times and paddles around. But mostly he sits just like we're doing now; always with a drink in one hand, watching. Once I offered to teach him to swim. He laughed. 'What the hell I want with swimming?' he says. Besides, he hates to get water in his nose. A couple of years ago my Mom got him one of those floating seats; you know, the kind with the little cut-outs in the arms where you rest your drink. He clears the pool with that thing. Nobody's allowed in until he's finished. He really likes that seat; he's murder with that seat."

"Anyway, end of the summer and my Dad finds out he has to have one of those covers for the pool. It's got to be covered, the inspector tells him, or somebody'll fall in and crack his head. I tell you, backyards are dangerous places. Besides, the thing is supposed to keep the pool clean until the next summer. So my Dad buys this pool cover. And the thing is huge! No joke, it is enormous. And it's made with this really thick plastic; must have weighed a ton. Finally this is something my Dad didn't really feel like doing himself. I know this is difficult for foreigners to understand, but stay with me."

"Charlie Canova lived down the street, Nulty lived next door to him, and Henry Maanard lived three houses the other way from Charlie. So they all come over about this pool cover. They've been swimming in the pool all summer anyway. And there was my Uncle Ed, my Dad, and me. And with the wives out there it was a regular party. And really, everybody was amazed, the pool cover was huge. My Mom was cracking up, yelling, 'You sure that's the right size, Art?' And my Dad grumbling while everybody laughs. There were six of us inside the pool wrestling with all this plastic about to have hernias, and all the men are heavy smokers. Including Nulty. People used to laugh about him and his funny headpiece when he wasn't around. He was pretty unreasonable about it."

"So we're inside the pool stretching and pulling all this plastic, everybody yelling directions and nobody following, just grunting and cursing. And the bottom of the pool is still wet. There were wet spots here and there at the bottom of the pool. So there's Nulty pulling on this cover just like the rest of us. And all of a sudden he yells, 'Shit!' Everybody turns around, and there's Nulty sprawled on his ass. And it must have been a really hard fall, because his wig was shifted. It didn't fall off, it just shifted around on his head. And everybody just laughed. There were tears in people's eyes they were laughing so hard. Nulty just looked so funny with that wig sitting sideways on his head. It just looked really funny. It was so funny to look at you just had to laugh. Maybe it was the worst day of his life, everybody laughing and him on his ass in the water with that piece of trash on his head."

Donald reaches for the wine bottle, spills a bit more as he fills his glass. And now I realize that insect, our only companion, is no longer beside those drops of wine. It is gone, escaped. At the edge of my vision a dark speck tumbles from the edge of the white metal table. In the hard light and sharp shadows beneath our chairs I lose sight of it. For some urgent reason I prepare to get down on my hands and knees to search; I must find it. Then something glints beside one of the white legs of Donald's chair. It ambles shakily out of the shadows, moves to the edge of the concrete, into the shrubs that boarder the sundeck, into the thick shadows, into the approaching night.

"Or maybe it was the time he was wrestling with his kid. The kid was maybe three or four years old, his name was Timothy. One afternoon Nulty and his kid were in their backyard and he was tickling his kid, or maybe they were wrestling. And suddenly the kid kicked him. Just gave him a really solid kick. One of those freak kicks or something. And the kid breaks Nulty's Achilles tendon. Only Nulty didn't realize it. Really, a very weird thing. So there he is stumbling around his backyard with this horrible grimace on his face. Charlie Canova happened to be in his backyard at the same time, and he sees Nulty hobbling and hopping around and he says, 'Hey Nulty, what the hell's wrong with your foot?' And the funny thing is, Timothy is really just this very little kid. And Nulty clenches his teeth and says, 'I think the little prick really fucked up my foot.' For a couple of days Nulty just walked around letting the thing get worse and worse because he didn't want to believe his kid, this little, little kid had seriously fucked up his foot. He was a ballsy old bastard, really. And he just couldn't believe his kid had hurt him so bad. After all, he was so little."

"I went to his house to watch when the ambulance came. He looked really terrible. They had to wheel him out on a gurney and they must have had him all shot-up with painkillers. So I'm watching and then it really flipped me out because I realized he didn't have his wig on. It was the only time I ever saw him without his fake hair. His wife Stacy was going to the hospital with him, and she asked him how something like this could have happened. Nulty hitches himself up on his elbows and says, 'That fucking little bastard of yours kicked me!' She started to cry right there. By then Nulty must have realized he didn't have his wig on and that he was all shot full of drugs, laying on that stupid gurney and now all these stupid people were standing around looking at him, and not having his wig was flipping him out completely. And really, he didn't look that bad without it. I mean, he still had a little hair on his head. But poor Nulty, it must have been so damned degrading, but I swear it was funny. What a clown. They had him in a cast for about eight weeks. And that cast was no joke; it went all the way to his hip. No kidding, an Achilles tendon is nothing to mess around with. He had a terrible time living it all down. And everybody saying, 'Yeah, that little kid is going to be a real motherfucker when he grows up.' Talk about degraded. But it must have been just one of those freak things. You know, they just sort of happen."

The sky has faded to a deepening blue, the sun is setting, and I am relieved. Too late to make a telephone call, speech over the telephone takes on an entirely different coloration after sunset. The breeze is thick with the smell of fresh-turned earth. It has become cooler. Grinning, Donald leans back. When he removes his sunglasses his eyes are glassy and protrude slightly. His hand moves slowly to his glass of wine. He misses once, grimaces, snares it with the second try. A smile of accomplishment.

Beneath the hum of the pool filter the silence is absolute. Even the birds are quiet as they return to roost. From far off the sound of a radio filters through closed curtains, then becomes silent. Donald belches, his smile replaced by a look of discomfort. He says, "So tell me something about your father." He slurs his words. He squints in my direction. In his eyes there are several of me, and he cannot decide which of us to address. Softening light disguises every gesture.

"My father was a civil engineer. He had been an officer in the army of France. He surrendered to the Prussians in 1870, and murdered Communards in '71. He expected me to study for the bar and become a lawyer and wealthy land-speculator like himself. When I announced I would go to Paris and study painting he called me a pervert, a degenerate and worst, a fool. To my face he claimed I could not be his natural son. He would no longer support me, he said, until I returned to my senses. When I told him I cared nothing for his bourgeois existence and that I would never need his filthy money, his face flushed, his cheeks blossomed red. He became drunken with rage. The civil engineer and former army officer broke his walking stick across my back. And I too became enraged; I hit him as hard as I could, in his face. Blood gushed, it poured from his nose and covered us both. He cried out then, and struck me with what was left of his walking stick." I point to a spot on my forehead. "You see there; he gave me that, my patrimony. My mother heard us, rushed into the room as he was about to strike again. She saw us covered with blood and screamed. I have never forgotten that sound, her scream. He threw me out of his house that night; everything that was mine, everything he had not paid for, was thrown out with me. Bourgeois to the very end, he would not keep what he had not paid for. Yet as I left I was not sad or even angry. I was relieved, I was elated. As I walked from his house I grew stronger; stronger and stronger with each step, my shoulders broadened and thickened, I grew inches taller. But listen, this is my last memory of him; standing at the front door of that house, the light fierce behind him, his silhouette cut with a black knife, arm upraised and shaking, screaming, 'Unnatural, unnatural', and the night so black I cannot see the blood as I wipe it from my face, but only feel it warm and congealing between my fingers. That is the last memory of him, the last time I saw him. My nineteenth summer. He lived to be quite old, but he has been dead a number of years now."

Donald's head wobbles on his neck. He studies me owlishly, a dazed light behind each of his eyes. After a long pause he says, "Sorry to hear that." Then carefully he stands. "Excuse me," he says pronouncing the words with care. He walks slowly toward the corner of the building behind us. When he reaches the corner of the building he leans one hand against it, bends slightly forward and becomes loudly sick. I should have believed him when he told me that drinking wine makes him ill. But he felt apologetic somehow for my father, and he had excused himself. This is what I like about Americans. Like Russians, they're never too drunk to apologize. Not like the French. His strangled grunts cut the silence as neatly as breaking glass. The sound must be heard everywhere, but I see no one at a window. Night has settled. I cannot see very well. Perhaps it is time for Donald to go home.

With my cane firmly in hand I make my way to where he is leaning. His head tilts at an angle that summons painful memories of times when I have been similarly afflicted. I am not steady, but I am steadier than Donald.

"Come along," I say. "My couch is not so bad for sleeping." He looks at me with broken eyes. He sighs loudly, clears his throat, blinks hard, shakes his head and then straightens. He takes my arm. Slowly we walk to the stairs, slowly we climb each step to my apartment. I do not like Donald; I do not admire him, or appreciate him, and my sympathy for him is limited to disasters such as this. He must possess some fine qualities but I simply do not know what they could be.

As I reach for my door, he steps back and leans upon the railing. For a moment I think he will turn and become sick again, but he stands watching me. When I have opened my door he smiles and nods greenly framed by the blue-dark night, beneath that yellow light bulb burning beside my door without fear or promise. "I'll see you tomorrow," he mutters trying to find me with his eyes and not succeeding.

"I doubt that," I say, but he has turned and begun to walk away. He sways from side to side, pauses occasionally, one hand steadied on the railing. He lives no far distance away. He will find his way home somehow, I have such firm faith. And I am relieved that I will not wake to see his slumped body, to listen to his resounding snores, his groaning misery in the morning.

When my front door is finally bolted shut, the lights are turned off and the drapes are drawn, I lay this ridiculous, useless body upon this bed, within this room, within this life. And finally, as dreamless drifting overwhelms me, I abandon myself to the pitch and roll, the gentle sway of my drunkenness and its painless, fearless despair, as each of my limbs detaches, one by one, until I am limbless, weightless, consciousness moving unburdened, untroubled as a cloud. All dualities resolve into a sweetly scented void. Floating empty through the aether to rise like a thin brown leaf above that which cannot be conquered. The rhythm of my heart becomes the rhythm of the world unobserved.

And I will not become sick until very much later.

CHAPTER TWO

WHAT I REMEMBER from that time is that nearly every day, when
the sun had turned the sky a yellowish white and the patio around our
swimming pool had filled with sunshine and young bodies, I enjoyed bringing
out my sketchbook. The heat and noise and stabbing reflections from the
water gradually filled me, untwisting the gnarled muscles of my hands and
tormenting the sluggish things inhabiting my skull. My hand would then
begin to twitch until I could feel something more than my descent into
dissolution. And then I could begin to draw. Drawing in my sketchbook, my
days passed pleasantly enough. While it is commonly agreed that with age our
memory becomes unreliable, these memories remain bright and sharp-edged.

What I enjoyed above all was that on that patio I was surrounded with life.
While there I suffered no lack of figures to draw. Hard flesh and glittering eyes
that unanimously agreed; we are un-ironic, un-satiric, and beneath our smiles
and firm flesh, so youthful and simple hearted, we will not be deceived; the
future is ours and we are very serious. The presence of such assurance thrilled
me. But while this memory is very clear, I now realize I did not sufficiently
understand where I was or what I was seeing. But my apartment at least
provided a precious retreat.

Though my apartment was sparsely furnished, I was quite comfortable.
Comprised of a single large room with a low ceiling, the bathroom a small

room to the right, kitchen appliances ranked along the back wall, several wide windows, and a pair of sliding glass doors which faced out onto a small balcony. The light there was good. So the apartment served well as space for the painting I did not do.

Conventional studio space in the arts building on campus had been given to me when I first arrived. And it was very nice studio space. I know this because I visited there once. But like many other things, that studio was a prize wasted on me. It demanded a journey of three or four miles from my apartment and I cannot drive an automobile, my most endearingly un-American failure. But I had no ambition for such space. The department recognized what I had known instantly, and I gave up that studio in exchange for my larger apartment.

The distance from the main campus proved to be an annoyance for those rare instances outside my weekly seminar when I needed to attend a department meeting or reception. But that distance provided one outstanding benefit: I had few visitors. Donald perhaps twice each week, along with occassional visits by Marla. Otherwise, over the previous two years John had paid me no more than four visits. In fact, of all the senior faculty, Vincent was the only one to visit me more than a few times.

But I enjoyed this isolation which spared me the presence of my colleagues, and yet that distance did not deprive me of human contact. The patio around the pool and its fountain of youth provided each day's entertainment, while in the evenings, those sounds of human activity I heard muted through adjoining walls reassured me. Quiet murmurs, bursts of sudden laughter, flushing toilets, shoes tapping across bare wooden floors. My apartment was sufficient and comfortable and adequate against the terror of absolute solitude. Thus, by every measure my accommodations were pleasant. But still, my nights were filled with troubled sleep.

The sun spent each day flattening the fields, but at sunset there arose a breeze, cool and smelling of the sea filtered through fresh turned earth. Stands of poplar and olive trees stirred, broad leaves green as midnight shivered as huge chestnut and juniper trees lining the roads bowed. But the cool damp air caused my shoulders to ache, sending me tossing from side to side in search of relief. Yet I bathed myself in that air. For then at least I could breathe. I released myself to that cooling air as I listened to men at work at the railroad switching yard nearby. No longer thinking, only remembered thinking, remembered dreaming. No object existed whose inscrutability was a source of profound torment, an exquisite torture. And then there were the nightmares. When finally I drifted into sleep I was assaulted by nightmares.

In conversations and letters to Martin I adopted the outrage of involuntary exile. But over time, truth became cliché, cliché became truth. The over-rich soil, lush trees and fat fruit. And so the swimming pool with its moiling horde of oversexed innocents around its watery altar. All of this treasure a gift simply of the weather, and particularly the sunlight, was offered to me, and I took it.

The quality of the light varied with the season, yet its beauty was not a color. The light itself was abundant, constant and always crystal pure. But a light that had shape and weight and texture.

Memory is stirred by sensations like the impact of light. The body releases as it absorbs images too pointed to be carried about day after day. Images reserved for the solemn soul-death of midnight suddenly erupt, overwhelm and devastate. Light and heat and smells and noise, and then memory overthrows every other thought. I struggled to convince myself that I had no real knowledge of the place, of those vigorous smiling faces, of that rich sweet land. And my failure thus sealed my fate.

The maze of years; a labyrinth of mirrors, of voices, memories caught spiraling like wind-devils, misplaced, spread across the sky, a kind of debris. And the sites of memory, the locations, those dreams within the dream, of miles ago and years. A chasm of breathing and eating and sleeping. Dreams and nightmares and a gasping of air. Summer nights heavy with the smells of broken earth and cool brine of the ocean just beyond the mountains.

Poor Dedo would have been happy there. The man known to my students as Amedeo Modigliani would have passed his life happily there. For the light, most certainly, and the air so clean and dry for his weak lungs; yes, he would have found it all pleasant. Dedo and I would have been pleasant old men together. We would have sat with our pencils in hand and bottles of wine between us, once again gratified simply to be drawing. Just the drawing and the silence and that sun. And at night we would have listened together to the baseball games on the radio as we played cards. And after the baseball game and the cards Dedo would have been sufficiently drunk to recite Dante and Petrarch and Baudelaire. And each day, all day, spent surrounded by the fair, smiling flesh of young women. And Dedo had been such a handsome man.

Being old with Dedo would have been pleasant. We would have been lecherous and charming old men. We would have been happy there. Far happier than I was without him, and without the others, too. All of the others gone, yet none of them as good as him. With him it would have been pleasant. Of all the others, it would have been most pleasant with him.

There was no crack in the ceiling above my bed, and this is an important point. I needed one so that at night as I listened to the railroad men throwing their switches and the locomotives straining and couplers clattered, I could have studied that fissure as closely as if it had come from my own hand. I could have reproduced it in my notebook, where it would never have appeared the same twice. I would have resigned myself to its inexplicability, its intractability. And so I would have pursued its decipherment into infinity. Such a pursuit would have been comforting, something substantial in a world uncontrollably itself. But my ceiling had no crack. Perhaps nothing that transpired later would have happened had I simply purchased a hammer.

CHAPTER THREE

VINCENT SAID, "Pretty soon we'll all be living in motels." And then he smiled. We sat in aluminum chairs beside the pool. The sun was not yet overhead, the morning air was still fresh.

"Will that be bad?" I asked.

He sighed and looked away, appalled by my naive foreigner's acceptance of everything new and modern and American. "Take a look at this place. Pile a couple of low-ceiling boxes on top of each other and put out a sign, 'Apartments.' Only difference between this place and a motel, you can't rent these places by the night." His laughter was firm and as wide as his smile.

"And because they have facilities for cooking," I said, determined to torment his smug self-confidence.

"Ah, they have motels with little places you can cook." Clearly he was displeased by my response. He snarled as he asked, "Guess how long it took to build this place."

I shrugged. What else was there to do? He was my guest.

"I used to do that kind of work so I can tell you. About two months. I know what I'm talking about; I used to do that work." Vincent settled surly into his chair and scanned the row of doors to the apartments on the other side of the pool as if one might open suddenly to reveal his worst enemy. "Like living in Woolworth's basement. Everything came out of the same Cracker-

Jack box. Sweep it away, nobody will know the difference."

"Perhaps we should all live in Egypt," I said. "Thirty years simply
to decide to build something. Would you prefer that; to live among the
pyramids of Egypt?"

"Why not?" Vincent muttered. "That's what Durrell did. Makes sense
when you think about it." I could not help but laugh. Vincent amused me far
more than Donald. An assistant professor and also a very fine painter, I liked
Vincent and felt sorry for him at the same time. He believed his life irksome
and spoke loudly about how unhappy he was. And at every opportunity he fled
back to the east coast.

Yet even I could see that, like many in the University's art department, his
life was far simpler than it would have been in the east. Had Vincent gone to
New York, he would have been eaten alive. When I once pointed this out he
said, "Better to be eaten by sharks than nibbled to death by minnows." But
Vincent had impressed me within hours of my arrival.

In his role as the head of our department, John Burston had arranged a
small reception at his home in my honor. He and his wife Janet are polite,
gracious people living in a simple and friendly home. About fifteen people
gathered there; other department members and their spouses along with a
sprinkling of graduate students undoubtedly eager to take the measure of the
new foreigner. I was introduced to all and instantly forgot every name. But
I put on my best face and circulated amiably, flattered to be the center of so
much unjustified attention. I ate and drank yet felt infinitely lost despite this
display of sincere hospitality. Certain that I was out of place, I wondered how
soon I might return to New York, that New York which might slip from the
globe without my presence. But a party should never be wasted.

Their living room was joined to their swimming pool by sliding glass doors
that opened to a broad, flagstone patio. I made my way through the cluster of
smiling faces and jostling shoulders, to its inviting space. Twilight had turned
the eastern horizon ultramarine, stars crystal bright and sharp. Alone I made a
silent toast to my friends, and to their celebration of my last Manhattan night.

I sat down in a metal chair beside their swimming pool, glass of wine
in hand, and watched the evening sky turn to velvet, a sky suddenly much
larger than I remembered, its stars almost lost in that expanse. The pool filter
hummed and clicked off.

Eventually the hour grew late and finally there were only four of us.

Grinning and a bit drunk, John slapped the arm of his chair for emphasis. "You were quite a hit! This is going to work out well. Thanks again for coming."

"Your invitation was as flattering as it was generous," I said, still unconvinced his assertion was true.

"Not at all. I was amazed your commitments back east would allow it."

Janet sat forward on her chair and chimed in. "John contacted your agent on a lark. He never thought he'd ever hear from you"

"Martin is ever-vigilant about my affairs," I said. "And he never misses an opportunity. When he told me of your offer, he began by saying that of course I would go." I laughed remembering the ferocious argument we had when I first refused. Martin is a patient man and I credit him even when his patience is self-serving.

"He's really charming," John said. "I'm sorry he couldn't accompany you out."

"I expect we'll all see Martin sooner rather than later."

John paused to light a cigarette as Janet stood up saying she would make another pot of coffee. Vincent had watched all of us carefully, eyes flitting back and forth as if he anticipated something.

"Your arrival," John said, "has started quite a stir." Blue smoke swirled before his smile. "The rest of the campus will soon be as excited about your work as we are." He leaned back with the thinnest smirk as the cigarette smoke drift sinuous in the soft air. "And I have to admit I was surprised to learn from your agent that your work has never been collected for a retrospective display."

I laughed, and my laughter seemed to startle both John and Vincent. "Your tone," I said, "suggests some crime has taken place. Martin exaggerates energetically, as is appropriate for an artist's agent. I've had several shows that included more than the most recent work. And every two or three years Martin decides I need a retrospective, like a child whose bath-time has arrived. But he is a fine and good friend."

John did his best to take my meaning and I knew it. He stroked his chin and puffed on his cigarette and then looked away. "Still, I'm surprised. I would have expected that something more enterprising would have been mounted already."

I shrugged. There was nothing to add and I could only murmur platitudes. "I have never seen any value in it. Besides, there is so much painting going on and so little space and time is spent on it. We cannot expect young people to survive on the shreds left by their elders." John's square-faced good looks darkened.

Janet appeared with tray and coffee. She glanced at each of us and then smiled. "John likes to see things stirred up. That's another reason he invited you out here."

Vincent added, "What Janet means is, support for your invitation was not unanimous." He watched us carefully, and I could not understand why. "More than a few faculty agree with you. Young talent goes begging for the space wasted on stuff that's no longer interesting."

"All the more reason," I said, "to forget these nostalgia shows." I had drunk enough wine to become excited. "It has been nearly ten years since I completed a canvas of any significance. What sort of display could be mounted, except something good only for a dissertation."

"What I have in mind," John said quietly, "is a true retrospective. Something that would span your career. It is precisely such a show that justifies an institution like ours. Your arrival presents an opportunity that must not be missed."

Janet spoke up when John seemed too frustrated to continue. "What he means is that we'd all like you to consider this suggestion seriously."

"Though I can only applaud you aspiration and thank you for your enthusiasim, when it comes to my work I cannot see that it really fits your description. I paint so rarely and have so little that is new, I could only be embarrassed by the sort of show you propose. And believe me, even old men can be embarrassed."

"You underestimate interest in your work," John said. "In any case, the last thing we'd want is to embarrass you. But such a show would give you a chance to display the work you most value."

Vincent added, "That by itself would be a great thing. For you and your reputation. And it would be a great thing for the University as well." Then he realized that his enthusiasm had betrayed him, and something inside shrank back. "After all, you've become something of a legend."

To this I could only laugh; laughter the only appropriate response. "Legends are always pure fictions."

Perhaps that conversation was the very beginning after all. Perhaps that one off-hand comment was the point upon which everything else turned. The plots and plans and deeds, along with the furious destruction that followed, seem to draw straight lines back to that one evening. I have thought about this a great deal. Although I remain uncertain, that explanation has an appealing tidiness about it.

"I agree with Vincent," John continued warmly. "Your arrival has caused a lot of interest. And this interest has gone beyond the department. There is the University's administration as well." Vincent sat forward poised and tensely balanced watching us.

John added, "The administration finds several reasons to be interested in you. But the arts college administrators are thinking as well. Perhaps they even believe they like your work. And they appear confident others will like your work as well. I don't know if there are any plans, but I hear that others have been thinking along this line."

Though it was impolite, I laughed. "I cannot imagine why anyone would bother. So much of the work you have in mind is out-dated, or merely preparatory. I am certain about what is most important about my work, and painfully conscious of how little of it would bear serious examination. So I am sure you have already seen all of it that is worth seeing." A sudden gust of night air, a chill, my tightened chest shivered, I grasped the coffee and held it close.

"And just imagine the party we would have." Janet's laughter possessed a singing quality that had immediately charmed me. "All those people coming out from the Bay Area. And think of the newspaper stories." Then her laughter became nervous. "It just seems so unusual for you to refuse to have your work collected this way."

I could only shrug with embarrassment. "What I find most unusual is that so many others tolerate the display of work they know is inferior. I find that amazing."

John said, "But your work demands a retrospective. Yours is work any painter would be proud of. I'm certain that anyone offered the chance would be eager to sponsor its display."

John and Janet watched me expectantly, Vincent stared off across the pool to a boarder of bright flowers along the edge of the fence. Unfortunately, at this point my patience had begun to unravel. "The work you are referring to is past. There are no more lessons to be learned from it, there is no more elegance to be discovered in it. Each piece has its own associations for me, but these are simply sentimental links to a past that is dead. I would rather be spared the confrontation with memories of my debts to those dead. So for me, that is all such a show would provide; reminding me again that all who I would want to be present are permanently absent. I would do quite anything to avoid that."

John continued to smile politely, but in Janet's eyes I saw a cloud of confusion. Vincent said, "Hardly seems reason enough to turn your back on the acclaim you deserve. High achievement, brilliant accomplishment; why push it all away?"

John clapped his hands once. "There you are, I couldn't have said it better myself. And I'll go one step further. Those associations you mentioned are reason enough themselves for this sort of show. Portraits of Modigliani and Matisse and Picasso, and the double portrait of Braque and Miro; beautiful portraits without question, but with historical value as well. No sir, you miss the point." He held his coffee cup high above his head in mock adulation. "Your work is both evidence of and testimony to a rich tradition. The more I think about it, the more convinced I am that such a show must be held. It would remind people just how important your work is."

"I have never felt any loyalty to, or affection for, traditions," I said, but the conversation had turned against me. I felt myself becoming surly, walls seemed to be closing in over me though we all sat in the open air. "Tradition is merely an excuse for laziness, incompetence and cowardice. A disguise for the lack of imagination. Ah yes, I care a great deal for those traditions; whenever they are waved in my face, I know something tawdry is being covered over. Traditions are a great camouflage which hides a multitude of sins. To retreat into the bosom of tradition is simply to confess that nothing more needs to be said, and all of the old ways are sufficient."

John's expression grew dark. Though I regret it now, perhaps I had intended to insult him. Perhaps I had meant to throw his generous gesture back into his face. But he did not react to that. He leaned back to light another cigarette and studied me. Finally it was time for Vincent to speak.

"I guess I'll agree with your conception," Vincent said, "but you push your point too far. Painting has a tradition based on accomplishments of the past. We don't burn our paintings once we've finished with them."

"And that is a pity," I said feeling a fight within me. "We do not because we are greedy and vain and foolish. With unembarassed desperation we try to sell our paintings even before their paint dries. We do not burn our canvases when they are complete, but that is not because they do not deserve to be burned. And it is not because that public loves them so much. The fact that they are not burned is testimony to our arrogance and avarice."

Janet laughed nervously, almost in spite of herself. "What a funny idea. Burn the Mona Lisa because it's out of date."

Pinned to the wall I shrugged. "Burn it tomorrow, I never liked the painting."

John stood and began to pace the concrete patio. His scowl drew creases all around his face, twisted his mouth. "Remarkable. You sound like one of our more addled-brained undergraduates. Reminds me of something a sophomore might cook up for an examination paper. I can't believe you're serious."

With my most solemn voice I said, "Believe me. I have never been more serious."

Vincent said, "And if this University decided to mount a retrospective of your work, you would refuse to cooperate? Is that what you'd really do?"

"Go further than that," I said. "I would do my best to guarantee such a project would not even be considered. Believe this much: I would do everything in my power to stop it."

In the long moment of silence that followed I met every glance without a flicker of humor or irony. I had said what I believed, and I demanded that every word of it be remembered.

Suddenly John began to laugh. "Well, this conversation has taken a strange direction. Especially with a topic so philosophical. A novel idea: to resist the display of one's most significant accomplishments. I tell you your addition to our faculty has already proved more stimulating than I could have hoped." He turned to Vincent and Janet still grinning. "Think he'll get along with Bill Thomas?" John laughed, clapped his hands together. He came to my chair and squeezed my shoulder. "You are a find, sir. A real gem."

Vincent smiled. "We certainly won't need to guess your opinion."

"I only want to avoid misunderstandings." My smile demanded serious effort.

Turning to Janet, Vincent said, "And you were afraid that being from back-east he might make dull company." All of us laughed. She turned to me then with bright eyes and a smile I could not decipher. Something in the sharpness of her gaze I found both flattering and discomforting. And something had been revealed to me which I did not understand.

Still smiling Janet stood. "Just the opposite. Our guest has turned out to be so interesting I'm exhausted. Sorry to say it but it's time to wish you all good night." With a meaningful look to me she added. "Please remember that our door is always open." I thanked her sincerely.

John stood beside her as he offered to drive me home. He and Janet left the patio so that for a short time Vincent and I were alone. The chill in the air had become more noticeable, and I found I had become nearly cold. Vincent stood and stepped beside the pool, hands in pockets and staring hard into the water, as if the pool was extremely deep, and deep within something moved. Years later I would still remember him standing there. Long after the worst had happened I would clearly remember him standing beside that swimming pool. And remembering him I would recall a legend. Among the fishermen of the Mediterranean it is believed that the souls of men who drown while fishing are captured by those fish they pursue, and are forced to swim with the fish until Jesus comes to free them. The fish keep these souls in the deepest, coldest part of the sea. And as I now recall Vincent standing beside the pool, he had that look about him. As if that swimming pool was deep enough to confine lost souls at its bottom. Standing alone he looked prepared to take responsibility for those souls. The purple night surrounded him like a cloak, light from the bottom of the pool shining up golden illuminated his face, blue shadows where his eyes and mouth might be, communing with the lost, the misplaced, the forgotten.

Several times Vincent talked to me about his dead brother, killed in Korea when Vincent was still very young. An early encounter with death is not always a bad thing. From it Vincent had taken something to crack his heart's teeth on, something that twisted him in the center of the night leaving his bed clothes a knotted prison. For Vincent, death was what was real. This was something to respect, something he and I could share.

CHAPTER FOUR

AS A YOUNG MAN I had tried to imagine what having attained this age would be like; I was wrong, it is nothing like that.

Unless I was badly hung over I sat out by mid-morning beside our swimming pool with my sketchbook in my lap. Because already there would be young people.

Everyone seemed to be a student of something. Instead of reducing the numbers of students, the University seemed intent on increasing their ranks. And when these students were not asleep, or in their classrooms, or both, they were beside me, around me, before me, under that sunshine.

I have at this age discovered gratitude for those simple things that are essential. Most particularly the sun, so bright I needed sunglasses simply to see the results of my pencil. With my sunglasses and my cane and my sketchbook, I, too had become something worth looking at.

But sunglasses are awful things, and I have never become comfortable with them. The eye is made for the sun, as surely as the sun is made for the eye. But everyone I encountered at the University wore them. Even John sometimes appeared with a pair of them perched huge on his narrow face. For me, the advantage of sunglasses was that they covered my eyes so as I sat beside the swimming pool it was not obvious who I studied or sketched.

Drawing is another essential thing, most essential because it is simply pleasurable. As a lycee student in Toulous I was known for work with pencil or pen. I take no pride in this, as I would take no pride in breathing or sleeping. But thus I began, and so I have returned. My skills, it appears, have come full circle. Still, I regretted that I could no longer paint. Youth is kind to many, while age is kind to very few. In the previous several years I had done only two small canvases, and even for these there had been much struggle, much pain. One day a truly great artist will create a portrait of the varieties of pain, give each its proper position in the Pantheon. This will be no small task, no casual commitment; it will demand an artist of enormous capacity. Fortunately, I am not that artist.

The University, which was also my employer, had hired Donald at very little expense to act as my assistant. Unremarkable in any way, but at least he, like most Americans, worked very hard; so hard, at times I had to order him to leave. I take it that he inherited this disease from his parents. Donald was a graduate-degree candidate in art history, which I expect is the reason he agreed to the humiliation of working for this twisted old man. No doubt he expected to write something academic in order to satisfy his degree requirements. I believe this because at first he asked many questions about what I remembered. I was grateful that at least he was polite as he probed my past, attempting to dredge lost memories. He seemed particularly to enjoy hearing stories of the Very Great; those people who have come to fill his fantasy of what Great Art is really like; people about whom monographs are written and whose names and dates must be memorized for examinations. Children must have their stories, so, I told him stories. Besides, what possible difference could it have made to me?

So I fed him tales of Renoir in his old age. I told him of my visit with him, already bound to his wheelchair, withered and slipping down in the woven-straw seat like a broken doll, his driving cap perched perfectly on his wizened skull, wires of white hair splaying from beneath and disappearing in his white beard. But for Donald's sake I tried to conjure an image of Art uncooked: of how, in Renoir's hand twisted with arthritis, was strapped a paint brush, and of how he sat before the large canvas, and of the look in his eyes, of the trembling hand painful merely to watch yet nonetheless creating brilliant short curls of color and light, luminous as they appeared upon the canvas. And how, young as I was, when I arrived he called me 'maitre', how he put his work aside, and how, for nearly an hour, we sipped cool wine from tall glasses together served by

Gabriella herself, and then what young Jean said when he joined us. And I told Donald those stories Renoir had told of himself and his adventures in the harems of Algeria, of his afternoons with Monet under the arbor, of the smells of the vineyard and barnyard, and the way the flowers and Gabriella had looked.

Donald was always genuinely attentive, so I lied mercilessly. I told him stories I did not know about people I had never met. At times he must have wondered if I was one hundred years old. But if he expected to make his reputation by talking to old men about the dead, he would need to take his chances. Just like the rest of us. I told him a story of Bonnard's visit to the villa I shared with Miro, another story about Picasso when he was out of money, another story about Gauguin burning with remorse and desire before he abandoned his wife and children. Donald always listened patiently. I strained my mind to fill these stories with color and light and action. Long elaborate tales of all-night carousing; drinking and painting and starving and fighting and still more painting with people whose names he recognized, connected in his mind with some two-by-four inch color reproduction seen for a moment in some enormous and over-priced monograph.

But he remained awake, and that was all I required.

It is a great relief that often I fail to recognize my own life; fail to note its discrepancies, those differences between an event and what I wish had been the event, that which I wish or fear had taken place. I wish I had met Bonnard; I saw him once at an exhibition of recent work comprising several rooms of lithographs at Nice in 1934 or '35. Did we even exchange greetings?

Under that sun and beside that swimming pool, I could dream a new past not unlike the old, not absolutely fraudulent, but different merely in incidentals. As if to recreate that which already had been, but transfigured. Like art. Perhaps the most perfectible art is memory. And certainly it seemed beside that swimming pool I had found a perfect place to practice.

And Donald seemed content to listen to all of my lies. The University paid him nearly nothing, as it paid me little more. My only contractual obligation was to meet with a half-dozen graduate students in a workshop once each week. So each week, large-eyed, fresh-faced and earnest in their paint-spattered clothes, those young bohemians like Donald listened patiently. And all the while thinking that if only they lived long enough, they would become me; all the while thinking in a few years, old man, I will badly need your job. Yes, I was filled with a certain awe, and dread too, walking into that classroom, every finger on my pulse, every eye on my respiration.

And I? I responded in the most gracious way I can imagine. I wished I could be them.

If only I had remained long enough, I am certain I would have found some sort of happiness living there, eventually.

CHAPTER FIVE

"I'VE GOT AN IDEA how to help you start some new canvases."

Donald was sitting with me beside the swimming pool. Usually he stayed away in the afternoons, only coming in the morning or late in the day. But he proved himself unreasonably dependable to a man who found few upon whom he could truly depend. Could time for him have been such a burden, and so easily discarded? Could his degree have meant so much to him, and could the world have meant so little? As a reward I told him lies to gratify an old man's ego, as twisted as Renoir's hands.

Old age has few compensations. One of my most precious is the freedom to demure from large undertakings without embarrassment or explanation. It is perhaps the only compensation, but I have clung to it with maddening determination. In response to his suggestion I said nothing. My silence seemed to provoke him.

"But look at all of this space," he said, arm spread describing an arc, as if our sundeck had suddenly become my apartment, or my apartment had become a world. "You couldn't pick a better place to paint. And the light." He turned to me with a look of earnest concern. "I've given this all a lot of thought." Donald spoke as if he sincerely believed something of value could be accomplished without pain. As if pain was merely an excuse which allowed me to give up painting. He was correct about one thing however; it was a pity to waste all of that space.

"I'm thinking," he continued, "that I could lean the canvas down while you work on it, and then lift it upright for you to study." His suggestion was not useful, but my silence seemed to provoke him. "Or maybe you could sketch the canvas and leave someone else to paint it in. You could make all the changes you want, add or take out whatever you like."

Although his insistence was nearly impertinence, I was flattered. I remained patient and did not become angry. And it was this restraint when dealing with Donald that pleased me most. Restraint is a young man's virtue, and an old man's vice. And while I could not admit as much to him, another canvas from my own hand would have pleased me.

The pleasure of working on canvas is sensual, and such sensuality will not be denied. Dedo once stole some pieces of cheap building stone from a construction site. With his hammer and chisel he carved and pounded on those cheap stones, filling the air around his head with a cloud of yellow dust, just because he wanted so badly to luxuriate in the physical, sensual pleasure of sculpting. To feel the cold hard chisel bite into the rough and ugly stone. And to feel, above all, the smooth elegant shape hidden and encased just beneath the stone's surface.

And despite the towel he wrapped around his mouth and nose, Dedo coughed and coughed and coughed until the front of the towel ran from pink to red with the blood brought up from his frail lungs. Coughing and hammering at his pieces of stone, invariably after less than an hour's work he would become exhausted. But he worked in stone and nothing could deny him. He would work in stone no matter what the cost. Because there is more to the pleasure of creation than merely what appears before the eye.

But for me, despite the assistance of pain drugs, even short periods of wielding a brush left my shoulders glowing with a grinding, sharp pain. As if the blood had flowed away from my hand; as if my blood had a will of its own, withdrawing, refusing, uninterested.

And what could Donald know of all that? Did he wake every morning with pain? Did his shoulders burn after thirty minutes effort? What could such a young man know? Perhaps he secretly believed I was simply one more old man living out the remainder of his life in the feeble glow of tarnished and dusty medals. And perhaps he was right. But perhaps he was jealous as well.

"Do me this great favor," I asked, "and leave me out of you fantasies."

He raked his fingers through his hair, peered at me above his sunglasses. "I don't understand, and I realize this is a serious fault. But just think about this. Whatever you paint will most likely be bought." He watched me closely.

I could only laugh. Donald was sometimes too amusing. He continued to study me, earnest and unsmiling, and this I found even more laughable. His delusions must be their own reward. It had become common knowledge that a group of my canvases was then on display at Freihof's in Munich. Apparently Donald believed that a few of those would be sold. The show, after all, had been noticed in the press. It seemed that many people had visited it though most did so simply out of surprise at hearing I was not yet dead. And I had been told that one or two delusional individuals had agreed to Martin's outrageous prices. Little could they know that Martin would have been delighted merely to recover the expense of transportation and insurance. Of course, Martin always insisted to me that he wanted more of my paintings. Perhaps he believed the value of those works would increase after my death. Martin claimed he would be pleased to see me paint a bit more before I made my grand exit. I expect that was at least partly true.

Slouched in his chair with me beside that pool, Donald grinned his American western-movie grin. "And think of the prestige of the department, of the University."

"I think of nothing so much as the prestige of our department and this great University. These considerations never leave my conscious mind." He grunted, suddenly aware he was being made fun of. "I am also aware of your prestige as well."

Donald moved to stand. I said, "Do not misunderstand. I am certain that if I decided to paint a large canvas, you would work very hard to help me. Such willingness must not to be taken lightly. Even I do not consider myself so energetic." I stood then to join him, and together we climbed the stairs to my apartment.

When we reached my door I insisted he come out to my balcony and drink with me in the dying light. Disapproval? Annoyance? He folded his sunglasses, slipped them into his shirt pocket. He invented an excuse to get away, while I invented an art-historical occasion. I told him that sixty-three years ago tonight I helped Picasso carry his enormous canvas of 'Les Demoiselles d'Avignon' through the streets of Paris to Vollard's gallery. Or had it been Salon d'Antin? And what a stir the painting caused even being carried in the street, the street-sweepers and boulevardiers calling out to ask when the painting would be finished. And what a heavy load it was to carry, and how far we had to carry it, sweating, relieved that the trip from Montmartre was downhill. And how, afterward, we sat together beneath the awning of Le Dome and drank wine. An evening, I assured Donald, just like this.

He did not believe my tale, but that night we drank together anyway. Already the air had begun to smell of damp earth. Softer than a thought the evening's cooling breeze arose.

There were still nights at that time when I did not wish to die. Beside that table I kept his glass full, began another story while I waited inside myself for those signs that the wine had done what it had done, what it had always done. And then perhaps I would ward off the dreams, and enjoy the delicious pleasure of a blank and empty sleep.

CHAPTER SIX

A DREAM OF THIGHS . . .

And black horses. Broad, heavy heads and broad, heavy haunches tossing gracefully, harnessed to an armada of glittering black carriages all moving slowly in the same direction through a sea of round black bowler hats . . .

Ranks of pale plane trees, regiments, bark mottled tan and green and gold, simple naked stumps, flat-ended and shorn of upper branches in preparation for winter . . .

And the ground thick with yellow and red and brown leaves that rise in waves at the passing carriages. Ahead looms a building that should be the Gare de l'Est but is not. I sit on a bench beneath the pale and amputated limbs of those naked trees with pencils and sketchbooks. A sudden breeze flutters the pages of my sketchbook, there is a large pile of them at my side, and sometimes they are not there . . .

Leaves swirl about my head, I sketch furiously each leaf as it sails past, the air is so thick with them I fear breathing them in. Frantically I sketch each new leaf, turn a page and draw another, turn another and draw another, my hands, my limbs jerk compulsively, each leaf another page. I realize that each of the sketchbooks at my side is filled with the same . . .

But when I look down, the drawing beneath my pencil is not of leaves but is of a thigh. A solid, vigorous, well-rounded thigh, a thigh of substance and careful shape. And when I turn back the pages, each carries another drawing of a thigh. Thighs from various directions, differing angles, thighs of weight, of energy restrained, profound thighs, subtle thighs, flirtatious thighs bound in black stockings or encircled by red lace garters or naked, fresh and sweet as ripe melons and pale as morning mist . . .

Suddenly the ground is littered with small heaps of my sketchbooks, while the air that swirls around my head is dense with huge red leaves, and suddenly I am certain I cannot remain in my bench any longer . . .

The sky becomes overcast, the predominant color of the half-light is dark green. Obscured by the swirling red leaves I cannot discover if I am standing in the street or on the walkway. The round black bowler hats milling about have changed into black silk top-hats. More carriages now circulate, turning and turning, as though with nowhere else to go, but unable to stop moving, and so compelled around and around, all in the same direction but slowing, becoming slower and slower, a carrousel gradually coming to a stop . . .

And her carriage floats among them. She sits by her carriage's window, lower lip pouting, the corners of her mouth bowed downward, an expression as if eternally smelling corruption. She sits frighteningly still; she might be a dress-makers mannequin though the color of her cheek breathes warmth, her eye is bright, and her blond hair curls to ringlets that sway provocatively beside her cheek and in rhythm with the powerful haunches of the horses around her . . .

Her carriage moves so slowly I count heartbeats between each clicking step of its horses. The air becomes visible, the carriage and horses and black silk top-hats shimmer and tremble as if seen through rising waves of heat . . .

The carriage moves slowly and the woman does not turn. I feel myself drawn, caught in her carriage's wake, beginning almost to levitate, to float behind in unwilled pursuit. I do not call out, and the woman does not turn. The carriage moves precisely, with infinite, maddening slowness. The slow swaying of the carriage, the slow roll of the horses haunches, the slow toss of their gleaming black heads, the infinitely graceful slow sway of their shimmering black tails, all movements resemble breathing . . .

Suddenly the dominant color becomes bright blue, it burns my eyes. A blue nearly electric that evokes the terrifying sensation of falling, of losing grip, a sort of vertigo. I swim toward her carriage as it passes, until I am beside her, my eyes level with her steely blue eyes, her breathing in my face like a sweet, warm wind . . .

And then I spit. On her cheek just below her eye, the spittle lies glistening, crystalline, descending very slowly as if it might be a tear leaving its bright trail down her pink and childish cheek . . .

And then her carriage has passed me, has moved beyond me . . .

In a moment I am looking at her black silhouette. Tight-curled ringlets fall black as eternity to her black shoulders. Beyond her outline, the glowing shine of crushed velvet, a red which lays between maroon and pinot noir, the quilted cushion of the seat directly across from her in that carriage . . .

And that carriage becomes our carriage. I am suddenly certain, it is as obvious as the stitching of its quilting, that the seat across from her was intended for me. It had been reserved in my name for numberless generations past. Our carriage is my carriage, as certainly as if my brass name-plate was affixed to the door upon which her hand has come to rest, her fingers curling ghostly pink, and that I could not be more awaited, could not be more anticipated, could not be more expected to occupy that seat. As if every mechanism and detour of history has conspired so that I will occupy the seat directly across from this captivating woman . . .

Yet somehow she has not recognized my absence. She does not turn to look for me, does not even lean forward to instruct the driver to slow and wait for me. I am frozen in a posture between inertia and action. I endure a motionless movement, a trembling of the air or a passage of light . . .

The carriage has suddenly become motionless as well and for the duration of several heartbeats, which themselves come slower and slower. The carriage appears so still it is like watching the sun set . . .

And suddenly I am mortally afraid. I have transgressed and I am frightened. I have broken a law, I have crossed a threshold and I am terribly afraid. Something is wrong, I need to flee . . .

Brilliant white light appears before me, and then directly beneath my feet and all around. This light envelopes me and blots out everything. A sudden raging wind tears at my face, lifts everything, uproots everything, rips away everything, a blast of bright white light coming from below claws at my eyes and I am rising swiftly upwards into a flat, hard blue vacuum of sky . . .

And then I awaken.

Even before I was quite awake, I knew the rest of the day would not be fruitful.

It would be a day I would willingly forego, and although as precious as each of my days had become, this day I would happily ignore.

Coffee is of no help on such mornings. For such mornings there is no help; no help at all.

CHAPTER SEVEN

VINCENT NEVER TALKED about his art, and for this small favor I was grateful.

He never told me what he thought art truly was. He did not tell me what art ought to be, or to do, or what art should concern itself with. But he talked about art nonetheless. He told me how many hours he had spent at his current canvas the previous day, or how many hours he would need to spend the following week. He debated the wisdom of having several canvases partially finished and available to work on, or whether it made more sense to work on a single canvas exclusively until it was finished. And he wondered aloud whether other painters "put in as much time" as their canvases needed. I asked who had most influenced his painting. He shrugged and then smiled. "Everything I know about art I learned from Tommy Morosci, and from my father."

We sat one searing-hot afternoon inside my apartment on hard straight chairs at my porcelain table, shielded from the heat by closed curtains and a noisy air-conditioner. Vincent's hands moved lightly over the tabletop as he spoke. "Morosci and me were buddies in high school. Sometimes I think he never taught me anything at all, except that it was possible to be an artist. We'd talk at each other for hours. I expect most of what he claimed he knew was bullshit. But it was serious bullshit; Tommy was a serious guy. He knew things; about painting and artists, and poetry, and even music. The music stuff

I already knew from my old man." He paused and hesitated and then shook his head with a reluctant smile.

"My old man. Pounding his fist at the dinner table, my mother yelling for him to shut up while he yelled that none of us practiced enough. Looming and pounding at the head of that big, dark oval table."

With the curtains drawn we breathed a muddy cavernous light edged with a nimbus of thick yellow.

"You might have liked him," Vincent said. I rubbed my leg, the muscles beneath skin that was loose and dry, yet remorseless as leather. "He liked hardly anybody except Uncle Salvatore who lived down the hall."

Vincent drank from his glass, returned it to the table, sparkling red beside our green bottle, the droning air-conditioner an accompaniment to our silence.

"He was a dispatcher for a soda bottling plant and sent the trucks out on deliveries every morning. He expected Louis, my oldest brother, to come work with him after he finished high school. Dad wanted to give him a job, to make that job a gift to him, talked about it all the time. Louis died in Korea. My mother said Louis's death changed my father. I was too young to notice. We were four brothers; Gino was the next oldest, then Frank and then me. After Louis died my father decided the rest of us would learn to play the violin, as if he figured he'd sacrificed enough to a world that didn't give a shit anyway."

Hearing this I became more interested in Vincent, and jealous as well. "So! I did not know that you played the violin. To play a musical instrument is a skill which alone makes a human being most human."

He smiled sourly. "One day that was all he would talk about, bragging that all his sons would play the violin. My Dad played the 'cello, you see. Studied it in high school, before he had to drop out when his own father died and he had to find a job to support his mother. Of all that tiny bit of education introduced him to, he kept up with playing the 'cello. He played with Uncle Salvatore, who played the viola. Some nights, instead of playing cards and drinking they played duets together for an hour or two in our living room. Salvatore would go down the hall to his apartment and come back with his viola, and Dad would bring his 'cello out of the bedroom. After fifteen minutes, my brothers would already be gone. Just my small dark mother sitting next to Salvatore's wife, Mrs. Petrillo, Augustina, large woman, light colored hair, Aunt Aggie. And me, stuck because I was the youngest and had no way to escape. They played these Baroque pieces and Italian love songs, some opera arias, some transcriptions. My mother and Aunt Aggie muttered together on the couch while my father and Uncle Salvatore played. I realized later that I'd slept through a lot of great music. A couple of times a week they'd get together, until we got the television. They'd get together sometimes on weekends except in the summer when it was too hot or there was a baseball game on the t.v."

Vincent's tale stirred memories, and I found something to share with this man. "Such a marvelous thing to have in childhood. A friend of my father's, a cavalry officer, played the piano. So beautiful. My mother loved it. Music is a gift. You are fortunate."

"So you think." Vincent laughed with annoyance at my stupidity. "My Dad wanted a string quartet made up of him and his sons. Uncle Salvatore didn't care what sort of band they made, he didn't have any children to offer to the goddess of music. We would play receptions, my Dad said, and make a little money. Uncle Salvatore never cared about working jobs and making money. But he liked this band idea. Uncle Salvatore was somebody I could talk to, somebody to back me up when my Dad got a crazy idea. But he got excited about this band. I realized this when, using my ten-year old brain, I suggested they start a rock-and-roll band like Bill Hailey and the Comets. Uncle Salvatore told me to shut up. That right there should've been a clue."

I drank more wine, drained the bottle and went to the cabinet under the sink, returned with another, refilled his glass and then my own. "So did you ever form your orchestra?"

Vincent shook his head. "My brothers and I were slow learners on the violin, so Uncle Salvatore brought his friend to the apartment. Mister DeSantis. He played the violin. Whenever he came to the apartment, my Dad would tell all of us, 'Now watch Mister DeSantis, watch how he plays.' They played trios together and my Dad really got to like Mister DeSantis. This went on maybe six months. Then Mister DeSantis said he had a friend who played the violin better than he did. The following week Mister Irwin appeared."

In my mind I saw four graying men surrounded by a loving family, smiling and nodding each to the other as they played. "Your father was very fortunate."

"You never played music yourself, did you?" Vincent asked this without expecting an answer. "I mean you never got involved in something like a band. It sounds funny, but more important than how much you practice, a musician has to co-operate with other people. That must sound strange to you, but it's all different from painting, music is. You really can't do it all yourself, there's always somebody else. Music is an art of collaboration; nothing like painting where you're all alone. At least in music there's somebody else with you." Vincent smiled.

"Here's the point. My mother and Aunt Aggie liked Mister DeSantis well enough, but they never liked Mister Irwin, even though he was a first-rate violinist. I liked him all right. He told jokes that made everyone laugh like crazy, and he was always staring at Aunt Aggie's breasts. But one Sunday after Mister DeSantis and Mister Irwin left, my Dad and the others began to talk about Mister Irwin. Aunt Aggie swore she could smell him across the room, so he must never take baths. I never could smell him, but my mother said Aunt Aggie was right. My Dad and Uncle Salvatore criticized his intonation and the way he held his bow. Then my Dad said something about the quality of his violin saying, 'Isn't it just like a Jew.' I guess they'd forgotten I was still at the table."

Vincent's gaze drifted to a spot high on the wall above my head. I said nothing. "And that man could play, even I knew that. And he played everybody's instrument just as well as his own, including my Dad's 'cello. And he played the piano. Whenever it was his turn to bring the score for a new piece, Mister Irwin went downtown to Presser's or Smith's or Henri Elkan's, and always came back with the fingerings marked already and everything. Nothing like my Dad, always pleading that he had forgot. All along he was too cheap to buy complete scores. My Dad was cheap. All the scores he had came from the Free Library. Whenever he wanted to seem absent-minded, he could do it good. If there ever was a man made to keep secrets, that was my Dad. And none of us ever knew that, all along, he was working on other things."

"What other things?"

Vincent smiled then, eyes narrowed, he waved his hand. "Gino, Frank and I took lessons on the violin at school. My Dad must have decided Mister Irwin didn't smell so bad that he couldn't give us private lessons in counter-point and sight-reading, neither of which he wanted to be bothered with teaching us, probably because he didn't know them very well. We all hated it equally, but Frank was the first to revolt. He could scream as loud as my Dad. Maybe all their fighting made me and Gino stay with the violin as long as we did. Because it had nothing to do with our skill. After Frank moved away to college my Dad got more unbearable. He was going to have his orchestra." Vincent laughed.

I was puzzled. "But he already had his orchestra with the others."

"He wanted his own orchestra," Vincent said, "like another guy would want his kids to take over his business. Like Louis and the job at the plant. Me and Gino were going to replace Mister DeSantis and Mister Irwin. Like the best stupid ideas, it got stuck in his head solid. The same year my Dad moved up to supervisor at his job, Gino started law school at Temple. Another screaming battle even if Gino couldn't scream as loud as Frank. Dad said he wouldn't give him any money to help out at school because he had crossed him up about the orchestra."

"And Gino just said, 'I'm going to do it anyway, old man, so go fuck yourself.' My Dad had this broad thick face, heavy features. His thick black eyebrows rose slowly, like a trowel had cleared the flesh from around his eyes, and suddenly he was all eyes, his face just these two huge eyes looking at Gino. Gino just stood up then, walked to the front door and left. My Dad had these thick fingers. I have small hands like my Dad's except my fingers are thinner than his. Maybe that's why he wanted us to play the violin; he loved the sound but his fingers were thick and the violin fingerboard is so fine and thin. He sat in his chair looking at the door Gino had just closed, eyebrows rising and thick fingers straining like he would crush those fat round chair arms. It was terrible, I had to leave the room." Suddenly looking around Vincent asked, "Is there any of that wine left?"

I refilled his glass, Vincent drank and then laughed. "I was in my bedroom listening. Dad paced the living room but after a while he went into his room and shut the door. Next thing I heard was classical music from his radio. I waited in my room for my mother to get home. I knew Gino wouldn't be back soon, if he thought twice he might never come back at all. When she finally got home and I told her what happened she went into the bedroom and closed the door. When she came out again she said nothing to me, just started making dinner. The three of us ate in silence, and as soon as we were finished Dad went back to his room, closed the door and turned on the radio again. And my mother washed every dish in the house, just bang and clatter and the sound of water. And all that noise just made the apartment more quiet."

"Close to midnight Gino walked in, right past us. Mom stood and charged after him as he walked toward my parent's bedroom. But before she could reach him, Gino opened the bedroom door, and to my Dad he said, 'I'm sorry.' He closed the door again without waiting for my Dad to answer, went to the bedroom we shared and closed that door behind him. Right in my mother's face. 'Gino,' she whispered to the closed door, 'it's your mother.' We could hear

Gino moving around in there. After a while she gave up and walked away. When I decided it was time I got some sleep I didn't know what to do, but I wasn't going to sleep on the couch. I leaned my head against the bedroom door and said, 'Hey Gino, I got to get some sleep. Let me in.' He opened the door then. I never asked, and he never said anything more about that night."

Vincent stood stretching as if tired and sore. The evening light had gone red; when he parted the curtains it poured into the room. He turned away and paced back and forth before my couch. "When my turn came, I didn't need to be told that I would audition for Curtis. With Frank at Penn State and Gino at Temple, I was my Dad's last hope. My mother took me aside while I was still a junior in high school. 'You're his last hope,' she said. My mother has black serious eyes. 'And you love the music. Don't break his heart like your brothers.' I didn't need to love the music to know there would be no argument this time. But day after day I sat in orchestra rehearsals with people who played really well. I mean those kids could play. I shared music stands with guys who were going to be plumbers like their fathers but who already played better than I ever would. But the old man wanted this audition. 'For your father,' she said, 'do this for your father.' She said it over and over, even after I was accepted at Pittsburgh College of Art. 'Don't let the poor man down,' she said. Once I asked if she wanted me to be a musician, too. She smiled and her dark eyes softened. She said, 'Do what makes you happy.'"

I said, "But you had been accepted into a college to study art." Curiosity had burrowed beneath the wine and pain. "Wasn't your father proud that you would study painting?"

Vincent waved his hand. "I did some drawing in high school, worked my way up to oil painting. Once I showed my father a couple of things. He looked, that was all. When I told him I was applying to art schools he shrugged. 'Anybody can go to an art school,' he said, 'but people will always pay good money to hear some nice music.'"

The burnt red rays of sunset had faded and gradually my apartment became smaller. Framed by his dark hair Vincent's face glowed, his skin become pale. His words echoed, like drops of water falling in a cave. A draft from the air-conditioner blew across my neck and I shivered. Vincent smiled.

"I'll tell you this one thing about Tommy. We cut class one day. We were juniors in high school and we'd taken an art class together. He said he had someplace he wanted to go. We were tight buddies then, I didn't argue, just

okay and we took off. On the bus he's all mystery. At the Parkway we got off
and started walking. I said, 'Hey Tommy, what the hell.' He just smiled his
goofy smile and pointed his finger. At the Art Museum. I had heard about the
place but I'd never been inside. So we'd cut classes to go to the Art Museum;
hoodlums in the galleries. Tommy made me stand in front of all these
paintings. He would read the label and then step back looking and say, 'Yeah,
just as I thought.' I looked at so much paint that day I got dizzy. Just looking at
that stuff, it took a while before all of it became real. But suddenly in my mind
I could see people, models and their painters, at every canvas. I saw each one
with somebody sitting in front of it with a brush and all the bottles and rags
and junk, painting. At that moment the act of painting became as real as this
table." He stood again, and returned to pacing.

"And this," I said, perhaps because I wanted to spare him feeling so isolated
and abandoned, "you could not explain to your father. You understood the
man but you could not explain this to him."

"I didn't understand him. Not then and not later." Vincent laughed and
dropped himself onto the couch, wine glass balanced carefully with one hand
on his stomach. "I've given up on the understanding-business." He paused then
before he continued.

"One Sunday afternoon weeks later I sat at the dining room table with
my old man, Mister DeSantis and Mister Irwin. We were waiting for Uncle
Salvatore. DeSantis sat to one side, Irwin on the other, my Dad between them
leaning forward in a closed-collar shirt, and all of them watching me. My Dad
said, 'The auditions at Curtis are coming up.' As if I need to be reminded. 'You
should practice more and you do not. You will need to work very hard and you
will need help. Mister DeSantis and Uncle Salvatore will help you with your
playing, and Mister Irwin will help with piano and theory. Now tell us, will
you study hard? Will you work to prepare for these auditions?'"

Vincent laughed again. "Just like always, my Dad had figured it out, he had
his plan. He was handing that plan to me and all he was waiting for was for me
to agree. All three of them stared at me and I couldn't open my mouth. Real
quiet like he doesn't want to wake my Dad, Mister Irwin leaned toward me
and said, 'It's a lot of work being a musician, and most of that work is practice.
Because performance is work, but not the bitter kind of work, the grinding,
discouraging kind of work that practice is.'"

With a broad grin, Vincent shook his head. "Mister Irwin was so serious, just sitting there with his hands folded motionless on the table. Like he'd control himself no matter what. And for a minute I gave it some thought; scared as I was, I listened to what Mister Irwin said. 'There are very fine musicians at Curtis. Among the finest in the world. And when you finish your studies there you will be famous. But to be accepted you must perform well at the audition. Which means a great deal of practice for the next year. For the next year, you understand this already, am I right? So tell us now what you want to do. How can we help you best?'"

Vincent leaned back to stare at the ceiling, again ran fingers roughly through his dark hair, then drained his glass. "See, being accepted at Curtis is an automatic scholarship. Nearly everything is paid for. And it was true what Mister Irwin said. That school had a tremendous reputation."

I said, "So this was a generous offer. These men were prepared to help you be accepted by this school. Do you feel guilt for all of that undeserved generosity?"

Vincent simply shook his head as if to shrug off a fly, then looked into my eyes. His smile reappeared. "I watched my Dad's eyes shifting back and forth, just waiting. And then all of a sudden he raised his hand, slammed it flat down onto the table. 'Dammit Max,' he said, 'you don't ask kids. If you had your own, you'd know.' Then he turned on me. 'You're a good violin player. And you'll get better once they get their hands on you at Curtis.' Mister Irwin put his hand on Dad's shoulder and said, 'You promised you'd leave this to me. Don't upset the boy.' The old man's ready to jump across the table, Mister Irwin is waiting patiently, and on the other side Mister DeSantis is completely quiet, nodding and sighing like this is the saddest movie ever. So I wondered how it could get any worse. It couldn't get worse, because Mister Irwin wouldn't let it get worse; I was counting on him there. That's when I told them all that I wanted to go to art school."

Vincent began to laugh and it was infectious. I laughed with him, simply from the exuberance of his hilarity. "Silence. Then very slowly my Dad began to stand, eyes glittering. He stared at me like I'd hit him with a truck. Mister DeSantis touched his arm. To me my Dad said, 'You sure about this? You sure this is what you want? Curtis isn't good enough for you. And you won't play the violin.' In a panic I said, 'I already play the violin about as well as I ever will. You know this, and Mister DeSantis knows this and Mister Irwin, too. I'm about as good as I'll ever get. But at least with the painting it's different.'"

"Suddenly I realized my face was wet. I didn't know I'd been crying. Mister DeSantis said to my Dad, 'I think the boy knows what he wants. And it's a good idea. What's wrong with going to art school? He knows already, Angelo; he knows what he wants.' My Dad jerked his arm away. 'Just a goddam kid! And he thinks he's going to tell me how it is. Me, his father, he's going to tell me. This is the thanks I get.' Then he started around the table for me. I backed away slow while he came at me, all the time thinking this can't be happening. Mister Irwin tried to grab his arm saying, 'Control yourself, he's just a kid,' but Dad's face was red. My mother came into the room then saying 'Angelo. Angelo.' In another minute the two of us are running in circles around that table. Mister Irwin and Mister DeSantis tried to catch my Dad by the arm, but he just pushed them away like bugs. My mother followed us calling out, 'Angelo! Angelo!' What a zoo. Running, screaming, crying, in circles around that table. Animals. Finally I'm finished, no more, so out the front door I go. In the hallway Uncle Salvatore was just coming from his apartment. He took one look at me and said, 'What's going on?' I couldn't look at his face. He said, 'Why the hell don't you leave the poor man alone. He's a genius and you want to put him in his grave. You and your fucking brothers.' And then he pushed me! Uncle Salvatore! The look on his face made my skin crawl. He went into our apartment and slammed the door. So I ran."

Vincent sat forward and his smile disappeared. Seated on the couch face in hands and elbows on knees, he spoke quietly to the floor. "I ran like crazy, until I got to the school yard at Barret. A couple of guys were shooting baskets, I stopped to catch my breath. Tommy wasn't there. I knew I had to leave home, just like that, never see anybody again. There was nothing more to say. As if I'd been thinking that over for a long time without knowing I was thinking about it. And now I didn't care. Maybe the old man was right, but I didn't care, about anybody or anything, except finding Tommy Morosci." Vincent laughed, suddenly embarrassed.

I said, "It is a terrible thing. No matter what the reason. To feel as if you must turn your back on your loved ones is a terrible thing."

"I thought the only person I could still trust was Tommy. I figured we'd just go. Get out, him and me, hitch-hike to New York or maybe out here. Anyway, I was ready, and anywhere was okay."

"Every conspiracy needs conspirators."

Vincent shook his head. "When I got to Tommy's house his mother said she didn't know where he was. I went to Torino's, couple of other places, nobody had seen him. Here I was, the big bust-out, and I couldn't find Tommy. I kept looking for him because I couldn't think of anything else to do. Finally I decided, what the hell, I'll go myself, get in touch with him later, pick a place we'll meet up. I was feeling pretty crazy. So I started walking up 16th Street. Nothing in my head, just walking north, toward something that would happen later. Just walking away, moving and moving, thinking about how it'd be, what the hell I'd do. The sun got low in the sky, I was still walking like I might walk right out the other end of the city. All I wore was this thin jacket, and when the sun went down it got cold fast. I went to a phone booth to call Morosci. I get inside and reach into my pocket. Nothing. Left the apartment with nothing in my pocket, not even bus fare. I was way up on Catherine Street, or Christian, only a couple of blocks below South. Then I thought, well, go ahead, turn around and go back, cold and broke, go back to your mommy and daddy. Sneak back into the apartment, knock on daddy's door, say, 'I'm sorry' and then they'll let you go to bed warm and safe."

Vincent's eyes were suddenly bright. He looked everywhere about the room except at me. "So I kept walking. And the further I got the better I liked it. By the time I got as far as the Parkway the sky was indigo running to black. Street lights hung along either side of the broad avenue, spotlights lit-up Eakins' fountain in the center. And in the distance the Art Museum glowed pink against the blue-black sky. And all of it, every bit of it, was utterly beautiful. I couldn't think how anything could be more beautiful than that at that moment. I was cold and as I got closer I went back to cursing Morosci. Because he should have been there. He should have seen all of that right there, just then. I followed the Parkway past the Eakins statues and something just filled me. Something passing, a feeling of something going away from within, going to surround everything. Something huge, and me walking though it like marching through a fog. Tommy and me were going to be buddies forever, and we would die young and famous. Yet there I was, climbing those huge steps up to the Art Museum alone. But at least I didn't feel cold any more, so I climbed slow enough to pause at each step. At the top, the Museum seemed immense with all the lights shining on it under that black sky. I felt crazy but it all seemed so beautiful. Behind me the city around the City Hall tower and William Penn glittered. I sat down on the top step and looked out over the city. Maybe the cold had frozen this smile on my face. Smiling and smiling, glad to be alive and just sitting right there."

Vincent looked up, his eyes suddenly searching my own. "I'm not keeping you from anything, am I? I mean I'll go if you want."

I shook my head, watched relief betray him.

"Anyway, the Museum was closed for the night, so I walked around the place two or three times still just amazed by something I couldn't name. I was certain something had happened, and I kept walking around waiting to figure out what it was. But after a while I was just cold again, and no understanding would keep me warm. I walked around to the back and down the steps toward the Aquarium and then further along the row of boat-houses. Big black cars were driving up to one of them and people were getting out; women in long dresses and men in dark suits. Two guys stood by the curb opening doors when the cars pulled up. I walked over to see what was going on. I was invulnerable, you see? Everything was interesting and nothing could happen to me. I walked past those guys and they acted like they didn't see me so I stopped for a while to look through the big window in the front with its curtains wide open. A party. The men and women were all dressed up, and I could see the room sparkling with lights. I stood for a while thinking if only Morosci was there to see all this. Especially the dolled-up women."

"Then one of the car-hops came over, asked what I was doing. When I wouldn't answer he called his buddy over. I told him I wasn't bothering anybody. The other guy said he'd call a cop if I didn't beat it. He was pretty unreasonable so I walked away, climbed the hill back up to the Museum. There were benches at the sides of the building so I sat down and just stared up at those peach-colored walls. By then it must have been past midnight and I was getting really cold. But at least I'd stopped thinking about going home. One of the benches was next to a bank of those big lights shining on the building. I got down beside those lights to get warm, all the while thinking about those two assholes and that party and all the beautiful young debs who'd gladly fuck me once I got famous, and that asshole Tommy and my bastard father, and a whole lot of other things just jumbled, everything running together in my head. Next thing I knew somebody was tapping the bottom of my foot."

"This big cop was looking down at me saying if I'm there when he gets back he'll lock me up as a vagrant. Somehow I'd fallen asleep. The sky was just getting bright. There didn't seem to be anything else for me to do so I walked home. By the time I got there my Dad had already gone to work. My mother was upset, asked me all kinds of questions. I ate breakfast and went to sleep, didn't wake up until after noon. I went to Torino's, finally found Tommy. First thing he wanted to know was where I'd been. Seems my Dad showed up at his place looking for me. I looked at him, and then I couldn't answer him. Couldn't say anything. This was different from sitting across the table from my father. So many things had happened and nothing had happened, but he hadn't been there and I couldn't explain it or tell him even the most important things. So I made up a story about meeting a girl. Because I felt sorry for Tommy. Hell of a thing. I felt bad for him so I made up a story. Maybe because he hadn't been there and it could never be like that again. Nothing could ever be like that again."

Vincent hesitated. I refilled his glass and he drank. "Tommy and me didn't hang out together so much after that. I guess I was still half-mad at him. And then I went off to college and he didn't." Hands flat on the tops of his thighs he slumped back.

"And what of your father?"

Vincent smiled, eyes suddenly animated. "I was in my room that night when he came home from work. I waited until he'd gone to his bedroom and then I knocked on his door. Before he could say anything I said, 'I'm sorry about last night. It won't happen again.' He looked at me and grunted. I was dismissed; from his room, from his life, completely. I expect he and Mom had talked about it, or maybe they didn't, but he never said anything more about the violin or music. I went off to art school the year after. Away from home two years and then I got the telegram: 'Father died. Heart attack. Please come home.'"

Vincent shook his head once, leaned back and closed his eyes. He sat very still.

When I no longer knew what he wanted or why he continued to sit I said, "And what was it these men taught you about art?"

Vincent opened his eyes slowly as a grin grew across his face. "I'll tell you; I learned that it doesn't matter what you do. Action is only a disguise, a veil that just allows reality to happen as it must. All that matters is what happens."

I could only nod and agree that he had learned a true thing. And I believed that I had learned something, too. But time had to pass before I understood what it was that I had learned. And by then it was too late.

CHAPTER EIGHT

FINALLY I WAS ALONE by the pool. Donald had just gone. He had been surprisingly talkative and I had feared he would never leave.

As we sat together under that scintillating sunshine he had burdened me with more of his talk, nearly all of it about that embarrassing retrospective, something I was determined to resist and had steeled myself to refuse. My insistence that I would not participate in anything like it seemed to make no difference to him. And so it appeared to me then that Donald finally had joined forces with Burston.

The first thing Donald had done when he arrived that afternoon was show me his list. This list must have cost Donald and Burston considerable effort to compile. In black and white, he had offered me a list of names and addresses of persons, collections and galleries in the area that held examples of my work. Glancing over it left me in a sort of depression, like a fog of anguish. It never occurred to either of them that I did not want to remember that I had painted those canvases, and I lived in fear someone would remind me that I remained responsible for their existence. I regretted the creation of each of those works offering merely the feeble plea of extenuating circumstances: depression, greed, alienation, hunger, lack of sleep, lack of compassion, lack of discipline. Anything that would disassociate me from them. But my pleas had no effect. Donald sat across from me, his sweat-glistening and self-congratulatory smile almost an embarrassment.

How could I explain that all he presented me with was a collection of embarrassments and failures? Nothing could improve any of them, I told him, except perhaps a kitchen match. Yet when I turned to him, what I saw was a grinning young man, sunglasses glinting in the bright sun, brawny tanned arms folded across his chest, radiant white teeth brilliant in his smile, overflowing with a delusional, guileless and utterly unjustifiable optimism.

Donald studied each of my drawings more carefully than necessary, and far more carefully than I did. Never critical, and offering nothing except praise and encouragement. His gestures of appreciation seemed to me a perverse mockery, and invariably tested my patience. Once some weeks before, he went so far as to restrain my hand when I decided to tear a page from my notebook. I recognized that the drawing was no good, but those fingers of his large hand curled like tan, firm talons and cupped themselves over my withered spotted hand making it appear even more death-like beside his. "No," he said, "leave that. I like it." I turned to him in silent surprise. "Hold off until tomorrow. Look at it again tomorrow." He smiled as if at the sight of his toothy grin I would fall suddenly helpless. "This one's good. I like it."

With all the restraint I could summon I said, "Tell me exactly why I should not throw this out. You must have a more substantial reason than that. Can you really like it that much?"

Questions of reason always stunned Donald, as if an appeal to reason was unreasonable. With a confused hesitation he said, "These sketches form a series you've created beside this pool. It'd be criminal to break their sequence. See what I'm getting at?"

A confused and inept liar; what could be more dangerous. Whenever I showed him something new, I stared directly into his eyes watching as they traveled over it and the corners of his eyes rose or tightened or stretched. In this way I knew that most of what I showed him he hated. He might lie, but he could not disguise. So inevitably his insistent talk about the retrospective strained my patience. Despite his determination to be encouraging, suddenly I knew I needed an excuse to send him immediately away.

So I asked him to run an errand for the purchase of large-size newsprint. The errand was neither difficult nor noxious, but still I felt a discomforting guilt. As compensation for this favor I suggested that with the change from the price of the drawing paper he should buy himself a quart of beer. This caused him to smile. I could tell this because the corners of his eyes tightened behind his sunglasses while the ends of his mustache turned slightly up.

But a little money finally had sent him on his way, and I had the patio to myself. I wished then that I had sent him away sooner. And what bothered me was that I had not. But I had managed to chase Donald away, and then I was alone beside the pool.

From open apartment windows around me came sounds; of radios and televisions and snatches of conversations and dinner dishes clacking together as they were washed. And every sound was softened by the thickening air.

My table was a few steps from the edge of the pool. Circular and of white-enameled metal, from the table's center a large green and white umbrella spouted conveniently. When the sun was low enough, its rays slipped beneath the umbrella's edge, striking the white enamel with a brassy golden red. That same light would strike the wine in my glass casting a muddy red reflection onto the table while the concrete of the patio continued to radiate the heat of the day. I could almost see the heat rise in waves against the cool, damp, heavier air spreading down.

Between two buildings of our apartment complex there was an open lot. If I positioned my chair properly, that space allowed me to watch the most marvelous sunsets. Patches of rose snagged on the bottoms of turquoise clouds, their edges like torn paper, bright pinks that turned insidious, tending toward a fiery gold, reddening, shifting through blue to violet. Vermillion, crimson, ultramarine, cobalt; manganese, viridian, cadmium orange and cadmium yellow; these were the colors of my sunsets.

Sunsets have never inspired me. No one but nature could do so little with so much. Even those cave-painters conjured colors more vibrant than what was found in a sunset. Perhaps this is why they painted inside caves. Nature, even at its best, is a weak imitation of Art.

No, a sunset is an event, but an event of drama rather than color; that battle between light and darkness. Color is merely the battlefield, shifts in hue and tint simple indications of the tide of that battle, the progress of that war. But sunsets are compelling, and watching them worse than a habit.

So what is it about them that most compels my attention? I will see a darkness one day which will never end; a day when darkness banishes light and color to flickering memory. Each battle at sunset is a foregone conclusion, yet I watch fascinated. The rest of us explain this fascination to ourselves as an enjoyment of the colors and their shapes, as if we were attempting to explain lightening to a child. In truth, it is this battle which brings me closer to acceptance of the inevitable, that smothering darkness beyond all light. Sunsets teach us acceptance; that acceptance which lies between the delusion of hope and the maw of fear. Or, if not acceptance, at least a humble resignation. A resignation at sunset.

Hideous thoughts; thoughts appropriate for a hideous old man.

CHAPTER NINE

EACH EVENING I reviewed that days' work while listening to music on my radio. I kept my collection of sketchbooks stacked in a corner of the apartment in rough chronological order, with those at the bottom filled when I first arrived. Gradually I had accumulated an impressive stack which stood in place of all the canvases I should have painted. So that stack depressed me as well. Yet I am grateful that music, like wine, bleaches out such darkness.

My radio generated light and warmth. From its back small holes offered a glimpse of an impossible world. The tubes inside glowed a liquid red-orange, a hellish color, a disturbing and erotic fluorescence, while exuding a draft of warm air that smelled of ozone and old dust. One could almost put one's arms around that radio, take it to one's bosom and warm one's stiff and chilly old hands over its back.

With Donald finally gone I discovered the radio was playing Beethoven; the cycle of Rasumovsky string quartets. Sublime music and a gift to raise the weight from every heavy heart. I had recently re-stocked with wine, so I was prepared to waste the rest of my evening reviewing sketches.

I discovered a perverse enjoyment in this sort of review because, as unlikely as it was, surprise remained possible. Even a sketch from several weeks past might suddenly present an unexpected revelation. So Donald's suggestion of restraint was not entirely unreasonable. Occasionally it demanded that much time for me to see finally what I had been looking at. But there were also disappointments; the discovery of a drawing I had regarded as successful, but now found almost sordid in its implacable failure.

But I continued these evening reviews because from time to time I discovered something that, with more work, might hold my attention. Yet even after additional work, most of those sketches remained stiff on the page, like repeated letters in a penmanship book. So I was relieved if even one stimulated my hand. Unfortunately, an evening of such review most often left me with a headache and regret.

But that evening, with Donald gone to accomplish his errand, a few pages of work I had completed days before suddenly held my attention until I struggled to recall when they had been done. An afternoon came to mind when Donald had sat across from me, a can of soda and a classroom's worth of student papers to mark, spread over our table.

The first four sketches were of a slim young man leaning over the shoulder of another who sat in a chair playing cards. I had worked on these figures in different ways, but only one had proved somewhat interesting. Following these were eight troche-style drawings of a young woman in a two-piece bathing suit. I moved past those to drawings of another woman wearing another bathing suit. This woman leaned against the diving board while she spoke with two men. I remembered her bathing suit and the way she had swayed gently as she talked to each of the men in turn, smiling up at the taller one and squinting half-blinded by the sun.

Those were followed by a sketch of a young man slouching down in his chair, legs extended and crossed ankle to knee, hands loosely holding a soft-drink can just below his navel. From the moment I had first looked at the blank page that shape was there, completely, in my hand and in my eye. I remembered drawing it without hesitation as its lines seemed to radiate from that soft-drink can. But when the man moved, the unfilled parts of the page became utterly blank, and that shape disappeared like a drop of water on hot concrete. Pencil poised, I had waited for the moment to pass and for the shape to return. But it did not, and then it did not matter. I had finished for that day, and I recognized it.

But those troche pieces from earlier captured my attention and held it. I paged back and forth over them surprised and somewhat confused. I approved of them without quite seeing why. The line from my pencil had been firm and convinced. And there was roughness in unexpected places, places where movement had come without effort. And there was a grace as well which almost approached elegance.

I turned back over the previous week's work looking for anything similar. Several drawings showed indications, as if eye and hand had struggled to find a movement of mind, a contortion of line that resembled inevitability. But nothing that preceded those drawings gave any hint of them. The troche drawings did not pretend more than they were; the harmonies of line, the shapes and their volumes were exciting and true though incomplete. It appalled me to realize it, but they were very nearly beautiful.

And then I realized those drawings were all of the same person. So I tried to remember her face, what she looked like, and became frustrated that I could not.

There were days when I sat beside that pool intoxicated by the heat and bright light. Sketches sometimes began and ended without clear intention. Lines could start by containing a volume, and suddenly that volume would disappear, emptied out, gone like smoke in a breeze. I could only look at those drawings later with consternation and embarrassment.

Though I struggled to remember that woman, I could only recall her in parts. The line of her calf from knee to ankle, the roundness of flesh on the inside of her arm, the length of her arm above the elbow. And her back. Three of the sketches were drawn from behind; two of her sitting on the edge of the diving board, another of her standing holding a towel in one hand. But when I tried again to remember her, all that came to mind was her muted, earth-green bathing suit. Sketches of her head were each incomplete, but stray lines suggested medium length hair which I remembered to be dark. But I was neither surprised nor concerned that I could not remember her face.

None of the sketches showed her complete face, only one attempted a profile. A thin nose, a sharp jaw, a slightly heavy chin. In one sketch, the chin and throat area were scratched over. I confess that sometimes the act of looking through my sketchbooks was like recalling a dream.

Memory tossed up segments of that woman, and those images moved with baffling speed. But they were there, undeniable evidence. I had not invented her.

With a charcoal-pencil I began to touch-over the shading of one of the drawings of her back while I tried to recall highlights of her face. But her face would not return to my memory, or perhaps it did and I could not recognize it. Suddenly I wanted Donald beside me. He would have recognized her, perhaps he already even knew her. But at least I could have tried with his help to puzzle it out. And just as suddenly I found myself thinking of Donald in a new way. I wondered about his girlfriend.

He had told me her name was Barbara, and he spoke of her with warmth and genuine loyalty, though physical passion never entered our conversation. Paging through that sketchbook, I realized I needed to meet Donald's girlfriend, because to meet her would be to know Donald in an entirely new way. I would sit beside her, drink wine with her, make caustic remarks about him in her presence and observe her reaction. Because Donald continued to elude me, and I had come nearly to resent this. Intelligent and manipulative but also somewhat talented, I could not understand why he remained at that University, or even in that town. A more provincial existence was difficult to imagine.

As I thought about all of this I realized that Donald and this mysterious woman from my sketchbook shared something profoundly important and deeply disturbing. As if she and Donald shared some ability that permitted the images of their faces to slip out of my memory completely the moment they had gone from my sight.

Or could this be all that remained of the crumbling mind of this old man? Could such a man, who had buried nearly all of his friends and nearly all of his lovers, arrive at a moment in his life when there was no room for additional faces? No face could be retained because there was no place to leave it aside. Had this miserable head become so cluttered with relics of the past that there was no room left for useful images of the present? A photo album with all of its pages filled? A sketchbook with no blank sheets left?

As I prepared for bed it seemed that something had been set into motion. The feeling of movement was undeniable, like sitting in the carriage of a train as it begins to move out of the station, the scenery at first moving slowly past my window, and then the speed increasing.

CHAPTER TEN

DONALD ARRIVED EARLY carrying under his arm the new drawing paper
I had asked for. I had not slept well and my head was still thick. This was my
reward for thinking. I drank two cups of coffee while he wandered around my
apartment waiting for me. I would have forced him to watch my third cup, but
his pacing finally came to irritate me. I asked him to gather my things and we
went out to the pool.

Seated at our table, I asked how his studies progressed. Through his
sunglasses I recognized his sudden irritation. I relished a bit of retribution. If
he could disturb me, I would disturb him in return.

"I'm doing an independent study with Burston."

"Fascinating. And have you made any momentous discoveries in this study?"

Donald shifted in his chair. "Discovery's not exactly the point."

"And does the history of art, the study of it, does this fascinate you? It
sounds interesting enough. I just wonder whether it excites you sufficiently to
give up your own painting and drawing to pursue it."

Donald became so uncomfortable I thought he might stand and leave.
After a long confused pause he laughed. "I haven't done any serious drawing
in years, but drawing was never something I was good at. I really liked
lithographs, and linoleum cuts. But I don't bother with that any more."

"Of course. Since the history of art really interests you, then so much the better. It just seems regrettable to give up such hard-earned skills. But confess something; for a long time didn't you very badly want to be famous, as a painter or engraver?" Donald hesitated, looked at me narrowly, his mistrust was almost palpable.

"Never mind," I said. "Teaching is a wise choice. After all, what are we if not first and foremost good teachers?"

Donald smiled behind his sunglasses, appeared to relax even as his foot hopped and jittered beneath our table.

"Once you have your degree," I continued, "you will be be able to teach anywhere you want."

He cleared his throat as if to announce his seriousness. "With any luck I'll find a job around here. I want to stay nearby even if it means teaching art history to farmers." He grinned at his own joke.

Our neighbors had begun to gather around the pool, and with careful glances I watched for her. People swam or reclined tanning, a few had books beside their chairs. I turned my chair to face into the sun, the heat striking hard on my chest.

I asked, "And what does your girlfriend say about all this?" Donald laughed in response but said nothing. "After all, I expect that with your plan to teach farmers you have decided to settle down, marry and all that."

"If you're asking when I plan to get married, nothing like that is exactly planned yet."

"Of course. And your fiancé no doubt has her own career in mind."

"She isn't my fiancé. I mean, we're not actually engaged."

"Fortunately for you both, when you've become a college professor there won't be an economic need for her to find work."

He sighed and leaned back as if this was a conversation he had already endured and still did not enjoy. "Barbara's in the school of pharmacology and she plans to go on to grad school. She wants to work at one of the hospitals." A blankness crossed his face, an exhaustion, and a touch of boredom.

"Sounds like an ambitious young woman. What kind of person is she?"

He looked at me carefully, and then he burst into laughter so loud several of our neighbors turned to stare. "That's a hell of a question." He continued to laugh though less noisily.

"Idle interest. Just an idle interest. You are here and I become curious." Donald slid lower in his chair, the sunlight heightened the sheen on his brow.

In my best conspiratorial tone I said, "This will seem an unlikely question, but have you ever met Barbara's mother?"

But before Donald had the chance to answer, I saw her, my model from the sketchbook.

She and another woman were just sitting in chairs several tables away that turned her in half-profile toward us. The two women performed the ritual laying-out of objects on the table, notebooks and towels and sunglasses and lotions, nodding as they talked. He watched while I opened the sketchbook and turned in their direction.

After a moment my model's companion stood and walked to the pool. I began to draw. Two drawings, hardly more than silhouettes, my hand trembled maddeningly. Then a third with fewer strokes. When I finished I shoved the pad toward Donald.

His look of surprise and chagrin annoyed me. He suspected he was being made a fool of, and perhaps he was right. Caught between boredom and annoyance, Donald eventually picked up the pencil.

His initial strokes were short, cautious, tending to curve in uneven waves, as if he awaited a mistake. Donald had not lied, his skills were very rough.

He turned the page and began another. The woman's friend called out to her several times from the pool to join her. My model waved and nodded but continued to read. While Donald drew I considered walking to her chair and introducing myself, in part to give myself an opportunity to study her face. She was not as tall as I recalled her from the drawings, nor as thick-limbed. But the line of her shoulders and the arch of her back as she leaned elbow to thigh; that shape I could have redrawn a thousand times.

Then from across the pool I heard a telephone ring. My model stood. Calling out to her friend, she picked up her towel and the rest of her things and walked quickly around the pool, climbed a set of stairs on the other side of the pool. Several doors to the right of the stairs she entered a door, closed it behind her. The telephone ringing stopped.

I slipped the sketchbook from under Donald's hands. "Should I deliver an insightful critique? Offer suggestions which might help you draw as I do? Would that please you?"

"Don't waste your time." His voice trailed off.

He had done four drawings. In each there were places where he had relaxed and fallen into a rhythm. Several good passages in one, in another the whole figure was placed well. I pointed out those places where he seemed sure of himself. In the end I said, "Bring your own sketchbook and pencils tomorrow and we will see what kind of progress you make. Perhaps you will sharpen your skills."

"Out of the question." He seemed seriously concerned. "Believe me, I've resigned myself." He forced a laugh, shifted uncomfortably in the sun, adjusted his sunglasses. "Besides, my time is tied up with graduate projects."

"Ridiculous. You will spend time here with me, anyway. Why not take advantage?"

More shifting in his seat, adjustment of sunglasses, as if he might be frightened by my suggestion.

"Fine," I said, "if your decision is final. But drawing would help us pass the time."

We spent the next two silent hours together beside the pool, with Donald grading papers as I sketched, until our neighbors began to drift back to their apartments while the sky hinted sunset. Then we stood and he walked with me to my door. I asked him what it was like to work with Burston. "Easy; he's brilliant in his field and he's head of the department." When I asked what Burston's academic specialty was, he said, "American Moderns. Loves Ashcan, Stewart Davis, the Cubists. Published a few articles on Thomas Hart Benton." Donald laughed again but more nervously, "And he's patient."

"Does he still talk about the retrospective?"

"He says he admires your work a lot." Donald shrugged and then looked back with impatience, as if he was stating the obvious, and the statement itself was a form of work. "And he wants to improve his position at the University. But a lot of others like the idea of that show as well."

"On the other hand," I said with a conspiratorial smile, "perhaps you and I can convince him that talented graduate students would benefit most from that sort of attention."

Donald shook his head over this, and I realized that my battle had already begun. As he turned to leave I said, "Bring your own paper and pencils tomorrow." I was feeling generous, even while I recognized that I had received a warning about the exhibition and the coming battle over it. Probably I even smiled.

CHAPTER ELEVEN

IF HISTORY MUST ALWAYS be memory and nothing more, why must it remain present? If it is immutable, why does it nonetheless appear to offer itself as if vulnerable to wish, plan or deed?

Donald and I arrived beside the swimming pool early again, perhaps because he had been out drinking the previous night. He certainly looked the worse for abuse. Even with the shield of his sunglasses his skin appeared yellow, the muscles around his mouth slack, his fingers gripped lazily. He suggested we remain in my kitchen a while longer but I would hear none of it. We left to take our seats under the hot sun beside our pool. In fact, he appeared to be in perfect condition for my experiment.

"This is something I only learned after I arrived in Paris and met Dedo. It was springtime and the Luxembourg seemed eternally beautiful. And all those young women; the nurses and laundresses and flower-sellers. Each day it seemed as if the whole world and every woman in it had been freshly made, and all were of exactly the same delectable age."

Donald moved his chair determined to sit where the sun could not find him. Undoubtedly it felt to him as if his brain was roasting, a feeling I know very well. "And everyone in Paris knew Dedo. Wherever we went, someone stopped us to speak with him. Especially the women. And this just added to my pleasure, because during that spring I fell in love nearly every day."

Donald's sketchbook on the table before him was bright green and corrosive orange. The pencils, blue and brown and green with blond ends and black tips, spread like colorful fingers in his shirt pocket. Sweat beaded on his forehead glistening in the golden light of mid-morning.

"Of course, Dedo and I had no money. You cannot know how little money we had. We had so little money, it was incalculable how little it amounted to. So there was never any money to pay models. Who could pay models when there was no coal to light a fire so that a naked body did not turn blue? Dedo sketched in the cafes around Place Pigalle for the price of a drink." I leaned toward Donald urgently. "I dare you to draw someone's portrait and then attempt to sell it to him. Even if it is only for a very small amount of money, this is a difficult thing."

Donald no longer looked in my direction. He drummed the table quietly with his fingertips, sighed, rubbed his forehead. Neighbors began to surround us; light, voices, the noise, everything becoming brighter. Gradually I began to enjoy myself.

"So he and I would sit together in the parks, particularly Place Willette below Sacre-Coeur. In this game we each took a turn choosing a model. Someone seated or standing in the park, and we would simultaneously draw that person. Then, the person who had originally chosen would call a stop. You understand? Dedo was so fast it made me furious. In those days I thought it important to take infinite pains with each line, every curve and shadow. But I would hardly finish an arm or a torso, while Dedo tossed off sheet after sheet, each time laughing, demanding to know when the Sistine Chapel would be finished. Now listen; he never wasted time looking carefully at my work. He understood how to encourage without instructing, but he insisted it was better to draw again than waste time making the last drawing perfect. I learned a great deal from him. About drawing, and so many other things as well."

Donald was gradually becoming miserable. Sweat trailed down either side of his face and he sat on the edge of his chair as if ready to leap. I chose someone for us to draw, and we began.

I worked slowly, paying little attention to what I was doing. But I listened closely to Donald's pencil scratching, audible even through all of the noise. I listened for length of line, for whatever excitement, whatever energy. And I listened for stops, reconsidered movements, hesitations. These are all observed better with the ear, which is not distracted by flaws of perspective, disjointed figures, lines and volumes gone awry. The ear identifies the only two qualities of any consequence; conviction and energy.

When the young man I had chosen stood to go swimming, I called a stop. I waited for Donald to choose. For a moment I was afraid he would simply hand me his sketchbook and leave. But he made his choice, a woman sitting alone on a blanket beside the diving board, and we resumed. I drew a bit, in case he decided to check my work. But I listened to his effort while I continued to watch for her.

Having made his choice, Donald worked furiously. As if by the act of choosing a model, he was now committed to fulfill his part. He seemed to understand what was wanted, but I had not expected him to carry it out so urgently. His body trembled and lurched, as if he hoped to place his shoulder behind his pencil. Donald's energy surprised me.

After several more drawings we rested. Donald offered to go back to the apartment and bring out something cold. I regretted there was no beer, but there were soft drinks and he left to get them.

In his absence I looked over what I had done, since it was easier to laugh at myself while he was gone. And I felt an odd relief when I realized I could throw all of my day's work away without regret.

I watched Donald approach carrying two soft-drink cans. Then, from the shadows immediately behind him, she stepped into the sunshine. She walked behind him as he turned toward our table. As he resumed his chair across from me she sat and then stretched out on a lounge chair just two steps away. He placed one of the open cans before me, then sat, his chair angled obliquely between the woman and me. I looked past his shoulder for a time and then my sketchbook was open.

As I began to draw I said, "Tell me a bit more about Barbara. I expect my request is rude, but just to satisfy my curiosity tell me some pleasant memory of her that you are saving. A memento you are determined to preserve for the days when you are both very old." Donald watched me clearly confused by my request. He slouched in his chair, content to rest while I drew. "Tell me about the first time you slept with her." His surprise at that request was obvious from the muscles around his mouth, and even under that bright sun he blushed. How charming, a blushing American. But whether from surprise or discretion or annoyance he remained silent.

Past his shoulder I watched the woman as she lounged, long legs extended, ankles folded one over the other, a book open in her lap. My hand moved without hesitation, those shapes not drawn but appearing under a pencil that behaved as if possessing its own consciousness.

The woman then leaned slightly forward as if watching for someone at the other side of the pool. As I drew I felt a tremor, as if under that scorching sun some chill wind had blown suddenly across my chest. Donald seemed not to notice. My hand moved without effort; as though all of the years and all of my practice had anticipated this one particular model whose lines seemed as familiar to my hand as my own signature.

I finished four good drawings before another woman sat down beside her and they began to talk. The gestures of the two women made it impossible to continue. I put aside my pencil and sat back to study and observe the curve of her arm, the shape of her neck and the way it joined to her shoulders, the way she dipped her left shoulder elegant as a duchess.

By this time our sundeck had become crowded. Donald suggested we resume but now I only cared to watch the light upon her back, and the blue-white of the swimming pool beyond. Whether he hoped for additional praise or a bit of advice, suddenly I recognized that my day was finished.

Then the woman and her companion stood. My model stretched arching her back, legs long and thighs firm, broadened at her hips that rolled like waves crashing, her back carved from fine alabaster and bright with oil, square shoulders which she carried like a ball-gown. A breathless exhaustion from our brilliant heat overwhelmed me. When she walked away, something of me left with her.

The others gathered around the pool became invisible to my pencil. Attracting the eye, they provided nothing for the hand; nothing lay beneath what was seen. To be alive and yet so old, this world merely a motion picture viewed through a keyhole.

When I told Donald I had finished for the day he appeared relieved, yet he protested. "Let's sit for a few more sketches."

"Draw as much as you like, but I am tired and must return to my apartment."

He stood. "Before you go, take a look at these." His hands fumbled with the book that he handed toward me. And suddenly I was angry. He needed to learn to like his own work, as much as he needed to dislike his own work, so that eventually he could distinguish between the two. Or so I insisted to myself. And I no longer wanted to look at anything at all.

"Practice," I said, "will improve your work, at least for a while. Give yourself that time. You have rediscovered satisfaction in the work itself. Enjoy that as well."

Disappointment gathered all about his mouth, but he agreed. My leg had begun to throb as the pain in my shoulders grew worse. I wished to leave and could not. My curiosity about Donald had evaporated. I became withdrawn and this made him uncomfortable. He sat motionless staring across the pool. I had finally bored myself. This day would end with self-loathing and self-pity, as days so often end. The day was dying slowly; it twisted around itself, it writhed and pounded its tail against the ground with dull thuds. Suddenly the air smelled fetid, overused, the light seemed soiled and flabby as rotted fruit. Only the breeze at twilight could wash us clean again. My gnarled hands, sore and thick, my arms, my whole body had collapsed and folded into that chair. Heat crawled down into my throat, claws digging deeper with each breath. I stood and returned to my apartment, it was just that simple. Eventually Donald followed.

At my door I reminded him to bring his book the next day. He looked at me oddly for a long moment. Whether he wanted to be invited inside, or merely hoped that I would pass him money for beer, I did neither and then he was gone.

I closed my door on him with the relief of a host after the departure of the last party guest. The air conditioner clanked metal against metal, roared and then purred, blowing a cool, mechanical flatulence. I walked the dozen steps to the refrigerator and my knees pinched and burned.

How much of that woman was a product of my imagination, and how much a gift from memory? This seemed important to determine. I lifted the bottle of wine, and was rewarded with sharp pain in my shoulder.

So little varied for me from one day to the next, I should not have forgotten her. Could I have been in her presence before and simply not remembered?

The air-conditioner pumped the combined smells of broiling meat and cat urine. My body weighed a thousand pounds, dull heart thudding, breathing twisted sighs, my lungs flopping inside my chest like sacks of mud. I turned on the radio in the hope there would be Mahler.

Once many years before, I rented an old farmhouse in southern France in the hills just north of Toulon. It rested against a small broad hill on the edge of a gnarled vineyard. I remember that first ride along its twisted dirt road several miles from the main road which passed on to Marseille, feeling relieved that I would enjoy such beautiful isolation. The vines planted around the house had been pruned low for the winter, and brown, dry weeds were thick between their rows. The vines resembled twisted fingers reaching up through the black dead earth. But the farmhouse was spacious and its setting was beautiful.

Matisse had been painting in the town of Collioure near the Spanish boarder and complained of having a terrible time, so I wrote to invite him to join me. There was so much room, I told him, and so much of it going to waste. And I told him about the grape-arbor standing a short distance from the side of the house. I had cleared away its weeds soon after I arrived. I told him of afternoons spent painting, or lounging, or watching clouds build huge and grey in the north, while to the south there was the bright blue ribbon of sea. And how every evening the wind blew directly from North Africa into my window. And the way the ground beyond the grape-arbor fell away sharply, leaving a view of the valley and the road beyond to Marseille winding between the hills like an impertinent black ribbon, and in the far distance the city of Toulon and the Mediterranean.

But Matisse had not warned me he intended to bring a companion, and then Jeanne was there and I could not protest. She was tall and slim with red hair, quiet, nearly sullen, and very young. For the first few days it seemed wherever Henri and I were, she was there, always slightly dissatisfied, a bit morose, a bourgeois out of her element and disdainful of everything not bourgeois.

He and I sometimes drew her together beneath the arbor, with patches of sunlight dappling the contours of her slim young body. For Jeanne was thin then, with a thin woman's face, eyes almost almond-shaped and large and dark, while from her head poured a mass of burnt-orange colored hair which she wore long and which she flipped defiantly in a terrifying arc whenever she was annoyed. Full lips and high gaunt cheeks, in a pensive, darkened mood she was nearly frightening. By then Henri had become more interested in rooms and interiors, and so he most frequently painted her in the large parlor. Each time I asked how he had met her, Matisse became mysterious. But at that time I felt no concern.

As the weather improved and the days grew longer and hotter I found myself more often inclined to ask Jeanne to sit for me outdoors. And more often Henri acquiesced.

Time spent with Henri; learning not by instruction or example but inspiration. And time spent watching her moods and postures and then listening to her soft voice. And so my growing sense of her frail and profound beauty.

Sometimes I think that even then, early in the game, Henri was laughing at me.

Despite the size of the house my room resembled a monk's cell. It was large but with only a single narrow bed, a small bureau, a work table and chair, and beside the window a broad fat reading chair. The pair of tall windows faced west and late in the day, golden sunlight exploded among my meager possessions. Some weeks after they arrived I suggested that Jeanne sit for me in that room, in that light. Over several days I drew her for about one hour each day. Bathed in yellow and gold and red light, she remained motionless for that hour, shadows around her growing violet and indigo and black until the light finally faded. We rarely spoke, except about Henri and his health, and then later even that topic became unimportant when we made love.

Perhaps Henri recognized what was merely growing, still half-formed; that I had come to be in love with his pretty, red-haired model. So sometimes I find myself certain he laughed at me. Upon reflection I suppose that was appropriate. Love, after all, had come suddenly, and I was unprepared.

Nearly every day the three of us ate our lunch together and drank our wine together under the blooms and blossoms of the arbor, even when we had not been working together. Ours became the sort of life artists dream will be theirs as soon as they have become famous. So there I was, enjoying fruits and rewards I had not even begun to earn.

Then one day Matisse announced he must return to Paris. When he first arrived he had said he intended to remain until fall. I do not know the source of his decision to leave. I could not understand why suddenly he preferred to endure the summer weather of Paris. And worse, he had given me little warning of this change of plan.

Though Henri had given no warning, I believe now that he recognized something I could not quit name. He and Jeanne were not lovers, of this I am certain, yet perhaps he felt something toward us that resembled jealousy.

So one afternoon he and I sat together beginning our lunch under the arbor, just us two. Jeanne was off somewhere, dismissed for the next several hours. It was an afternoon of immaculate light. Sounds cluttered the air; insects, birds in the meadow, while far off a dog barked, and was answered by another. That afternoon I was still full of having slept with Jeanne, of having drawn her, and the anticipation of sleeping with her again, and the smell of her throat in the darkness of my arms.

Over bread and wine and cheese and sausages Henri began by telling me how impressed he was by the work I had been doing, and what a good effect this sojourn had been for me. As he spoke he watched me carefully, too, perhaps even counting the glasses of wine.

With a wistful smile Henri said, "It appears I need to return to Paris." Yellow sunlight bathed his face, he turned from his glass of bright red wine squinting toward me. "Bernheim-Jeune wants to re-negotiate my contract." He laughed with the self-confidence of a man who knows his own value better than those he is expected to trust. "Two years we have waited but finally they have agreed to increase my prices. Two years!" He slapped the table. "As if I was a child needing discipline."

Of course I was pleased for him. I asked when he planned to leave and he said, "Wednesday; four days. I need to be in Paris on Friday."

"And when will you return?"

He waved his hand. "I do not assume the papers will be ready for my signature." He shook his large square head and sunlight glinted from his eye-glasses. He turned away to face down the valley, bright light flooding its eastern side, the west bathed in blue shadows. "Not less than a month and certainly no more than three. If negotiations carry on past July, I will leave Paris, contract or not, and return. So you can be certain to see me in August." He smiled broadly, squinting.

And I smiled too, pleased for Henri and his good fortune. This was not the result of simple luck; for a long time his work had fetched good prices. But I smiled as well with the sudden recognition of my own good fortune. Jeanne and I would be alone at the farmhouse as summer deepened. Time to be productive, to paint and draw, draw and paint, morning until nightfall, and then as dusk colored the tops of the hills with indigo, there would be love.

Then Henri added, "Of course, Jeanne must accompany me." He must have studied my face then and recognized precisely how possessed I had become by this woman. And how much more possessed I was about to become.

Thus I played the ass in a comedy of manners; a bedroom farce not unworthy of Moliere himself, as if he had written my dialogue and created every thought in my head. I smiled while my knees trembled. I expect I said something about my own work and how the time with the two of them away would allow me to complete it. There were more glasses of wine, and with each glass the light changed, the air changed, everything re-molded itself. Jeanne did not reappear, and then I did not notice her absence. Henri and I began to talk together as we had not since his arrival.

Much of our talk was about painters and their paintings, styles and techniques and who was working well or in interesting ways. We talked this way until the sun had reached the horizon between two hills, and the shadows around us had deepened and lengthened as the light turned, yellow to gold and then red. My head became filled with the sound of his voice muted by that wine he continued to pour demanding that I drink.

Finally in answer to a half-articulated question he promised he would bring Jeanne back as soon as he was able. But for now she must visit her parents, he said. He felt obligated, Henri confessed, to bring her to her parents so they could be assured she was well. And besides, he also had planned canvases that depended on her presence, and he was as eager that she return as I was.

But I never believed him; nor do I think he expected me to. It was sufficient that I lacked the courage to deny what he said, but also lacked the courage to believe. At that moment, with my heart so thoroughly turned, I would avoid understanding what I certainly knew.

So we talked on and on. Later, Jeanne did not join us for dinner, and still later she did not join me in my bed. I became very drunk that night. Yet not drunk enough to forget, only too drunk to be fearful.

In the morning Henri was already working, Jeanne seated under the arbor. I wanted very badly to see her alone, but I could only sit beside Henri with a silent pencil. Even with my head throbbing and my nausea, I noted the passage of the hours, moments slipping past until they would depart. I scratched at the paper waiting to be alone with her, in the darkness, to share with her my silence and my grief.

But not that day, nor that evening, nor even that night. Each day and each night, Jeanne was here or she was there, or she was with Henri, but she and I were never alone.

Until that last evening before they planned to leave. Paul was already on his way driving Henri's big grey car, had probably reached Toulouse. He was expected to arrive at the farm early and would join the three of us for a meal. They would then leave together and I would be left alone. In my mind

I rehearsed the passage of those hours, forced myself to believe that despite all that had been planned they would return together. I insisted this to myself because reality had become too awful.

And that last day Jeanne remained elusive, as if already practicing the avoidance of my embrace, or my whispered words of love and despair, as if she was already gone.

In preparation for his departure Henri carefully cleaned brushes, wrapped canvas and folded his clothes into his suitcase. I suspected he helped Jeanne pack her things as well, and I was jealous even of this. I wanted that privilege of touching for the last time her intimate things; those small objects she had kept beside her bed, to feel every article of her clothing, to find the proper place for each in her bags, and to handle each small thing one last time.

But finally I was alone with her. As I suspect of everything that happened that spring, this meeting, too, was Henri's doing. Had he perhaps even urged her to see me?

She and I sat together under the arbor. The moon was full to bursting, heavy and pale, and the black sky surrounding it sparkled with slivers of light. Jeanne sat leaning back into deep shadows. Though she was inches from me she was almost invisible. Unable to see her face clearly I held her thin soft hand to be certain she would not disappear without my knowledge.

And there I opened my heart to her, offering every scrap of phrase I thought might be true. I spoke every word that came into my head. She remained silent, as if listening. I could not see her eyes but I believe that from time to time she looked at me.

When I finished there were only those secret sounds of the night. But finally Jeanne spoke. "The moon is restless," she said, "it has no mouth and it must speak." And she said, "The moon is sad, it gives love unevenly. The color of the night leaves the moon without hope. The clear light of the stars, arms embracing, reach even into the jungle, even deep into the earth. The moon has eyes, its arms are forgiving, even in the jungles of our hearts."

She trembled. A warm breeze carried the odors of summer earth and sounds of invisible life. Her hand was dry as I held it, and I listened to her breathe. Looking to the sky she said, "There is Mars. And there is Venus. Heaven is alive and moves, the subtle movement of an ever-breathing beast. The planets are alive, they breathe, and they hate us. They watch us and they see, and in the love of their hearts, in the joy of their embrace, they hate us. They see we are not beautiful and we cannot love, and they loathe us, a merciless contempt. To them we are as spiders. We disgust them so thoroughly they pity us. Even you, merely because you create, you are no less contemptible, ugly, worm-like, just as blind and just as ignorant. While they up there are even more beautiful than the sun. So they suffer for us here."

She leaned further into the darkness with the slightest smile as she withdrew her hand and curled her knees beneath her. Somehow she seemed for a moment to radiate a pale blue light.

As she suggested, I searched the sky for some sign. She had found that sign she needed, something that helped her to continue. So I searched for something that would allow me to continue as well. She was so young, I could only marvel at her understanding.

I said, "Promise me only that you will return with Henri. Tell me that when you have finished in Paris you will return with Henri." I had no counter, no alternative. I was so shaken, so abject and empty.

After a long pause she said, "Mars is guided by the smell of blood. Our earth attracts its attention. It is a predator that knows we are here and prepares to attack. We are such loathsome creatures. The beauty within our souls has been drained by all those machines which suckle us, and nourish us, until they lead us by the hand to our chill, damp graves. Mars understands the spirit of machines so all machines obey the god of war." She leaned forward into the silver light of the fat moon, her grin haunting. "And you? What of you? Will you join the machines? When Mars beckons, will you answer and obey as well?" With that question still on her lips she stood, held herself very still, white highlights sparkled in her hair and upon her sharp cheeks. She breathed evenly, poised to be seen before moving. Did I sigh? Or was that sound of despair the rustle of her dress as she moved, or merely the sound of that which was hidden within the night?

She strode across the dark lawn with long, young legs toward the lighted doorway. The open door bathed her for an instant in yellow light. She did not hesitate in that pale light, but stepped though and was gone.

The air thickened slowly around that door. The farmhouse became encased in another time as it appeared to retreat, and suddenly it and I were separated by centuries. As if already I was merely recalling a dry and hollow past. A gulf opened separating us, all of us, the past become tangible, a continent dividing us, its outlines indelible under the cool, pale light of the moon. What had just passed was now utterly gone.

I remained under the arbor, weighed down within that chair, watching each of the lights in the house blink out. The moon traversed its slow path, and the stars followed in honorable silence. Hushed footsteps of ghosts passed across the field and came to stand beside me to watch as I wept. Slowly the black night turned grey. Mist stole through the vineyard, grey tendrils curling about the staked black vines. Goats wandered on the opposite hill, their bells echoing and brayed to each other as I wept.

The mist-grey sky lightened until a rising breeze announced dawn and carried the gold-tinged smell of the sea. I went to the house, and without undressing laid down in my empty bed to drown in profound and awful sleep.

Suddenly Henri was beside me saying, "We're going now. We're leaving." He pushed gently on my shoulder, leaned down over my face smiling, eye-glasses glinting in the full sunlight. "We're leaving now," he repeated. He wore the grey tweeds he called his driving habit and his little chauffeur's cap.

With an effort I cleared my eyes until I looked directly into his. "Are you her lover?" I demanded. "Tell me now and I will believe whatever you say. Are you her lover?"

The grin left his face; his look darkened and then became terrible. And I became terrible. Words came from my lips which I had never thought before. In the course of that torrent, how did he restrain himself from violence? How did he not beat me bloody?

Instead, he simply snarled, shoved my shoulder hard and then left the room. I listened to his footsteps ring clear on the stone steps, then thud dully on the wood floor through the house, and eventually emerge crunching on the gravel drive. I listened to the car door close, the automobile engine cough and then start.

By the time I stood and reached the window, wheels were moving slowly over the noisy gravel. The engine roared gaining speed and then the car approached the gate. There was just enough time to recognize profiles, and know certainly that she was with them. At the gate the car turned left, increased speed and then they were gone. No profile turned in my direction.

In the days that followed I discovered the value of sleeping until well after noon, of wanders over the grounds of the farm, of the distinct unburdening of idleness. The days appeared stacked like playing cards unreeling with the arbitrary beauty of a solitaire hand. The heat of the day challenged my concentration, while the cool voluptuousness that drifted through the windows at night tormented my memory, sending nettles of desire that would not let me rest. And worse, in some concatenation of what I feared and what I desired, a fantasy gradually overwhelmed me, until finally I convinced myself that at any moment she might return. With that I found myself drawing again.

My fantasy was so miserably unbelievable, so perfectly impossible that I could pretend it without fear or hope. I pretended that at any moment Jeanne would flee Matisse, flee Paris, leave whatever her life had come to, and fall into my arms. In preparation for this impossible event, I returned to painting even as I continued to sleep until mid-day. The light through those windows as dusk approached was glorious, and as it faded I chased blue and indigo and violet, until darkness obliterated all. At night, working by candlelight, I drew with chalk and crayon in pursuit of the colors of the fire; gold-orange, yellow, sienna and ocher. Otherwise I slept or read, but when I drew I did so furiously, sheet after sheet. Somehow I convinced myself she was about to return, and would be delirious with satisfaction by what she would discover I had accomplished.

Days passed until that month became the next, followed by another. The summer was a dry abundance, a horde of golden light in which everything glittered. When the evening air became so thick one could drown breathing, I finally regained enough strength to abandon my hope, and simply revel in its memory. And then the large grey car turned into the drive and passed through the gate.

In silhouette, Paul hunched behind the wheel, Henri beside him gripping the dashboard with both hands, face nearly to the windshield. A tremor rippled over me. When I could see further into the car I recognized that she was not with them. I had prepared myself for this likelihood, but not well enough.

After quick embraces of greeting, Paul and I carried his and Henri's bags to the big room on the second floor. He and Paul planned to continue on to Nice the next day. "You must come with us," Henri insisted. "There is the air and the hills and the sea. Please. It will give your eyes a treat." Their arrival brought relief to my brooding solitude. But I could not yet accept that generous offer.

Over wine Paul described the perils of their auto trip, the breakdowns, the farmhouse just beyond Avignon where they had been forced to take shelter. When, at the last part of the evening, I could no longer restrain my curiosity I asked Henri about Jeanne and her stay in Paris. He looked at me a long moment and then laughed. "My good friend, you would be so much happier collecting used and empty tubes of paint than trying to collect your models."

Paul stood then, excused himself saying he needed sleep. They would leave at seven, he said, and he hoped I would join them. I listened to his hollow footsteps climb the wooden stairs, and then the bedroom door close.

Finally alone with Henri I insisted he tell me everything he knew. Again he laughed a quiet, gentle laugh that chilled me. A laugh that said he understood my unhappiness completely, and that there was no help for it. With the smile still tracing his lips, his voice lowered to a whisper. "Listen to me. If we are to paint well we must love all of our models, each and every one. A rock, a mountain, a sky, a bowel of fruit or a lovely woman. We must love each to the utmost of our capacity. The act of painting is an act of love. Each act of love is a way of seeing, a way of recognizing that which is most beautiful around us. A lover is a model of convenience, just as a model is a lover of convenience, useful because available if she is patient and sympathetic. But a lover is no longer a useful model when the love for her that you need to paint beautifully is no longer there, has become simply another act of possession. Listen to this old man's advice; you have a great deal yet to accomplish. Paris does not wait for you, do not wait for Paris." His laughter was as gentle as I could want, yet it caused me to shiver again. His laugh said, we now understand each other so well we will never need to speak of this again.

I stayed in Nice with Paul and Henri for two weeks; a time of additional and more elaborate idleness in which I enjoyed the city, the night life and the cafes. In the mornings I watched the fishermen outfit their armada and crest the waves to test their fates. But eventually I became eager to return to the farmhouse, and to painting. Paul announced that he needed to drive to Lyon. I asked if he would drive me to the farmhouse on his way. Henri listened without expression, watched in compassionate silence while I packed my things. When I had placed my bags in the car he took me aside. "Do not forget that I am here. You should give up the isolation from time to time. It is such a short drive. Paul can be at the farmhouse to rescue you very quickly. Stay busy, my friend, but when you need a spree, remember us here."

Paul was an excellent driver and we drove rapidly along the narrow roads and for a long time we drove in silence. In spite of my friendship and affection for Henri, it was up to Paul to tell me what I most wanted to know. Shortly after she arrived in Paris, Jeanne was introduced to Dedo. Did I need to know more? Of course. She had modeled for several painters, had enrolled in a painting class where Dedo found her. After a while she modeled only for him.

They became lovers and now they lived together in Rue la Peche. Did I need to know more? Perhaps not. Paul and I did not speak again until we arrived at the farmhouse.

I remained in Toulon for six months more. I needed to paint, and still I could not face returning to Paris and meeting them, Jeanne and Dedo, together. There would be quarrels; I knew them both at least that well. I imagined myself sitting across a café table from a drunken Dedo to hear his complaints of her weaknesses, her dullness, her malleability and her infidelities. As such thoughts came to me I felt my heart grow weak and beat more softly. I would never find the strength to console him. I could never take his side against her, could never listen patiently and offer him my sympathy.

During the rest of my stay at the farmhouse Henri and I exchanged occasional visits. Then, that spring before the Armistice, he came to take a long, careful look at my canvases. That year had resulted in more than twenty, and nearly all of them seemed to please him. His enthusiasm for my paintings gave me courage to return to Paris and try for a show. And during that year, too, I gradually grew accustomed to thinking of Jeanne and Dedo together.

When I returned to Paris in the fall I found life was exactly as I had expected; parties, fights, meetings, evasions, desperation, doubt, misery, humiliation, reconciliation, and joy, too. I had visualized all of it in my solitude; a remarkable clairvoyance which gave me no pleasure. And just as I had feared, I was cast frequently into the role of peace-maker for the two lovers.

What I had never anticipated was my devotion to their happiness; the energy and patience and good humor I brought to their squabbles startled me.

But then all of us, even Picasso whose disinterest in such matters verged on the diabolical, all of us tried to help them. We did this because we saw how good, how energetic and how serious she was to help Dedo. And because above all, we loved him.

Dedo was beautiful and weak and self-destructive and strong and assertive and protective. And we loved him. So, as it became obvious he was truly about to die the death we had always predicted, we loved them both even more. We recognized things in him to which we could only aspire: profligate energy, indomitable pride, disdain for mediocrity, casual ease in the face of desperate circumstances, but most of all his complete and unshakable conviction that he was indeed a great artist.

And when those last days came and we watched Jeanne, pregnant now

and running frantically from one doctor to the next for them both and fiercely
holding off death, something close to amazement filled us all.

The girl was born even as Dedo wheezed and coughed, spitting blood, his
beautiful head even more beautiful in his pallid weakness, and we loved them
all now, all three even as something within us was slowly passing away. Dedo
was stealing something from each of us. Some bit of our lives was disappearing
within his sunken and tormented chest. We could merely watch Jeanne
fight with her thin pale arms, fighting and fighting for all there was in this
monstrous world worthy of her to love. All of that love she fought to keep, and
no one, not her parents and not God, would steal this love from her without a
battle. Squalor and beauty and devotion and pain; we watched him slide faster
and faster, away from all of us, without hope.

But somehow she held him. Jeanne held the child and she held him, both
together, with a strength we had never suspected her capable of. She shamed
us. We were awed and shamed by her whom we had disdained; the effete
bourgeois. Her frantic determination to replace what Dedo gradually drained
amazed us and humbled us.

Perhaps it was our youth. Perhaps in the midst of all this we suddenly
realized that we were no longer so young. And a recognition that no matter
what the future, we were all about to be somewhat less, our confidence
somewhat diminished. Each of our endings stood out more sharply, and those
endings were not so far off after all.

Many who stood by Jeanne and Dedo are now dead. But for each of us, our
own deaths began the day Dedo died.

Because it was not enough that he died.

Finally we came to accept this death, his ending. With his gradual decline
there had been time to understand and salvage a shred of peace. So when he
died we were prepared to mourn, to hold each other, to console each other, and
then to carry on. All of this without thinking of anything else.

The next morning, the morning after he died, despairing of ever living
completely without Dedo in her arms, Jeanne leaped from a high window to
her own death. This, the grotesque, destroyed us completely.

We might have withstood. We were, after all, somewhat prepared for
Dedo's death. But for Jeanne to be gone, by her own hand and of her own grief.
And there was still the child.

We walked arm-in-arm to Pere-Lachaise in some terrible, stupid rain, mourning ourselves and what we had already begun to re-invent as the glorious past, regaling ourselves with guilt and glory, a self-indulgence, an ecstasy of self-hatred, self-loathing. They had died; a stupid fact and as meaningless as the fact that we continued to live. But we had been marked. Other things happened, the future happened, that world of events none of us could have imagined. Yet this above all marked us. We mourned their meaningless passage, and a love we could only envy.

All of us marked, forever.

Old men think such things. Memory comes unbidden, like death, and cannot be cast aside by the movement of a wrist, the turn of an eye, the flutter of a page.

My graduate students came to me eager for something they could not name but were certain they needed. I looked at their work, the things they spent their time and energy completing, wondering what I could give them that would be of any value. Would I show them tricks? Would that replace the urgency, the desperation, to love by painting? Where would they find the thickly-muscled hearts they would need?

My day finally stood at the threshold of night and darkness. I paged over those drawings of the woman beside our swimming pool. I wanted her to be different and yet to be all of the models in all of the lights under all of the suns waiting to be discovered, that which is least discoverable; the self-evident.

My leg continued to ache as my heart pounded in my ears and my eyes would no longer focus. The air-conditioner blew a swampish heat. It seemed I could not catch my breath. The radio meanwhile would only give me Brahms. Perhaps that was why those drawings seemed to smear and blur. Shadows became a mound of raw black earth covered by cut, long-stem flowers strewn chaotic and wilting under a sky low and grey, cold rain falling heavier. Old men should not speculate upon life, they are least prepared.

Carefully I tore those drawings of her and her swimming pool out of the sketchbook, arranged them on the wall. Daylight was fading quickly, but wth my glass refilled and my cane in hand I hobbled out to the pool side.

One more sunset.

CHAPTER TWELVE

DONALD KNEW that I was expected at the faculty meeting, and that he was expected to provide a ride for me. It did not matter that I cared nothing for those exercises of petty animosities, but my attendance was part of my contractual obligation.

Scheduled to begin at two, by one-thirty Donald still had not arrived. I called his apartment twice. When I recognized I would not reach him in time, I should have called Marla immediately. But instead I called Burston. Since he and I so often disagreed, he was easily convinced that once again my presence at this meeting would benefit no one. In the midst of our phone conversation he asked about Donald. I insisted to him that the responsibility for my absence was entirely my own. I had come to suspect he had found a new favorite among his graduate students who he expected would replace Donald. I found Donald's companionship difficult enough, but at least he was thoroughly trained. Always prefer the devil you know.

But his absence that day still surprised me. In the past he had arranged his absences in advance. He appreciated an occasional holiday, and he had my sympathy for the dull job of attending an old man.

So it was late in the day before I finished making phone calls and absolving myself of further bureaucratic obligations, and then, sketchbook under-arm, I made my appearance beside the pool. The sun was already low, a disk of lurid orange. Although most had already gone, several of our neighbors still lay about. But she was not among them.

I opened my sketchbook, flipped through its pages, hesitated at those ragged edges left by those torn drawings that now decorated my wall, until I reached the next blank sheet. The moment I took up the pencil my hand moved blindly, as if in a sudden dozing dream, filled with aimless motion, abrupt and pointless stops, lines carved over and over, all of it fueled by a sense of helpless yet alert lethargy and frustration. I could only conclude that the day had begun badly, and there was no likelihood of its improvement. Nothing stirred my eye, or moved it to move my hand. Nothing, except bright white light, and blue and green.

I began to wonder about her. At first I merely wondered where she was, but then I found myself wondering about her more particularly. I glanced up repeatedly to that door she had entered the last time I had seen her, and wondered further. Was that her apartment? And why had I not noticed her before? How had she come to my attention without my awareness? That door became a screen upon which I projected images, a lens of sorts, or perhaps a prism. And at that moment I began to draw.

The oblique angle from which I could see the door, the parallel lines of the door's frame, the window-frames at either side of it, even the roof-line; all appeared determined to converge and failed. Her apartment? Her friend's apartment? Her boyfriend's apartment? Had I stopped noticing such things? Did that matter? And if it did, to whom did it matter most?

The moment I began to sketch my hand started to tremble, and despite that heat and sunlight its disorderly movement frustrated me and made me furious. Sharp pains bloomed between my shoulders. In less than a moment I recognized that I had sketched an absurdist's mess, and the sheet of paper before me was now only useful for cleaning brushes. The door-frame at the center of the sheet remained too open and could not hold the edges. What was needed was a sinuous line, a shapely and proportioned form to relieve the tension of relentlessly telescoping lines. Perhaps I could add a man bent with age and with a cane supporting him.

I looked away to stare into the deepest shadows beside the pool, a respite for my eyes from that overabundance of light. I imagined her stepping out through that doorway, her hair pulled severely-back from her face and wearing a pale summer dress, she and the dress moving even as she reached backward, behind her, stretching awkward with the door-handle barely within her fingertips, reaching to pull the door shut, fixed in that moment within that door frame, pulling it closed behind her, in a swirl of pastel movement. Thus I tried to draw. When finally the image blossomed beneath my hand I knew I could smile.

The woman was an occasion. I would recognize that fact and eventually even accept it. She was an opportunity, a sort of doorway, but even for this I would be grateful. Of course I did my best to purge myself of illusions; she existed independent of any drawing or painting or photograph fueled by my desire, unconstrained by any encapsulation or limitation within any frame I might draw. But still she was for me an occasion, and nothing less. And a lens of sorts, through which light and shape and color and movement all converged in a passionate and colorful energy, a hurricane of visibility, the ravenous eye's mouth's feasting. My drawings existed independent of her, yet dependent upon some fortuitous combination of luck and will. The drawing was that which truly existed, unchanging over time. Whatever else appeared to endure, appearance itself endured.

With another glance around the pool I discovered myself so exhausted I wondered if I might be unable to walk back to my apartment. I recognized what a mess that drawing was, how stupid and loveless and without hope, so I tore it into pieces. The air was suddenly greasy, grey and thick, and I could no longer breathe.

The sky had gone milky blue as torn white clouds slid along the horizon, the bottom of each tinted a sweet vulgar pink. The rising breeze fluttered the other pages of the sketchbook, sending my pencil rolling across the table. I stood and released those bits of white paper clutched in my hand. They danced in the air to the surface of the pool where they fell to float like white magnolia petals. This moment seemed suddenly so right it was almost perfect, and so I gathered my things from the table.

Restlessness gradually began to bloom behind my eyes. A desire grew in me to feel movement, to see motion, a kind of soothing drone for the heart. But of course; Marla and her pick-up truck.

Marla was a painter for whom straw and sweat were colors, and farmer's hands and farmer's wives were medium. Thinking of her I remembered Donald's remark; a career teaching art to farmers. Small, slim and dark-eyed, talented and shrewd, generous and serious and funny as she directed her degenerated, collapsing truck through time and space. Could Marla's father have learned art? From anyone? Even Marla? And could she have taught any farmer about art? Was there something of that in her which could accomplish such a feat, and with pride?

But I needed a journey, even if that journey only amounted to going as far as the campus and then returning. I decided to call Marla the next day and suggest we drive once again into the foothills beyond the town. Twice we had driven as far as the ocean while she told stories of her father and her four brothers, and of their South Dakota farm.

Sitting in that metal chair beside the pool so long my leg had become numb, as if it had already been replaced by a shaft of wood. So I stood then, tucked my sketchbook under my arm and my pencils into my shirt pocket, and then climbed to my second-floor walkway. Sweating and moving slowly pummeled by what remained of a searing sun, I imagined myself a tortoise carrying his house and all of his belongings, moving slowly one foot before the other and terrified of being flipped onto its back. Before my mind's eye arose the image of my bald, toothless head, my scrawny neck, and my collection of awkward and deficient limbs.

But as I climbed the wooden stairs to the second level, fatigue made me cautious until for a moment I was overwhelmed by a piercing sense of vulnerability. As though, if I failed to pay attention, I might forget and leave my body aside.

Standing halfway to the top of the stairs I heard another apartment door above me and just out of my sight suddenly open, and then close. Light, quick footsteps tapped an approach and then stopped at the top of the stairs ahead of me. I looked up, but already she was nearly upon me, hurrying, passing, and on her way. It was her. I stopped, overcome with an oddly breathless surprise. Intending to step aside to allow her to pass, I found that I could not move. As if I had fallen into a trance, unable to will movement or make her stop, incapable even of attracting her attention.

While her long legs flew by me, my own legs turned to mud. The sky swirled with colors. I opened my mouth but, deafened by the roar of her movement, I could release no sound. My heart had suddenly been stuffed with cotton, with nothing.

I watched her turn at the corner of our building toward the parking lot. Though she was gone from my sight, I listened to the sound of her footsteps, gravel under foot and then tapping firmly on concrete, until the sound was swallowed by the night. Then I resumed my slow climb.

In this life there is infinite time for regret; she had passed and I had allowed it.

Embarrassment. Had I returned to that schoolboy in short pants who hoped the little girl across the way would eventually notice? Had I become a complete fool?

Perched half-way up the stairs I lingered over that moment of timidity, an instant of uncertainty that depressed me. I wondered if there had been an opportunity to captivate her, to snare her attention with fraudulent elegance, with a foreign accent and practiced charm, with flattering interest.

But I had simply watched as she passed. Her swirling, delightful flight down the stairs provided a contrast to the bald and toothless turtle gapping at the young maiden in her summer dress. She had not turned to look at me but she might have seen me. My eyesight, after all, is no longer perfect. Our eyes might for a moment have met. The more I thought about it the more certain I became. Then I began to speculate upon intention. Had there been a gleam in her glance, a hint of awareness, of observation, some tremor of recognition?

Eventually my awkwardness and timidity came to infuriate me. To be so easily cast into confusion, into self-doubt and embarrassment, and by someone whose name I did not know. Thus I discovered I needed a distraction intended not merely to amuse. A distraction of a physical sort; perhaps a ride inside a big, noisy truck.

When finally over the telephone I heard Marla's voice, I felt something close to relief. But without waiting for me to make my request she announced, "Too bad you weren't at today's meeting." She paused with a quiet chuckle. "They got started on your show again. Burston took over the meeting since you weren't there. He announced that your work is being displayed at a gallery in Munich."

"Come over in your truck and you can tell me all about it."

Disappointment flavored her voice because I would not immediately explain, but she promised to meet me in a half hour.

When our conversation was finished I sat down immediately at my kitchen table, because there was time for one more thought. I worked quickly, allowed the pencil to remember those lines of her face; shape of mouth, thickness of lips, position of cheekbones and nose, the contour of her eyebrows. Images fade, the pencil wanders, it can not remember everything, but it most quickly forgets that which is beautiful.

When finally all memories had evaporated and become lost forever I closed the sketchbook, pushed the pencils to one side of the table and left the apartment, to make my slow way to the parking lot, and to Marla's truck.

CHAPTER THIRTEEN

MARLA'S OLD TRUCK was gorgeous. Scratched, battered and patterned
with mud over a color that could have been dark blue unless it had been dark
green. Its left fender was folded directly beside the wheel, raw gaps of red-
orange rust trimmed the edge below the doors, a long crack in the passenger
side windshield sparkled, while its tailgate bowed inward at the center like a
toothless smile. Through both sides of the floor were holes large enough to
glimpse the asphalt passing beneath. A truck of character, of unpretentious
pride, a machine to be trusted.

From our high seats the view was regal and I enjoyed looking down into
automobiles around us as they passed. Beyond the highway, broad, flat fields
and dark clusters of trees flew by. But it was the sensation of speed that most
pleased me. Sweet air poured through the windows as we passed fields black-
green in the hard blue twilight, and flooded irrigation channels that flashed
silver beneath towers looming black against the indigo sky.

Marla enjoyed cowboy-music blasting from her radio, her choice for our
velvet night. In that great noisy machine I could almost imagine myself just
another farmer living within uncomplicated rows; a simple life of straight lines
and perfect right angles, driving through the warm night, passive and complete.

Brushing a rebellious lock of wind-blown dark hair from her eyes Marla
said, "You missed a real party." The green dashboard light tinted her chin and

ghostly eye sockets. "They argued about that show again."

Annoyed by her reminder I said, "Another weighty problem for my colleagues to wrestle with. They should spend their days the way they expect their students to: by painting."

Marla's smile was both sympathetic and mischievous. "Sometimes they ask me what I think would change your mind. Why, I have no idea, but I tell them the same thing every time; 'I don't know.' It never helps and they ask again anyway." With a quick, grinning glance she added, "Help me out here and think of something else for me to say."

"Are there no problems more urgent?"

"A big show smells of political advantage. There'd be a lot of prestige involved for whoever pulled it off." She shook her head. "By the way, what's all this I'm hearing about some show in Munich? You never said anything about that. You could have mentioned it at least. I thought we were friends."

I looked away annoyed. "Twenty canvases, each twice as old as you are, and none even remotely as beautiful. Martin made the arrangements. I wanted nothing to do with it and now I regret having given my permission."

"Well, it's getting at lot of attention. Everybody at the meeting has read about it in the magazines. So it's got them thinking again about the University's own show. And they've overcome their usual inclination to give up at the first refusal. I think you've got them so confused they may have forgotten how to give up."

That thought made me uncomfortable. Save me from the bureaucrat who ignores his limitations. "I am surprised a show in Munich could create so much turmoil in a country that speaks nothing but English. And badly, at that. I consistently underestimate you Americans. Martin had promised it would all go off very quietly. So much for his promise." Once again Martin had helped me into trouble. I doubt we would ever have become friends had he not been my agent. But he was, and we were.

Marla steered the truck north so that with the ebbing light at our left, the foothills ranged ahead appeared black as castle walls. "Prestige," Marla said with a shake of her head and yelling to be heard above the roar of the engine. "The University, the department, and anyone who can hang their name to the project. But especially John." Her derisive laughter tugged at her throat.

"What makes all of this seem so funny?"

"They'll all look bad enough when their plans fall through. Because you won't agree, not now. I know you that well at least."

"And so much better than my colleagues. But tell me what you think I should do. Should I appear at the next meeting and curse the lot of them?"

But something had made me sad, and I no longer wanted to talk about addled people and their perverse designs. Retrospectives are for the dead, and I have no curiosity about what others might admire after I am dead.

"A lot of people are excited by your work," she said, more a repetition of another's words than a conviction. "Maybe they deserve a chance to see it."

"You begin to sound like John, innocent of all self-interest. How can I combat all of this thoughtful innocence?"

Driven by the wind Marla's dark hair swirled impatiently about her face and shimmered in the headlights of on-coming cars. Sweet air beat around my face, beat against my ears and flared my nostrils, until it filled me. I breathed deeply enjoying its pressure against my flesh and the way it rushed into my lungs; all of that dark air thickening in uncomplicated space.

With a gentle tap on my knee she asked, "And how's your leg been feeling?"

"Instead of answering my question, you ask another. So I will grunt in response."

"Take good care of it," she said ignoring me. "My grandfather had the same trouble. One night we're driving the horses into the corral and Grandpa held the gate. As they trotted by one skittered. Burdened with horse-stupidity it decided it didn't want to go through the gate. And it sort of flicked a hoof toward Grandpa. You know, just like you might shake water from your hand. It didn't knock him down, just opened this hole in his leg. Right then Dad wanted him to take it to the doctor because of all the blood. But Grandpa said it was just a cut, so he washed it out himself and wrapped it. He had bad circulation, but he just walked it around. After a week he could hardly stand up. When he couldn't stomach the smell anymore he let Mom took a look at it. What a sight! The doctor sent him to the hospital right away. But they had to cut off his leg at the knee, anyway. Bad circulation." She shook her head with a bitter smile. "And that horse. A horse is stupider than a man. Not by much, understand. You should have seen his leg, all infected, just terrible." Nodding she said, "Believe me, with certain things you can't be too careful."

After a while I asked, "Have you seen Donald today?"

She nodded. "Sitting with some woman," she said, rolling the words as if to savor them. "They must have been talking about something important, or at least Donald was. Something serious from the looks on their faces. Maybe they were having a fight." Marla had a good laugh, warm and darkly-shaded, and it filled the space around us like smoke.

I asked, "Someone you recognized?"

"You mean, was it his girlfriend?" She brushed another rebellious strand of hair from her face. "How would I know? Maybe Donald isn't all that interesting."

She slowed the truck as she steered from the road. We moved over onto a gravel parking lot. At the center of the lot and set back stood a small, low building, with no light coming from within or any sign announcing its purpose. Beside the building stood a small shed. Between the two buildings, a tall lamppost leaned awkwardly, the source of a single cone of yellow light. The larger building appeared to recede into its own shadow. At the sharp edge of that half-light I could no longer be certain of Marla's eyes or the shape of her mouth.

She steered to a spot beside the shed and stopped and then turned off the engine. She leaned forward over the steering wheel as if studying the building before us. I motioned to open the door. "Hang on," she said, her voice was soft and clear. The engine of our truck ticked as it cooled while crickets sang in the tall grass and trees at the edge of the gravel. In the distance I heard the songs of a croaking chorus of frogs. Within the cone of yellow light, fluttering moths flapping huge dark wings darted and dived in a mad dance, a calligraphy in yellow light.

Marla sighed. "One thing I've learned; men are stubborn and stupid. They think stubborn is the same as being strong, and that being stubborn about something stupid makes them even stronger. Besides my Dad and Grandpa I have four brothers, so I know something about stupid. In fact I'm probably an expert on stupidity. And one thing I'm certain of; you are the stupidest smart person I've ever met."

Her conclusion offered nothing of interest to me so I asked, "Has John convinced you, too?"

She made a disgusted face. "What could he tell me? Another stupid man. If he ever knew anything, he's probably forgotten it, and then forgotten that he forgot."

"And what is it you think I have forgotten?"

"At least you're smart enough to suspect when things are going wrong."

Recovering my annoyance I could only snarl, "I have no such suspicion. What I know is that I am not permitted to carry on my work in peace."

Marla's laughter was thick with derision. "Who works in peace? Who has ever worked in peace?" Her laughter continued. It entranced me, I suppose, because I could think of no good response. "If that was all you really wanted, you could set up shop on some island. Travel to someplace weird where nobody knew you, and paint your brains out."

"That is not the point," I answered without reflection. "My work is no longer my own. My paintings, my skill and effort, will be used to promote men I do not respect in designs I do not approve and toward ends I cannot tolerate. Merely to consider compromise is already to agree to it. No matter how humble and unpromising my work may be, if it has no integrity it is nothing at all."

She leaned back from the steering wheel and her face became lost in the darkness. With flat certainty she said "No one has asked you to compromise. About anything. Your work is attracting attention. Listen to me now and I'll explain what I understand. The department and the University see a chance to profit from your work. Nobody expects you to paint especially for the show, and nobody wants you to change anything you've painted."

"Admit you have been talking with John again."

With a sudden flare of grim annoyance she said, "I'm speaking my mind, and I'd be glad if you'd admit I'm smart enough to be flat wrong all on my own. If you don't like what I have to say, fair enough. But if it's wrong, at least I made it all up myself." Marla's temper was short and razor-sharp.

I said, "Believe me, I have no doubt you are intelligent enough to be wrong."

"Sarcasm won't save this situation."

"Once again," I said, "you may be wrong. Sarcasm and ridicule may be my very best weapons."

Marla shifted around in her seat to look at me directly. "If you expect me to go into these meetings and defend you, give me something more than condescension and ridicule."

"I appreciate your concern, but I can defend myself well enough. In any case, you seem already to have gone over to their opinion."

"You really should come to the next meeting." Marla's voice became dry with exasperation and its sound floated within our shell. "You should hear what your colleagues say about you. As it is, all Bill Thomas wants to know is how the department can get its hands on your work. He suggested they just convince your agent to ship your paintings."

"Thomas is a walking fraud, so I am not surprised he made that suggestion."

Marla slapped the steering wheel. "You see! I tell you they're ready to steal your work if you force them to, and you answer with condescension. What goddamn difference does it make how lousy any of them are as painters? Suppose they become so frustrated arguing with you that they give up. You think eventually they'll give up the argument, but don't kid yourself. They're way past that."

Not being surprised by bad news is not the same as accepting it. "I have battled against this sort of person all of my life. I have beaten such flabby and gutless opponents even before the parents of your oldest classmates were born. Of course I am no longer young, but these desk-warmers are not as tough as those men I have fought."

"Wonderful." Marla again slapped her palm against the steering wheel. "More condescension. Pretending these people can't defeat you is simple blindness. Whistle past the graveyard loud as you like, but face up to it before you're eaten alive."

We sat wrapped in noisy silence. The buildings and lamp post stood alone in the darkness, frozen in time and waiting.

She sighed. "Okay. I realize you have reasons that satisfy you for refusing the show. Fine. Give me some excuse that'll sink into their tiny heads. So that even if they don't agree with you, at least they'll leave you alone."

Like a disturbance in the air I felt her lean toward me, eyes large and sharp and digging into my face. And I waited too. I waited for words and to hear that explanation my colleagues would understand. So I waited. Words seemed to fly about us like those moths within the cone of yellow light. More words joined them, moving wildly, until finally they attached themselves to each other.

"A painting," I said, "is a living thing as it is being painted. Imagine the paint as blood, with the stretchers as bones and the canvas as its flesh. The blood vitalizes that which is motionless until finally the canvas comes alive. The painting breathes with every stroke of the brush, growing and changing as the paint is applied. I can only help it. The image within sharpens until it becomes precise and acquires hard edges. Even as I daub and splash I must watch to see where the paint must go, where it needs blood to become strong. So I watch. I am an accomplice, you see, not a creator. I help the work to become whole and find its completion. But at that moment of completion, the life of the work comes to an end. The painting dies because completion is death. A completed painting is a beautiful dead thing, an exquisite corpse. It can no longer grow. Nothing more can be added to it or taken from it. One can admire a dead thing and one can examine it thoughtfully, attempting to probe its secrets. One can become fascinated with, even seduced by, that which is dead. But one must not love the dead thing. This retrospective my colleagues so earnestly desire is merely an homage to dead things. And I, least of all, can afford an infatuation with dead things." I stopped, then, because finally I had run out of words. "Now, I have explained to you my problem."

Within the yellow cone of light under the lamp post, bats joined the swooping moths, their darting an insistent staccato to the sinuous flights of the moths as they snatched them one after the other.

Eventually Marla shook her head. "All I see is somebody who's real smart and just as crazy. How do you expect me to explain all that? Do you understand what you're saying? You're making them all out to be necrophiles." This time her laughter was sweet.

I could not repress a smile. "And perhaps that is how I mean them to understand it."

Marla's laughter became harsher. "You need help, you really do. You don't want it, you probably wouldn't know what to do with it, but you really need it." She shook her head. "Like my oldest brother. That's who you remind me of sometimes. We always knew he was in trouble when the bragging got loud. Jimmy and his goddamn motorcycle and his goddamn motorcycle buddies." She brought her face suddenly close to mine, her eyes flat and black and terrible in the darkness. "We'd sit at the dinner table listening to his brags, mister know-everything. And the noise, all that noise, knowing he was going out, and what he'd probably do, and what kind of shape he'd be in when he got back, and how long it would take for him to get better." She sighed. "I'll bet you like to break hearts, too."

Marla did not wait for me to respond. She leaned forward, started the engine and switched on the lights. She shook her head as if chasing a discomforting thought. She put the truck in gear, slowly we moved ahead. We bounced along the edge of the parking lot, headlights shooting up and diving down, sweeping madly, looking for the path back to the road.

I had explained myself to her as best I could, but my explanation had merely left her annoyed. Perhaps what I demanded was inconceivable, or unjustifiable, or just so sophomoric it was indefensible. But at least I had tried to make myself clear.

She leaned forward and turned on the radio loud. Twanging guitars and whining voices throbbed over lost love and humiliation and self-pity, revenge and death and broken hearts. Marla stared over the dashboard as if watching the road.

Against our headlights the darkness was endlessly retreating as we hurtled into it encased in our fragile truck. I turned back, the lamp post receded, grew smaller, and then disappeared. We gained speed, its pressure a gentle caress as the engine whined louder, reached for a higher pitch, and then still higher to strain like a throat that must scream. Our truck trembled and each rut in the road sent us bouncing. I rested my hand lightly on the dashboard. The white lines zipped beside us. Marla hunched forward as if peering through a fog, the straining tendons of her fingers outlined in the weak light.

Then something dark suddenly flashed into our headlights. Marla jerked the wheel hard and we swerved sharply. A dull thud and then our truck began to careen back and forth across the white line. Marla wrestled with the steering wheel while the tires screamed. I flew about, thrown from side to side and then thrust forward until my face was close to the windshield. And then very slowly we began to spin. Skidding to the edge of the road, my side of the truck tipped high into the air. I felt myself rising, tumbling toward Marla. Then, as if caught by some great hand, we remained for one heartbeat suspended. In the next moment my side of the truck dropped hard onto the road. But we had stopped.

The engine idled throaty and dull, our headlights shone into a tangled hedge-row of weeds. I could not look at her even to see if she was all right. My legs had become soft, and I turned to my open window thinking I might become sick.

Marla was panting, head tipped back and eyes closed, hands draped lightly over the steering wheel. She turned her head toward me expressionless and lips tight.

"Rabbit," she said finally.

After a pause I said, "A posthumous retrospective might be acceptable." She smiled then, or tried to, and the result was a painful grimace. I looked away.

After a few moments she put the truck in gear, we moved ahead slowly and turned. We drove more slowly after that and eventually reached my apartment.

One of the tail lights of Marla's truck was cracked. A thin bright shaft of yellow pierced the red around it. I watched her truck pull away from the parking lot of our complex. Even after the red lights had receded and dimmed, that shaft of light continued to find me until it too winked out. Standing in our parking lot as I watched her drive away, suddenly I felt a desire to take-in great mouthfuls of air. Across my face a soft breeze suddenly arose and calmed me. Something in the air or in my chest constricted my lungs. Beneath my feet the earth labored, I felt it. The earth's axis needed lubrication, grinding resistance sent spiraling waves of tension that radiated vibrations. The blue-black air quivered to some low, deep-pitched groan, the sound of an enormous gate very slowly closing. Automobiles I could not see whispered along our narrow lane. The street murmured as the highway beyond hummed, and invisible children called out in high-pitched voices. But I remained rooted and unmoving.

Each moment became separated from the next acquiring its own color and shade, its own music as a separate cadence, dancing to its own rhythm. As though the language of memory was self-effacing so that each moment was simply a word attaching itself to a new meaning, and all became discontinuous, as if invented for that moment alone. And after that moment had passed, the entire ensemble of syllables collapsed becoming unintelligible to the moment which followed. The earth's trembling grew louder, more violent until the earth beneath my feet heaved. And in that instant, finally I was shaken loose as if I had been freed.

But standing at the center of all of that darkness, the dark sky and the dark ground, I realized that after all that had happened I was merely older, and nothing more than a ripple in the eternal continuum.

Making my slow ascent of the steps to my apartment, my thoughts returned to that thrilling young woman in her summer dress. Later at my kitchen table with a glass of wine in hand, my leg again began to throb while my head filled with a clutter of images. With no collaboration on my part, this universe suddenly presented me with a configuration that left me breathless.

But with each glass of wine I cared less, so that by the time I had finished the bottle of wine I was both unable to undress and indifferent to the fact that I laid down on my bed.

That image appeared before me as suddenly as lightening and complete, each element bound to the next, its outline so hard-edged and clear I thought I had truly seen it. Three men standing in a half-circle around a woman standing naked facing them, all beneath a single cone of yellow light. And the darkness beyond hiding two trucks. The men leaned back on their heels, motionless as if overwhelmed. The three men, arms at their sides, and the woman being seen. And in the deepest part of the darkness an invisible crowd, silent and frozen.

As suddenly as it arose the image was gone, and my ceiling again was merely an indeterminate white.

Later there was communing with ghosts, much conjuring of pasts, ghouls and monsters howling. Chains rattled and teeth gnashed, as if the dead were determined to rise and to fly. This became the program for the remained of my evening, and I its captive audience.

CHAPTER FOURTEEN

BEFORE I HAD swallowed my first cup of coffee Donald was at my door
with his sketchbook under his arm. My head was still so filled with screaming
ghosts I could not speak. Before I could offer him a cup of his own, he began.

"Sorry about yesterday." He sprawled in the chair long legs stretched before
him looking genuinely tired, but grinning, as if only he understood the joke.
Beneath his tanned skin a hint of grey, eyes puffed and red, as if he had stayed
up very late drinking a great deal. For a moment I almost imagined a bond
flowed between us. "A friend," he said cryptically. "I should tell you about him.
Came through on his way to Corvallis. We were friends at State. He never even
called. Complete surprise. Great guy. Hadn't seen him in a couple of years.
Stayed until late and then he was gone. That was last night."

I said, "That was last night. What does that have to do with yesterday
afternoon?" He had awakened me early and what he had told me was of no
matter, so I would torment him a bit. "There was a commotion when I was
not present for the meeting."

Something between a nod and a shrug, it was a gesture neither of us would
recognize. He said, "Heard all about that too."

But I did not care about his friend, or about not being at the meeting.
Demons swirled behind my eyes and my heart was chapped and dry. I poured
a cup of coffee and passed it to him. "In the future, be sure you call. I do it

resentfully but I pay the telephone bill to keep myself available."

When he did not laugh I should have sent him away. As if all of his energy suddenly had disappeared he slouched lower into his chair. Eyes hooded and slightly glazed he appeared to want something from me; perhaps human company, or just absolution for a sin unacknowledged. But now he was wasting my time, so I would waste his.

"I once knew a photographer. She understood talent, understood the demands of talent." Mildly curious, his eyes became glassy. Was it simply lack sleep, or dull-witted boredom? "Heidi Berenson. She was well-known for a time. Heard of her?"

"Yes," he said and his brightened expression confirmed his curiosity. He leaned forward in his chair, tipped his chin over his folded arms. "You say you knew her?"

"For a brief time we were friends. Her photographs were very good and she impressed me greatly. Have you seen any of her work?"

Why did I not simply tell him I had work to do and send him away? I wanted to like Donald. I wanted to trust him, to take him into my confidence, to share ideas and opinions. But the distance between us was unsettling. In the end I found him difficult to like and his effort to create an excuse for his absence simply made liking him harder. Had he fabricated this story about this friend? What was I left to believe? Difficult man; and when he tried to be helpful and perhaps even likable, I found him even more offensive. Had I managed to like him I might eventually appreciate him. And then perhaps I might even value him.

The world has grown too large. Friends who are not dead now live a continent away. There is too much space between us all, and that distance frightens me. So Marla, and Vincent, and Donald as well, and John, and all of the others. Could I hold them, freeze them long enough so that they might become important to me? Perhaps something in that water, or in that air, or that light, or those buildings, the entire town and its roads, perhaps even the very land upon which we stood, prevented any of that from happening. There was something ephemeral, even imaginary, about our existence. Had I awoke one morning to find all of it gone, I would not have been surprised. Perhaps in some unlikely way, Vincent was right.

With his face as naked and open as a pair of fried eggs Donald appeared to present himself as simply himself. Yet I could not discern, in all that cheery and unembarrassed space, why he remained at my table. Weary and drawn, did he believe he might acquire something from me?

"You look very tired," I said. "We should continue tomorrow."

"Berenson?" His eyes were heavy and half-closed, but the tone of his voice modulated with curiosity.

I hesitated before I responded. "There was a series of shows in Berlin. Though I had little money I was very fortunate. Our association was entirely accidental. We were both shown by the same gallery. She was already becoming well-known in Berlin when I met her. I attended several of her shows."

Eyes sharper, Donald lifted his chin in his hand. "What was she like?"

I was compelled to laugh, and its sound arose without reflection. "Such an American question. As if Heidi could be summarized. Perhaps instead you should ask what I was like. What were my own feelings? Such a web of emotions, so many contradictions. You ask me to lift the lid on a boiling pot, or open some mysterious door. What is anything like? Shall I ask what Barbara is like?" I could not restrain my laughter. When I knew his curiosity had been frustrated I asked to see his sketchbook. He picked it up from the floor beside his chair, passed it to me reluctantly. I flipped through the pages. "To be alive is to know that every day there is work to be done." I looked up. Donald's slack face had tightened. Finally he was tempted to leave.

"Look here," I said pointing to four attempts from the same model, a young man, arms crossed over his chest, standing in three-quarters profile. "These are rather good. There is energy here, and your facility improves." I could not decide if he was still conscious, although he appeared to continue to breathe. "Paint what you like and die happy. When you discover your true subject, then you will do great things, attain shattering inspirations. Years are spent in the quest for the true subject, centuries are wasted. Waste as much time as you need, as long as you are certain discovery will come."

Donald squirmed sleepily, a man fighting within his own dream. And what could I care? Too many with talent starve, while those without prosper. Fool to come to me for advice, greater fool to miss my foolishness.

"On the other hand," I added, "perhaps you would be happier selling insurance to farmers. Consider this now, before it is too late and you realize you have missed your opportunity." I returned his sketchbook and stood. Because finally I was ready, and the day remained for us both to waste. Voices from the swimming pool already drifted through my open window. "Never ask a critic what he thinks," I said. We descended the stairs, Donald leading the way.

A festive air, bright sunshine, some sort of holiday. Many more people moved about talking and laughing. I saw no books. Everywhere and everyone in contrast to our table. Were we noticed? Did we draw sidelong glances? Did I become self-conscious?

Using Donald's drawings as examples I created lessons for him, suggestions and imperatives. Avoid this, never do that because it becomes automatic. Eventually he would care more for the drawing than for his vanity. As a painter I am no-good. My talent is the pencil, and the pencil is all I am certain of. But with knowledge of the pencil, all the rest follows. Like breathing.

"Are you friendly with Marla Stewart?" I asked.

Suspicious of my question he nodded. "I see her around the department sometimes."

"Talk to her, ask her to look at a few things." His face hardened, and then it emptied, as if momentarily I was no longer beside him. "If she can spare the time I'm sure she'd provide useful suggestions. She is quite good." Donald winced, and even his sunglasses could not disguise it. If his desire for guidance was earnest, I could not suggest a more talented associate. In any case, he presumed a great deal. Marla was busy enough and would not drop everything she was working on simply to help him. And if she had free time she still might not be inclined to help him. His bruised ego was itself simply another vanity.

For half an hour Donald scribbled and yawned, fending off the sunlight and sleep while making unremarkable marks on his very white paper. My own pencil lay motionless in my hand. But then I saw all of them again, that vision suddenly as clear as light. Beside a road under a single lamp post, the yellow light smeared as if reflected in turbulent water. Surrounded by a thickness of light encased in darkness, light reflected into darkness, devoured by darkness. That group stood in darkness directly before me even while our sun-dazzled students walked among them without disturbance. The gleam from the water overlaid with all of that darkness.

Sparkling water, heat, voices, sounds, were all a constant pressure on my senses. Donald continued to pretend to draw while I was left alone in that bottomless night beside that solitary lamp post. A grand canvas, but a simple formation. Five figures in the darkness; four men, not three, and that woman, submerged in darkness. Just the four, their backs to me and surprised before the one.

They face her surrounded by darkness so thick it might be the pelt of an animal. They are mute. Beyond surprise their gestures are empty. The men overshadow her; their shapes are distorted, built up from heaps of color. The woman stands alone, slim and silver, a flame shimmering in a heat mirage, a dagger of bright flesh, luminescent.

The canvas that I imagined seemed to sprawl yards high and more yards wide.

Suddenly Donald said, "Maybe we should think a little more about this drawing business." He slouched down suddenly in his chair exasperated, tossed the pencil to the table. I watched it roll to the edge and then fall clattering to the concrete.

And then they were gone. He shifted, rubbed his eyes, leaned to the side and retrieved the pencil.

With the pencil flipping nervously in his hand Donald said, "They talked about your show again." He grinned. His mention of the show caught me unprepared, and he recognized this as his grin grew wider. "They're getting tired of you, I think. They know you'll agree to do their show eventually. You're just play-acting as far as they're concerned and it's begun to piss them off."

"Marla told me all about their meeting last night." Perhaps a result of the sunlight and the heat, but gradually I too had slipped into a lethargy.

Donald leaned forward. "In case you haven't figured it out yet, every one of them wants a show just like that. And each of them is sure they deserve one. Even John. Even your buddy, Vince." Donald laughed with quiet derision. He glanced distractedly over his shoulder, in his left hand his pencil now tapped rapidly against the top of his thigh. "I know they're going about this all wrong. What I can't figure is why you don't work something out with them." He sighed without condescension.

I muttered, "Je vous enmerde." Donald leaned forward, and a smile that could belong only to him crept over his chin toward his lips. I asked, "Do you know what that means?"

Martin pesters me from time to time that I should paint another large canvas. And several times Donald has suggested the same thing, even insisting he could help. Martin demands that it be something of substance so it will shut people up, whatever he might mean by that. But from Martin, that request is at least unremarkable. He, after all, is my agent.

"Dedo's favorite expression," I said. "Whenever events conspired against his wishes or plans, he would put the demons to flight by shaking his fist at the air and say, 'Je vous enmerde'."

A huge canvas, seven feet by twelve, perhaps even larger, principle figures proportionally small, swaths of ultramarine and deep violet and black. And two pick-up trucks, one deep green with yellow headlights. The other? The trucks should appear reduced, even smaller than the figures. And all of it with a low horizon line. On a large canvas, all of that space. Just that lamppost and all of that space.

Donald eyed me with increasing suspicion. I said, "When I fail to appear at next month's meeting, and John asks you if my decision has changed, you tell him that I say 'Je vous enmerde.'"

He squirmed in his chair so vigorously I thought he might fall. Too bad that I would not be quoted exactly.

With Heidi and Leon on Kurfurstendamm, and Heidi shaking her head laughing. "Give up the little mistakes," was her favorite expression. "No more little mistakes." Shaking her cascade of warmly golden-hair, her smile flashing brighter than the entire boulevard on that sparkling night, as she said, "Big mistakes or nothing." Big mistakes or nothing. She would have liked Dedo, but then again most women did. And Dedo would have liked her, as he did so many others. The two of them could have made big mistakes together; big mistakes that would have recreated the world.

Yes, Heidi, big mistakes or nothing.

CHAPTER FIFTEEN

THAT BERLIN WINTER.

Rain every day. It must have been rain. It was wet, everything it touched grew darker. Its sound was incessant; on the roof, on the windows, gurgling from the gutter beside Heidi's door. Whenever it is cold and grey and raining, I think of Berlin.

And Heidi. In those boots she was an inch taller than I. Without them she was still several years older, far more talented and charming and better-looking. But what was most often remarked by others was that she was taller than I. Those black riding boots that made her appear so tall became remarkable simply because they belonged to Heidi.

Hurrying along Fredrichstrasse through a soft rain she took my arm, leaned her weight staring down as though she was eleven feet tall and offered a pained expression. We had been talking of Willy and her admiration of him as an artist, but what we had not yet talked about was her infatuation. All of that would come later. I said, "I expect he is popular with the young actresses."

In response Heidi whispered hoarsely in a fair British accent, "But really, darling, you have no idea."

On this she was correct. We then talked of other things, arrived at our destination just as the rain became heavy. But she was as usual correct. Nearly every time, nearly every thing, she was correct. Nearly every time.

She frightened me the first time I met her. The opening for a group show where Leon had a few pieces on display. She knifed into the room clicking across the brightly polished floor, black riding boots nearly to her knee, those riding boots, and narrow white trousers, black silk shirt open nearly to her navel. Skin so pale as if never seen by the sun and large, blue, perpetually-injured eyes. Beneath her chin and beside her ear intricate patters of opaque blue veins, white-blond hair close-cut and combed boyishly to one side. I find no difficulty in remembering Heidi very well.

A tall, thick-set man arrived with her and stood by her side. Heavy featured, oily lank nearly-black hair falling across his eyes, he and this startling woman spoke quietly together as they surveyed the room. I looked away, stared without seeing as I passed one framed piece after another, until I was only a few steps from them. Leon suddenly stepped up beside me.

"Freddy has three more cases of champagne on the way." Leon's round, pink face shined with perspiration as he giggled like a school-boy. "He passed himself off as Herr Markel on the telephone. Freddy understands what it means to have a real party."

I nodded in the direction of the woman and her companion. Leon glanced, his sharp, dark eyes returned to mine smiling. "You wish to be introduced? Personally, I would take great pleasure."

"Only just tell me about her."

Leon shrugged. "She has already asked about you, what more is there to tell? It would be so much simpler if I introduced you. You will fall in love with her anyway. Perhaps she will be unfortunate enough to fall in love with you." Bullet-headed and balding, Leon looked as cherubic that night as I was ever to see him. He clapped his hands together grinning, as if joy bloomed in his chest like tiny explosions. "Berlin is an amusing city and you will find much amusement here. Tragedy here is only bathos. We stop all seriousness at Potsdam." With a loud laugh and a slap on my back he walked away. I looked up to discover that Heidi had been watching us.

In the joyous melee over the arriving champagne I made my escape. Several parties later Heidi asked why I had so secretly fled. "Poor planning," I said.

Days of cold rain seeping, dripping, from skies uneven and unequally grey. Dark hallways, stone stairways to fifth-floor walk-ups behind double locked doors, all-night trips in automobiles full of strangers, to Potsdam or Weimar or the docks of Hamburg where arriving ships brought North Africans and drugs. Long intricate nights without sleep, sunrise a mere brightening, a lighter grey in the eastern sky. Long walks to meet nameless men, listen to hopeless plans, return to friends operating short-wave radios, cutting mounds of cocaine, phone calls arranging for purchases: a printing press, some motion picture equipment, a jazz band, a French whore.

Long black overcoats and grey snap-brim hats. Lank, chain-smoking women, ashtrays filled with half-finished cigarette-ends stained with lip-stick; purple or green or black. Street-cars clanging along Fredrichstrasse, pushing past clusters of ragged and dark unemployed men swimming suspended in the festively lurid neon of the cabaret bars in Alexanderplatz, and here and there small mounds of ash-blackened snow.

"You will fall in love with Berlin." Herr Markel had made his statement sound like a promise. Fingers hooked lightly into his charcoal waistcoat pockets he leaned back on his heels, brilliant fragments of light from the chandelier overhead multiplied in his wire-framed eye-glasses. His left hand was badly scared and had the color of cooked shrimp. "She is moody and difficult, and sometimes so cool to your desire you will think she wishes you gone. Not like the southern cities, so responsive, so unrestrained, so vulgar and available." He followed my glance, removed his hands from his pockets and interlocked them behind his back.

"Berlin is a community of a different species of people. A people both generous and careful. And a people not without enthusiasm, not without moments of ecstasy. Our people have reached a new elevation in culture to which others can only aspire. And we are moving further. The German artist is about to create masterpieces which will transform everything that has come before. You are fortunate to be young and alive and here, at this critical moment. Here you will find that appreciative and loyal audience you have hoped for."

Herr Markel leaned back on his heels, brought his arms forward and folded them over his chest. "Who can say, but perhaps you will find us so enchanting you will wish never to leave."

I smiled. "And perhaps I have already fallen in love." Markel surveyed the room smiling to no one and everyone.

A serving man appeared carrying a silver tray and stood beside him. On the tray was an ivory colored envelope. With his scared pink hand Herr Markel

handed that envelope to me. I slipped it into my jacket pocket. With a deep
and grateful bow I left.

My first one-man show outside France, this was 1928. Martin introduced
me to Herr Markel at a group show at Le Coc d'Or in Paris. He insisted
on bringing Herr Markel to my studio. Deaf to my complaints of invasion,
unimpressed by my absolute refusal, Martin had had his vision. Even if that
man had to be a German, he was about to make Martin terribly happy. Martin
was certain at least of this.

In response to my indignation, Martin reminded me that half of his gallery
was cluttered with examples of my work. I reminded him that he displayed
none of my recent work. He said he would only care for the new work when
the old work had disappeared from his ledger. "Besides," he added, "there is
no more money. You have finally driven me broke. Have mercy and let me sell
something. At least permit one of us to eat."

"Bring that man to my studio," I said, "and it will cost us both a great
deal." I had loosed my only arrow, an obscure but terrible threat.

"You are a fool," Martin responded with boredom, "which is bad enough.
But now you wish me to appear to be a fool as well. And that is infinitely
worse." An indulgent smile appeared suddenly. "We have a contract, you and I,
until I decide to tear it up. Do something about this visit and do it now."

There was a warehouse opposite the alley behind the bank at the end of
my street. It took some time to find the person with keys to open its door. I
gathered my finished canvases and a stack of drawings, and in the warehouse
set them up under the best light I could find. Herr Markel arrived as requested,
and Martin wrung his hands. Martin had good reason to wring his hands.

Herr Markel affected darkened eye-glasses in the most inappropriate
situations, including badly-lit warehouses. I had chosen a section of the
building directly across from its largest window, then used movable screens to
break-up and redirect the light. Markel stepped slowly from one work to the
next, removed his eye-glasses to squint as his fingers moved a small dark cloth
restlessly over each lens. He paused at several pieces, a few he returned to again.
The drawings he ignored. Martin wrung his hands and he had good reason to
do so. Several times I sneezed from the dust.

When finally Herr Markel came to stand before Martin and myself, his eyes
seemed to retreat from the light and its saturation of color, as if the light passing

through them would abrade his eyes and wear them down. He replaced his dark glasses, and then slowly a thin, tight smile appeared on his face. His smile went first to Martin, and then to me. Martin stopped wringing his hands.

For the first two months, Berlin was yellow and red and brown and green under blue and white skies of sharp and startling light. The air at night was chilly enough to brighten our faces as stars perched silver and sharp beyond the streetlamps. Bright colors and warm sunshine, and in the evening chill sweet winds. For nearly two months.

And then, for several days just before it truly began to rain, the sky went nearly black and the wind blew sharp. In shops, on busses and in offices, people spoke together quietly. After that, it began.

Day after day cold, black and wet, as if black oil fell from the sky. Sounds became twisted, reflections appeared everywhere. Sparkling light doubled from the surface of the street, seeing and hearing became games of chance. At night, in the rain, all autos are black.

The rain arrived, and with it the light changed completely. Though the window of my room was large, what little light reached the canvas seemed to soil it rather than illuminate. For days a grey film covered my eyes.

In the darkness and cold of the early hours there were things half-heard along with things nearly seen. Returning from the cafes, drink-sweating, weaving past the tribe of unemployed men sleeping along Potsdam Bridge, a progress of sorts, what was seen was expected to be forgotten because it was understood to be impossible. But how to forget? Certainly not the violin-playing street musician dressed as Charlie Chaplin standing beside the little boy dressed as Jackie Coogan. Or the hissing of rain-slick auto tires under Brandenburg Gate, or the roar of arriving and departing airplanes over Templehof, or the wide-open doorways of cabarets pouring out bright light and negro jazz and the moaning of their cabaret singer. And everywhere, the undulant movement of shadows.

It began to rain in Berlin two months after I arrived. As far as I know, it is still raining.

"You think such things are not possible? I have important friends. You think I do not have important friends?" Face flushed and sweating, Leon leaned his wide face across our table. A café on Kurfurstendamm. "With important friends, anything is possible." It was very late; with Leon the hour was always very late. "I have such a friend," he said. "You have money?"

I still had some money then. But Leon was rich with friends. He insisted that his wealth was measured in friends. "Friends are wealth. And with wealthy friends one can accomplish even the impossible."

Kurfurstendamm; a strand jeweled by a thousand hotly-lit cafes, a boulevard of red and blue and pink and orange neon, its kaleidoscope of light slashing the chill, rain-sodden air. And the voices, the calls, and the automobile horns.

"We do not have much time," Leon said. He took my arm, steered us through the crowd with quick and nimble steps. "Opportunities for such encounters are self-limiting, and limited by the police as well."

Not far along the boulevard we entered another café. Leon walked directly to the bar and asked for a telephone. The bartender brought it instantly from under the bar. Leon turned his back on the café and began to use it. I asked for wine. I do not know how many times he used the telephone, but after my second glass of that awful German wine he replaced the telephone and grabbed my arm. There was hardly time to pay the bartender.

On the street Leon hailed a taxi and we climbed inside. "You have enough to pay for this ride as well? Because riding in a taxi in Berlin is not cheap." I thanked him for his concern.

At Café des Westens we stepped from the taxi. Leon quietly asked me for a sum of money. Like a good bourgeois I hesitated. He leaned toward my ear. "I am your friend. Do not doubt that every good thing is worth its price."

Inside he left me alone at a table near the door, walked to the back and sat at a table with a young man narrow and ruddy-faced. They talked. When a waiter came to my table I waved him away. The two men continued to talk until finally Leon stood. He signaled as he passed my table and I followed him out.

Another taxi. After giving an address to the driver Leon leaned far back in his seat, wrapped his coat collar tighter. Very near the Russian Embassy we stopped. The Aldon Hotel. We walked to the waiter's entrance at the side of the building. I waited as Leon went in. The wind began to blow colder threatening another icy rain. The thick mist around each streetlight became a halo of silver. No one walked the street. It seemed I waited a long time.

When he reappeared we walked together quickly and on Wilhelmstrasse hailed another taxi. The trees along Unter den Linden blurred past. In a slow arc we passed the Imperial Palace, the Town Hall, and then we were turning again under the glaring lights of Alexanderplatz. Beyond the Police Headquarters we turned into Landsburgstrasse.

We drove nearly to the end of the street, then the taxi moved to the curb. A storefront, children's clothes. A route, a street, a storefront I would come to know well. Even down to the cracked forest-green paint just above the buzzer that Leon's index-finger pressed.

From the third floor windows we heard the bell ring. And then footsteps.

The open door revealed a tall man, gruff-voiced, asking Leon what had taken him so long, then breaking into a large smile. Leon turned his smiling face to me. "Albert," Leon cried, "meet our benefactor for the evening." To me he said, "Albert is the best printer in Berlin." Another tall, thin German with a narrow face, Albert's smile grew wider. He squeezed Leon's shoulder affectionately and stepped aside. We climbed a long narrow flight of stairs, past weakly-lit landings, murmuring heard through thin walls.

When the apartment door opened a cry went up for Leon. Much tobacco smoke, the Victrola roared incomprehensibly, while all about the small room men and women stood together in knots.

Leon walked to the low table near the center of the room, tossed down a package wrapped in brown paper. Voices melted away until only the Victrola remained boisterous. All eyes went to the package. Nodding in my direction Leon announced, "Pay him."

With a nonchalance that annoyed me I said, "There will be time enough for that."

"So!" A throaty woman's voice. To Leon she said, "You were not wrong; we shall have a party tonight after all." Again, Heidi.

All of this was followed by the cutting; whispering as though the white and glittering powder might awaken. And then came the dividing as metal clicked bright against glass. And all of it to the nervous quiet of chirping voices.

I sat on the couch directly across from Leon watching his fingers move over the bright white powder and the glass. Heidi stepped from her corner and sat down beside me. When her thigh rubbed against mine sparks pierced my chest. In a chair to Leon's right sat the same lank-haired, heavy man I had seen accompanying Heidi at the exhibition. His name, I had learned eventually, was Michael. His eyes followed Leon's hands darkly, as if watching a dog defecate. Then he shook his head and spoke quietly. "Our city is overwhelmed with penniless men, battered women, orphaned children, and you spend your money on that." He looked up into my eyes and laughed bitterly.

Leon crushed and cut and divided. He spoke without looking up and almost without breathing. "At the expense of our friend here, a few of the poor and several of the wealthy have improved their financial well-being tonight. You should at least acknowledge that." Leon's laugh was a whisper.

"You ease your conscience," Michael said, "with a bedtime story. Ask those men sleeping under the bushes beside the fish-pond at Teirgarten if they would like some cocaine. Or would they prefer an overcoat, a serious meal, a clean, dry bed for the night. You can ask anytime, they are always there. Unless the police have beaten them and chased them off."

Leon paused and looked up wearily, and then he smiled. "Do you think any of them would walk away from a line of this?" His hand began to tremble distorting his careful lines. Heidi tapped Leon's arm and said, "I have been practicing." With great care he passed the glass and its heap of white powder to her.

Michael's dark look shot to her. "If I were to spill all of that now, none of you would appreciate my generous favor."

"Now, Michael." A short woman with a broad, over-decorated face and wearing a shimmering green dress called from across the room. "If you don't behave, you'll be asked to leave." Her laugh was like shattering crystal. "Besides, why else have you come here?" Michael's face froze, his grimace turned to Heidi. As usual, I failed to understand.

Heidi then laughed breathlessly while her hand moved along the edge of the glass. "Michael has all of our best interests at heart, Anna. He wants to protect our better selves from our worse each-other's."

"Why must I always fail as a communist?" Leon asked rhetorically. "Because they mistrust anyone having a good time which is unjustified."

"Leave him alone," Heidi said wearily to Leon. "Michael is doing his best. Having a good time is a skill he has not yet mastered. Like every skill, it takes time to learn. But he is improving."

Leon grinned. Michael leaned back into his chair. He said, "I will derive my pleasure from watching."

"Exactly as I would expect." Leon laughed.

Michael said, "Such a desperate path simply to have a good time."

"Is it only the money that disturbs you?" Anna asked this with a teasing smile. "You are in such a vile mood, Michael, that no one will have a good time while you are here." In the silence that followed we all could hear a man and woman arguing in the street below. Michael began to twist and knead his hands. He looked at Heidi for a long, pained moment, but she did not look up to see his eyes. Then he stood and walked to the door. Heidi glanced up once to see his back. When the door closed behind him the room sighed. All except Heidi.

Someone restarted the Victrola, voices returned to conversation. In her soft low croon, Heidi then asked me about my painting. She mentioned a visit to my show, how impressed she was with the works displayed; she used the word 'devastating'. She asked then about Paris; had I met Matisse, did I know Picasso, how did the women dress? I began to lose interest.

Then she began to speak of her own work; I had not needed to ask. She spoke of hours in her dark room, long nights peering into weak light, fluids and powders and their smells. And her obsession with the scale of grey-to-black and the mystery of light.

Heidi leaned forward toward the glass, her face nearly to the table top. Through her thin, dark sweater the knobs of her spine curved gracefully as a string of dark pearls. She straightened then, the lines of white powder inviting in their furious uniformity. She turned to me then and asked, "Do you love your painting?"

Her question was asked without expression, as if she had asked the time of day. Before I could answer she handed the glass to me, a small straw lying to one side. I took the glass from her saying, "I love my painting even more than I love this."

Heidi laughed brightly. She had small, yellow teeth, like kernels of corn, stained with tobacco. Eyes alight she asked, "Do you love your painting more than you love me?"

I did not hesitate. "Yes, but of course."

Heidi laughed and laughed. Leon turned to her saying, "At least he does not lie to you. That is something different."

"Such optimism," she said, "coming from you. You may be right, but I doubt it. He will lie to me, or he will lie about me, and most likely he will do both. Tolstoy was right; all happy love stories end the same; it is all the unhappy love stories that end differently."

I said, "I believe you have mistaken the quotation."

It was Leon's turn to laugh. "He will prove amusing, Heidi. And he will improve your Tolstoy."

Later, after everyone had gone and she and I laid together in her enormous

bed she spoke of the pleasure of working in absolute darkness, of having to
rely on the touch of her fingertips, on her memory of placement, of watching
a pure white slowly grey under the enlarger, and then greyer, and then black,
and of the chemicals, the acids which burned, which ate away the skin of her
fingertips, of the rawness of her eyes and throat from the vapors. I imagined
her a brooding alchemist of the Middle Ages.

Between words we made love and took cocaine, we talked and took more
cocaine and made love again. By the time we finally ran out of words and
cocaine and love, the eastern sky had brightened. She turned to me pale and
slim and languorous in that morning light saying, "There is something wrong
in you, and I find it very interesting. Something about you demands close
examination. Very interesting." Her large blue eyes were shadowed luminous in
the half-dark room as they probed my face.

So, for a time, Heidi found me interesting. For a brief time in my life,
Heidi Berenson found me interesting.

Heidi took pictures endlessly.

Of everyone, of everything; a sort of hysterical desperation, reprinting
from a single negative time after time, demanding love from each image,
demanding knowledge and passion. She claimed to have printed every
negative she ever took; stacks, piles of photographic prints were everywhere.
To move about in her workroom risked an avalanche of glossy black and white
sheets. A row of 6-drawer file cabinets with still more stacks piled on top, piles
in the tall, narrow kitchen closet, boxes filled the space under her bed. For her
to abandon an image was impossible. That was not her discipline, not the way
she used her eyes.

So I assumed she would have been incapable of making a motion picture.
How would she ever edit her film? She would never allow even one image to
become disconnected from the others. How would she tolerate images reduced
to shards, to scraps, a perversion of their original sequence, or the violation of
that movement implied between frames?

No, I thought, that was not her discipline, that was not her personal
challenge. Or so I believed.

As a token of her interest, Heidi took photographs of me.

I was certain she would grow bored squinting at me through that tiny glass

window. And eventually I came to loath having my photograph taken. I tried
to explain this to Heidi. She found my discomfort vastly amusing, and took
more photographs.

Before I left Berlin that final time, I asked Heidi about those photographs
of me. There had been a small box of them. I asked because now there was no
question, she no longer found me interesting. Otherwise there was nothing else
left for me in the city. So I asked her about those photographs, the detritus of
my existence there, and our love. Did she still have them, and did she intend to
keep them?

She laughed huskily. "Do not worry, darling. I burned them. They have all
become smoke and ash." She laughed again. "Does that please you? Are you
relieved?" I said nothing. She asked, "Don't you believe me? Have you no faith
left at all?" This I could not answer either. There was so little left to say, more
words hardly seemed to matter. There did not seem to be words that small.

Of course, after all of that there was the war.

But from the beginning to the end there was Leon. Always, until nearly the
very end, there was Leon.

Watch him move, so large yet with so much speed and grace, passing
through a crowded café from one table to the next, dancing as lightly as a
prize-fighter. Leon, the painter who never appeared to have enough time to
paint, a professional waiter who rarely held a job very long, the poor man of
expensive habits.

Leon believed in favors. Leon lived by favors and for favors. Life itself was a
favor, and his life was that favor provided by Fate to everyone who knew him.
"Just this one time," he would say twisting the French happily. "Just this one
favor and nothing more, ever again."

While I had the studio on Potsdammerplatz near the train station, Leon
visited me every two or three days. And if he did not see me for several days
at Cafe Kanzler in Kaiser Wilhelm, then it did not matter if it was four in
the morning, he would ring my buzzer, climb the four flights to my door
grumbling, and then embrace me in the doorway, overwhelmed with relief,
as if he had half expected to find me dead. Under a single naked light bulb
we would sit across from each other in those hard wooden chairs, smoking
cigarettes and drinking whatever he had been able to steal from the restaurant
he currently worked in. He would wear his overcoat, insist it was not necessary

to remove because he could not possibly stay long. He had other things to do. And so he would sit, for two hours or longer, wearing his overcoat, red-faced and sweating, smoking and drinking and talking.

Sometimes he brought drugs; cocaine when he could, hashish when he could find nothing better. But under that bare bulb with cups of cheap wine in hand, his visits were always a great relief.

The light was bad that year, or at least I was unprepared for it. My studio had southern light; from it I should have gotten bad light but at least a great deal of it. Perhaps even too much, but certainly enough to work with. But those thick oily-black clouds came and stayed, and I could only shake my head. The canvases I had brought from Paris leaned against a wall unfinished. With light so bad, inevitably I gave up the brush to work entirely in crayon and charcoal-pencil.

Max Ruddge was a good friend of Leon's, and Max owed Leon a favor. He owned a printing company including his press and was doing work for several artists in Teirgarten and Charlottenberg. After Leon spoke to him on my behalf, Max suggested to me several poems by Heine he wanted to combine with a series of my own lithographs. Within a week I had twelve good drawings that he agreed to put out in a folio of lithographs. Max was a master-pressman and did beautiful work; short-tempered in negotiations, he was relentlessly methodical in his printing. The folio sold reasonably well and we received offers for several projects, enough so that we set up a small design studio. "Working at a studio," Max insisted warmly, "and away from where you sleep will do you good. And with some steady income you can properly entertain your women." In this way, Leon repaid his favors with more favors.

Near the time my exhibition of paintings was to close, Heidi and I agreed to spend Christmas in Paris with my friends, and then return to Berlin to celebrate the New Year with hers.

Christmas in Paris was a disaster, but we returned to Berlin certain we had made a new beginning, the New Year would bring us only good luck, and that we no longer needed to worry.

I moved my belongings into Heidi's apartment the first week of the new year. By then I had already begun working with Max at his studio. After fourteen weeks, all of my things had been removed from Heidi's flat, and I was no longer speaking to Max. In those days, life changed very quickly.

And there was Leon. When I moved my things to Heidi's, his visits stopped. Was he simply being discreet? Or was he somehow, for some reason, upset? I saw him occasionally in the cafes or restaurants. Neither of us spoke of Heidi or the end of his visits, and I was sufficiently enamored with her that I was relieved to allow that topic to fade. But eventually I came to suspect that something I had said or done had alienated Leon and made him uncomfortable in my presence. But all of that was much later, and by then I had become so unhappy with Heidi, and my life in Berlin had become so depressing, I did not try so hard to understand, and did not care so much whether I did.

After I had moved my things from Heidi's to a new flat I saw Leon only twice; once, the day before his last arrest, and another time before he was supposed to have committed suicide. From time to time, mutual friends reported seeing him with people they never recognized. The consensus grew that his circle of associates had changed. So I was not the only person who suddenly found it difficult to maintain contact with him. But by then I was so unhappy I failed to recognize the unhappiness of others. So I did not try so hard to find him; in fact I did not try at all. And then he committed suicide, or at least everyone agreed that it was suicide. In this way I found myself with nothing, or with too much. Remorse, but most of all unspeakable regret.

And after that I moved my things, finally and for all, back to Paris. And of course, after that there was the war.

"You are certain you want to do this?"

"It is such an opportunity. And he is a very interesting person. And so young."

"So young?"

"To be doing what he is doing. So much responsibility. Only three films and already he has become their most valuable director."

"And you are certain this is the work you want to do."

"I don't know. He is so young. And so interesting. Very talented."

"But do you want to operate a camera? Because that is what he wants. Do you want to operate a motion picture camera?"

"There is so much money. If I operate the camera there will be a lot of money. And afterward I'll be asked to work on other films. He will be sure to offer more work."

"Is that what you want?"

"I thought you wanted to spend the winter in Italy. Didn't you say this? To move to Italy to paint? And I would continue my photography. Isn't that what you want?"

"I don't understand what this man has to do with our plan to go to Italy."

"You understand that if we don't have enough money we cannot go to Italy. What more is there to understand?"

"But won't working with this man take time away from your photography?"

"What I do not understand is why I must be the one to invent schemes to get us money. But I am willing to try. I do not understand this, but I will work for him and his company. I will help them make their film so that we will go to Italy."

"But is this what you want? Do you want to make films?"

"What does that matter? You say we must leave here, that you cannot work here, that something in the light is keeping you from your painting. I will help us both. Besides, perhaps I will be very good at this. Perhaps I will be so good we will go to America and I will make films for Charlie Chaplin and Douglas Fairbanks. We will live in California and you will paint and I will make films. Do you think that would be exciting?"

"And what would happen to your photography? Would you still make photographs?"

"I don't understand you. You continue to repeat the same question as if I had not already explained. You pretend not to understand. Besides, suppose this job is not offered to me after all. This argument will be for nothing. Will that please you?"

"You would not ask such a question if there was a chance he would not offer you this job. You are preparing me, I understand this much"

"I am doing what?"

"Never mind; think nothing of it, I am prepared."

"What in heaven are you talking about?"

"Never mind. But I do not believe you want to make motion pictures. I do not believe you wish to go to UFA, to their studio instead of your own, day after day, watching through their lens instead of your own. And you say he is very young?"

"What are you suggesting?"

"You are not doing this to make a movie."

"Be very careful, you are about to make me angry."

"That's quite all right. You are valuable to me when you are angry. I trust you when you are angry."

"I believe you are jealous." Heidi said this with genuine surprise and began to laugh.

"Perhaps I am. That is possible."

"I think you are jealous that I will become famous and everyone will love my films and I will make so much money. At least show the decency to admit it." Her laughter became louder.

"Perhaps you are right," I said. "Perhaps you understand me perfectly."

"I knew I was right. I know you; I know you perfectly."

Nearly every time, nearly everything Heidi said was correct. Nearly everything.

Immediately behind the grey-green control tower at Templehof airfield there was a cafe. It was on the roof of the reception building, in the open air, open to the sky, and it was called the Flughafen restaurant. The sky was clear this day; cold but without wind so that sitting quite still in the sunshine one became warm. Heidi and I shared a table with Willy. Dark-haired, dark-eyed, he fingered his lit cigarette annoyingly. Nervousness makes me nervous. He smoked cigarette after cigarette. His lips were thin, they curved nervously, especially when Heidi looked at him. Occasionally his eyes left Heidi, once or twice he actually looked into my eyes. She looked at him often, watched him as she might a bird in a cage.

I asked, "And have you met Lillian Havey?"

Willy nodded with disinterest. "Everyone admires her." He spoke barely moving his thin lips, I was appropriately impressed. "Fine person, a serious and accomplished actress; I am not surprised you inquire about her. She'll soon begin to work on a new film: 'Keusche Susanne'. Very gay, very risqué. Marvelous person, really very beautiful."

To me Heidi added, "He knows all about your British actress, but he would rather work with good German actresses." She turned to Willy in a way that made me very sad.

Willy said, "Our decadence has reached such depths we now prefer foreign actresses, even some that are not so very good, rather than watch our very fine German artists. So many German artists starve while rich Germans buy work created by foreigners." He looked from me to Heidi with barely suppressed boredom. Perhaps he did not know why he was there with us. Perhaps he did know and simply wanted to be somewhere else.

Each of us gazed up into that bright sky, the first clear sky in days, and watched the planes, their engines roaring louder and louder gliding toward us or away, their wheels poised on the tarmac below us as graceful as dragonflies. A half-smile appeared on Willy's lips. He watched Heidi and me distantly, as he might watch actors moving across a stage.

Heidi sighed. "Perfectly beautiful day." Turning to Willy she added, "Perfectly beautiful because he is not painting. He hasn't painted in weeks. He takes my money and hangs about the cafes with his communist friends. And then he comes home drunk. That is how they make art in Paris. Rest easily in the sunshine while their women work, day after day. The first rule for being famous in Paris: do no painting. Second rule: let the woman make the money."

Willy shifted uncomfortably in his chair. I asked him, "Do you ever go to Potsdam?"

Heidi's eyes widened as she became very still.

Willy nodded. "It is a wonderful city."

"I agree with you there; a city filled with beautiful views."

Willy and Heidi remained silent watching me, watching my lips.

"Heidi and I paid a visit to the city quite recently. By the way, if you don't mind my asking; when you go to Potsdam, which hotel do you prefer?"

Willy shrugged, an aristocratic indifference, a beautiful indifference. He was indeed good-looking. "Probably Zum Einsiedler."

"Extraordinary. But of course," I said quite pleased. Heidi leaned back in her chair. "We stayed there a month ago. Was it only a month ago, my love? Heidi insisted we go there though I had never heard of the place." She watched me carefully, and recognized something that my face revealed. She looked away then, eyes directed to the horizon, the blue sky, perhaps on watch for airplanes. "First-rate hotel, quite elegant though its decorations are somewhat old-fashioned. Still, very tasteful. Ornate, for my taste, ostentatious in many ways, but elegant still. Even its bathroom fixtures have a certain joi de vivre. Pardon my asking, but which floor was your room on?"

"Second, as I recall." Willy's expression became suspicious, waiting, anticipation in the sunshine.

"Ah, too bad. You should really take a room on the top floor. Ours was a corner room. Chilly at night, but the light, particularly in the afternoon. Well, it was marvelous. Wasn't it, Heidi?" Her large blue eyes remained fixed on the horizon, and on sights I could not see. Willy's eyes shifted from her to me and then to her again. As though something between them suddenly had been agreed.

"I had brought my drawing materials, and of course Heidi had her camera. The light in the afternoon was quite marvelous. A certain color of gold or brass; and the wallpaper in our room was a russet that turned nearly blood red in that light. Quite beautiful." Turning in my chair toward Heidi I said, "Tell Willy what sort of work we finished that afternoon."

She said nothing, did not even acknowledge that I had spoken.

"We had planned an outing to San Souci," I said, "but due to a variety of distractions our morning drifted away. Sometime in the afternoon I made some attempts to draw Heidi. And she had the inspiration to photograph me. But we both failed, doomed I suppose by that wealth of light. Heidi could not sit long enough for me to draw, and I did not move sufficiently to give her a variety of postures. A curious irony, don't you think? And as you must know, Heidi likes to move around, to pace back and forth, as though constantly testing her vision. I admire that quality in her work greatly. So she was the first to notice the marvelous way the light at that moment flooded into the bathroom. Dark marble and white enamel tile, blue-green glass patterns etched into the windows. Forgive me, but I forget that you are already familiar with that hotel's decor."

But no apology was needed. Willy by now had become so bored he would not have even recognize an affront.

"This particular day," I continued, "the light poured through those windows into our bathroom, reflecting from every shining surface and turning the wood to the color of butter. The light touched everywhere like a veil of fire. Heidi went to the bathtub and turned on the taps, and the flowing water appeared nearly blue in the white enamel. I sat on a stool beside her and drew three sketches. Heidi fitted her camera with a special lens and then holding it with one hand she took photographs of the water as it poured from the spigot onto her free hand, moving the hand back and forth through the water while it churned and boiled crystalline white. My darling is very talented and a brave artist."

Heidi stood, walked quickly to the stairway. "She took a number of these photographs," I said ignoring her departure, "and they are very good photographs; very beautiful in their own way. Certainly you have seen them in her portfolio. Erlich at the Waldtheim printing house plans to bring them out in folio. He is certain they will be popular. And Heidi's agent, Gustemeyer, I'm sure you've met him, he predicts she will have a great success."

Willy stood and watched Heidi descend the stairs. He glanced back at me once, a grin like a death's-head masque slashed across his mouth. Then he left the table to follow her and was gone.

"The worst part," I said to the waiter just coming to our table, "everyone is anxious to see this folio of photographs, but no one appears interested in drawings of Heidi taking those photographs. In that wonderfully lighted room with the white and green marble and the bright brass and dark wood, and the white enamel. All of that light."

The daylight faded as the waiter added one saucer to another each time he returned. With the darkness the airplanes droned invisibly. When they flew low enough and close enough to the runway, searchlights would find them. Those big planes would then appear within cones of yellow light as suddenly as sea monsters, gliding slowly down, lower and lower, the sound of their engines growing louder, pitch becoming deeper, resounding.

Wrapped in my great warm overcoat I wondered about airplanes and why they did not fall, and about angels and how they could exist and yet have no bodies.

"Listen to me." Leon spoke across our table at the center of the crowded Salamander café in Oranienplatz. He looked grey and soft and defeated. When I offered to lend him money he pulled from his pocket an imposing roll of Reichmarks. He was employed again, he said, now a waiter at Marakesh in Fredrichstrasse but he had been ill. He breathed heavily, his eyes moved along the floor, the walls, the ceiling. I wanted to know what had happened at his police interrogation. I wanted to know what they had asked, whether they had beaten him and had he been hurt, and who he thought might have exposed him. He would only shake his head, a gloom like the shadow cast by a cathedral, his face glittering with sweat yet composed, eyes surveying, fearless, mouth carefully set.

"Listen to me: people will say it was because of too much. Listen to my words and go back to Paris. The Angel of Death perches above Kaiser Wilhelm cathedral. And the angel has its heart set on Berlin. People will say it is because of too much. People will say there is too much, and that we deserved a visitation, a punishment from God, because there is too much. Too much drugs and too much freedom and too much sex and too much money and too much movies and too much Charleston-dancing. And too many men like me, and like you, too. The Pope anticipates this visitation with pleasure and gratified that it will drive us all back to his church."

I could not hear his laughter, but only see it smeared across his mouth through the cigarette smoke. In all of that noise no one could have heard us, because even I could hardly hear us. And then I watched Leon's face change, his breathing become labored, suddenly there was not enough air for him to breath, not in the entire world.

"But what they say will be a lie," Leon continued. Sweat glazed his forehead and his eyes swept restlessly from window to door. "They will say it is because of too much and they will be wrong. The visitation will come, believe me, it will come. But it will come because there is not enough. Not nearly enough. Drugs? Not enough! Freedom? Not enough! Money? Not nearly enough! Movies? Not enough! Sex? Not nearly enough either! Charleston-dancing? Least of all that. Charleston dancing makes one more human, and more generous and caring of other humans. No, not nearly enough." He slapped the table with the flat of his hand. His hand trembled, his smile disappeared.

How to reassure him; what could I say to Leon? What would convince him there was no cause for alarm?

I said, "Now I will take my turn to make a prediction," because I was drunk, and because Leon had genuinely frightened me, "and you must listen to me. I will tell you what is true and how it will be. You and I will always be young, always be healthy, always be friends. There will always be enough paint, enough canvas, enough drugs, and always enough sex. There really is nothing to worry about."

Leon stared at me without anger, a gentle look without a smile but indulgent. He spread his fistful of Reichmarks on the table between us.

As we drank Leon spoke cautiously of recent assaults against friends, confrontations with the police or worse, the street-armies, thugs who spread pain and havoc with only apparent randomness. He described arrests he had seen in Kurfurstendamm, in Fredrickstrasse, even inside Marakesh itself, in Leipsigstrasse, and beatings of the miserable whores working in Teirgarten. Headlines in the newspapers every morning demanded a cleansing of the streets to protect the German family. Finally Leon's sweating insistence drained me and left me brooding.

But Leon must have recognized this. Suddenly he grabbed my arm, heavy body heaving he stood, dragged me to a passing taxi. We rode to Templehof.

Although the waiters there still served, the café was empty. It was late, the two remaining waiters sat together at a table smoking. Leon and I took a table in the darkest corner, and silently drank. We listened to the overloaded Luft-Hansas labor overhead, watched searchlight beams like yellow pencils laid on black paper follow their landings and takeoffs. The wind blew their sound away as the planes circled roaring in a sky that was utterly black.

And I would not believe Leon, not that night, nor even after his second arrest. I loved him, he was a great and generous man, but I had been unable to believe him. I could never believe he knew what he was talking about. After all, he was an artist. What could a painter know of politics? So once again I proved myself an abysmal fool. And worse than a fool, much worse than merely a fool.

Perhaps, in order for me to believe Leon and recognize what was about to take place, it was necessary that he throw himself into the river Spree. Simply in order that we, who loved him when he least loved himself, might prove our love by our insistence to public authorities that he would never have done such a thing, not voluntarily, ever. Why these protestations, these demonstrations of loyalty? Just so that from that time forward, all of us would walk the streets, day or night, certain a pair of hands had pushed Leon. So that each of us would wonder if the same pair of hands awaited us as well.

Christmas with Heidi in Paris.

The concierge at Maurice's apartment building was a grey stump of an old woman with a grey mustache on a twisted face, a face from a painting by Bosch. And she still hated Germans, even female Germans. Every day, at least twice a day, Heidi had to walk past this woman's open door, hear her muttered curses, a foul-mouthed crone. But in Paris we had nowhere else to stay.

Maurice had only been living in that apartment a month, forced out of his old studio by Sylvie. "She was stealing everything I had," he said after meeting us at Gare de l'Est. "Anything lying around she was likely to steal. Canvas, tubes of paint, and especially brushes." Arms waving, windmills in the cold, blue-grey winter evening as we walked to his flat. I breathed deep, my first return home, and found even the air in my lungs different. "That damned slut. A brat on each teat, that's all she's good for." Heidi said nothing, but by the length of her stride and the way she held her shoulders, I knew that a subtle fury was upon her that would not depart until we left Paris.

But I did not yet understand. Maurice amused me enormously. We had been friends for years, and Sylvie nearly as long. "Where is she now?" I asked, knowing she would never remiain too far from him for very long.

"Point de Neuilly. With the Spaniard, the poet, what's his name?" Maurice scratched his head feigning confusion about the name of the man who regularly had tried to bed Sylvie, only succeeding occasionally. "Sebastian! That's the fool's name. We shall make him a saint. St. Sebastian of the Fornicators. He has rescued me. I'll send flowers and a note, something to warn him. It is only fair he should be warned." He slapped me hard on the back. "Sylvie plans to use the material she stole from me actually to paint with. She's only going to pawn part of it to get some money, but stupidly she expects to paint. Canvas and paint are expensive enough without the likes of her driving prices higher."

Maurice shook his thickly-curled black hair with good-humored disgust. He continued, "I should be grateful she is gone, what with the cost of canvas. A model is cheaper than the paint to paint her." Streetlights winked on, bright pearls flickering into the distance. "I cannot force paint back into the tube from which it has come." Suddenly turning to Heidi he asked, "You wouldn't happen to have the price of some canvas and spirits? My supplier's shop is just around the corner. We could drop in, just for a minute." I began to laugh as if he had made a joke but Heidi did not join me.

Days later, Heidi and I lay in the tiny bed just beneath the window that faced onto Place Clichy, old Moncey on a pedestal outside still holding off the Germans and Russians from the rape of Paris, a bright sun peered around billowed white clouds. Heidi's large blue eyes; I could sometimes imagine living within those eyes, so large and their color so thick, like undiluted pigment. So many times we lay with our faces close, and so much talk, so many things argued. But those eyes, and their determination to see.

Friends in Paris and Berlin, just like her, seeing even with eyes closed, seeing around corners, seeing over the horizon, seeing beyond every boundary. Even as they made their purchases, their mundane acquisitions; automobiles and cocaine, opium and vegetables, tablecloths and town-houses, buying the future and the past, buying the dreams and the nightmares, without ever losing sight of the futility, the banality, the vaguely ridiculous, and that bilious horizon rimmed in black crepe.

What we did not realize was how thoroughly we knew these things; how perfectly and completely we recognized them, with what crystalline eyes, what perfectly-sharpened sight, we watched all of these things approach with nearly bloodless curiosity.

Later that afternoon I left Heidi alone in the apartment. Alone I climbed the hill to Sacre-Coeur, and to Pere-Lachaise.

There were no flowers at his stone but the sun was shining. This pleased me. I had brought no flowers of my own so I stole some from another grave and laid them for Dedo. I wondered if Dedo would recognize us all, now that we had become so modern, even more modern than Dedo. Sitting beside his remains and thinking about him, as if we might be speaking together, all this warmed me in that bright yet fading winter light.

And so I sat, until the arms of those naked trees above me were black against the blue violet sky, and shadows had covered everything, each corner and hollow, until the very tops of the monuments had disappeared, pearl-gray as an undertaker's trousers. For a moment this Universe held its breath.

Then streetlights blinked on one by one and the headlights of taxis moved faster, joined by others from every corner of Paris. Then it was time; time to find friends, time to find a bistro, time to find some wine, some food.

The German-hating concierge threw me a black look when I came in. But I had Maurice's key. I climbed the six flights and used it in the lock. As the door swung inward I saw directly into Maurice's bedroom, Maurice asleep in his bed, Heidi asleep beside him. I closed the door quietly, waited several thick heartbeats, and then left. At the bottom of the stairs the concierge was nowhere to be seen.

Like a metronome, the click of Heidi's camera seemed to beat out the rhythm of our visit to Paris.

I had come nearly to the end of my money. I had sold two paintings in Berlin, and I still owed money to Martin from his last loan. Heidi and I had just enough money to ship my belongings and paintings back with us to Berlin. So like good bourgeois we clutched our purses tightly and counted every centime.

A party nearly every night, rarely enough time to sleep and rest and then dress for the next. Friends had heard about my Berlin exhibition and had read favorable reviews. This surprised me, but wherever we went someone was there to congratulate me. As if overnight, simply by leaving the city, I had become a tremendous success. As if suddenly my empty pockets had become stuffed with money. No one except Maurice knew I possessed only a five-franc note and my return ticket to Berlin.

Everyone asked, and my answer was always the same; I was not happy to leave Paris. If asked in earnest I would have said I was going back to Berlin for love. But as always, the truth was of no matter. And the memory of love? Yes, madness to leave Paris, and madness to leave for love.

My dreams in Paris were peopled by those men sleeping under Fredrichstrasse Bridge. Later Heidi would confess her certainty that I would die in a flaming automobile wreck.

Meanwhile, Heidi's star had begun its rise, and faster and farther than either of us had expected. We both understood this, or at least claimed we did. Privately I was dissatisfied with both the kind of work she had been doing, and the people who were buying it. Heidi vaguely agreed, but insisted she was only doing this for a time. It was inevitable that she would return to her own photography.

"What are you thinking of me? You think I enjoy this work? When I have put some money aside I will thumb my nose at them. While they go to hell, you and I, darling, will go to southern France. And Italy. You still want that, don't you?" She laughed, we laughed together. Very often over that Christmas in Paris we laughed together. And I believed her. She believed herself so I believed her. If there were other things, there was also love. Not a love doomed to fade and perish, but a love to be ingested, to be consumed. A love.

We made our plan to move my life to Berlin. Because she was there. But when anyone asks why I moved to Berlin, I do not tell them about Heidi. When anyone asks why I went to Berlin, I tell them it was for art.

Christmas Eve, Jacques Hibbert and his wife Nancy invited us for dinner. Just the four of us. By then there had been too many parties, and Heidi and I were finally defeated by exhaustion. And Heidi had become sentimental. It was Christmas, after all.

During dinner Nancy said, "I'm told I have an uncle living in America. My father says they were both hardly seventeen when Uncle Marc went away. As we were growing up, father rarely mentioned him. But now that he is old, my father insists he talks to Uncle Marc. You know, sits in his room and speaking as if Uncle Marc sat beside him. 'Why did you go away?' he asks. He repeats that question as if expecting an answer." Nancy shook her head. "They were both so young. What would make a young boy go so far away? I've wondered why he left; and what has happened to him."

Turning to me Jacques said, "We are going to America in the springtime. We will find Nancy's Uncle Marc and he will be rich, and he will give us a pile of American money."

Brightly Heidi said, "In America a young woman can become famous in one night, and world-famous in a week." She turned to me then, threw a comradely arm over my shoulder. "I would like that. I would do anything to be famous like that, to be loved like that."

Jacque turned to her and half-earnestly said, "But you could never be truly happy that way. Not without a husband, not without children." He turned then toward Nancy, but she missed his glance. She watched Heidi.

Heidi laughed. "With all of that fame and all of that money, who would lack husbands?" Her eyes sparkled. "And to be loved like that. To travel like a comet, trailing beautiful planets, silver stars, and leaving a wake of breathless faces and broken hearts. That would be something. That might be something more than children."

Jacques eyes for a moment became wide. Then he suggested it was time for desert. Nancy stood to help him.

Heidi laughed softly. When they were gone she turned to me. "Perhaps I also have an uncle in America. Perhaps he is simply waiting for us to arrive so that he can give us piles of money."

I said, "We should write for him to send us money so that we can visit him."

Heidi laughed more, perhaps even too much.

At midnight we stood and toasted the holiday and then exchanged small gifts. After another hour Heidi and I left. It had stopped raining but the streets were still wet and bright with lights from windows and doorways. Revelers prowled the streets singing and roaring with laughter, celebrating with eerie insistence.

She and I were already asleep when Maurice burst in upon us. "Happy Noel," he cried shaking the footboard to our bed. His eyes rolled to the ceiling, he could barely see us. He swayed. "Happy Noel," he cried, "I am destroyed." He swayed to his own words as if dancing. "Never met one like her," he cried. The tenant above pounded down on our ceiling.

"Happy Noel," Maurice cried in reply. "Must she return with you? Can you condemn her to such a life in that pig's hole of a city? Leave her with me, you go to Berlin. I'll take care of her." Then he moved toward the toilet. "Happy Noel. How can I live without her? You are my friend and you do this to me."

I could watch without standing as he knelt down beside the toilet, and then became sick. I called out, "Happy Noel."

"Happy Noel," he cried between fits of retching, chin resting on the edge of the toilet.

"Happy Noel," I said as I stood. When I reached him his eyes rolled in my direction. He panted for breath, his face a disgusting mess. "Happy Noel," he gasped.

It occurred to me that it would have been easy to kill him just then; simply bash his drunken head against the porcelain. It would have been too easy.

I took a fistful of his hair, he did not even wince, and held his chin over the toilet as he became sick again. "Happy Noel," I said.

"Happy Noel," he groaned. I held his head.

"Happy Noel," I said.

Heidi did not move from the bed. She lay with the blanket to her nose and did not stir, did not open her eyes. As if she could have been asleep.

Two days later my belongings, my paintings, my miserable life secured within three stacks was loaded onto the train for Berlin.

Of course, this was before Heidi had become the protégé of the film director Willy Sudderman. And of course, all of this was before the war.

Just before the end of the great war, the first great war, Dedo came to visit me in Montpellier. His doctor had sent him south once again, hope against hope that his lungs might clear, and that he might rest, away from the friends and the bistros.

Stepping from the train he looked terrible, which was beautiful. Weaker than I remembered, but his spirits were very high. He said he had just begun a new series of nudes, he was full of plans, ready to work, even in his broken state, to paint every inch of canvas in the world.

I rented a room for him at the Hotel Henri IV. Across from the hotel was the municipal park, Les Arceaux. We walked there one afternoon. Late in the fall, the sky was bright and clear. We watched children kicking the piles of copper leaves that surrounded already-naked trees. The air was brisk and blew softly. We walked slowly as he described his plans, the canvases he would do, the women who might model for him, and whether Zborowski was cheating him with his advances.

We walked in the park: Les Arceaux, the arches. The remains of a Roman aqueduct, tall, graceful arches, one after the other, towered above us, a straight line of masonry disappearing into the hills north of the city. Beside one of those stone pillars an old gypsy woman sat at a folding table covered with a bright red cloth. Spread over the cloth lay an assortment of paint supplies.

Dedo circled her table several times. He had left his painting materials in Paris. He walked around the table in silence, looking.

She was a small woman, black and grey hair pulled severely back from a rough, wrinkled, nut-brown face, sharply hooked nose, large black eyes. She sat on a chair beside the table knitting with dark green wool.

"Can you draw, mother?" Dedo asked politely.

The woman did not look up from her knitting. "No, Monsieur," she said. "But Monsieur must be a very great painter." When she spoke her teeth were difficult to see.

Amused Dedo asked, "How have you come to be surrounded by these toys?"

Finally the woman put aside her knitting and looked up at Dedo. Her voice was dry and hard. "My son is also a great painter, a great artist. He is as great an artist as Monsieur."

Dedo glanced at me before he said, "With you as his mother, he must be a very fine painter indeed."

"Yes, Monsieur," she said, "he is a very skilful painter. He could paint flowers that would break a lover's heart, birds which flew instantly from his brush into the sky. But that was not enough for him, Monsieur. He left everything, even his paint, even his sister, even me." The woman looked down and signed herself with the cross. "I wish his heart peace. But one day he will come here and see his things, and he will want them again. I know that he is painting, Monsieur. Wherever he is, he is painting. He painted as a small child, and even if he is in heaven he is still painting." The woman signed herself again.

"You must be very proud," Dedo said. "One day he will return to thank you. He will show you his paintings, and in his purse will be much money, and he will give it all to you. And other painters will come from far away to ask your son to teach them how it is. And you will be very proud. And he will never go away again."

A distance away a group of children played, chasing each other shouting with pleasure. The woman lifted her head, eyes now dry, and sighed pitiably. "If Monsieur was my son I would cry all day. Surely your death will come very soon. To die is to go very far away. But perhaps Monsieur is like my son, an adventurer who is careless of the pain of those who can only await his return.

My son did not need to go away to be a fine painter. But he is gone. Perhaps he is already dead. Or perhaps like Monsieur he merely waits for death. Or perhaps he simply wishes to be dead."

Dedo's face changed, he became quite pale. I said, "Sometimes a mother is glad her son has gone away. Sometimes it is easier to adore one who is not here; easier to admire one whose mistakes and failures are unseen."

The old woman turned her face to me. Her eyes vanished. And where her eyes and cheeks and chin had been, in their place appeared a dark blue absence more remarkable than what it replaced. A void that opened into another void. From that emptiness a voice said, "Monsieur expects one day he will have a son. Perhaps Monsieur takes his birthright for granted." And then somehow that void smiled.

Dedo tossed a large coin onto the table saying, "Mother-love protects every son, but God's love protects us all."

We stepped away then, walked quickly, and neither of us looked back.

Beside the old Medical School there was a small hill sheathed in dry, brown grass. We stopped there finally to rest. Dedo's face was flush bright, he gasped for air, its sound was wretched. He sat down on the dry grass wheezing and panting. I sat down beside him. After a time his breathing gradually eased. And then he began to laugh, though laughter made his breathing worse. Spasms of coughing interrupted his laughter.

Still laughing and in mocking imitation of me he said, "Perhaps mother is glad her son is gone." More spasms of coughing, until he regained his breath to ask, "Whatever came over you?" He shook his head. "We should bring her with us back to Paris. A treasure. 'Monsieur takes his birthright too much for granted.'" He lay back, rolled onto his side on the ground still laughing. "If I hadn't given her that coin she would have put malocchio on us both."

When finally he could stand again he threw one arm across my shoulders. "Protecting me from the old gypsy woman, is that it? Afraid the she-dog might bite?" He laughed more quietly, breathing ruined, and coughed-up a small bit of blood. "Perhaps you should reach into your pocket; be sure the she-dog didn't bite off your birthright."

From there we climbed the long, steep, cobbled street beside the University. Dedo suddenly decided he was thirsty and suggested we stop in a nearby café. But there was a bar in his hotel, and I knew he was better off getting drunk where he had only to climb two flights of stairs to his bed.

As we made our way back to his hotel we stopped for a moment before the display window of an artist's supply shop. A dozen different paint boxes were arranged on a long piece of bright maroon satin. Each had some unique use of interior space, or included some device for doing something unnecessary. Each had a lid painted a different color, some had small pastoral scenes painted on their sides, others had scenes of Greek or Roman gods and goddesses The display filled the window, as thought the world of painting depended completely on brightly-decorated paint boxes. Dedo leaned his forehead against the window staring as he struggled to retrieve his breath.

"Too bad I don't need another paint box," he said. "I hardly ever need a new paint box. Except last year. You remember? That woman, what was her name with the tattoo? Rose. You remember how she threw all of my things into the Seine. And to my great sadness the paint box did not float. Everything else floated except the paint box."

"Perhaps," I said, "you should only buy paint boxes guaranteed to float."

He laughed weakly. "If I had a new paint box I would have to start painting again. And the doctor has warned me." He laughed. "I should introduce the doctor to the old she-dog; she would have something to say to him." He leaned away from the window, his eyes gone soft and melancholic. "But I will go back to painting, damn the doctor. And the sculpture; yes, damn them all. Wouldn't it be grand to sculpt even one beautiful piece of stone, something huge, and then sell it to some fat-assed bourgeois and his fat-assed bourgeois wife. Wouldn't that be fine? And for a lot of money. With that money I would buy a paint box whenever I liked. I would buy every paint box in this window. I would have piles of paint boxes."

"We should go," I said. The air had turned colder as the light began to fade. And finally I was hungry. We would have dinner together at Dedo's hotel.

"Yes," he said as we began the easy walk back down the hill, "piles and piles of paint boxes. Each a different color, a different design, all piled together in the middle of a field, a huge pile under the bright sun. Yes, paint boxes", he said coughing, bringing out a handkerchief pink in places with blood. "That way, all of this, every bit of this, would not have been for nothing."

Heidi was at UFA every day, I saw her rarely in the evening, and even less often on weekends. From the very first she was often busy. "Shooting is behind schedule," she would say. Or, "I'm going to Bremmen to look over a location." Or, "I've been called in to help with the edit; miles of rushes and so little time." But most often there was simply no answer to her telephone. If I had stood beside the UFA gates I was more likely to see her. So eventually I removed myself from Heidi's flat, and moved into my own studio. But at least I no longer worried whether she was sleeping with Willy. That, above all, was no longer something I worried about.

My new studio was a single room. Very small, it had one large window that faced north, a good direction for light everywhere else in Europe. But in Berlin it merely allowed me to study the clouds as they climbed high, shifted, bumped each other, shoved each other aside, and all that rain as it fell. I sat beside my stove in that room waiting for light, waiting for warmth, waiting to be dry, and always waiting for money. It was, I discovered, a studio for waiting.

I spent too much money walking around the city, so I settled in at the Romanische café. When I had a few marks more than I needed to buy coal, I took them to the Romanische. Marvelous, nearly religious occasions. For the price of three glasses of wine, I witnessed the most brilliant conversations, the most beautiful women, the most bizarre behavior; an atmosphere thick with the certainty that here was Something. At the Romanische, the evening was always just about to begin.

When my few marks were gone and I could find no one to advance me the price of one more drink, leave-taking broke my heart. No matter how late the hour, the air remained filled with anticipation, yet I would stumble alone back to that bleak studio.

But finally Herr Markel promised money. On the weight of his promise, money was nearly in my hand. He stood before me in the Strum-Galere absently cleaning his glasses, staring myopically into my chin and promising that despite my refusal of his clients' access to my studio, the arrangement was nearly complete. The sale of ten canvases for a single price. Herr Markel was a precise man carefully hiding his disappointment at my inexcusably bad business sense. The entire batch, all of that work for a single price; he insisted his offer was good. There was real money involved, no question about it.

And I was utterly broke. I should have offered those same canvases to Martin. As my agent by contract, he still had right of first refusal, which fortunately for me he rarely exercised. Perhaps I was so certain he would accept anything which Markel might reject, it never occurred to me that Martin's feelings might be hurt as well as resent the loss of those sales. Checks from Martin still found me from time to time for the sale of some drawings or a small canvas remaining in his store-room, or a late payment for something sold months before. His loyalty was never in doubt. So I should have offered those canvases first to Martin. At least if he bought them I would be sure of getting paid.

The sum Markel offered seemed enormous. It was only later that his offer became less enticing. Ten paintings involved a great expense for materials. Measured against those costs, Markel's offer became less magical. But all of that cash, all at once, all together.

Time and again I walked the early-hour deserted streets cursing misery, cursing friends, cursing Heidi. I even cursed Leon, the only honest friend I had left. But finally to be rid of those paintings lying about. Herr Markel would take them all, the ones I no longer liked along with the ones I liked too well, get rid of them, clear all of them out of my studio, out of my life. A fresh slate upon which to start new projects. Cash for what was finished to start new projects, a new life.

First things first; I ran up a huge bar-tab at Romanische. I told everyone who would listen that I was about to sell a pile of canvas to a dealer. Eyes turned to me.

In a few days strangers began to greet me as I walked through the door, others detached themselves from conversations to sit beside me, to let me buy their drinks. In those days we were all very game to drink each others drinks.

When all the money was gone, it was time to meet with Herr Markel. We met at his home, in a room the size of an aristocrat's boudoir. We sat like sweethearts together on his couch. Six canvases had been delivered, three others were nearly complete. But one canvas he especially wanted, a canvas several years old but for which I had become very fond. I had agreed to sell it, and I had intended to give it over with the rest. But the more I savored that painting, the more resentful I became. So I had begun to wander the streets again. We spoke together about that painting for a time, what other accommodations might be made.

Herr Markel was a patient man with flat eyes. I found immense pleasure knowing he valued these canvases even more than I, although a valuation entirely different from my own. But he was wise enough to resist pressing certain issues.

We were men of the world, after all, he said. He then asked if I had made any plans.

At that moment I could see no future. Or, more exactly, I expected to remain in Berlin, keep painting, scratch out an existence, and have as good a time as possible. Or perhaps the future was not even that clear. No plan except continue to pay the rent. He leaned back into the couch not concealing his boredom, and again cleaned his glasses with a small, dark handkerchief while he awaited my response. So I said, "Berlin grows colder by the hour. I have decided to return to Paris."

Markel leaned forward and displayed his teeth in a grimace. "But how can this be? You have made so many friends here. When these canvases are finally displayed you will acquire a serious reputation. And of course, I will continue to be eager to acquire your work. Without doubt its value will increase in a very short time."

"Their financial value, strictly speaking. Merely one measure of value."

Herr Markel pressed a button by his arm, a man appeared. Markel requested drinks be brought in. For several minutes we sat frozen together in silence. The man returned pushing a small cart. Markel stood, damaged hand already reaching for the decanter as he dismissed the man.

"You are young," he said, "and anxious to get into serious trouble. No great art without serious trouble, am I correct?" I waited. He said, "But trouble comes all on its own, it needs no invitation. And once it arrives it is a guest difficult to be rid of. Here your work is recognized, and you have the opportunities you need, even for trouble. People admire your work, and they buy it. There are one or two things I can do to assist, but you have already done the most difficult part. Your work sells slowly, but you have begun to gain a following. Patience is what is needed here, not adolescent impulsiveness." With a glance at the cart he asked, "Care for something?"

I requested, he poured as he continued. "If the question of your remaining in Berlin is only a matter of money, we might lower our commission. Quite likely you have out-spent your allowance; a young man's tastes."

He carried my drink back to the couch in his damaged hand and then sat again beside me.

I had not realized that I wanted to return to Paris. And even at that moment I was uncertain how I had reached the conclusion. There would be humiliation in my return; there would be apologies, and embarrassment and sneering condescension. But my worst fear; that somehow I had already used up Paris. That I had left because it had already become empty for me and could not be re-filled. As though a certain Paris had ceased to exist.

Yet I had responded to his question immediately, as if, without knowing it, I had been thinking about it for a long time.

Markel spoke as he again cleaned his glasses. "You must admit there is nothing left in Paris, at least artistically speaking. Its days of glory were twenty years ago, thirty years ago." He spoke so softly I needed to lean toward him. "Nothing of any of that is left. Today everything, great art, great music, even motion pictures, all is here in Berlin. The truly New World is here, that world you have worked so earnestly to prepare yourself for. In any case, what chance do you have to establish a reputation by hanging beside works by Picasso, Braque or Matisse? Yet, they are the old school, while you are the new. They have run out of places to hide the despair of their own failures and have become merely frightened old men. Your youth assures that you are truly modern. Besides, very soon, everyone will wish to be here in Berlin, and to live just as we live." His eyes without their glasses burned vaguely grey, his soft voice was reedy, producing words like soap bubbles perfectly shaped by his lips that expanded over our heads. Finally he returned his glasses to his face and then leaned back, the light from the crystal chandelier shattered on their lenses.

I said, "You are probably right. This is quite likely the modern world. But my decision will not change." There was no longer any good reason to remain in that city, and several good reasons to leave. The glass in my hand suddenly grew very cold.

Markel shrugged. "I do not understand you, but perhaps it would count as your failure if I did understand you." He laughed quietly. "All of us know of your attachment to Heidi Berenson. It should not surprise you that I know even more than you are likely to credit me. I am careful of my investments, after all. Fraulein Berenson is extremely talented, certainly head-strong, perhaps a bit mad. But she has acquired some reputation. Those around her will likely gain attention as well. I think of her as a comet with a very long, wide tail."

He leaned forward, his voice lowered, I had to lean even further forward to hear him. "It is only fair that you know your association with her can only bring you more attention. And where the spotlight falls, there the rainbow begins. Bear with me another moment and do not prejudge either of us."

"Fraulein Berenson has created a small storm. Soon she will be among the front ranks of popular film makers. Willy Suddermann has been extremely useful to her. I expect she is quite grateful, but gratitude does not go on forever. Once we have offered our thanks, every debt becomes a burden." Markel's fingers tapped lightly on my forearm.

"You are a talented painter. Skill and emotional depth shine in your work. Even without a crystal ball I say in five years your work will sell simply on your reputation alone. No longer will you need to prove or argue. In five years you will be recognized by every gallery in Germany. Your success is inevitable, but I offer that success sooner than you imagine."

He leaned back then and looked away. From a small side-table by his injured hand he brought over a box of cigars and offered it to me. I refused and he chose one for himself. He spent time and care trimming the end, and more time and care lighting it. Did he enjoy watching me, the insect that had come to rest in his web? When his cigar plumed grey smoke he patted my arm.

"There are things worse than success." He laughed warmly. "Success goes to those who know its darkest secret. And that secret is, success goes to those who share it." His eyes narrowed, a look of scrupulous wisdom, a vast sagacity. "You will no doubt object that sometimes a man succeeds who is isolated, alone, independent of the judgment of others. And I agree, success sometimes comes to one disdainful of it, one who does not welcome its arrival and insure its comfort, nor shares it with those closest to him. But success does not remain, my friend. Unlike trouble, success will not abide where it is not wanted. And it never, ever comes back."

Markel rolled the grey ember of his cigar against the edge of a green glass ashtray, carefully forming it into a cone. "Let me be blunt. Your association with Fraulein Berenson has created a receptive area in people's minds no other artist at this moment can claim. People have become curious and will want to see your work. I am confident that what they see, they will want to buy."

"And what they will want," I added without sarcasm, "will appreciate in price, the more of them who want it."

He looked at me carefully, his smile was slow in forming. "Understand me when I tell you all of us enjoy the success of others most when that success directly benefits ourselves. The more we benefit, the happier we are for that successful person. Those most successful recognize the self-interest of those around them, or they cease to succeed." He stood. "Can I re-fill your glass?"

As I handed it to him I asked, "And if I still do not wish to remain in

Berlin? What of my success then?"

Markel shrugged as he refilled the glass and returned to the couch. "Do not over-estimate your value, my friend. The group of investors I represent is prepared to keep you comfortable in Berlin. However, if Paris tempts you too strongly, fair enough and so be it. Germany does not yet force people to remain. There are quite a few others here nearly as talented as you." His laugh was tinted with condescension. "But you and I will settle this once and for all. We have chosen you because your work is superior, but not merely superior. Your career is connected to the meteoric rise of another artist. Thus your work is doubly valuable." He leaned back smiling as contented clouds of grey cigar smoke circled his face dulling the glint of light from his glasses.

"And if I still do not wish to remain in Berlin? If I decide to refuse your offer?"

His smile disappeared, replaced by barely controlled patience, a frustrated tolerance. "You are a very young man, but don't you ever concern yourself with your old age? You are creating a body of work here, a testimony to your skill and artistic courage. You have embarked upon great work. Do not play childish games when a life is at stake. We have offered you an opportunity because we are certain of your success."

Markel studied my face as if to invade my thoughts. His offer was generous. It would enable me to paint with an easy conscience and sleep without care for tomorrow for the better part of a year. There would certainly be money, and perhaps all of the other things he had said would come true. And perhaps, eventually, Heidi would again find me interesting.

He tired of watching me. "You are very close friends with Leon Reichtmann, this I know from mutual friends. Do you want to know what is wrong with his paintings, why no one buys them, why no one will ever buy them? Because he paints too dark." He smirked then as he leaned away. "You think I am crazy? You look at me and see some soulless bourgeois? I have been in this business forty years and I tell you no one will ever buy his paintings because he paints too dark. He's good, of course, no question, perhaps even brilliant. But this you must understand most thoroughly; 'good' is never enough, never will be enough."

Markel allowed his words to spin and drift upward with his grey cigar smoke. "But I will make a compromise with you. If you agree to our plan, I will arrange an exhibition of Reichtmann's black paintings. This must satisfy you. Of course it will loose money and I will not sell a single piece. But here you will do something good for yourself, and also for your dear friend Reichtmann as well. You see how success is?" he said with a laugh. "It has already spread beyond us, even against my better judgment. So now, I ask you once more; what of my proposal?"

It took a moment but I had to confess. "Leon changes everything," I said. "I need to speak to him. Only twenty-four hours. I do not wish to insult your offer, but I do not want to make a mistake either. I should as well call Martin in Paris."

Markel snorted, clenched the cigar tightly in his teeth. "Prevarication." In his voice I could hear his patience nearing its limit. "An opportunity other painters dream about. This is absurd." He stood angrily. "Am I wasting my time or not?"

I waited.

"This is absurd, this is pure stupidity. I am half-embarrassed. You say you need time to think, to talk to this painter and that agent and then God only knows who else. Should we perhaps call your mother?"

"I am adventurous on canvas," I said, "but business matters are always more treacherous."

Herr Markel removed his glasses and began to clean them again as he slowly smiled. In a moment he had come to a conclusion, and that was what his smile meant. He had recognized something, and now he knew that everything would be all right.

"Believe me, this is not a proposal of marriage," he said with a laugh. "You are a fine painter and I am a fine dealer. I make you a better offer than God himself." He stood, paced slowly before the couch, his smile no longer quite on his lips, merely around his eyes and rippling around his mouth. He reached into his jacket, brought out a pen and small book. "I understand your kind, you see, and I know precisely what it is you need." In a few moments his pink, tortured hand held a small, narrow sheet of pale pink paper. "Consider this a down payment, and from this moment consider yourself under contract." The ink still wet, a check for twice our originally agreed upon advance. "Be in my office with the rest of those paintings promptly at nine tomorrow, or don't be in Berlin at all. Because if you refuse this, no one else in this city will touch your work, ever." He shook himself, his smile disappeared, he stared at the floor. "I have staked everything on you, sir, and I am beginning to regret that fact."

Herr Markel turned and pressed a button on the desk, in a moment the butler entered. To me he said, "As our interview is over you must excuse me. I have a pleasant dinner engagement which you have ruined. Remember; my gallery at nine. Neither you nor Reichtmann will ever regret this, although I already have begun to." He shook my hand with his good one, and then smiled. "Such a pleasure doing business with someone so knowledgeable in the ways of business."

I followed the butler out of the room, down the long hallway, to the front door.

On the street I knew at once I must find Leon. I had faith he would know what needed to be done.

I walked the few blocks north of the train station through a weak chilling rain to his apartment and tried his doorbell; no answer. Stepping back into the street I saw that his windows were dark. But his apartment was a good distance from my own, so I debated the wisdom of going to my own apartment and then returning in an hour or two. There was a café a short distance from Leon's apartment. I decided to wait there, return every half-hour until I had found him. Life had suddenly become that urgent.

Thus I walked several times between Leon's place and that café. But by midnight I had no money left, except that check so large only a bank could cash it. Soon I would need to return to my apartment if only to sleep. So I walked to Leon's apartment one final time.

Perhaps I now wish I had given up finding him; gone home, and the next day gone to Herr Markel's office with those paintings ready to sign his agreement. So many things would have been different if I had simply given up on Leon.

But as I approached his apartment I was relieved; lights were visible in his room. I leaned on his doorbell a long time, listened to it ring loudly above my head. When no one came to the door I decided he must have returned and then left again without turning off his lights. Another opportunity to have gone and moved on without Leon. But I tried his bell again and again, as if I was determined not to be denied.

Suddenly the door opened to reveal a woman's face peering at me. It took a moment for me to realize it was Anna's face.

"What do you want?" she asked, unable or uncaring to disguise her fear.

"I must speak to Leon. It is urgent."

"It must be terribly urgent," she said, and then her eyes filled suddenly with tears. The rain had stopped and the air had become quite cold and the wind had begun to blow; soon it would snow. She held the door as if resisting the wind, and prevented me from coming in.

"What is wrong?"

Anna sighed so loud it could be heard over the wind. "No one has told you? You come here so quickly, pretending you do not know." A change in the light and I could see her face more clearly. Make-up smeared, eyes so shattered they might have been removed, the muscles of her mouth tired and lax, even her voice was stretched taunt. "I hope you did not come here for money. I hope he did not owe you money."

"What has happened?"

Her eyes suddenly went wide as she stared at me. "Only two hours ago. The police boat pulled his body from the river. The police said there were witnesses." She spoke as if spiting something vile from her mouth. "They said the witnesses tried to stop him. They said they tried to pull him down from the railing. They said Leon fought and screamed that he wanted to die. And then he did."

She sighed again exhausted, her voice as if rising from the deepest part of her soul. "There were other witnesses. They said Leon screamed something else."

Then her eyes emptied. "Listen to me and do everyone here a favor. Go back to Paris. Do not wait for anyone else to tell you, just go!" She tried to shove the door closed, but I jammed my foot into the space. Her eyes widened. "Who are you to come here? The man is dead; don't you understand? Dead!" Her tears fell as she tried again to close the door.

"Tell me what you know," I said. "At least tell me that."

"You will go then?" Her face suddenly hardened, became massive, each crease and corner square, eyes dry and furious.

I did not reply. She said, "You know what he was. Always his friends and his deals. The rats and cockroaches of Berlin knew him by name. To look at him you would think he never opened a newspaper. So it could have been anyone. The men standing by as he went into that black water could have been anyone from the streets. Because Leon never protected himself. Anyone could have as much of him as they liked. Gangsters with drugs? Or one of the pimps? Or maybe just an ordinary policeman. What difference does it make now?" She clung to the door frame and began to weep in earnest, a loud and furious wail.

"What bloody difference?" she screamed as she pounded the door frame with her fist. "Who cares? Who cares about him?" She stared at me as if seeing me for the first time. "Did you care about him? Is that why you are here? Or are you working for them, too? Are you here to make sure? Do you work for them now?" She glared at me and then she began to laugh maniacally. "Has someone come to his door to give him money this time, instead of take it away? They pushed him, you know. Off the bridge. Into that icy water. They pushed him and then no one tried to help him. Was it so cold? No one would become wet to save Leon. Where are your friends now, Leon?" She laughed nearly mad, screeching, the sound tore from her throat. "They would not save you from that river. All the kind, thoughtful, decent friends you bragged so much about. Where are they now, Leon? All of your precious, miserable friends are gone. You needed them and they are gone, lost, and you are forgotten."

Suddenly a fury possessed her; she began to slam the door against my foot, screaming. "Go away! Get out of here! Go back to Paris! We don't need you here. Your only friend is dead, do you understand? No one wants you here. Not even Heidi! Go back to your whores in Paris!"

And I ran away.

At my apartment I packed everything that would fit into two suitcases and three boxes, strapped the canvases together in a bundle. I could not take everything, three canvases I left, and two grey clay figures. The rest fit into several parcels, my life was such then.

A taxi. We loaded all of it, my entire life, and then we were gone.

Approaching the train station we crossed the Spree; I asked the driver to stop. I did not know which of the bridges he had fallen from, but it was the same river. Despite the proverb, this remained the same river, and always would be. I walked to the middle of the bridge. In the rough wind Markel's slip of pink paper snapped and danced like a flag; neatly, brightly, precisely. Large white flakes of snow blew, the wind froze my hands, my fingers became cramped and stiff.

And I tore that piece of pale, pink paper with its curled black numbers, tore it as it danced in the raw and careless wind. I tore it into the smallest pieces my numb fingers could create. Hands cupped I tossed the scraps high, the wind caught them, indistinguishable from the fat snowflakes, they fluttered and twisted down toward the oily, glistening water. Leon painted too dark, he used too much black. The fragments looked like rose petals on black lacquer. For a moment they floated, tossed back and forth, clustered by the rushing air. In a few moments they were gone, drifted off into the darkness.

Forever I will lean forward over the railing of that bridge, and forever there will be that bitter wind within which to weep.

My train was scheduled to leave an hour or so later, a long wait. The sky was flat without stars, the flakes grew larger and more numerous, they spun like fairies, it became colder still. As if there might not be anything, anywhere, not outside or in.

At the train station I bought a sheet of paper, an envelope and a stamp. At first I knew precisely what I would write, how I would phrase what I would say. But the moment the pen touched paper it disappeared, all gone from my head as if it had never been. And then I did not want to write anything. Sudenly I wanted to find her, I wanted torture, I wanted revenge.

I took up the pen and wrote; "When you next come to Paris, be certain you bring Leon." My hand trembled as I addressed it and dropped it into the mail. I remember very well how my hand shook.

With my things collected I climbed aboard the train and found my seat. I waited counting heartbeats until the conductor blew his whistle. There was the rapid succession of slamming coach doors, a moment of terror, a moment of panic, the train shuddered as if throwing off a nightmare, and I fell back into my seat. And then we moved.

The train crawled, a journey of tremors that threatened to last until eternity. We moved so slowly I shivered with the certainty I would never see Paris again. As if our train had entered a dream-world of interminable movement. I wondered about my friends in Paris, my burden of shame, of my failure in their eyes. But I deserved no less. There was Leon, after all, a corpse now bloated and gray, still floating in the darkest, longest night of all. I had failed in ways my friends in Paris could never know.

My memory now is that I cried; that I spent a long time staring into the black, peaceful night, and that I cried. I have not always remembered that night in the same way. For years I believed I was sad but resigned, and that I was optimistic as I stepped from the train. And for a certain time in my life I believed that as the train arrived at Gare de l'Est the sun was shining, and I smiled.

But my memory now is that I wept; that I found my seat as the conductor blew his whistle and the doors slammed shut and the train jolted into motion, and that I cried. That I cried and that it was raining in Paris when I arrived; that I cried for days as it rained and that I cried even when it no longer rained.

Because something terrible had happened and I knew this, and because something even more terrible was about to happen, and I knew that too.

After that, of course, there was the war.

CHAPTER SIXTEEN

WE SAT BESIDE THE POOL as Donald sketched while I pretended. I had become desperate, and the most desperate measures had come to mind.

Only a few days before, in the hall of the Fine Arts Building, Vincent took me aside. He spoke quietly. "I know what you think about this retrospective, but let me ask you one question, just as Burston asked me. If we really have such great regard for your work, don't we have an obligation to make it available to a wider public?" Vincent stared into my eyes waiting. So I laughed. I laughed so loudly heads turned. Vincent flushed and walked away.

To Donald I said, "Have you spoken to Vincent recently?"

Sunglasses glinting in the fierce sun, he looked in my direction and shrugged.

"And what about Burston? Have you spoken to him?" He paused to shrug again and went back to his scratching. As obscure as the gesture was, I understood that he had spoken with them both.

I wrestled with my frustration, unable to decipher even the contour of my own thoughts, because that woman was not there beside our pool, under our bright sun. So I told Donald a story.

"I arrived in New York a year before the war began. I was alone with only the money I had squeezed from Martin, and my solitude was terrible. And I was angry with everyone and everything, even with him. Against my specific instructions he had sold several canvases from his Paris gallery which I had

asked that he store until I had sent for them from America. I should not have
been so harsh. The money from those sales allowed me a bit more luxury in my
stay. But I hated New York. No city could possibly have been as miserable and
unsympathetic a place as I pretended New York was. All because my own life
was in tatters, while we all recognized that the world itself would soon be in
flames. There were nights that first year of the War when I was certain that if
I walked to the end of Manhattan island and looked east, I would actually see
the glow of the inferno devouring Europe, smell the burning and rotting flesh.
They were terrible years, and I spent them clinging to the smallest bit of the
edge of another continent. But worst of all, I was not painting."

"I had rented a decent, warm apartment, and I did not lack materials. And
there was often good light, particularly in the morning. But I did not paint.
For a time I convinced myself I had lost the ability to see shapes, and that
colors no longer made sense. My hand moved badly, and I had frequent and
powerful headaches. This went on almost two years. I made attempts, started
a new canvas every month or two, continued to draw nearly every day, even
adopted several new techniques. But it was as if I needed to re-learn to tie my
own shoes."

"Amazingly, with Paris on the verge of siege, Martin continued to find
people willing to spend good money on my work. Later he came to New York,
claiming earnestly that, like me, he intended to stay only through the War.
So much for good intentions. But not even his arrival shook the dullness from
mind. The chill in my heart, like a minor head-cold, evolved into an artistic
pneumonia."

"One day in the reflection from a store-front window I recognized myself,
advancing past middle age without anything worth saying, uninterested in
others or in myself, no longer capable of interest in anything. It was then that
I began to think in the way one thinks when considering a retrospective. I
began, so to speak, to count paintings. The exercise was not pleasant, my state
of mind did not improve, and so after a time I stopped."

Donald looked away, his finger tips stroked the white metal table top.
I leaned forward as close to him as our table would allow. "What finally
rescued me was this recognition. There will be enough time to count all of
my paintings once I am dead. And the realization as well that I am the most
fortunate of men, because the chore of gathering and organizing and all the
rest will never fall to me. Those whose job that will be, will do all of it gladly,

of this I am certain. There are, after all, those born to do just that. And if it is not my life they will poke about in, it will be another's. Such a life is the only one some are capable of. In any case, they will do it, encouraged or not."

Donald stared across the pool. I followed his gaze. He pretended interest in a gathering of people standing in the shade of a tall tree. I said, "I assume you expect to do the catalog for this exhibition."

When finally he turned, he was smiling. "What would make you think that?"

I said, "If I needed a catalog, I can think of no one I would rather have prepare it." This was most certainly true. At some things Donald was very good.

"But would you not prefer that I continue simply to paint? Would you rather read about my past work, or look at my newest? Never mind what John wants. He would prefer a library full of books to being forced to look at another new painting, react earnestly to a new aesthetic. Answer me this, because this is very important to me. Are you not the least bit curious to see what else I might paint? Are you not eager to see what I paint next?"

Donald removed his sunglasses, rubbed his face as he squinted into the sun. "The problem with you is, you refuse to understand how important this show is to all of us."

"No, no. It is you, and those others, who refuse to recognize how degrading such a show would be. We all agree that this show is important. But for me it is poison." My voice rose, I heard it echo from the walls around us. Several faces turned to watch. I moved my chair closer.

"A sculptor you do not know, August Picard, an artist of an earlier, no-longer modern style, lost to your catalogers, but a friend dear to me. So, he lived with a model, a beautiful young woman, her name was Rosa. For thirty years they had endured poverty and infidelity and fury, yet remained in love. So you might think this woman deserved to share in the honors bestowed upon August. So, five days before Picard died, with all the ceremony of the church and pomp of the great and adoring nation of France, she became married to him. Are you not touched?" I waited, Donald remained quite still.

"I ask you now, is it so important that our lives be made tidy? Should we spend precious moments re-knotting loose ends, as if life was a middle-class living room, the bits of a life neatly arranged on shelves for display and carefully dusted, constantly prepared to receive guests who never arrive? So, a catalog and a retrospective. But for me? I will likely spend too much time wondering why the lost has not been found, why the destroyed has not been rebuilt, why the dead are no longer living, and why it is I recognize no friend's face, anywhere, any more."

Donald glanced up. His sunglasses completed his disguise, he looked away.

To prune my work. Snip off unsightly ends, attach appropriate labels, filed, indexed and set on shelves, the best place to collect dust. Could I make him understand? Do whatever you wish when I am dead, simply wait until I am dead to do it. This seems a simple desire.

I wanted badly to look at that woman again, there, showered by bright, caressing light. To look at her would have refreshed me, just as staring into a deep stand of green trees relaxes the eye.

Several days had passed since I had last seen her, sufficient time to settle my plans for large canvases. Their images had begun to clear, along with their disposition of elements. Over several nights I had laid in my bed watched them form on my ceiling. But I needed her presence to complete them. In a way that frightened me, they would also become part of her, as she became part of them. Whatever pleasure there was, the burden of my dependency on her depressed me.

Because it was not simply her help I needed. I had needed other models before. But I needed to depend upon other hands, other eyes. Those paintings growing in my mind could not be completed without assistance.

The sun was about to blister the backs of my hands. Donald resumed his pencil-scratching exercise with a concentration I found almost convincing. I watched the end of his pencil bob and dip as his elbow moved like a 'cellist's. Waves of heat from the concrete hovered around us. Pearls of sweat gathered under his eyes.

I reached suddenly across the table and pulled the sketchbook from under his hand. He released it reluctantly, flipped his sunglasses back over his eyes, then leaned back in his chair folding his hands across his stomach. An expression of boredom appeared around his mouth.

Resolved to look carefully at each drawing I turned back to the first page.

Over-determined shapes, meaningless, as if he might hide behind the act of drawing itself. Pages he had drawn as we sat beside the pool the previous day, thick, black lines, hard-edged, tight angles. And then other drawings in unfamiliar settings. Obviously he had taken his drawing seriously enough to carry his materials to other locations. Finally I began to see Donald's drawings. I came to several of a man in a chair; dark lines thicker, heavier, cross patterns more dense, tight angles erratic, as though the figure was covered by a net of black ropes.

More drawings of that man followed, head tipped in one direction and then another, hand raised or lowered, shoulders turned to one side, hand resting on the top of his cane, sunglasses abandoned on the table before him, a flat book open, pencils scattered beside it.

"The likeness is not bad," I said finally and looked up. Donald turned away. "But you should only choose models who inspire. The other kind are everywhere and always available. But inspiration, on the other hand, is rare."

When Donald said nothing, I continued. "You have a choice. Help me with my paintings, or bury me with your catalog."

Behind his sunglasses I could not catch the look of his eyes. He did not move. He said, "I am not an artist, and I never will be." He paused and I waited for him to continue. His lips moved as if forming new words, other thoughts. But his silence continued until I could no longer bear it.

I said, "Perhaps you presume too much. An artist is someone who makes art. A catalog is not art, but a painting can be. One learns to make art by making art, not catalogs. One does not choose to be an artist, but one can choose to make art."

"That choice has already been made," he said, "and years ago. Or maybe there was no choice at all."

"No choice is eternal. Except the choice of death."

Donald finally smiled, turned to look at me and then quietly he laughed. "Maybe that's exactly what I chose. Maybe I burned my brushes years ago."

I asked, "Was the funeral beautiful? Was it artistic?"

His smile disappeared and he turned away.

I yawned and stretched and stood. "This day is dying and I am tired. Your problem is not easily solved. I wait for your answer."

He turned to face me, his face was golden with the setting sun. "I can't help you," he said with flat certainty. "There is nothing in these hands that can be of any value to you. You like to watch me struggle with these things; fine and fair enough. But you want me to become your accomplice. You think if I help your painting, I'll abandon the catalog. And then I'll try that much harder to discourage the retrospective. Let me remind you, if I prepare the catalog and your exhibition is a success, I could make something of that. But suppose I help with your painting? So maybe you sell a few canvases, and maybe the committee gives up this retrospective. Where will all that leave me in the end?"

"I would invite you to prepare the catalog for the display of my newest work. And, having worked on those drawings and canvases yourself, yours would be a unique perspective. This would be useful to your reputation among other artists and dealers. Yet I believe you favor the department. Perhaps all you really want is the glory and gratitude of the department."

Frustration, anger, impatience? Whatever it was rushed to the surface of his face, even disguised by his sunglasses there could be no mistake. I continued, "But perhaps your decision is simpler than you realize. Perhaps you simply need to decide whether you would prefer to act, to do the painting, to create, to imagine for yourself, or would you rather sit by and watch someone else do it for you. Because if you want a challenge, there it is."

Donald did not turn away. But by now the bright, harsh sunlight had given me a headache. Or perhaps it was the toxin of my frustration. "Come back tomorrow. I have made you a generous offer, do not waste my time. If you will not help me I must find someone who can. And very soon. So go home." Donald stood abruptly, turned and strode away. Was his fury directed at me, or at himself? Or was it the entire world that made him furious? But with young people, who can tell?

CHAPTER SEVENTEEN

THE LIGHT IN MY WINDOW turned from burning orange to brilliant gold, softened to rose and then hardened in blue. My head felt ten feet wide and weighed down with chains. From my bed I watched every hue, every saturation, a movement as graceful as a sigh. I felt exactly as if I suffered a hang-over.

I did not recall having drunk so much after Donald left. Yet I felt as if a vampire had come in the night and drained me of every ambition, even to open my eyes. No time seemed to pass while a band of light like the leading edge of the incoming tide slid at an angle along the white sill of the window. I dozed as if submerged in warm fluid.

Rapid knocking at my door finally saved me. I could think of no one who might need me at that absurd mid-day hour. Over-burdened with curiosity I stood and opened the door.

Until well-after mid-day my doorway always flooded with sunlight when the sun finally dipped below the roof-line of the building across the way. But until then, golden pink light washed over my threshold, just as it did as I opened the door, all of that light blotting out the figure that entered. A loud greeting, an excited hand thrust toward my sun-blinded eyes.

"Typical of you foreigners," Vincent said bright with humor. "Sleep until noon while pretending to paint." He laughed nervously, as if his own excitement was insufficient, and he needed my excitement as well.

"Shut up and drink coffee," I said relieved it was only him, "or get out."

He said, "Since you're making the coffee, it's probably safe to drink." Vincent sat down at my table and said nothing more until the coffee had been poured, until it had cooled and he had drunk half of his cup. His presence annoyed me and he ignored the fact of my displeasure. But finally he decided to allow me to know what was on his mind.

"The latest rumor has Burston phoning all his rich friends." Vincent interlaced his fingers around his coffee cup. They looked clumsy, thick and awkward beside my own fingers, thin as bands of light through narrow slatted blinds, and nearly as useless. "Seems there're more than twenty of your paintings and drawings held in different collections nearby. See? Burston could mount a show just from local collections. He won't need to track all over to find enough to hang." He leaned back with a satisfied expression, as if it was all working according to his prediction. "Things, as they say, are working out."

"And you come here expecting my response? I feel no gratitude that my work is so widely available. Now tell me now why you are really here?"

Vincent stood and went to the stove, returned carrying the coffee pot and used it to refill both our cups. "You're ignoring the significant. Burston has put the wheels into motion. By the time your help is asked for, all you'll need to do is make sure everything hangs straight." His thick black eyebrows rose with condescending mirth. "Of course you're right and this show is worse than a bad idea. idea." He smiled. "But you fail to grasp the inevitable."

His glee was bitter and unrestrained; as if he was as annoyed as he was relieved that his cynical expectations had been confirmed.

He anticipated my outrage, so I did not disappoint. "I could offer my own paintings in the company of those of my colleagues. Let everyone stare at one of Burston's canvases hanging next to one of mine." Words made my head throb, but the thought of our two canvases hanging side-by-side almost made me laugh.

With my suggestion Vincent's smile disappeared and he lowered his voice. "The public relations office for the University has gotten through to the Chancellor who's finally become convinced your show would get international coverage; a plus for the department, and for the University." Vincent leaned back, crossed his arms behind his head and looked up as if addressing the ceiling. "They all assume you're not as naive as you pretend. Some people probably sympathize with you, but the show in Munich is getting a lot of attention, so expect things to get worse."

"And they can all go to the devil," I said, because I could think of nothing else.

Vincent laughed. Did he enjoy my discomfort? "If I can't change your mind, that's the end of it as far as I'm concerned. But for the others, it's only a matter of time until you agree."

I muttered a curse. What else could I do? And Vincent smiled. What else could he do? "Suppose," I said, "I denounce these maniacs to the press? Slander everyone at the University. What value would this retrospective have for them then? In any case, the Munich show is nothing compared to the circus the University plans." Despite my headache and my despair, I was gradually becoming furious. "I will be damned by God Himself before I allow any of them to make a fool of me."

His dark eyes studied me the way a tailor might before offering a suit of clothes. At the corners of his eyes I saw deep and tan creases. Suddenly he appeared no longer so young. Perhaps his years at the University and their compromises had begun to weigh upon him. But his eyes were also crafty, lids slightly closed. Quietly he said, "John offered the catalog to Donald."

I shook my head. "I have assumed this all along. Has Donald agreed?"

"Told John he needed to think it over. I figured he'd talk it over with you."

I laughed. "Meanwhile John goes ahead with his plans, one right after the other, ignoring my refusal."

"The farther along a truck goes, the tougher it is to stop."

"Even down to who will write the catalog."

"John isn't kidding. He figures with Donald writing it, that's just a bit more candy to tempt you. Because with Donald, John's giving you complete control. That's just his way of demonstrating his respect for you."

"And he expects me to be grateful for this opportunity to become my own propagandist. The opportunity to offer my soul to a captivated public. How tempting."

Vincent tossed a hand as if to dispel a noxious vapor. "Everybody agrees, but all this agreement doesn't do you any damned good. Time for you to wake up. If you expect to stop this train, you need to tear up the tracks."

My head continued to throb. At the base of my neck something clamped the muscles and nerves, and slowly squeezed. I wanted badly to lie down, close my eyes, and for Vincent simply to disappear. Shadows had grown deep, violet to a black edged with silver. Daylight pained my eyes. I said, "Does Donald seem an appropriate pawn? Does he seem the type?"

He shrugged. "Forget Donald, he's just a cypher. Burston's erasing your alternatives. Whatever you think of his painting, he's a clever guy."

I studied Vincent's fingers, their cracked, paint-stained calluses, more shards of paint black beneath his nails, the inelegant way his hands folded one within the other. I said, "Has Donald told you I am planning new work?"

When I looked up, his expression suggested he had not. Could Donald have successfully kept my plan to himself? Could it be that John did not know? Or simply that John had not told Vincent? "Projects of size and number," I said. "Significant work. I have become ambitious. A half-dozen canvases, perhaps ten. Works of real size."

I watched Vincent's hands become very still, no longer reaching and relaxed. I said, "But this work demands a free mind. Planning for the exhibition must stop." I paused and hesitated. "So tell me what would happen if I threatened to abandon these new paintings? Suppose I took a vacation, a trip to New York or to Munich, or perhaps a long journey to Paris."

Vincent remained still, his eyes blank. He recognized the depth of my desperation. Some things Vincent understood very well. He stood, went to the counter and again returned with the coffee pot.

"As we grow older," Vincent said, "each of us learns when and how to be careful." He poured the steaming coffee into our cups with exaggerated care. "Being careful means paying close attention to whatever you are doing, even as you are doing it." Replacing the pot he returned and sat down. "Never underestimate your own foolishness; that's what I've learned. If you're more foolish than Burston, you lose. He doesn't understand your reluctance and too bad for him he never will. He's certain he's doing you a great favor. Your refusal just convinces him you're too naïve or deluded or obstinate to appreciate his help." Vincent's thick eyebrows arched and then flexed, finally turning up into a smile.

"Besides," he continued, "he thinks he'll get this show going without your help. But don't think I haven't wondered which of you guys is the most loony. And one more thing you should keep in mind. Self-interest may have grown beyond even Burston's ability to control. Somebody above him may have taken this project to heart. Convincing Burston might not even be enough anymore. But go ahead and threaten your brains out if that makes you feel better."

Vincent leaned back head tipped to one side, as if he might be hearing termites in the floor-boards. A glimmer moved within his eyes. I said, "We are not toy dolls for bureaucrats to move about. If the history of this century demonstrates anything, it is that none of us needs to play the pawn without complaint or protest. This is not a circus for performing animals, or so I have been assured." His expression did not change but the light in his eyes weakened, a flame guttering in a candle.

Vincent tapped his knee once and then stood quickly, a sudden display of energy, as if to demonstrate that our discussion no longer held his attention. His strong hand reached for my own. "Anyway, Donald's not a bad kid. By the time this is over, you'll really need him. But just remember that I warned you." Vincent laughed loudly.

I could not resist antagonism. "Given the alternative of depending on you, I would want Donald at my side."

Though he laughed, his eyes narrowed. "Are you really doing new work?"

Finally it was my turn to shrug. "Only sketches so far, but I could begin stretching canvas within three months."

His narrowed eyes held me a moment longer than I wanted. "It's hard to imagine John letting go of this show when he's already got his teeth in so deep." We shook hands again. Was his grasp gentler, or was I more tired than when he arrived?

The sun had already reached the tops of the building across the pool. Its yellow light had paled to cream. Vincent studied risks like a good card player. In this I nearly admired him, but also mistrusted him, so I would not underestimate his political position.

The day had begun badly and, had I been wise I would have returned to my bed. Without hope of salvaging whatever remained of the day, I was overcome and suddenly exhausted. As if something Vincent had said, or left unsaid, had sucked my body dry.

Vincent once told me he admired my work so much he thought it deserved a retrospective, but Vincent was not Burston. I would not confuse their motives. But if Vincent became outspoken in support of the new work, interest in that other show might fade.

The telephone rang several times. It sat on the floor squat and black. I walked to it, stood over it, a giant staring down at a nasty spider. I felt neither curiosity nor compassion for whoever was making my telephone ring. Its bell banged in my ear even as the throbbing in my head diminished. Moving between rings so as not to disturb that spirit immanent within its black plastic shell, I took up the sketchbook, my cane, sunglasses and pencils. When I closed my front door and listened to the telephone ring muffled through those firm walls protecting me from its vicious bite, that throbbing in my head suddenly lifted, replaced by a lightness, almost a vertigo of fresh air. Against my better judgment, I smiled.

The crowd beside the pool that day was large, yet not large enough to include her. Christmas was approaching. The weather had turned cooler and soon there would be year-end examinations. Everyone beside the pool had at least a small stack of books. Subdued voices, notebooks exchanged, heads leaning together; it was all rather depressing. Although it was not cold, there was a chill beneath the gathering of grey clouds. All seemed dreary despite the light. As if everything around me had been painted with a grey wash and every color was reduced. With no sound except the hum of the pool filter, it seemed as if my head was swathed in white bandages, and everyone around the pool had become as motionless as a dream.

Without even opening the sketchbook, I reached for the image and found it. They stood as if waiting for me, patient and unassuming, and their movements graceful and slow. The water and our concrete stage lay bathed by that light of clouds passing before the sun. In my sketchbook the figures remained as if expected and waiting patiently. A tableau under that light; a sampling of the light at each moment. An earthen yellow light the color of dry adobe separated each of those shapes; sinuous figures against powdery dry air. A ballet beside the pool, a dance of light and shade, a pas de deux with the sun.

Sketchbook in my lap and the weak sun in my eyes I knew I had discovered the image. Was my desire to paint purified by its urgency? Or did I simply disguise myself from my despair?

Ten canvases, each of them large. I realized there would need to be at least ten. So the question became; how much can this old man accomplish?

I would offer Marla the opportunity to work very hard for an ungrateful old man. There would be enough work for Donald as well, and perhaps he would even agree to do it.

With a final decision made I stood feeling suddenly refreshed and prepared. Then I heard them; three voices talking excitedly as they descended the stairs. I watched them from behind my dark glasses.

Her blue jeans clung to her thighs and hips and her white blouse was open at the throat highlighting her broad shoulders. Her dark hair was drawn back by a wide green ribbon. Beside her two friends she settled in a chair at the far end of the pool.

Watching her move about, stand and walk and then lean and then sit, my eyes became calm and my breathing eased. She would model for these paintings, and realizing this assured me their work would be completed. There would be no self-doubt, no hesitation. And those canvases would become a chronicle of my captivity to her.

With sketchbook and cane in hand I stood. I was ready to begin. I climbed those stairs slowly. When I reached the door to my apartment I paused again to look out across the pool to watch her head move, her shoulders turn. Unfortunately, the light had grown too weak for me to see if she saw me, and if so, whether she smiled.

A retrospective could bring only sadness and a great deal of it. But if my colleagues were genuinely hungry for great art, the canvases I planned would stuff their faces with it. And that idea pleased me.

Inside my apartment I called Marla. When I explained my decision she paused a long while before she spoke. "You're talking about a full years' work, maybe more. I should really spend that time on my own painting. You know how that is."

I knew precisely the position my suggestion put her in. And in her position I would have rather done anything than work on another painter's canvases. But there was no one else I could trust, and I confessed just that.

After another long pause she asked, "Why not Donald? He would take your coaching just as well as I would."

"He is less skillful than you are," I admitted. "Besides, Burston offered him the catalog for the retrospective. Working on that will leave him no time for painting. He is well-meaning, but that is no longer enough."

"And you think I offer more than good intentions?"

I told her that even her questions were more valuable than Donald's. When she hesitated, I suggested she draw up her own schedule. If she decided to work on her own material for several weeks, that would be satisfactory. We would start whenever she felt ready. But I assured her these would be large works so they would demand a lot of her time and energy.

Finally she asked, "If I agree, when would we start?"

I explained how far along my plans had proceeded. "Not for another two months."

I imagined Marla curled around her telephone studying a spot high on the wall, eyebrows knit into a ridge of consternated flesh, upper lip curled down over the chewed lower. She said, "When you have those sketches finished, call me. I'll come by and take a look. Meantime, I'll hurry my own work along. But understand that none of this will get you what you want. You won't get anything good this way. I don't like the show any more than you do, but what you've decided is a hundred times worse. You don't understand me and you won't believe me, but nothing good can come from this. Just remember that I told you so."

When I replaced the receiver I was not relieved and I did not feel better. Pressed against the receiver as I listened to my own voice, my ear had become hot and sore, my mouth dry. I stood exhausted, as if I had been climbing stairs for a long time.

The evening air had turned nearly cold. It startled me, as if I had just awakened. The sky in the west was the color of raspberry tea. Below, the patio was deserted, and that was just as well. A stream of pink clouds fringed the darkening horizon. Dry leaves rattled in the corners of the walkway. Perhaps Marla was right and this was the worst way to approach new work. Perhaps I had already placed a curse upon that work, and my motives had already betrayed it.

A gust of wind suddenly pulled the door from my fingers and slammed it shut with an explosion. A world growing dark, the cold, creeping wind blowing everywhere and restless. Not as cold nor as dark as other nights, in other places, so cold every Christmas. The cold and dark and wind. It whispered at the windows, a bleak darkness, a sparkling darkness. And the cold. I wished suddenly for a roaring fire.

CHAPTER EIGHTEEN

FROM THE MOMENT he turned the corner I watched Donald's approach. The sky was grey and its light washed out every other color. But the air was mild and dry. Tempted out earlier by a suggestion the sun might appear, I sat at the table beside the pool cursing this sordid light and nature and God. And then Donald appeared. I watched him walk slowly, shoulders bent as if draped with a heavy blanket. Did he see me watching? Did he wonder, what is that old man watching?

But when he reached my table he smiled and sarcastically asked, "Working on your sun tan?"

"Some days," I said, "even bad light is good." He sat in a chair across from me and with the pool behind him. The look of simulated amusement in his eyes was even clearer at this distance, their sparkle more silver and less blue. "I did not expect to see you today." And this was true. The holiday season and resulting exodus of students meant the end of regular schedules.

"I'm leaving for home tomorrow. Going down state for a few days. Just thought I'd stop by."

I thanked him for his thoughtfulness, asked if his examinations had gone well, had he found time to draw, and did he plan any outings during the holidays. He said that things had gone well, but he looked forward to a quiet holiday. More relaxed than I had ever seen him, good humor refused to leave his face.

"Are you going home to your parents?" I asked. He nodded. "And your girlfriend; have you made plans to be with her, too?"

I watched his smile fade as the lines of his lips and cheeks and chin turned down. A shadow passed over his face. "We'll get together a few times over Christmas." Then he laughed. "I still have her Christmas gift."

I said, "I want to begin stretching canvas soon after the beginning of the new year. Will you trade writing a bibliography for wrestling with twelve foot sections of canvas?" The moment he looked up I realized he would not refuse. I continued, "So, is there anything to keep you from this work?"

Donald shook his head but said nothing. I waited for him to satisfy my curiosity. But he looked at me as if anticipating the next question. Gradually his face reddened and then he said, "If you're worried Barbara will somehow interrupt things, don't be."

"If you tell me I have nothing to fear, I will fear nothing." I stood then, took up my cane, lifted my sketchbook and turned toward the stairs. "But I need a definite answer." After a few steps Donald was beside me but he moved as if his flesh was wrapped uncomfortably around his bones. I stopped. "Do you expect me to believe this only involves Barbara?"

He shrugged as if he was freezing. "You take some things too lightly."

Impatience overwhelmed me. "Understand one thing; there will be no retrospective. Any work you do on the catalog, no matter how brilliantly incisive, will be without value. On the other hand, the paintings I have in mind will be completed. Now, which of these projects would impress her more?"

"You don't understand. It isn't that simple." He resumed climbing the stairs and continued past me toward my door. "I'll need recommendations from the department if I expect to do anything with my degree after I get out of here. I need them to talk about me. I need them to value me"

"I will write your recommendation," I volunteered, a generous gesture under any circumstance. "What could be simpler?"

Donald laughed without malice. "You think your recommendation would be more useful than one from John?"

I stepped past Donald. "So the source of your hesitation is your careerist aspirations and how John would prove more useful to you than I would. Am I correct?"

"You are contemptuous of something valuable. You speak lightly of something that is very serious." When we reached my door, he was breathing hard as a glaze of sweat covered his brow despite the cool air. Suddenly I found myself thinking of him as someone with a problem. Trouble is humanizing. Americans, I have found, believe in failure, see failure as a constant possibility, a material trap along the path of life. And they appreciate the grotesque depravity at the heart of failure.

I unlocked my door, motioned him to come in. He glanced inside and then at me. Quietly he said, "I'd like to work on your projects. But given everything that's going on, there just doesn't seem to be any point."

"Come inside," I said. "Perhaps I misjudge your affection for painting."

I turned on a light, turned on the radio. Donald sat down at my table. From beside the refrigerator I brought out an unopened bottle of burgundy. I said, "You are not telling the complete truth. Your unhappiness you regard as romantic, yet unhappiness with Barbara merely disguises your unhappiness with yourself."

He smiled sourly. I said, "You think such a problem is unique to you? You think I am so old I forget certain things, or that these things have just been invented by you?" I wanted him to laugh, at least at himself, but he did not. "Perhaps you use Barbara as an excuse so that you will avoid having to try your hand at this work. Perhaps you are even afraid." I filled two glasses with wine, slid one across the table.

He fingered his glass. We dank in silence. On the table beside his hand was one of my old linoleum knives. He picked it up, tested its blade with his thumb, returned it to the table. He asked, "You do any print-making, any linoleum cuts with this?"

I shook my head. "I use it to cut string or pieces of canvas; there are some things it is still sharp enough to cut." When finally he began to speak, it was not about Barbara.

"I learned to do linoleum cuts in high school. Before that, I did all the usual kid stuff, but then I started doing those blocks. I just loved the way they looked and how fast you could do them. A couple were printed in the high school magazine. But I was doing all kinds of things with them, you know, really experimented."

Donald laughed and his eyes sparkled with an impish delight. "My fingers were always cut up and gouged from the knives. And I didn't own a shirt or a pair of pants that weren't stained with some ink, or blood, or both. My folks never knew what to make of any of it. But I kept at it. I hung onto some of those prints, kept them in a box, but I've got no idea where they've gone."

"So you no longer make them."

He shrugged but his face darkened. "I never really decided to stop, I guess I just lost interest." He shook his head. "Senior year in high school, I started dating Diana. Her father owned a trucking company in Burlingame and she was headed to law school at Stanford; her family had money. Small and blond, in that blue two-piece bathing suit she looked like Sandra Dee just stepped out of a movie. Real popular, and grey eyes that could look right inside my head."

A cloud of the thinnest grey smoke seemed to fill the space between us rich with the aroma of rosemary.

"Dating Diana pushed me right into the high school social circuit. From Christmas through that summer we were a hot number. She was my date for the senior prom." His memory filled his eyes.

"The summer after graduation Diana's father put up a bunch of money so she and her girlfriends could rent a beach house near Santa Cruz." His laugh was thick and came from deep in his throat. "From Memorial Day to Labor Day, wall-to-wall people and drinking. Cases of beer, quarts or six-packs and sometimes a keg. And whiskey. Cigarette butts floating in the dregs the next morning, and head-splitting hang-overs. Sunday mornings the place groaned. Sand and salt on everything you touched, the smell of sun-tan lotion and medicated creams. Everybody had at least a part-time job, except Diana and a couple of her girlfriends. So there was money to blow on alcohol. Hours spent drinking. Surfing in the sunshine and drinking at night. And then the fights."

I refilled our glasses. The grey sun had set unnoticed, and shadows began to fill my apartment. Donald sipped from his glass and smiled.

"She liked telling people I was an artist. That's always how she introduced me. I never figured out why, but she got a real charge out of saying it. She liked the idea, so everybody else did. But it was like that. Whatever Diana liked, a bunch of those people would like it, too. Some people figured me for a weird-o, but she liked it."

"Eventually there was a friend of a friend, and then there was a boat and people started going out for the afternoon on this boat. I hate boats, hate being on top of all that water. And always so hot. I went out once or twice, but that was it. So aside from the time I spent with Diana I was getting sort of bored. That's when I brought some of my drawing stuff and my litho equipment from home and set up the press and worktable in her room."

"But you were not actually living there, with her?"

Mock horror touched him, and then he smiled. "That's all her father would need to hear, that a guy was living there. Of course eventually I had so much of my stuff there it was like I lived there. Anyway, after dinner one night everybody was just sort of laid-out and beat so I set the press up in the kitchen, you know, just for fun. Pretty soon a couple of people wanted to take a turn at making a print. People seemed to have a good time that night. That was a fun night." A smile of genuine pleasure suffused Donald's face as he reached for the bottle and refilled his glass, then motioned toward mine. I nodded.

"That was the summer I got the brilliant idea of going to art school. I hadn't thought much about anything before, but everybody else had made a plan except me, and I guess I just wanted something to tell people I was doing. And I decided to go even though my family didn't have any money. Stupidly I gotten it into my head that art was fun and something you did with your friends, and that girls liked it when you did it. So I knew I wanted to make art." He laughed then so fully I joined him.

Suddenly and with enough yearning to surprise me he said, "Oh Diana." He shook his head as if chasing a bad dream. "Sometimes it comes back to me, on that beach lying beside her, the surf and the piercing sun, the smile she'd turn on me like a breeze that smelled of flowers, and the jewels of sweat between her breasts." He shook himself again and then grinned with embarrassment. I motioned with the bottle toward his glass. He shook his head.

"But what a hard-head. And aggressive in her own way. She was born to be a lawyer." He lifted his glass and drank. "And what could I know about lawyers? The only ones I've know were Diana and Bruce Garvin. And he never really became a lawyer, as far as I know." He leaned forward, lowered his voice. "Garvin was going to Stanford, too. They would be law-students together. But I never thought anything about that until it was too late." His laughter grew slowly, until it filled with a macabre humor. "And she was such a hard-head. First, she was a hard-head about having nothing to do with Bruce, until she became a hard-head about being with him everywhere. What a time." Donald's smile remained, but around his eyes and at the corners of his mouth his flesh tightened. I could not read his eyes. He turned his glass slowly between his fingers.

After a long pause I said, "Drink up! I will open another." He sipped from his glass, returned it to the table still half-full. He leaned forward, weight on his forearms, large hands folded. He stared down into the plastic surface of the table, the crumbs and stains and scratches of its surface. And the light, or at least the reflection. When I had the fresh bottle open I waved it toward his glass. He ignored me. I said, "You were jealous of this man, of course. She was your lover, and this other fellow was your friend. You were hurt."

"Garvin was never my friend." He spoke quietly but managed to retain his smile. "He'd been dating one of the other house-mates so he was around that house a lot. Anyway, by the end of July Diana and I were fighting. A lot of romances about that time hit the rocks. Or maybe you only notice what happens to you." He shook his head. "I kept hoping eventually she'd drop him. When she didn't, I decided we needed to talk." His look sharpened but he continued to smile. "You look at me like you can hardly believe how stupid I am."

"Not true. But it seems that every time such a thing happens, it appears as new."

Donald stared at me, and I could not discover whether he was annoyed or amused. "Maybe the appearance is the reality. Maybe it's always new, always different."

I waved my hand to dismiss the thought. "So you came to believe a conversation would clear the air and put things to rest."

"No, I never believed anything like that. What I needed was just the act, stripped of everything; hope and fear and everything else. Speaking, just to sit and talk."

Again I motioned with the bottle. His glass was empty but he ignored my gesture. "I don't remember how it worked out, but one afternoon we were alone, just her and me. At that point she would never have planned to be alone with me, but there we were. I was getting ready to get all my stuff out of there. And honestly, I'd been doing some drinking that afternoon. But she was there and I was there, so eventually we got into an argument. Stupidly I insisted she stop hanging around with Garvin. And of course she refused. But something about that refusal crushed me. Completely flat." He reached across the table, took up the lino knife again, turned it in his hand thumb on the blade.

"I wasn't working on a block just then but I found one of the knives lying on the table, away from those others I usually kept together in a closed box. I sat down on the couch thinking, 'Don't forget, put this away, what's this doing out, just put this back, don't forget.' She and I argued and it just got louder. Suddenly she was standing beside the door saying, 'Forget it, just forget it.' She reached for the door. And just as suddenly, I couldn't just stand by and watch her leave. I probably said something like, 'You can't go', or 'Don't go yet', or something like that. And then I took her arm, just put my hand over it. She pulled away, furious, called me a creep. I reached out for her with my other hand to hold her arm back."

When he paused our darkness was already complete and I did not move. His voice became very soft. "There was a jolt, a tug on my fingers. The knife slashed lengthwise along her forearm, hooked at her wrist. But so fast I couldn't believe it happened. And she kept moving, heading through the door. I yelled or groaned something wretched. Suddenly blood was coming from her arm, just so much blood. When she saw it her face went white. But she never screamed. She held her arm out toward me without a word but with this utterly horrified expression. And the blood just poured."

"This was a beach house so towels were everywhere. I grabbed every one I could reach and squeezed them to her arm. But she just kept bleeding. Towel after towel, but she kept bleeding. Then her body started to tremble, her face was terrible, and real quiet she began to cry. I was going nuts, but I tied a couple of towels together, got the blood to slow down, and then got into her car. That ride was a horror. The whole trip she laid on the back seat whimpering. Somehow I got us to the emergency room. When she got out of the car there was a small puddle of blood on the car floor."

He shook his head slowly, closed his eyes once. "I sat in the emergency room like I wasn't really there, couldn't even feel my body. No idea how long. But finally she stepped through a door and walked toward me. She looked terrible, her face, and this big white bandage that covered her forearm. But she was walking. She nearly walked past me, hardly even looked in my direction. I stood up, got in step beside her. In this weird zombie monotone she said they'd put in twelve stitches, that I'd come real close to the artery. Walking back to the car she turned to glance up at me, the first time she'd looked at me, and she said, 'They wanted to know what happened. And who you were. I told them it was an accident and you weren't even in the house.' That's all she said. We'd never agreed on a story, you see, she did that all herself. A real lawyer thing. All I had to do was shut up. I never figured out why."

He paused. I said, "Terrible things are done for love."

And then he surprised me. He laughed. "Love didn't have anything to do with that. Too much had happened. But if there was love there was more self-preservation. And maybe some misshaped loyalty, some twisted pride. I've had a lot of time to think about it." He leaned forward, each hair of his moustache sparkled. "Somewhere she'd caught herself in a mirror and got a look at something. But everything was over. Our romance, that summer, that beach house, those friends, everything. Maybe I was having the same thoughts, or maybe I've decided that my thoughts were her thoughts. But she must have known. Like I realized later, if she'd told the story straight there'd have been questions, and then police. So none of it would ever have finished." He leaned back and closed his eyes. "Or maybe not. Maybe that part just makes me feel better."

I said, "Understanding is not consolation." I offered the wine bottle but he did not appear to notice. "The past leaves us impotent precisely because it is beyond our power."

His smile became broader. Something appeared in his eyes, a hint of superiority or condescension, and I winced with anger. "When we got out of the emergency room it was late. I helped her into the car. She started to tremble like she couldn't get warm. I got out a blanket, got the heater going, we sat for a while with the motor running. All wrapped in that blanket, she said she didn't want to go home yet, that she wanted to go for a ride. I told her she was too sick and that I should get her home right away. But she repeated it like she wasn't fooling. She said to take her to this place we used to go to when we first started going out, a place maybe twenty minutes south, almost to Salinas. Off Route One across from a hamburger stand there was a dirt road that snaked north through some sand dunes, and then opened out to the beach. You could drive right to the edge of the ocean. We used to go there after classes or a movie to make-out."

"All the way there I tried to convince her she was sick. Inside I was frantic. I had to get my stuff out of her place right away, that night. I tried to think of who'd help me, who owed me a favor, where I'd dump my stuff. But finally we were bumping around in the sand, Diana tossing beside me in the front seat. I drove to our spot, a space between sand dunes."

"I expected a tirade, but nothing, just nothing. Her eyes were closed and she sat very still. Curled up half against the door, blanket still around her, darkness except for her light hair and that white bandage on her arm. I put my arm around her but she shoved it away. I'd already repeated all of my stupid apologies a hundred times. Other than those apologies, there didn't seem to be anything to say. And she said nothing at all."

His hands opened wide. "Silence except for the ticking of the engine as it cooled, and the sound of the surf, like the breathing of a giant." His hands seemed to grow larger. As though hinged together, they opened like jaws and then closed.

"And then out of nowhere she started to laugh. It was a quiet laugh that scared me. There was a catch in her voice. I thought maybe she'd flipped out. The crazy edge to her laughter faded and I started to laugh with her. The tension or pressure, or something, who knows. Even while I was thinking about how to get my stuff out of her place, I laughed with her."

"But then, she stretched suddenly, threw the blanket off and tossed it onto the back seat, and then turned to me saying, 'Get out!' Clear and strong, there was no hesitation in her voice. When I didn't move she sat up straight and screeched, 'Get out!' A look came into her face, not just anger, but rage. 'Out,' she said again, and then she kicked me. When I still didn't move she started to scream, 'Get out! Get out!' What else could I do? So I got out of the car. She slid across the front seat. In one motion she slammed the door closed and started the engine. And just that quick she had the car spinning around, rooster tails of blond sand spouted under the moonlight. I had to jump out of the way or she'd have run me down. And then I watched those red tail-lights get smaller. All I could do was watch."

Donald laughed, perhaps as much to relieve his own anxiety as to display his sense of humor. "When those tail-lights disappeared I started to walk. I cursed her screaming into the surf like some kind of nut. When I reached the highway I tried to hitch a ride but it was late and nobody stopped. Those sandals I was wearing were killing my feet, and wearing just a t-shirt and cut-offs, I got cold. But I kept my thumb out figuring any minute somebody'd stop. Finally I walked to the phone booth beside the hamburger stand. I called a friend in Los Gatos whose brother had a truck. No answer. I stood in the phone booth trying that number until finally I got him. He said okay, he'd come out but it would take a while. It felt like I was going to be stuck out there forever. Waiting in the middle of nowhere messes up your sense of time. Anyway, eventually he pulled up."

"By now it was near three in the morning. Doug, that was the guy's name, tried to talk me into going straight to his place for the rest of the night and then collecting my stuff the next morning. But I was sure something more was about to happen, so we drove. The minute we turned the corner I knew we were too late. I almost told him to turn around."

"On the front lawn was this pile. At first I figured, oh well, and then I started to pile the stuff all into the truck. But everything I touched had been cut or busted. Shirts and clothes, books, all my 45's, everything was cut and sliced and torn. What a mess. And my press. The prints, the lino blocks too, all gouged and scared. Especially the lino blocks; she'd gotten every one. Must have spent a good hour cutting all that stuff up. So as pissed off as I was, I was amazed, too."

"The windows of the house were all dark. I walked around to the side door, tried it, tried all the others because I didn't have my keys. I walked around certain she was inside hiding and watching me. If she'd come out I don't know what I'd have said to her. What was left to say?"

"We got all my stuff, or what was left of it, no reason to hang around." Donald laughed, as if the weight of his thoughts had finally left him; his laughter sounded relieved. "What a night! I dumped everything at Doug's and waited. Every day I expected cops on the doorstep. Weird summer."

My eyes had become heavy. They had developed corners, like cubes, and they moved painfully in my face. They needed darkness, and quiet.

"For that last month of the summer I became Doug's roommate, and he got me a job at a record shop. Later on, everybody else went away to college. Garvin washed out of Stanford first year, but I heard that Diana did all right. Meanwhile, I waited to go to art school. Never did any drawing or painting, never touched a linoleum knife again. I just waited to go to art school. After the record shop, I got a job in a coat factory lugging armfuls of coats in hundred and ten degree weather. That was lots of fun. Then a job as a maintenance man in an apartment building in Burlingame, another joyful period. But eventually I got into San Francisco State. With the little bit of money I'd saved I got my art school."

He looked up then, stared deeply into my eyes. "You don't understand any of this, do you." It was not an accusation and he was not angry. It was a flat statement of fact and he was certain of the words he spoke. The knife lay on the table beside his hand. He brought it directly before him, with two fingers he set it spinning.

"Ever play spin-the-bottle when you were a kid?"

I shook my head. "What is that?"

Smiling he said, "We played it at parties. You get a pop bottle or something and you spin it. Whoever it points to, that's who you get to kiss. And somebody else takes a turn and maybe you're the one that gets kissed." Donald continued to spin the knife. Each time it stopped he spun it again.

Almost addressing the knife Donald said, "You think I don't want to help you. You think I don't care whether you finish those paintings. You think all I want is to write the catalog. You think maybe I really just want to be Burston's pal." The knife stopped, he spun it again. "And guess what? Maybe that's true. On the other hand, maybe I'm more scared of failing to help you work on your canvases than I am of washing-out of this program." He sighed with frustration. "Because if I piss-off Burston enough, he could have me thrown out. You know he can do that, don't you?"

His eyes darkened. He spun the knife faster. "Anyway, just who the hell are you? It's cost me a lot to get this far. I hurt a lot and I gave up a lot to get here, sitting at this table with you tonight. Did you ever think of that? Did that ever occur to you, how much helping you could cost me?" He no longer watched me, but he watched the spinning knife with great care. Then his smile returned.

"You Europeans are supposed to be suave gamblers. So here's my deal. I spin this knife; if it points to you I'll do your work. But if it points to me I stay with Burston's catalog." I said nothing.

Eyes grown brighter he said, "Tell you what. Just to be fair I'll spin it three times. Two out of three. How's that sound?" I still found nothing to say.

"Here we go," and he said and spun the knife. When it stopped turning, it pointed toward Donald. "Two out of three," he whispered and then spun it again. The knife spun slowly, and when it stopped it pointed at him again. Eyes fixed on the knife he leaned forward.

I stood then and stretched; with relief or annoyance, I could not tell. I said, "And perhaps we should change to three opportunities out of five." The throbbing in my head combined with pain in my leg. "And perhaps if you leave your allegiance to a spin of a knife, I am more fortunate without you than Burston is with you."

Did I smile? I remember relief and a certainty that now merely breathing would release the pressure. Donald remained sitting at the table very still.

I walked to the sliding door of my patio, opened it wide allowing cool air to pour in filling the space around us. Donald spoke to my back. "Here's the deal. I'll help out with everything except the painting. You want stretchers? Okay. You want a canvas prepared; I'll do that. Errands? Fine. And in exchange, you tell me everything I need to know to finish Burton's catalog." I turned, his eyes were blankly earnest. Lies are always instructive.

I said, "To the extent we prove useful to each other, and only that long. You should not presume that your help is so precious." I tried to remain firm and unimpressed, but somehow Donald had exhausted me. And in our exchange he had gained something. Cool, damp air from the open doors flowed over my back, over my neck, a haze in the room seemed to dissolve. But finally I was finished with this conversation, and with Donald. I walked to the front door and opened it. "I need sleep."

Donald remained seated. He studied me as if seeing something he had not seen before. I believe there was something he wanted to say to me, but he pursed his lips and then stood. "Thanks for the wine," he said. He reached the door without stumbling. His smile grew. "I'm going home tomorrow for the holiday; won't be back for a few days. Did I tell you that before? Anyway, I'll call you when I get back."

I shrugged because it no longer mattered. As he passed through the door I patted his shoulder. "Have a good holiday," I said. He tottered where he stood, eyes confused, they could not hold me but slipped from my shoulders and dropped to the floor. He nodded without looking up. He smiled as he reached for my shoulder but missed, and then he was gone.

I closed the door on his back, and suddenly I felt quite awake, suddenly relieved. Something had disappeared from the air. I opened the door again, stepped out onto the walkway and filled my chest with cool sweet air. It carried a touch of fog and the scent of burning wood, a taste as palpable as baking bread. Leaning both hands on the railing I breathed heavily, furiously, as if I might inflate, become lighter; perhaps if I tried very hard I might have floated away.

My memory of his face as he departed: lines of yellow and green and blue etched over his cheeks and jaw, and his carved-out eyes. He had looked as if he had lived ten years confined within a windowless basement. And yet he stepped more lightly, as if he had been suddenly relieved of a burden.

The evening had passed into deep night, and I needed to close my eyes. I needed to retrieve them and put them away. A world growing dark, the wind a tiger with crystal talons. A sparkling, diamond darkness.

CHAPTER NINETEEN

EXCEPT FOR THE OCCASIONAL solitary student too impoverished to enjoy a holiday, our apartment complex was deserted, leaving a world of blank, dark windows and firmly locked doors. Most of the students had vanished several days before and our walls and floors lost their resonance, as if our buildings had stopped breathing.

When the weather was good I continued to sit beside our swimming pool making sketches for the large canvas. But the weather was rarely good. Still, I accumulated sketches. Earlier pages of the sketchbook provided additional figures with which to surround the pool.

And she remained at the center of every image; a fact that was more than sufficient to cause me concern. Was it simply the way she held her head erect, shoulders square, the play of muscles along her spine, the deep declivity between two thick bands of flesh tapering down? A dancers' body after all, but a dancer of strength, a dancer of weight, of heavy limbs and rounded hips and arching calves, muscled arms held away from her sides, and elegant hands offered gracefully.

Since that time I have wondered if I had been genuinely helpless. Certainly nothing other than her visits to our pool had made the rising and setting of the sun of much importance to me. I had discovered that drawing her figure was as much a pleasure of the hand as of the eye. Her presence had come to me unearned, and was therefore that much more precious. I had stumbled upon her as a tremor of light, this dancer of the mind's-eye, and regretted every thought of inevitably losing her.

I awoke each morning certain there was serious work, and with less than sufficient time to complete it. Already I had sufficient sketches to lay-out four large canvases, but frequently I discovered or imagined additional sketches.Before he left for his holiday, Donald had already completed crating those few small paintings I had kept at the apartment. They were now distractions, and it was a relief when finally they had been shipped back east to Martin for storage.

So, on that day particularly grey and chilly for our part of the world, I was already thinking of Martin. Despite his foolish willingness to represent my work, Martin remained a good dealer. And at that moment, in the center of that holiday season of light and its promise of a new and unsoiled year, I had begun to feel mildly optimistic, and perhaps even a bit sentimental. So when the telephone rang, its sound almost pleased me. That was perhaps a mistake.

Martin and I exchanged hearty greetings and enthusiastic best wishes for the new year. I was surprised to discover I was relieved to hear his voice. It was unfortunate that our conversation so quickly turned to business. When I explained the reason I had sent those paintings to him he became silent. After a long pause he asked why I refused to cooperate with that retrospective. "Because such a show would cause me to retrospect." I spoke into the telephone loudly, as if I might not be heard in New York any other way.

I told him which among those canvases I was returning he must not offer for sale. For Martin, any suggestion that a canvas might be withheld from sale was a decision expressed in some unimaginable language. Foolishly I then related my most recent conversations about the retrospective. We sat, each on his own edge of a continent, whispering to the other without faith in comprehension, and responding to calls half-deciphered.

He paused and then laughed. "For grey-beards like us, shyness is obscene. In one breath you describe to me this great opportunity for an exhibition, and then you dismiss it as not merely annoying but contemptible. My friend, once again and as usual, you have left me speechless. I am overwhelmed with the certitude that my own stupidity is immeasurable. Here I have completely deluded myself into thinking that not only would such an exhibition benefit us both financially, but it would assure that your critical reputation finally would be secured. For those reasons alone, such an exhibition would gratify me enormously. But I confess all of this simply to demonstrate how thoroughly ignorant I have become concerning matters of art."

"You flatter yourself," I said. Martin knows how to irritate.

"On the contrary, my friend. It is you who flatters me with your wisdom and unerring good sense."

"Then do not allow this flattery to go to your head. I need your help. I need your cooperation and your own good sense as well."

"Quite clearly you need these," he said laughing, "since they are qualities you most thoroughly lack. But allow me to flaunt my abysmal ignorance and ask; are you unshakably intent upon impoverishing us both? Allow me the bad taste to remind you that time and money are not so completely interchangeable. The checks I have sent you were invariably cashed, while you rarely grace my establishment with additional samples of your genius."

"Be patient, since I will be dead soon enough."

"Soon enough for whom?"

"All of my paintings will then belong to you, to do with as you wish." Martin's silences are remarkable because they are so loud. "But I have good news. I have begun work on several large paintings. Imagine how quickly your pockets will fill when finally you take possession of them. What more could any agent wish for? Still, you must understand that I can only complete these paintings if this retrospective can be postponed until well after my demise."

Again Martin laughed. The holiday season had apparently put him in a jolly mood. "You have become a barbarian, and the signs of that could not be more obvious. You have lived in this country so long, my friend, that you are not embarrassed by your own ingratitude."

"Not so barbaric as to attempt to bury a living man. Not so barbaric as to suck the living man dry."

"This is melodrama, my friend, while we need to discuss these issues seriously. Our salon possesses a number of your canvases for which you have been paid but which have not yet been sold." Martin's voice turned dark and heavy. "But I am certain that if I made just a few phone calls I could quickly mount my own modest retrospective of your work. And perhaps as a result, even earn a bit of money. A small amount, no doubt, but enough to retire a bit more of your debt."

"This threat is couched in such enticing terms I find it difficult to resist."

"Spare me your sarcasm." All playfulness drained from Martin's voice. "This University fellow is kind enough to take a serious interest in your work.

And what do you do? How do you respond? You slap the foolish man in the face. I have become accustomed to your high-handedness, but this poor fellow probably labored under the delusion that he was helping you. God help him if he expected gratitude." Martin has a musical laugh that rings in the ear.

I said, "Your own platitudes hardly stand closer scrutiny. Besides, there is more than mere principle involved. I have work already begun which this exhibition will jeopardize."

"If I were beside you right now I would wash out your mouth with some dreadful California wine. Do not forget I have seen your fingers, my friend, I have seen your hands. And as I remember, they are no cleaner than any others. And this exercise in posturing means little to your reviewers. I am certain by now you have heard that the exhibition in Munich has been well-received." Martin invariably exaggerates the popularity of my work to his clients. In our conversations Martin sometimes forgets I know more about it than they.

"Perhaps you are right," I said, "but in this case being right does not matter. What concerns me is the future of the work I have begun. I had assumed that you would appreciate this." I lied, of course. Martin could have no such concern, but I hoped at least to arouse his curiosity. When he asked, I described the canvases, exaggerated their sizes, their number, and the amount of effort that would be demanded for their completion. But Martin seemed to anticipate such exaggeration. He often did the same himself, and I believe if I had not exaggerated, he would have worried that I did not display enthusiasm sufficient to complete them.

Martin said, "You have always been a charmless fool, otherwise you would not be my client. I am gratified to act as your agent because I know the reward that awaits me in heaven. The Good Lord will reward me for having protected someone as helpless and head-strong as you. As your agent and benefactor, I am certain of a heavenly reward, because assuredly there is nothing for it here on earth. And now, just when we have this opportunity for a reward comparable to that which awaits us, you decide to play the clown."

My anger began to rise. "Nothing on this earth could possibly compare to the reward that awaits you."

"I certainly hope you are right. But my friend, a bit of advice; beware of the wolves. Keep guard against those wolves of the forest."

As I replaced the receiver I paused to consider how much work would need to be done.

Just past mid-day the sun was bright in a hazy sky, cool and without a breeze. I looked down from my walkway at our sundeck, saw my chair and table. Then turning I looked back into the apartment to see my sketchbook and pencils. At that moment I could almost imagine this world without my presence. And that thought did not distress me.

CHAPTER TWENTY

VISION IS NOT A PRODUCT. Reshaped, over-wrought, its light eventually
begins to fade. And then its life begins to fade. Colors mute and become
motionless, until it is time to put that vision aside as one puts aside a vase filled
with faded flowers; the end of a future.

Classes eventually resumed, and with them the crowd returned to our
swimming pool as the sun grew warmer. But she had not returned. Though I
knew I had nothing to fear, a wave of exhaustion, kept me staring through my
opened door out to our patio.

One day standing before my graduate seminar, I lectured on the necessity
that a true work of art reflect nothing of its outside circumstance. Only in this
way could a work be purified of its temporality, its dependency on its occasion.
And further, I insisted that art's beauty was its timelessness. In response to my
pontification, one of my more talented students argued a rousing insistence
upon committed art. Gradually over the course of the discussion that followed,
I suddenly recognized my own fears for the paintings I carried in my mind.
And I did not enjoy that fear, I did not find it instructive.

Seated at our patio, I worked largely on those sketches for the pool scene,
that painting least dependent on her presence. And with each revision, the
painting seemed to grow larger. Its forest of bodies and faces thickened,
clustered around the gradually disappearing swimming pool. Some figures

I discovered in the sketchbook seemed to demand their inclusion, even as I fought to reduce the number of figures. The frame of the painting had become a congested passageway, with more of its figures struggling to pass through. Paintings, like children, often enjoy periods of being hateful.

Gradually I came to imagine a canvas of impossible size enclosing a kaleidoscope of figures arranged with uninteresting symmetries. And then Marla paid me a visit.

Several times she and I had discussed the swimming pool painting. But the day she arrived, its completed sketch lay on my table with the sketchbooks spread all around it. While she scrutinized the sketch, brow puckered and her dark eyes sharp as pins, I complained that the crowd within it had become a mob. She sighed then and shrugged.

"You should think about doing entirely separate canvases."

I pretended not to understand.

"And why not? Same point of view but different figures in different positions. Keep the lighting the same, unless you want to change that, too." Her keen eyes found mine; what did I think of her suggestion?

"Impossible. Besides, it is not the image that I am eager to create." Marla shrugged without looking at me, wandered away from the table. "I want this group unified," I said, "with the figures all within the same frame. Even at the risk of this impossible clutter."

She sat down on the couch, crossed her legs, looked up at me and smiled.

I looked back at the sketch again because I could no longer look at Marla. Besides, it demanded less than a moment to recognize the advantages of her suggestion, and conjure its possibilities. Finally I said, "Perhaps it could be done. A triptych. Three panels, three separate groups of figures, each panel reflecting and referring to the others. Certain figures repeated and re-positioned in each panel, with others added or removed. I suppose it could be done that way."

Marla did not laugh. "Don't listen to me! I'm only suggesting more work for myself. And more complicated work. In fact, now that I think about it, you're right. There really should be only one canvas. Work on as few as possible."

Marla offered a solution which, had I not been so old and stupid, I would have recognized immediately. And then I had hurt her feelings. Our collaboration had not begun well.

But in this way our collaboration did begin. I had visited Marla's studio several times to look over her work and see what I might expect once we began in earnest.

The preliminary sketches progressed, and Marla proved herself frequently resourceful as well as reliable. As for Donald's less-frequent visits, he remained amiable yet sufficiently aloof to stay out from under foot. And because I had not heard from Burston for weeks, I began to suspect he was actively avoiding me. So, aside from a plague of dreams, I confess now that I was nearly content.

The dreams came, night after night, and when they did, they assured me that the painting was going well. But they were not pleasant dreams, and I did not enjoy them. They frightened me and left me confused and uncomfortable in the morning. My dreams were an illness like a fever of the soul, particularly those which never quite began or ended, and in which whole sections repeated maddeningly. Or there were gaps, large blank spaces, grand gray voids, as though they remained suspended in a state of non-being. Dreams from which I would revive, but not quite awake.

And the worst of them —

. . . my front door opens suddenly, floods with light, a black shadow fills the doorway, bright light rich as amber, as honey, filters around the figure, that light becomes nearly white, the black figure whispers without speech, I stand, move slowly toward the door. The doorway opens onto a long gallery, I follow it, move along it without moving. The walls of the gallery pass me even as the door ahead becomes larger. Beyond it, the light is searing white softening into blue, I pass through that door to find blue light everywhere. I discover myself standing at the top of a hill, the blue above me with the white light of an enormous sun, it fills half the sky and its light burns my face, burns directly into my eyes. I look away below me to a valley, my eyes move above the valley like birds in search of food. My eyes swoop and soar offering the sight of the entire valley. My eyes see me, eyeless on the top of the hill, my eyes turn and soar and then swoop again, lower. Suddenly my eyes see her. My eyes return to me and I know where she is, in the distance and yet so close. The hill I stand upon is high, its sides form a long broad meadow sheathed with lurid green grass. The unearthly green grass is high and very thick. I run down that long broad meadow toward her. She is seated with her back naked and brilliant in that light, her beautiful, square-shouldered back, dark chestnut hair long down her back lifted and billowing playfully with the soft breeze. And forever she is about to turn to face me, to see me run through the lush grass toward her. The thick grass grows higher as I approach her seated forever with her back toward me. Everything around her grows larger, the grass grows higher. Long, wide blades of bright grass begin to knot over my feet. I stumble as the grass grows still higher. It begins to cling to my ankles, my legs, even while she is infinitely about to turn to see me. The grass begins to entangle my knees, then it wraps about my thighs. My legs are held back, suddenly I am at the bottom of the ocean and seaweed has entangled my legs. The mermaid's curled dark hair rocks weightlessly like seaweed across her broad pale shoulders, and more seaweed tightens about my legs. I can no longer breathe. The seaweed enwraps my waist as enormous dark fish begin to circle above me blocking the light, their broad shadows black across my face. I look down, my eyes dive down upon me, see that my thighs, my legs are entrapped, my waist encircled. I realize that I hold my last breath. I can no longer move and there is no way to breathe. Yet she sits so close I can call to her, and she must hear me. Panic constricts my throat, I open my mouth. She does not turn. She is infinitely about to turn, her broad shoulders angled over and slightly down toward me. Her face in another moment will turn toward mine. A soundless torrent of sparkling white bubbles rises before my eyes. I empty my lungs in a final scream, its sound rings in my ears, the sound of the last breath. I empty my lungs and force out every bit of air screaming, waiting for her to turn. And now my lungs are empty, and still she has not turned. In just another moment she will turn, just another moment as seaweed laces over my shoulders, around my neck. My lungs are empty, I stare at her as she sits about to turn to see me. I know that in just another moment I will begin to breathe in the bitter salt water while seaweed wraps tighter around my throat. But in just another moment she will turn to see me. I feel the acid burn of salt water rushing into my throat, into my chest, my chest expanding as it fills with sea water, and then the light dimming, the darkness, thick mud of darkness, falling, and the water, down . . .

And thus I awoke shaking and sweating, and with the sound of my own scream still ringing in my ears. Someone was rapping firmly on my door. "Yes," I responded as loudly as I could.

"Everything all right in there?" A deep voice, a male voice, someone from the apartment next door.

I cleared my throat and said that yes, everything was all right. The voice wished me good night then, and I listened to footsteps moving away. Yes, everything was all right. Everything imaginable was quite all right. It was as all right as it would ever be.

CHAPTER TWENTY–ONE

DONALD WORKED VERY HARD stretching my canvases, so I tormented him with instructions, advice, and warnings. Exhausting himself on my behalf, Donald embarrassed me. He worked far harder than I ever would have, even for someone else, even for money. These Americans are hard workers.

I believe now that he worked hard in part because he was earnestly curious about the new paintings. He had seen my sketches and understood my plans, but still he was curious to see what I might accomplish. And so was I. So his energy, his persistence, and his curiosity all offended me.

I was certain that Donald also made reports. Although I had no evidence, I was confident that he kept Burston informed of my progress, or its lack. Was it more important for him to know that I had slept well, or that I had begun to read Nietzsche again?

Donald offered to photograph a record of the progress of the paintings. Small color images of each canvas as it developed, as if this might have some value for me. Despite his frustration with me, Donald was admirably dependable, and I could find no fault. But there were times when his silent insensibility drove me nearly to send him away. Yet because of his help, I was able to disturb Burston without having to meet with him. Curiosity over my schemes gave them both a great deal of work to do. But believe me, I admire these hard-working Americans.

Donald never spoke while he worked, he simply worked. He moved methodically around the stretchers, applied each staple with a crisp snap-snap, always making certain he had stapled properly. When finally he leaned the last prepared canvas against the wall, I brought out one of my sketchbooks.

"Do you remember this one?" I offered him one of my drawings of half that woman's face, her face. He squinted as if the drawing's lines might move, or as if he was searching his memory.

"I guess so," he said. "Yeah, I think I've seen her."

"Have you seen her recently?"

Donald glanced up to search my eyes. Once again in his presence I felt like a fool, a jester created within a younger mind. When he did not respond I asked, "And how is your own painting coming along?" Because I could no longer tolerate my thoughts of his thoughts.

He looked away and laughed. I nodded my old-man nod; that movement when the head dips gently as a balloon, the sympathetic defense, the temporizing maneuver, the understanding-old-man nod.

I asked, "When you painted, did you prefer landscapes or still-life, or nudes?"

Donald thought for a moment, or at least his brow knit as if pretending to. "People," he announced. He nodded as if finally in agreement with himself.

"Did you put these people in complicated backgrounds, or did you like groups, or did you prefer single figures?" I had to laugh at myself, my own retreat to formal generalities discomforted even me.

"Well, I guess simple figures with simple backgrounds." Donald scratched his head, as if he had confused himself, or one of us had confused him. "But I've never rationalized my painting that way."

"You should find a model that inspires." He looked at me with suspicion but said nothing.

"After all, the University pays for a model. So your difficulty cannot be the expense."

He shrugged. "Even if I found the right model, I've got classes to teach and papers to mark, and then my own papers to write. So where would the time come from?"

"Of course. There is no time to paint. So it is good that you have given it up. Everything is cheap, except for time and bad health. But tell me; have you not seen something recently, or met someone, you suddenly wanted badly to paint? Have you seen anything or anyone which demanded to be painted?

Has no one impaled your eyes, or enchanted you, so that you found yourself thinking, even for only just a moment, I must paint this or die?"

Donald's look of confusion embarrassed us both. His eyes clouded as he recognized his own embarrassment.

"And Barbara?" I asked.

His confusion cleared. Thought he remained silent, once again he was seeing me.

I asked, "Have you ever painted her?"

When he did not respond, I asked, "Have you ever even wanted to paint her?"

When Donald still said nothing, I began to laugh. At first he seemed almost curious. But then he caught himself and made his face look bored, as if a dense cloud of ennui had gathered suddenly about his head. "Maybe she just isn't that interesting to look at."

His response only made me laugh harder. I said, "I expect she would be quite unhappy to hear you say that. But then again, there is so much else in life that needs to be accomplished, and one has only so much time. And after all, if she has no desire to be painted by you, what is the point of argument?" Laughter clung to my throat like a smoker's cough.

Donald's boredom turned somewhat green. "She's very self-conscious about her looks. Even in front of a camera. And she'd get bored sitting for something like that."

"So you think?"

"You don't know her like I do."

"Perhaps you do not know her so well, either."

He shrugged and then shook his head. "That wouldn't surprise me."

"How can the thought of painting her not appeal to you?" I could not resist my own curiosity. I dug into his thoughts with a rusty nail and ignored his discomfort. "Can you not want even one single drawing of her?"

His determination to misunderstand my questions only drove me further. "You love this woman and yet you pretend no desire to paint her. Not even one single nude drawing? I know this is not your intention, but you leave me feeling thoroughly stupid."

Donald laughed. "You don't know her like I do." He smiled as if he had sat down on something hard and sharp. "Some things I've just stopped worrying about. And besides, I stopped worrying about painting long before I met Barb. So when I met her I already knew I didn't care about that other stuff anymore.

And she never showed any interest in any of it, so everything was fine." He paused watching me without inviting me to respond. "As presumptuous as it may sound," he added, "there are some things I understand which you never will."

There seemed nothing more to say. Donald cherished his opacity, a veil separating different parts of himself from himself, and I had no way to dispel it.

He studied me in a way that suggested he was able to overhear my thoughts. The movements of his eyes seemed to outline my judgment. He shook his head as he leaned back. "Know anybody who's a Pentecostal?" When I admitted I did not, he asked, "And how about any Baptists? Or maybe Jehovah's Witnesses?" When I still said nothing he continued, "It makes a difference how you're brought up. I can't tell you about that stuff like other people can, but it makes a difference. So let me tell you one thing about Barbara. The house where she grew up was eighty miles from the nearest movie theater. Can you understand that? Drive almost two hours just to see a ninety-minute movie, and then another two hours to get home? You're smiling, which means you have no idea what I'm talking about. What I'm trying to say is, the place where Barbara came from is a big country but a small world." He paused watching me. "See, I knew you'd laugh." But I had not laughed.

There was nothing left for me except embarrassment. If Donald felt the need to defend Barbara to me, he had done it so well I could no longer challenge him. He stroked his moustache smirking. He would tolerate my ignorance if it allowed him to offer enlightenment. He continued, "The idea that someone who said he loved her would also want to draw her naked would make no sense to her at all. It matters how you're brought up. And the way she was brought up never included even the possibility of that kind of love; drawing a picture of her naked body could be an expression of love." He sat back then. "But you're right about one thing; I wonder if we've missed something more important than she realizes. Just don't think she's some intellectually-deprived student. She's a smart and honest person, without much pretension or vanity, but with a lot of interest in other people. And I'll confess there isn't much of that I'd want to change."

I shook my head. "You describe her coming from a world more narrow than I can imagine. This is my flaw, without question, and I offer no excuse for it. But I cannot understand what any of that has to do with your practice of drawing."

He shrugged. "If I start drawing, first thing she'll think is that she's going to be poor again and back in those mountains. And nothing's going to drag her back there. To hear her, you'd think there was this big vacuum-cleaner in the sky trying to force her back into that world. As if she had to hold onto the furniture or she'd wake up one morning in her old bedroom, and with her mother and father snoring next door. I start drawing and she'll get the idea I'm ready to waste real time. She can't trust it. As if the practice of drawing could take over my brain or something."

"Barbara sounds like a person not entirely assured of this existence."

Donald turned his hands palm up. "I don't kid myself. It's important to know where your talent lies and then to follow it. You want me to fool myself into believing otherwise just because you need help." His smile beamed with tolerance.

But my own patience had finally run out. "So, can it be the case that you have nothing more to say with your drawing? You want me to believe that there is nothing you want your fellow humans to know so that something important is not left unsaid; something which would enlarge these fellow humans, and perhaps even reduce the burden of their lives. You have nothing to add. All that is important or useful has already been said, or will be said, by others, and better than you could. Do I understand you correctly?"

His smile said nothing. I said, "Tell me just this then; what is it that would make you take up drawing again? Because I cannot believe you have put it aside completely."

"Why?" he asked in a whisper as quiet as a lover's.

"Because an old man dares you."

Donald watched my eyes. I said, "All right, I admit it. I confess to all you suspect. Start painting again simply because an old man needs your help."

His smile grew slowly, his eyes softened and his brow smoothed. "No," he said.

I said, "I am certain you will prove yourself useful in capacities neither of us imagines. And one of those will be a bit of drawing."

"There you're wrong. That stuff is out." He leaned back then, chin set firmly.

Which of us was most tired. His eyes peered huge and dark in his face as if prepared without fear for my next assault.

"I think you are merely afraid," I said. He smiled, a reflex, a special smile meant to hold me at arm's length and end our discussion.

But I continued. "I want to meet the person who can keep you from doing something you sincerely want to do. And I want Barbara to explain to me why she does not want you to paint. But most of all I want to see what she looks like. Because I cannot understand how visions of the woman you love do not burn your eyes, do not destroy your sleep. Honestly, you have made me curious."

He stood suddenly, as if determined to be released. His impatience became visible, and I could only watch him. I believe he understood all of this because then he left.

For a time I watched the door through which Donald had passed, but then I stood and began to arrange those blank canvases he had stretched to lean against the walls. And I found that they all but filled the room. Two were so large, the only way to get them out of the apartment would be through the sliding glass doors to the balcony, and then lowered to the ground. Or broken into smaller pieces. Donald had done his work well and I was satisfied with it. But our talk left me troubled. He had used Barbara as a shield. But in doing so my curiosity had been aroused, and now I wanted to know more about them both. I sat admiring the expanse of white, blank and empty canvas before me.

As if rolling and rippling in a mild breeze, lines began to appear on those canvases. Spaces shifted, opened across areas that hinted at their volumes, their shapes fore-shortened, swaths of different shades of grey appeared running from edge to edge. With more arrogance than courage I stood and took up a stick of charcoal pencil, began to mark-out divisions of the canvas establishing their proportions. As I reached my hand to the top of the swimming pool canvas, a bolt of pain shot through my shoulder and into my neck. Suddenly my hand became numb and the stick of charcoal dropped from my fingers. By this I was again reminded that I could work only enough to suggest what I saw. So I would need to trust that Marla would see precisely what I could render only vaguely.

My mouth now filled with defeat. I returned to my chair and from that vantage point the charcoal marks I had attempted appeared hardly more than a smudge on the canvas. Resigned to my impotence, I began again to wonder about that woman, the woman I must lure into my lair in order to complete these paintings. It seemed that Donald would not help me, but I still hoped that Marla would do so. If she was successful, it would then be up to me to convince her to remain, and to cooperate.

I realized that I must resign myself to a dependency so profound there was no room for the slightest doubt, the least hesitancy, concerning the persons around me. Though this thought left me furious, it was obvious that my body could no longer be trusted to accomplish even the smallest challenge. And after all, what is the value of a body if it does not obey, if it can not accomplish that which most needs to be done?

CHAPTER TWENTY–TWO

VERY SLOWLY, with glacial slowness, with geometric slowness, I emptied
the second bottle of wine. I had finished the first in some distantly geological
epoch which I could no longer recall. But now I was successfully and even
remarkably, but certainly thoroughly, drunk. Because of course I was not
desperate.

Despite being quite drunk I was still capable of categorical statements. And
since indecision leads to desperation, I could not therefore be desperate. I looked
constantly for that woman, my model, and had yet to see her anywhere about our
apartment complex. Wine is the very best medicine against desperation, since it
is a most certain solvent against indecision. And surely I was not desperate.

Sketchbooks lay scattered about the room, their pages open with their images
merging and melding, a pleasant chaos of shapely fragments. I could see them all
commingling frantically from where I sat with my glass of wine.

I was not desperate in part because I had discovered sketches of her from
different sittings. Their number surprised me, but also left me rather embarrassed.
Although the quantity of these sketches suggested something unseemly, that
quantity saved me from a panicked desperation at her absence. The quantity of
sketches along with two bottles of wine.

So, with sketches and wine and memory I would create on canvas. Or that
is, Marla would create for me on canvas. So why did I endure such urgency

that the woman sit for me? Simply so that she would see me work and admire my greatness?

One day I asked Marla to drive me around the campus. After only a few minutes of making turns and retracing our paths she turned and asked, "Who are we looking for?"

"What I am looking for is a pleasant campus scene. Some landscape to provide an attractive background."

"Some scene you could hang in the Regents' lunch room?" The pitch of Marla's laughter began high, then descended, each interval slightly longer, a pleasantly soothing sound. My confusion had been entirely my own fault. I had insisted that the woman beside our swimming pool remain impossibly anonymous, completely self-contained and apart from me and my aspirations. But that anonymity, which had been so attractive, finally became a barely-tolerable burden.

As we drove, Marla told me that she had heard that over the holidays, Donald's affair with Barbara had come to some trouble. My first thought was to wonder if he would now be free to help my projects, or would he be even less free to help even in those small ways he already had? Those questions remained unanswered but after a bottle or two of wine they became easily ignored.

Through the bottom of my empty glass I surveyed those sketches, a wealth of sketches, or perhaps a swamp. The large sketches were nearly complete. When Donald finished stretching canvases, Marla had begun making regular appearances and asking questions, as if she too was finally prepared to begin.

Those bottles I drained had been brought to me by Vincent. An hour after Marla had dropped me at my apartment following our unsatisfying search, Vincent had appeared at my door, a brown paper bag of wine bottles clutched tightly under his arm. As I ushered him thought my maze of disorder, he surveyed the floor. "I heard you plan to begin painting again," he said. "Word's gotten around, and Burston wants to know what you're going to do with all that linseed oil." Vincent laughed with embarrassment as he set the bag on the table.

The existence of those canvases had provided sufficient reason for him to come snoop around and pry into my plans. The day had become very warm, almost hot although it was still early in the spring, a preview of another dusty summer.

So, as Vincent dropped into his chair he wiped sweat from his face. "Talked to a guy from public relations a couple of days ago. He said there's been a meeting with John and some people from the administration. I thought I'd stop by and warn you." Elbows propped on the table and face in his hands Vincent's smile faded, his voice dropped to earnest seriousness. "They really want this show."

"And you came all this way to tell me that?" I could not restrain my laughter. "I thank you for your thoughtful warning, but did you think I had been asleep for these past months?" I should not have laughed, my laughter offended Vincent.

"The University's determined to have that show." Polite Vincent, determined to remain patient with a witless old man. "And they're not just thinking about it. They really don't care about any new work because they figure it'll all just be absorbed into this show." He paused and looked hard into my eyes. "Nobody will even wonder why you've suddenly decided to start new canvases. So I'm here to let you know there's nothing you can do to stop it." He shook his head then and looked away. "At least that's what the guy from public relations told me."

For a moment his information left me speechless. I know precisely what a bureaucratic administration can accomplish. But I still found Vincent's message amusing. "So they believe I will simply sit by in my rocking chair and wait for them to come and take away any of my work they wish. I am an old man, this is certainly true, but can they honestly believe that I am helpless? What can they possibly be thinking?"

Vincent shrugged and then, as he opened the first bottle, asked where I kept glasses. "You aren't alone," he said, "despite appearances or your own conviction. But John wants this exhibition, and he's convinced the administration to go along. Nobody I've talked to sees any way out. This must sound a little stupid to you, but that's what I'm here to tell you." Then he lifted his filled glass in my direction. "And by the way, congratulations on your investment in these supplies. The art-supply industry of America thanks you, and it remains honored to serve you."

"An investment in canvas is a gesture of optimism in the future."

Vincent smiled as we each sipped the wine he had provided. An unremarkable burgundy, but allowed to breath it might have been a bit smoother. We stared past each other for a time. I wished that he was more determined to be useful as an ally, while he probably wished I was less contentious and more malleable. I watched his eyes slide past me to those vacant canvases, watched as they moved over their large, still-unsullied rectangles of white. "Nobody would blame you if you decided to give-up on these. Or that you decided to keep them out of the show."

"You have spent too much time in the sun. You need rest. You are suggesting I might stop painting simply because some officious bureaucrat intends to steal it. And you say you would not be surprised if I stopped. You do not know me very well. I do not doubt that your intentions are honorable, but do us both a favor and avoid the absurd. It can only corrupt what may already be very fragile."

Vincent smiled. In the warm light of his smile I realized I understood him even less well than he understood me. Finally he said, "I admire you. Don't look embarrassed. I admire integrity and diligence and patience. Your example is an inspiration to all of us." Again I could hardly restrain my laughter. A young man full of praises, all of them spoken as if certain they would be believed. I laughed without embarrassment or restraint.

Annoyed by my laughter Vincent continued, "I agree with you about this show. And believe me, if there was some way to help you, I would." He shrugged his shoulders and looked away. "Burston isn't a bad guy. I've worked with him for seven years. You couldn't know what I know about him. I'll admit I don't understand what he expects to come from all of this. He's never seemed a real ambitious man. Maybe his ambition isn't so much for himself as for the department, odd as that must sound to you. Or maybe he's just realized he's getting old, and he's got things to protect. I don't know what to say except that at heart I know he's a good man. But you shouldn't doubt he's convinced himself this show will benefit everybody."

My glass was once again empty, "Such a generous and dedicated artist. Misguided for some reason but a good man none-the-less." I reached across the table and refilled my glass. "And you believe that with these fine phrases my revulsion will evaporate. I say, shit on him. In fact, shit on all of them. And shit on you, too, for supposing me such a fool. To be led around by this old, fat nose, and all of it for my own good, no doubt."

Vincent retreated behind his face, behind his eyes. Eyebrows rising in defensive surprise, his voice cracked in panic. "Who would force you to show your own paintings? All I'm asking is that you shouldn't prejudge John's motives." Our first bottle of wine had emptied quickly.

"Shit on his motives," I said because finally I had begun to enjoy my indignation. "My intentions, my aspirations, are all merely impediments to him and obstacles to his grand and grandiose schemes. I have already spoken to him, explained myself to him as patiently as a priest. What was his inevitable reaction? Burston put his arm across my shoulders and smiled the smile of superior understanding. Such presumption! I have survived worse than him, though happily none with such sterling intentions." But finally I had grown tired of this sword-play. "Drink up and we will toast to your own good fortune. And I thank you for such good cheap wine."

We drank after that in silence. The buzzing in my head sounded like a bottle full of bees. Vincent stared at a spot above my head until a smile rippled weakly over his lips. He said, "Someone like me would do pretty much anything for the sort of opportunity you're tossing aside. I suppose you already understand this."

Finally it was my opportunity to smile enigmatically. "This is because you do not recognize what it is I am refusing. To you a retrospective is a marvelous thing. Understand that at your age I had nothing worthy of such attention. But this exhibition, the paintings they hope to display, all of it is work I am relieved to have passed beyond. Yet it is precisely this work that they are determined to offer. Paintings I forgot long go and have not thought about in many years are suddenly thrust into my face, as if I was a dog that has misbehaved." I could only tremble with frustration. "Believe me when I tell you that I know precisely what is at stake. So just consider the possibility that you do not."

Vincent's narrow, dark-eyed face creased and wrinkled in a kind of bemused defense. "Why worry about any of that? The exhibit'll add to your fame and reputation as well as your fortune. What more could you want?"

He seemed determined to misunderstand me, and suddenly I found myself just as determined to explain myself until even he could understand. "I have not spent my years painting simply in order to gain a reputation. I paint in order to see. I paint because that is what I need to do in order to see. Reputation means less to me than it does to John, because I paint in order to see more clearly. I cannot see until I have painted. On the other hand, I must assume that John already sees in a way that is satisfactory to him. He sees enough, and well enough, and so endures no desire to challenge his sight. But I cannot see until I have painted. John is free to choose my canvas or to pass it by for something else, but I have no such privilege. These paintings are what they are and look the way they look because that is all there is. All I can paint is that which becomes visible to me, and without tricks. I am not a confused tourist in the land of great art, and I am certainly not a bargain-shopper in the grand supermarket of beauty. My painting looks the way it must simply because it must, and because I cannot create it in any other way. Now, drink up!"

Something distorted Vincent's face. He stared directly into my eyes until a grin appeared and then grew, and then his laughter burst above our heads like sunlight. He shook his head, a signal of disbelief and amused incomprehension.

He said, "I must have told you once about how my Dad wanted me to be a musician. He wanted me to play the violin but I turned him down and ran away to art school. He was an amateur but actually pretty good. But good or not never mattered to him; what mattered was that he played and had a good time. It's been almost fifteen years since he died, but there's something I want to tell you about, just so you'll know. I was still in art school when I got the telegram. I packed my bags and I was home the next day. There'd been no warning, no long illness or any reason to suspect, but suddenly he was dead. Me and my brothers stayed with Mom for a couple of weeks afterward to help her get things straightened out; sort through his clothes and decide what to keep and who would keep it. This all happened early in February, and after those two weeks we each took off. With Uncle Salvatore and Aunt Aggie still living down the hall we knew that Mom wouldn't be completely alone. I went back to art school and had a terrible time. Everything I touched turned to shit no matter what I did. But eventually that semester ended and then I was back home again for the summer. By that time Mom had gone through most of Dad's things, or at least she thought she had. So we were both surprised poking around in one of the deep hall-closets when I found a big box hidden away back on a high shelf."

Vincent shook his head, a look of amused bewilderment around his eyes, lifted his glass and drained it. He refilled his glass, waved the bottle toward me and I nodded. "Mom claimed she never saw that box before and had no idea what was inside it, so I brought it down. And as soon as I opened it, she started to cry. Piles of sheet music all stacked nice and neat; page after page of manuscript paper covered with neatly drawn musical notation. Pile after pile. I kept lifting the stuff out, but it seemed to go on forever. My Dad's compositions, you see? Each one copied out carefully in long-hand. The box was absolutely full. Mom stood to one side looking from me to the box and back to me, crying. Four symphonies, eight 'cello concertos with long poems attached, along with a pile of musical sketches. And a lot of duets and trios, short pieces for piano or violin or 'cello."

I said, "Even the dead are capable of surprises. Even our dead loved ones."

His smile seemed to fix on the wall above my head. "I brought a couple of the short pieces to the piano. I don't know what we expected to hear. His voice, maybe, or some sound of his voice singing, like some tape recording? Mom sat down beside me on the piano bench watching as if I was a child holding a crystal glass. And we both wanted the music to be beautiful, marvelous, like nothing we'd ever heard before."

My surprise was genuine. "And neither of you had any idea this music existed?"

Vincent shook his head. "After all those years, and there they were. If he'd kept a mistress all those years I couldn't have been more surprised. I played through one piece, and then another. Mom sat listening with tears rolling down her cheeks. Each time I finished she asked me to play another. For my Mom that music must have swirled around her like the scent of flowers and she was content as she listened. I guess for her it was like my Dad had reached back into time to stroke her head, to caress her face, and she was responding. I stumbled through that music while my mother listened as though I wasn't even there."

Lost for a moment in memory he paused and then smiled. "So I did finally get to play his music, and so Dad got a little of what he'd wanted. After I finished each piece, Mom would ask me wasn't that beautiful, wasn't that perfectly beautiful, and tell me that he had been a man with such a soul. And I said yes, it was all wonderful, just wonderful. We must have been at it a couple of hours, but then she asked me what we should do with all that music, and wasn't there some way to get it all published and maybe even performed. That's when I realized I had to talk to Uncle Salvatore."

"Had he known about these compositions?"

Vincent nodded. "Even helped him with the stuff. He said, 'Your father asked me to go over them, play through some of the hard parts, check the fingerings, stuff like that. I even helped him write out some orchestrations. But he never really needed any help from me. Your father was a genius. But what the hell can you know; you're just a kid, what the hell can you know. That's some beautiful music your father wrote. He could really write beautiful melodies. I wondered when somebody was going to find that stuff. I was just waiting for somebody to find them.' And then he asked me, 'So what are you going to do with them now? What will you do with them now?' When I told him Mom wanted to know how to get them published, Uncle Salvatore just shook his head. He said, 'At least she has some sense and some respect. At least she doesn't want to throw them the hell out.' We stood in his doorway looking at each other a long time. He was a short man and I remembered him from when I was young, and now standing in front of him I realized how old he'd gotten and how I had to look down as he looked up at me. Or maybe it had already been that way for a long time. He said, 'He wanted you kids to grow up and play it; you know, not to make himself famous, but so that maybe you all would love the stuff as much as he did. And there he is dead, and here you are and you don't love the stuff, not at all. Just trying to figure out how to get rid of it. There's no fucking justice in this life. You're just a kid, what the hell can you know? He broke his heart writing that stuff and he broke it again over you and your brothers. Now here you are just getting all sentimental about your old man. Like somehow you'll make it all up to him now if you just cry a little bit. Fucking kids, get all goddamn sentimental just when you're too fucking old or fucking dead. I just thank God I never had any.' Then he shoved me back out into the hallway and slammed his door."

Vincent laughed. "Such a weird old guy, but I really liked him. Last time I was home he was sitting between Aunt Aggie and my Mom in the living-room watching Ed Sullivan, grousing about what weirdo creeps the Beatles are, and if he had kids with hair like that he'd kill them. And saying the same thing he had said about Presley; 'All you need in this life is a goddamn gimmick.'"

In the thick gray smoke of silence we each weighted the same thought. Then with a nervous, chattering laugh Vincent said, "Maybe it's true; maybe all of us get the endings we deserve." I confessed I did not understand. Vincent said, "Maybe if he hadn't kept his music such a secret, one of us might have stayed with it. If any of us had known how hard he was trying, maybe we would have tried harder, too."

His was an interesting thought, but I could only shrug. The afternoon stretched itself and yawned and then shifted, rolled onto its back. And I had drunk too much wine. "So what happened to the manuscripts?"

"Mom keeps them in a solid wooden chest, this big heavy thing she bought especially. Francis wants us just to pay for the publication ourselves. You know, pay for the printing and all that. Gino's got the money so someday we probably will. You know, in time for Mom before she dies."

Through shimmering waves of accumulated drunkenness a feeling of what Vincent was about to say grew in my heart. I felt his mind wrestle with it, awkward in its unwieldiness, the obvious coarseness. He would detect the sentimentality like a coating of grease over whatever he thought or knew. The muscles of his face moved slowly. Or perhaps it was the wine. Once again he smiled; an expression ironic and detached and yet earnest.

He said, "I want you to know I admire the fact that you still work at your art. Maybe that doesn't make much sense to you. I'd be glad to help in any way. If something comes up, give me a call." He looked away then, as if waiting for something to happen. Did he anticipate my gratitude? Could he think I would be flattered?

My glass was empty, and I stood intending to go to the refrigerator. But after one step my leg suddenly began to throb, a burning beneath the skin and deep in the muscle, a sort of paralysis, all sensation gone below my thigh. And in front of Vincent I stumbled. My fall was ridiculous, like any old drunken fool. The pain was nearly intolerable, but the humiliation was even worse.

He stood, took a step and leaned forward over me. "Are you all right? Do you feel okay?"

With one hand on a chair I steadied myself and then stood, pain still throbbing but finally I could put weight on my leg. A body so rotted, so decayed, and I was angry; with my leg, with this head, and all the rest of it. I reached for my cane and could not find it. Vincent handed it down to me. Then he picked up my unbroken glass.

"I have enough help now," I said, "and for the future." Even in pain I was the soul of infuriating yet earnest ingratitude. Earnestness is a highly valued commodity in this country; America is earnest, and so I did not smile.

But just as suddenly I needed to sit down. My head spun, the room tipped to one side. The sofa was nearby, and I needed to use it. Vincent carried a full glass of water from the faucet, placed it on the low table before me. Again I lifted that stupid leg, this time onto the table, just as the doctor always advised.

He said, "I should probably go now," but then he sat down beside me and leaned back. Gradually my vision cleared, the spinning sensation ceased, and then the pain in my leg eased. Vincent stared off though my front window. The room glowed deeply orange, its light cast blue-grey shadows over his face. I watched light flow into his eyes, watched him see and not remember, remember and not see.

But finally I was able to stand. "It is getting late," I said, "and I have work to finish this evening. I thank you for your visit, and for your offer of help."

Startled, Vincent stood from the couch beside me. He finished his glass of wine and then we walked together slowly to the door. When the door opened, cool air exploded through the warm and stale room. Once again the day was dying. Below us the pool was pristine in its shape and weight and color, unaltered, undamaged by the momentary presence of some eye-arresting figure. The lounge furniture had all been removed. The concrete had been cleaned, and the pool's water appeared particularly bright.

Vincent stepped up beside me, looked intently into my eyes. "I can help you because I understand what you're going through." He took my old, thin hand and squeezed with the sound of rustling dry leaves. I winced. "The one thing we both understand," he said, "is great sacrifice, great pain." Still squeezing he continued to stare as my hand began to sweat within his. Finally he released me and bid me good night. I remained on the balcony watching him go, and then watching the color of the light change, finally confident the evening could only improve.

Vincent was not a madman; I understood this regardless of the temptation to think otherwise. A carrier of pain wherever he went, guilt-driven, he still made me nervous, like having a spider-web high in the corner of the ceiling when the spider vanishes.

I wanted to descend the stairs and sit beside the pool, stare down into the water. I wanted to feel the evening breeze blow over me, over my bald and naked head, over my weak, shallow and wheezing chest. I wanted to breathe air that was filled with the smell of the fields.

But the lounge furniture had been removed so there was nowhere to rest. Our patio was as naked as an empty dance floor. Nothing remained there to soothe a twisted consciousness, nothing to offer relief for a trembling body, nowhere to lean or lay. No place had been left for the spirit to hide. I was left with its plain line-drawing of perfect geometry.

Perhaps I was wrong, and Vincent was truly and genuinely mad. Or perhaps it only needed that I insist he be mad. But at that moment he certainly seemed crazy to me.

CHAPTER TWENTY–THREE

"ARE YOU SURE YOU WANT TO DO THIS?" Marla stood with her hands on her hips and dark eyes half-hidden by those strands of hair escaping from under a small yellow bow. One of my sketchbooks lay opened to the most recent draft, while another large sketch was pinned to the wall. This painting would be of two figures, male and female, wrestling in the rear seat of a car. Within the frame, and just visible in the distance, the figure of a nude woman stands with her back to the viewer.

Marla asked, "And what about Donald?"

"He has seen most of these sketches already."

She shook her head. "So that's the secret; the great artists reach into the misery of their assistants for their inspiration."

"Nothing inspires like misery."

But perhaps I gave the lie to my own optimism, misunderstood even my own inspiration. Marla stood by waiting for my instructions while I hesitated, overwhelmed with a noxious uncertainty. I paced as my head ballooned with self-doubt until too much time had passed. A day of false starts, instructions to Marla that turned out wrong, until eventually I was forced to concede that it all needed to be done over. By that time I had stared at that expanse of white for so long I had become lost within it.

Over the previous weeks we had begun work on three canvases. But to accomplish this I discovered that I needed most of all to trust Marla's judgment, and I never was able to do so comfortably. There were parts of each image that physically only she could finish, yet my dependency had not become easier. I needed to trust her absolutely, and I did not.

After looking at that vacant canvas so long my eyes had gone nearly white, I took a charcoal in hand and made some marks. The black stick cut the whiteness as palpably as a razor through flesh. Like cutting into some huge, white fruit, and leaving a trail as unmistakable as blood.

Sudden pain in my shoulder left it feeling bathed in a liquid heat, a sort of lava. The pencil moves itself, it comes alive and it decides. The pencil moves with its own will and, if one is fortunate, with its own passion. My hand merely follows the pencil, and I remain its audience. Forms shape themselves at the end of the pencil as if they had always been there, just below that skin of white gesso and the act had merely scrapped away its surface. The piece of charcoal between my fingers tingled; it buzzed in my hand, a wonderful thrilling sensation.

But then there was more pain. I handed the charcoal to Marla, led her back from the canvas so we might both recognize what had begun to appear. With a bit of coaxing eventually she recognized what I saw. After that the work became less hard. After another hour the figures began to recede from my eyes and every extension became false, every path a wrong turn. Time to stop.

Beyond the sliding glass door, my patio was just wide enough for two chairs. The patio faced the lawn and the street beyond, and because it did not overlook the swimming pool I hardly ever used it. The lawn below us was green even in winter, flat and uneventful to the hedge-row that defended us from the street. I brought my sketchbook out with us, Marla sat in a chair across from me, and I began to draw. As if by silent agreement she did not protest, but relaxed her posture as I sketched. When she changed her position I turned another page and started again. The pain in my shoulder was no longer very bad.

The moments floated past like those clouds along our horizon, and several of the drawings were nearly satisfying, there was something to enjoy in each. Then Marla stretched and shifted as if determined to leave. I flipped back through pages looking until I found a good likeness of that woman and then held its sketch toward her. "Have you ever seen her? I mean, around campus?"

Marla took the book from my hand and leaned back to study. I watched a tiny black ant walk slowly along the railing of the sundeck. Finally Marla's laugh exploded. "April," she said.

Impossible to hide my surprise and I did not try. The shock was complete.

"She used to live here." Marla's voice was mildly amused. "In this complex. That's where you drew these. Right?"

The ant reached the edge of the rail and walked back and forth searching for an escape. Its search became frantic as gradually it began to realize it was trapped.

Warmed by the light of the declining sun, amused curiosity painted Marla's face in bright colors and dramatic shadows. A smile drifted across her lips. She looked again at the sketch, flipped further back to previous drawings. Along the street hidden beyond the tall hedge-row, autos passed whispering.

She said, "She's living on Alvarado with a girlfriend." She closed the sketchbook, passed it back to me and looked up directly into my eyes as if waiting for me to respond. When I did not, she stood and turned her back to me, stepped to the high railing. As if lost in thought she leaned forward looking down although there was nothing below us to see. Finally she said, "April always seemed the type, but I never expected it to be you." She laughed with warm derision.

"I want her to become become our model. And I am asking you now if you will help arrange that." My growing frustration annoyed me.

"Are you asking me to work with her, or to get her for you?"

"Yes," I said, "to both."

Her confusion was replaced by annoyance. And I did not defend myself from her insinuation. She shook her head. "If I know her, she'd be willing to try." She smiled in a way that made my skin tingle. "If you're sure about this I'll talk to her. But you should think this over, and I'm not kidding."

I said nothing. She said, "April is the kind of person who has this way of causing good friends to fight with each other. Know what I mean?"

When I said nothing she added, "I'm warning you right now. If you're in a hurry to finish these paintings she'll just slow you down and maybe without even realizing it."

Finally confident of my decision, I said, "I want her as my model. Her presence will allow me to complete these canvases. So what do you propose? How can I gain her cooperate?" Marla looked at me as if she saw something unremarkable, but which she would note and remember. In the long silence that followed my question, I felt myself under a scrutiny I could not tolerate, and which I might not survive. I stood as if to call an end to the day, returned to the apartment and Marla followed. As she collected her things we discussed when she would return. I was relieved that she did not ask any more questions about April, and relieved I would not say something more to further upset her.

But her name was April. Was I, even for a moment, enchanted? Did I smile when Marla had gone and I was alone? April had already proved problematic. First, a problem knowing when she might appear beside the pool. Then, a problem to find her when she failed to appear beside the pool. And now, if Marla became impatient or angry with her and refused to contiune, that would provide its own problem. But there was at least the relief of finally knowing her name. Did I convince myself there would be no traps or dangers in the decision that April should be my model? But had I not, simply by deciding to begin new work to thwart the retrospective, already opened myself to a swarm of difficulties? That decision alone led to a long train of possible hazards. But I was determined to avoid illusions, the dark woods are always treacherous. Besides, considering the complications I already faced, April would have to go a great distance to make my life more difficult than it had become.

When Donald arrived the next day he appeared startled to see progress on the canvases. He scratched his head. "I didn't think you'd do it." He paced before the most recent canvas, stepping forward to peer intently and scrutinize a detail. "I suppose I don't really care. But I don't know; there just seems something wrong with all this here."

The moment Donald entered the room and saw the canvas of the couple fighting within the car, his consternation was obvious in his eyes. So I had no doubt he found something wrong with all of it. He moved to turn and look away. But that cluster of canvases, perhaps merely by their size, would not allow it. He said, "The thing's just damned weird." Pointing to the figure in the background he said, "And I don't know what she's supposed to be doing there."

"You have a problem because it does not look the way you expected it would? Familiar as you are with every piece of my work that has survived? You are upset because this does not fit your understanding of my work. Be honest for once and agree with me."

He scratched his head again and then shrugged. "Maybe you're right. But I still think something's gone wrong."

"Wrong with the piece," I asked with heavy sarcasm, "or wrong with you?"

He turned and faced me. "Don't misunderstand, but just look at the thing. I mean, it's just so weird." He turned to look at it again shaking his head. "It's so different from the rest of your work. Even the subject. It's just all so different."

The violence of Donald's reaction pleased me. Above all, such a striking a reaction from someone who knew my work so well. "Look more carefully," I said. "Is it so different from the work I did when I first came to New York?" The distortion of figures resembled some early efforts, but I intended these canvases to be different, an extrapolation from previous work, a sort of retrospective within themselves. I had worked hard to make each of them different from my previous work. So his confusion confirmed my success.

"And what's that?" Donald again pointed to that figure in the background partly sketched and waiting for Marla to arrange April's sitting, a figure impossible to finish until then.

"Should something else stand in its place?" Cane in hand I tottered to the canvas. "That is what it is because I put it there." Using my cane as a pointer I said, "A part of the composition. You know from composition? That figure is there because it needs to be there." My impatience startled Donald; it certainly startled me. "Did you think these shapes fell accidentally into my paintings?" Reduce him to silent embarrassment even though he did not deserve it.

He looked from the canvas to me, and then back to the canvas. "I still can't make any sense of it." He stalked back to the canvas seemingly unable to leave it alone. "I just can't see how you've come to these proportions. It's all just beyond me."

"At least you have the honor of your honesty," I said. "A quality hardly universal among your colleagues."

I thought again of Martin. Would he prove even more resistant to the possibilities, and more intransigent against them?

At least he now had something remarkable to tell John. They could laugh together that the old man finally had fallen overboard, once again frantically making paintings no one will like. Would John's curiosity compel him to invite himself to my apartment to see how badly everything was turning out? Surprisingly, only Marla seemed unsurprised by the direction these paintings had taken. Only she seemed so satisfied with the work that she could make suggestions which even I found extreme.

Three partly finished canvases leaned, one against each wall of my apartment; the sections of the Swimming Pool Triptych. I wanted each of them advanced as far as possible so that whenever April arrived, her portion would be completed quickly. But the image had grown muddled. And now the underlying structure had nearly collapsed under the weight of all that I demanded it carry, and I no longer recognized how to fix it. At first, the various figures had rioted over the canvasses, even while there were a dozen or more sketches demanding to be incorporated into it. But my enthusiasm for these paintings had gradually fled. Marla insisted she still liked them, but even she no longer seemed certain how to proceed. Something about them eluded us both. And I was no longer certain that when April finally joined us, her presence would clarify what needed to be done.

So Donald's reaction to the paintings of the triptych pleased me and revived my interest in them. Beneath his cautious exterior there was perhaps merely another philistine heart. But even that could be used to some good end. As he paced about the apartment I brought out the sketch for another painting.

"Look here, perhaps you can help me with this. Sketch some of these figures on the canvas so that I can see them grouped together full-size." He glanced at the sketch and then at me. After a pause he shook his head.

I said, "But you seem to have such definite ideas about these paintings. And believe me, I badly need fresh eyes right now." Again he shook his head, walked over to the sliding doors and looked out. I laughed. "Can you be afraid you will compromise your work for the catalog?"

His back stiffened but he did not turn. Instead he addressed his words to the glass of the sliding door. "We already agreed I wouldn't be asked to help with the drawing."

"I am asking you to do only something very rough. I find myself in trouble, and I merely ask that you transfer that drawing onto the canvas. Do this and certain things about the paintings will become clearer to me. And if you are able to offer a suggestion that advances the work, I promise to tell no one." I waited while he continued to stare out the window. "If anyone asks, I merely offered you the opportunity to practice your drawing skills."

Finally Donald rubbed the back of his neck and sighed. "What the hell; I guess it's not a big deal after all. But I'll tell you right now, I don't like this. Maybe you're right, and maybe I don't want to risk the catalog. Or maybe I just don't like being made a fool of. So I'll tell you right now, I'll do it just this one time and then we'll leave it at that. Never again. You're racing a deadline that's of no interest to me. That exhibition will go on, regardless of how much I help."

I could only laugh. "I am a certain fatalist, but if I had an outlook such as yours I would be depressed for the rest of my life."

He moved the canvas to the brightest corner of the room while I retrieved the sketchbook, and then we began. He worked in silence, and even my remarks and suggestions brought no response. His casual indifference made me furious, but it also forced me to go slowly, to study every turn. But we did not advance far before the light changed, my eyes grew weak and then I knew it was time to stop.

I wrote out a list of those supplies I would need for the next several days saying, "L'art pour l'art." Unamused by my jest, he left, and I was relieved.

I moved a chair directly in front of that canvas and then sat down to study it. The sketch had offered suggestions. And now, those suggestions seemed to multiply. Too many, or perhaps not enough. The top third seemed to need something, perhaps a figure I could not visualize. The area was not completely open, several figures were already planned for the space. But even in the sketch, those figures seemed insufficient; as if that space might inflate and the whole painting float away from its companions. Something substantial was needed to provide an anchor, something to suggest the canvas had looped vertically back into itself. A long brooding hour staring, waiting but not seeing, shapes superimposed that faded without clinging, unattached, dissipating like smoke in the night. Like wisps of cool blue smoke. The rest of that evening passed like a wisp of blue smoke.

CHAPTER TWENTY–FOUR

I PICKED UP the telephone and dialed, felt relief when I heard Marla's voice respond. Did she have time to drive with me out again to those farm-fields west of town? She hesitated, but then agreed to come by in another hour. I was not in any hurry; there were still two hours until sunset. Time enough.

I thought again about Martin's threat to come out and visit me and observe my progress. Could I predict his reaction to those new paintings? They certainly did not reflect the current trend, and Martin has always bothered himself about the current trend. And I suppose that is as it should be. But he already owned enough of my canvasses which could be easily categorized for quick sale.

Marla arrived much later than I had hoped; by the time her truck churned the dirt roads beside those fields it trailed a brown cloud smearing the fat, red sun that had begun to slip below the horizon. By then the eastern sky had darkened, stars dotting an outline of the distant mountains. But I was easily discouraged that evening, and with so little light remaining I suggested we start back.

She turned the truck beside a field of irrigation sprayers that hissed rhythmically into violet shadows. Soon our headlights burst through a thick stand of trees ranged like a black wall, and then the flat land beyond spread and disappeared. In the far distance a lone street-lamp shown yellow as a beacon. We approached it rapidly. For a moment the road became as familiar as a dream that I could not completely recall. But then I did, and then I was certain.

"Up ahead," I said. "That parking lot. We should stop there." Marla's eyes darkened but she said nothing.

"An opportunity to refresh my memory," I said. I did not admit it was for that other painting, the one not yet begun, its canvas turned to face the wall, its image hovering like a mirage only awaiting its opportunity. But she guessed correctly anyway.

She asked, "You still plan to paint that one?"

"In my mind it has already been painted, and perfectly."

She paused. "Suppose I asked you not to paint it."

The quiet drone of the engine surrounded us. Shrouded in that deepening blue, all contours disappeared into a thickening black. A moment of vertigo. "Why?"

"Nothing in particular. Just wondered what you'd say." She spoke as innocent of intention as a bird.

"Can you think of some reason that should cause me consider it?"

She laughed with embarrassment. "Never mind. I can't think of a convincing reason. But what reason do you have for painting it?"

"Do I need a reason to paint?" Her question set my teeth on edge. Suddenly I needed to get away from her. "I am thirsty, my thirst is my justification for drinking, the need that will be fulfilled. My eyes are on fire, so I paint. But that is all beside the point. You have helped me with these sketches from the beginning. So what can you be thinking?" My anger startled her, but it surprised me even more. "If you find something objectionable about these paintings, at least speak to me honestly."

"Sorry I brought it up." She waved her hand, brought it down to rake through her hair. "Forget I mentioned it." But she intended no apology. She spoke as if she had known to say nothing, but had failed.

And I became more curious than wise. I said, "I still do not understand. What reason can there be to abandon that painting?"

She slowed the truck as we approached the parking lot. "Where should we stop?"

And now my frustration had overcome me. "Keep driving, just keep driving."

Instead, she drove slowly to a spot at the far-end of the lot and parked. She shut off the engine, and hands still on the steering wheel she leaned back.

Full night had fallen. Darkness expanded all around us, beyond us. Resigned, I could not look at her, my thoughts jumbled with missed opportunities and memories of failed designs. Marla asked, "Have you ever had to abandon a painting because your model screwed up?"

Now I could not help but laugh. "The paintings left incomplete because something happened with the model would fill their own museum." Once, with only a few days more work remaining to complete a canvas that I genuinely loved, my model died. It is a story without charm and its misery I carry as a rotting carcas. I did not repeat that story to Marla.

Indifferent to my silence she said, "I met April in sophomore year through a friend in the department. After six sittings as its model my painting was just about finished. And then one day she stopped showing up. I was frantic and it took me two weeks to find her. When I confronted her, she said she'd had a fight with this guy, another painter in the department. She refused to come to my studio because she didn't want to run into him in the building. So I said, well, look, I understand all that but I've got this canvas to finish, what do you think I should do? Her best idea was that I find someone else. I said no, that won't work at all. I said we could get together when he wasn't around, but she said no, that won't work because he knew she'd been sitting for me and he'd come around and bug her. I said I'd talk to him and he'd understand about finishing the painting, but she said she didn't think that would help. I tried talking to him anyway, and I was sorry. Over the phone I told that guy I had this goddamn painting and I couldn't just let all that work go to shit, and he said if you painted her it's already shit, and he hung up." She shook her head with a bitter smile. "I began to understand why some painters work from photographs."

She continued, "Then, for two more weeks I couldn't even get her on the phone. I asked around but nobody knew anything and I was afraid maybe he'd killed her. I even called the old boyfriend, but he said he didn't know anything and hung up. Well, I really liked that painting and I'd put a lot of time and work into it, so I put it aside and started work on something else. Four months later I saw her in the Fine Arts building. I reminded her about that painting and asked if she'd sit so I could finish. She stalled around but I sort of threatened her so finally she agreed."

"And this other man from the department?" Her tale challenged my patience but I was her guest and was not free to leave.

"He already had a new girlfriend. So the day April promised she would arrive I took out the canvas, made some decisions about what I liked and didn't, made plans for what I'd do. I waited a long time. It took two more days until I found her. She had a new boyfriend but this one wouldn't let her sit. This guy had some weird thing about his girlfriend being seen without her clothes on. I screamed at her about why she was letting this jerk tell her what to do. By this time I didn't care about her or him, but I had a painting I wanted to finish, and what difference did it make without her clothes. I talked to her for a while, but all along I knew I should just dump that canvas and move on to something else. But I'd gotten attached to the thing. She just kept saying, no, no, no, so I hung up just furious and put the painting away. Then three weeks and just out of the blue, she called."

"Perhaps she really had wanted to sit for that painting after all."

Marla shrugged. "After some point I didn't care what she wanted. But she told me she was finished with this other guy, didn't care if he jumped off a building, and did I still want her to sit. I set a date and to my surprise she actually showed up. Another week of hard work and the painting was nearly finished. The academic year was almost over, year-end critiques were coming up and I wanted that painting for the judges. So one day and once again she didn't show up. I called her on the telephone and got her on the first try. She said she was back with this other guy, the other one who wouldn't let her sit. I went crazy. She said, what can I do, he wants to marry me, we're getting married. I said, I've got a critique coming up. You can get married anytime. I was so mad when I hung up that phone I grabbed whatever was sharp and cut that canvas to shreds." Marla laughed as though the wound was still fresh. "I cut it so small you couldn't make a pillow with what was left." She laughed again, that rich sweet laugh in our soft, blue-black night. "Of course, the real kick was that she and that guy only lasted another couple of weeks. Months later she asked what I'd done with the painting, so I told her. And she surprised me because I think she was really disappointed."

Marla turned the key then and started the engine. We glided forward slowly past the lamppost perched over the crushed-stone parking lot. When we reached the road she leaned back, left arm cocked on the window frame, right arm draped over the steering wheel. The engine whined louder, her right hand dropped down to take the gearshift, the engine whined still louder, she shifted with a thud, our speed increased. She raked her fingers again through her short dark hair. Gradually the light from the lamppost disappeared behind us.

I asked, "Why have you told me this?"

"I just want to know how much you're willing to risk with April."

I shrugged with surprise. "Is that a rhetorical question, or does she have another boyfriend?"

Marla laughed. "You've pinned a lot on her. That isn't rhetorical. I'm asking if you understand well enough to make these plans?"

"So I should begin with you. What do you think she will do?"

Marla shook her head. I said, "I depend on your opinion about so much else, why not this as well?"

Headlights of on-coming cars bathed her face in yellow light, eyes rimmed black. "You don't know much about what's going on. You only know what others decide to tell you."

"What is there to know? None of that is of any interest to me, or of any value. Given what little time remains to me, I have more important things to consider." I turned to her then feeling suddenly generous and philosophical. "In the shadow of death, what is important stares one more plainly in the face."

We began to pass familiar landmarks as I realized we were approaching my apartment. She said, "I wouldn't know anything about that." The silence that followed annoyed and depressed me. Perhaps with more time and a bit of wine she might have told me what I most urgently needed to know. She leaned over the steering wheel as if her thoughts were speeding ahead of our headlights.

We pulled up behind my building and stopped and then I stood on the asphalt of our parking lot beside the open door of her truck. The engine stuttered as it idled. She sat high behind the steering wheel not looking at me. I asked if she would come to help me the next day.

She nodded. "Sure."

"About eleven?"

She paused before she said, "Should I bring along April?" And she grinned.

Once again she had caught me unprepared. "Of course. If she will come."

Marla nodded again, put the truck in gear while I closed the door. In another moment she and her truck were gone.

During the slow walk back to the apartment I thought, and in thinking realized she was right and I understood nothing. The more I think, the less I know. Quite an accomplishment.

The telephone was ringing as I opened my door. I lifted the receiver, put it to my ear. From the other end I heard blurred speech, as if the conversation had already begun. But the words rambled, and I could not make it all out. I recognized that it was John speaking, our department head and official representative; even drunk and muttering I could not mistake his voice. With the intention of replacing the receiver I blurted out, "Good night!"

But suddenly he asked, "Where did you take her?"

"You are drunk," I answered. "I have no idea what you are talking about. And neither do you. Now, I am going to hang up."

"C'mon you old bastard, don't act dumb with me. You've been angling for months to get your bony hands on her. She told me all about it. Staring at her every time she came out to the pool. That's why she moved. That's why she isn't living there anymore. I know all about you." Burston cackled drunkenly. "So just tell me where you took her. Just tell me."

"When you are sober you will call me again and then you will apologize. But I am exhausted now and I am going to bed. Call me tomorrow."

"Stay away from her. I know her, and you're no good for her." I pushed down the receiver button cutting off his words. My hand trembled as I replaced the receiver.

From the bottle in the refrigerator I filled a glass with wine, set it aside to warm. American refrigerators make everything so cold.

In this way a blindfold had been lifted from my eyes only to reveal another blindfold. My precious and inspiring model was not my own discovery, neither plucked from obscurity nor redeemed by Art. Had she modeled for John? By appearance at least, she must have. And had Marla spoken to him about her, or about us? I did not want to consider that she might have compromised our confidence. That possibility made me gasp for air.

I slid back the sliding door. The night breeze billowed the curtain, a sail to my rudderless ship. I did not wish to think any longer, about anything. I had misunderstood much, perhaps nearly everything, but I was still not so foolish as to believe that simple questions would yield simple answers.

CHAPTER TWENTY–FIVE

WHEN I DESCRIBED what John had said to me over the telephone, Marla seemed surprised. "Why would he call you about her?"

I tried to move my arm in a smooth arc, but my shoulder groaned loudly and its pain rang in my ear. The line I was able to draw resembled nothing so much as the graph of an earthquake. In my frustration I would have crushed the soft frail stick of charcoal in my fingers, if only those fingers still had the strength to do so.

But this was all only a prelude to my asking if she had contacted April. "I called her a half-dozen times." Marla sat on a stool behind me, waiting for my interrogation to end and the day's work begin.

"Does she have a roommate? I thought you said she had a roommate." I moved to the lower left area where the successful arc would terminate. I tried that arc in reverse, moving my arm carefully across my chest all the while feeling ridiculous, like a child forced to turn the coloring book upside down in order to color the feet. When my hand was just above my shoulder the pain was suddenly terrible, as if a piece of broken glass was grinding within the joint.

Marla answered, "Either nobody was home, or nobody was bored enough to answer. It was a Friday night, remember?" She said this as if the work-week was the universal determinant of behavior.

"Do you expect to hear from her today?"

Marla shrugged. "It's Saturday. Why would she call today?"

I asked if she carried April's phone number with her. Marla shifted on her stool, then stood and walked resentfully to her handbag. After thumbing through a small notebook she concluded that she must have left it at her apartment.

"And you cannot remember her telephone number?" Marla shook her head. I said, "Do me this favor. Call me when you arrive home and let me have her number."

Marla turned slowly on her stool and spoke with obvious annoyance. "Don't worry. I'll call her again when I get home. I expect she'll be home tonight."

"But how could you possibly be sure? After all, it will still be Saturday night." Sarcasm sometimes bursts forth unbidden.

Annoyed, again she shifted. "If she isn't home for me, she won't be home for you either." Then she smiled.

The arc I labored to draw would define the limit of that corona of light from the streetlamp. I intended a deep, dark blue there with streaks of yellow and green, touches of red and white. But the pain in my shoulder had finally become distracting. I called Marla to the canvas. "You can see where this is going. Finish it for me, would you please?"

In a moment the arc was complete. Marla moved so beautifully, so smoothly, as if dancing before a blank white screen, her hand a comet leaving a thin trail of black. I said, "By the way, when did you last speak to John?"

"John?" she repeated without turning.

"John, our department head, you know."

"He left a message that he wanted to talk to me. It was in my department mail box."

I stepped to the canvas and took up the pointer. "The peak of the road house roof should begin here and move like this." The pointer trembled in my hand, but the shape and direction were right. Perhaps I should have put a piece of charcoal at the end of the pointer as Matisse had done. Marla stepped forward and inscribed the line. The angle was wrong and we tried again, and then again. I stepped back. It was nearly right, I felt myself giving up. It would have to do.

I asked, "Did you mention anything to him about April?" She turned to study my face, the student studying the instructor's eyes hoping to recognize the correct response. "He must have asked questions about how these paintings were progressing. I simply want to know what most piqued his interest."

Confusion darkened her eyes. She shrugged. "He asked how I liked working with you. And yes, he asked how the painting was coming along. Just general things, as far as I can remember."

"And you mentioned nothing to him about April?" Before she could respond I took up the pointer. "Try moving the peak here, put one leg of the hip roof along here."

She worked so casually, yet so carefully; and so damnably self-confident. Her arm swung into the shape as if the shape was already there; not just in her mind or her eye but inside her hand. She stepped back from the canvas without turning. She said, "'Maybe you should ask Burston yourself."

We worked for several hours that day, and I asked no more about John or April, until finally the flat canvas had been divided and broken into work areas. I would find out nothing more about either of them anyway, and I still had several paintings to finish. And now I could at least see this one more plainly, its proportions becoming clearer, its overall shape beginning to emerge. I could see where heads and shoulders would range, the space April's shape would occupy, where the streetlamp like a monumental arch would overhang. And finally I was tired.

Yet Marla seemed even more full of energy than when she had first arrived. I asked, "Do you think I will ever finish any of this?"

Something in the question seemed suddenly to deflate her. She walked to the couch, sat down heavily without looking up. Her silence made me impatient, almost resentful, but I could not be angry. She said, "I think the odds are against you. You've set yourself all kinds of difficulties. I'm helping because this work seems worth doing. But a lot of it I can't do for you. And it doesn't help if you insist on making stupid decisions, or becoming paranoid so you can't tell your friends from your enemies. I don't understand why you need to involve April. It isn't that I don't understand why she appeals to you. But why do you need her?"

I said, "You know more about her than you have told me. How can this be helpful to me?"

Marla smiled. "You really should talk to April yourself. She would tell you everything you want to know. I'll bet she'd even enjoy it." Then she asked if we were finished for the day and I could only nod and then watch as she collected her things and left.

My leg had bothered me for most of our session. I sat down on the couch, propped my leg on a chair, and rubbed. I leaned back, stared at the ceiling, at the soft whiteness slipping into grey shadow at the corners, and awaited my very own premonition. The ceiling appeared smooth and even, but if I had moved close enough I would have seen them, all of those thousand tiny cracks.

Simply by her questions Marla had reminded me how thoroughly I had permitted myself to depend on April. But I was confident John was too cowardly to interfere directly in my work. The fact that he had waited until he was quite drunk before he called me suggested how uncomfortable he was about his own intentions. Perhaps I exerted more influence over his decisions than I had thought. And from his behavior, I tantalized myself that there was a genuine possibility of overturning the retrospective exhibition, and thinking this I dozed until I fell asleep.

The ringing of the telephone woke me suddenly, and my head remained filled with the leadenness of a dreamless sleep.

"I am flying next month to Los Angeles for de Kooning's show." It was Martin's voice, although our connection was noisy. "The time has come for me to see the progress of your projects you have told me so much about. Suppose I fly up to San Francisco. We could meet at the Saint Francis hotel for dinner."

"It is good to hear your voice again," I said. And truly I was relieved to hear him. "But this is a very bad time to see the work. All of it remains half-formed, and very far from completion. You understand."

Martin laughed. "Have I ever asked to see your work when you have agreed immediately? Or happily? But tell me how I can form any idea of your progress unless I see them? I have wondered about nothing as much as these new paintings of yours. I have even lost precious sleep over them. Be kind, my friend, be merciful. I need to savor their shape and color and size. How else will I know how properly to represent them?"

I enjoyed this opportunity to laugh. "If I could answer those questions I could dispense with my agent; do you agree?"

"Do not jest. I am up to my ears with de Kooning's show and he has become unfortunately surly in his old age. But even he does not demand so much of my patience. I request an opportunity to reassure you that, as always, you are doing very fine work, work which will sell to your enthusiastic audience. Is mine such an unreasonable request?"

"We have an agreement. And part of that agreement involves those paintings I have already sent to you. We have already agreed upon which of those you will offer for sale, and which you will place securely in storage."

"Of course," Martin responded impatiently. "One would think I have no feelings about these matters. But I travel so infrequently. This seems a fine opportunity to see you. And the years pass so much more quickly than before."

"Sentiment aside, Martin, you believe I am attempting to hide something from you. You suspect I am concocting some enormous joke at your expense."

"My friend, certainly not."

"Believe me that the paintings progress, but I cannot allow you to see any of them right now. You and I have been along this path too many times before. And we know precisely how valuable patience is to any worthwhile undertaking."

He sighed. "Perhaps you are right. And perhaps I have become too old to understand certain things. Some nights I no longer recognize my own image in the mirror. Does that ever happen to you? Do you ever see a face there which you do not recognize?"

For a long time we were silent. The clicks and hisses I listened to so intently through the telephone created a sense of widening space, as if perhaps I was already dead and attempting to communicate with the living, my room suddenly become small and airless. Finally, Martin spoke.

"You know the gallery where de Kooning's work will be shown. If you change your mind, contact me there after the nineteenth of next month. Nothing would give me more pleasure than to extend my stay and visit you. I envy you living out there, have I ever told you that? So beautiful; not like New York. I have been thinking that next year I might finally move my organization, perhaps to Los Angeles. A very nice city. And the weather, so beautiful."

"Visit me in three months. The paintings will be far-along by then. And then yours will be a very pleasant visit."

"Of course." Martin's voice became suddenly heavy and dry. "As in the old days, I must beseech you for an audience. Yes, the old days. Is it very nice there in the autumn?"

"We will go to Napa," I said, "and we will tour the valley. After the grape harvest we will visit the wineries. It is very beautiful there, you will see."

"Yes," he said emphatically, "that idea I like. We will do this, and we will talk about the old days." He paused then, and into that pause I poured all of my relief, months more without his prying interference.

"On the other hand, perhaps I should look again at my schedule. Perhaps there is time for me to surprise you one day with a visit. When you least expect me, you will find me rapping on your door. Would that be marvelous? Just like in the old days."

"We would enjoy your visit so much more if you waited until autumn."

"You are adamant. One might almost suspect you had found a lover and were hiding her from your friends."

I could only laugh. "Were that the case, I would invite you here immediately. For a man of my age, that would be reason enough to call the newspapers."

With a sigh of resignation Martin said, "I suppose there is nothing for me to do but continue to attempt to sell your paintings and look forward to autumn. I can hardly contain my curiosity. But mark my words: one day you will again need my help."

I laughed. "If I did not know you so well I would suspect you of the worst sort of shameless melodrama."

"You of all people accuse me of melodramatic invention. But we will not argue. To hear the master is to obey the Universe." Martin began to laugh. "But should I suddenly appear at your doorstep, you must not refuse me shelter. It is the least you can do."

When finally we had rung off I went to the refrigerator. The bottle inside held only enough for two or three glasses.

Light was finally gone and no more work would be done. With my glass and my cane I stepped out onto the back balcony to listen to the passing automobiles. With its portrait in progress I felt no desire to sit beside our swimming pool. Looking across the cool dark lawn I recognized a delicate tension within myself that was more than merely the residue of my conversation with Martin.

Had I become wary of April, perhaps even afraid? Had I taken Marla's cautionary tale too seriously? And had John's sudden outburst put me too thoroughly on my guard? Gradually I realized that the person who I had depended upon as a source of inspiration had become a temptation to failure, a trap capable of diverting me into disaster. As if at that moment her presence could only complicate everything which it was intended to clarify. I would need to proceed cautiously if I was to discover what needed to be done. And all of this came suddenly to depress me. I felt its discouragement spread like oil upon water, thin yet pervasive, reaching even into the farthest corners of my life.

Suddenly all of the colors around me became harsher, even as the air softened. And just as suddenly I began to weep. The sight of an old man crying can only be demoralizing. And if April had seen me at that moment and for some reason managed to empathize with my objectless grief, she would have crossed that thin yet sturdy membrane which separates us all. And as complicated as my situation was, that would have made it infinitely and terribly worse.

CHAPTER TWENTY–SIX

THE POUNDING at my door was sharp and rapid. I struggled awake in
the deep blue light of dawn. I opened the door and Donald filled its frame.
Shivering, dark circles beneath his eyes, haunted, as if he had been tormented
the entire night. I said, "I am about to make a pot of coffee, and you look as if
you could use it more than I."

"Can't stay long," he said as he entered and sat down at my table. "I've got
to go soon." He shook his head. "What a goddamn mess." He dragged fingers
through rumpled hair, and then he began to laugh. I had heard Donald laugh
before, but this sound frightened me.

I said, "Rather early in the day for a crisis."

This caused him to laugh again. Hands twisted, fingers twined, he looked
about the room as if gathering words from the air. "I was going to call first
but then I figured to just come over and tell you." Panic overtook his confused
eyes. "This is real sudden, I know, but something's come up. It'll be tough on
you for a while, but how hard could it be to find somebody to do what I do?"
His voice trailed off. He looked away, half-muttered something, and then his
eyes softened, as if exhaustion was taking over.

I busied myself with spoons and coffee and boiling water. "And your degree?
Will you leave the graduate program entirely?" A glitter returned to his eyes. He
laughed harder than before, and so full of panic I expected him to stand and

run out my door.

He caught his breath to say, "Hadn't thought about that. Not that it matters." He paused and looked over at me. "I know this must sound weird." His smile suddenly disappeared. He stood, eyes darting about the room and flinched at each of those canvases leaning against the walls without pause until they touched the doorway. And I too felt a sudden panic and a kind of paralysis; knees gone soft as wet sponges, while I remained transfixed watching him. Then the boiling kettle screamed.

At its sound Donald stood and reached my door in two long stride. He turned to face me. "Somebody old and cynical as you; what made me think you'd understand?" His voice became frantic and angry. "I want to marry her. What's wrong with that?" Suddenly I was seeing Donald from a great distance. As if my vision had telescoped, and he and the room, and the whole world had receded into a small bright circle of light and color, surrounded by a nimbus of impenetrable black. What I remember is Donald's eyes blinking and blinking as if forcing back tears.

"Where will you go? Do you have money?"

"Money isn't what I came here for."

"Nobody does not need money. And will Barbara go with you?" At the mention of her name tears fell. He did not shiver or sob. He stood quite still as the tears traced brightly over his cheeks.

The sight of his tears somehow calmed me. "Sit. The coffee is nearly ready."

He shook his head though he returned slowly to the table and collapsed into a chair. "Already had too much coffee." Exhaustion made his voice hollow and his words were spoken without inflection. I placed a cup on the table before him. He looked at it once and then sipped. I sat down across from him.

He said, "She's going back home; to Idaho." He paused as if still trying to understand his own words. "Ever hear of Pocatello? She's pregnant. She has my kid, understand? It's my baby, too. She's going home and she doesn't want me along. She won't marry me, won't even admit the kid's mine." More tears perched at the corners of his eyes but these did not fall. "She says she's going home to have the baby, and that she's going to keep it. My kid, too, understand? But it's like she's running away from me, like she has to keep the kid away from me. I love her, I want to marry her. You understand? And I want that kid."

I said nothing. There was nothing to say.

"But she swears her father will kill me if he sees me. And she says that if we marry now, eventually we'll hate each other. She talks about that part all the time. 'You'll hate me', she says. 'You'll stop loving me and then you'll stop loving our child. Then what happens?'" He spoke to the top of the table as he shook his head. "Who the hell knows; maybe being pregnant makes you crazy. Maybe she isn't thinking at all. Everybody tells me to give it all up because Barbara won't believe I can support her and the kid." He slammed his hand so hard on the table our coffee cups trembled.

"What the hell do I know? All I want is to be with her. We could be in Las Vegas in a couple of hours, I told her. We could go to her parents married already. Who would give us trouble then? But no, that's not good enough for her. So I'll wait until she leaves, get on the bus right after hers. She can't stop me from taking a bus to Idaho. This is a free country. She can't stop me from going if I want. And she can't stop me from seeing my kid. At least once." With slowly dawning amazement he said, "My kid." The torture within his expression, days of torment, as if he no longer even slept but thought only of this trip. And his sense of amazement overwhelmed all of it. He looked up suddenly directly into my eyes, his own eyes so haggard and yet he appeared almost happy. "Have any children?"

"No," I said. He looked at me with sudden pity. "How much money will you need for this journey?"

He laughed. "I know all about your finances. Where the hell would you find money?"

"If I ask whether you need money it is my own business." I stood and walked to my bureau. There were several large bills, all that was in my possession. "Take these. If you need more, call Vincent. Tell him I will repay whatever he gives you."

He took the bills from my hand and fingered them as if to confirm their material existence. Or perhaps he was thinking something else, listening to music only he could hear. Very quietly he said, "Thank you, but I didn't come here to take your money. I won't need it, but thanks for the offer." He put the bills on the table and again stood.

"How will you get out there?" Each second removed something of his presence, as if he was fading, becoming less material, as if he might be dying.

"Like I said, there's a bus runs up there. Right after the one she gets on." He moved as if sleep-walking to the door.

"You know my telephone number. If you find yourself in trouble feel free to call." He turned, smiled weakly, a smile whose despair took my breath away. Then he was gone.

For a long time I watched the door. I expected him to return, as suddenly as he had left. Perhaps merely a poorly-placed faith in the movement of the Universe. The world moves only in one direction, and it can be no other way. And just so, Donald would return. Motion of the planets would carry him back.

Brightening sunlight penetrated the narrow space between closed curtains. Dawn. Its light formed a four-sided patch of yellow, a rhomboid of gold, high on the opposite wall. Very slowly that patch of gold slid down the wall, onto the carpeted floor. With infinite slowness it moved further along the floor, then climbed the corner of the dull green couch, undulating over each obstacle and over every shape.

Those brown and twisted black and grey hairs on the backs of my hands beside the smaller hairs along each finger did not move, did not shift along, with that creeping rhomboid. Hands which I had depended upon and which had done my bidding lay useless as if in a coma or worse. There was instead some subtle movement beneath, motion of the unseen, a throb within the light as if marking the passage of some radiant yet invisible energy. The room remained motionless and flat as the rhomboid moved silent as a dream.

With my throbbing head I tried to make sense of Donald. He had struggled mightily and for a long time to achieve his meager position within the University, yet now he was almost eager to throw all of it away in order to pursue something he could never have. This baffled me.

I wondered if he might be collaborating with John, and this crisis was simply another attempt to cripple my paintings. But such a grand strategy seemed more than either of them could successfully conceive. And in any case, Donald's panic appeared genuine. Suddenly I began to wonder about her, that pregnant child, the child-bride big with child. He had accepted its responsibility eagerly, unlike many others I have known. So I began to pity him since he appeared to be out of his mind.

When the telephone rang I expected to hear Donald's voice.

"What's the schedule?" Marla asked. "Do I come over?"

"Not today. A bit under the weather, if you know what I mean." Her laughter clicked with static. She did not protest and even seemed relieved when I asked that she come the next day instead. Our conversation ended with her cheery goodbye.

The events of the morning had pushed me closer to the edge of some void. The paintings suddenly seemed to loom over me. A single false step and I would be swallowed by them, lost forever and condemned to wander inside their cacophony of fractured and incomplete figures. Each leaned staring at me with its own accusation. Each flaunted those smears and daubs of paint futilely applied. Ridiculous, all of that mess gone completely wrong and of no earthly interest to anyone. Looking at them left me disgusted. They deserved their destruction. Each was a mindless, useless attempt to conquer the white void and so declare victory against death itself. My stomach churned with a justifiable nausea. The purity of their unsullied whiteness seemed the more appropriate object of worship. Hence the temptation; to scrape and gesso and repaint with the purest titanium every one. Only that gesture would rescue them from a torture I was determined to inflict upon them. Their violation appalled me. Paint them white and return them to their purity. Either that or flee. Run until no one could connect them with me.

But I could not avert my eyes. A power within those color-spattered windows of canvas rooted me to that chair. I was bound down with chains of line and color. I wished for sleep, for the cessation of consciousness. I wanted to ignore my obligation to breathe continuously. I wanted a willful rejection of will. I wanted the power to reject consciousness.

The light continuing to leak into my apartment became muddy with red. Not maroon, nor sable, not nearly enough burnt umber, or enough sienna. Twilight; already my startlingly brief day was drawing to its close, and I could look forward to salvation. I had somehow permitted the entire day to pass, and had done nothing to resist that passage; one more day wasted.

When finally I could stand I went to the refrigerator. The bottle of wine inside was nearly empty, only enough to fill a glass which I drank and then returned to the table. That glass occupied its appropriate space, unlike me, displacing the appropriate volume of the rest of the material world without conflict or resistance. Its cylinder of reality was contiguous with the rest of the room, the rest of the Universe, as it perched on the edge of that table contiguous with Time. The white table top formed part of a frame and the brown rug beneath it could have been a river. As the shaft of red twilight slipping between pale curtains faded approaching the wall, its slash of light deposited a diagonal of red enwrapped by a shadow of pale violet. The light shone against the wall like a message. I returned the glass to the table as the final note of a symphony. Perhaps Donald would never return. Perhaps he would decide to live forever in Idaho, with his Idaho wife and their Idaho child. Perhaps that was the way his life was predestined to end. Perhaps that is the way all lives end, with the urgent wish for a wife and child in Idaho.

Suddenly I wanted to call John Burston. I was certain that he knew what I needed to know about Donald. John appeared to occupy that peculiar place within the Universe from which all complications arise. The mystery of April, of course, and now the tragic-comedy of Donald. As if John operated a device by which any of our lives might become twisted and turned and redirected along some unexpected channel. In the end I could only conclude he would provide no help. But perhaps at that moment no help existed and so nothing could be assuaged. Although it remained incomplete, my day was over and I was exhausted. My only hope was to cultivate the patience to wait, and not wait in fear.

CHAPTER TWENTY–SEVEN

THE SUN WAS BRIGHT and hot even under my umbrella. The crowd of young people beside our pool possessed careless and infuriating energy. No eyes frantically searched a book, no heads were scratched over hastily scribbled notes; only swimming and radio music, horseplay and laughter. It all left me so depressed I was compelled to leave. Those voices followed my slow steps back to my cave and ignored my closed door. Only in the eye-soothing dimness of my four walls could I halt and reflect and breathe easily.

Even after two weeks of Donald's absence, his frantic eyes, his trembling voice and his shivering body seemed to follow me everywhere. But it had demanded those two weeks for me to discover pity for him.

Before going out earlier to the pool, I had called Vincent's office only to be told he had gone and left his office for the day. I called his home then but received no answer. So I convinced myself that I needed to speak to John directly.

By forces that had spun far out of my control my relationship with John had become burdensome and complicated. And because of this, his courteous nods when passing me in the halls of the fine arts building had come to seem to me terrible insults.

But circumstance had moved away from us both, and this I could no longer doubt. Objects, thoughts, images, sounds, in fact every element of the material world had moved beyond my grasp to some irretrievable periphery. The tide of reality was receding, and what remained was an absence, a vacuum. Some noxious vapor or bitterly corrosive fluid had seeped into my sanctuaries to violate my most certain convictions.

The air conditioner rumbled and then roared, and its sound instantly blanketed the revelry beyond my walls. My ears, I discovered, had become delicate. Every sound seemed a voice speaking quietly of something incoherent but of fearsome importance. Yet with every voice equally loud, I could not decipher what any single voice was saying.

As if exhaustion and such dark confusion was not enough, once again my head had begun to throb with a subtle panic. My refrigerator was nearly empty since I still lacked an able and dependable assistant. So perhaps it was not exhaustion; perhaps it was merely an exquisite form of fearsome despair.

When I failed after several attempts to contact Vincent I was overwhelmed by a putrescent debility and laid down on my bed. But from that position, wherever I turned my head I looked into the humiliation of another unfinished canvas. And then I would overflow with useless and impotent rage. So much wasted material, so much wasted energy, so much wasted pain along with that enormous waste of precious time. Elaborately contrived, projects with no hope of completion filled my eyes. If there was indeed some sliver of justice in the world, undoubtedly I would be tied down to an operating table for the slow torture of experiments performed for the advancement of art. Could anything that sounded so innocuous prove to be so perverse and so destructive?

That retrospective exhibition I despised would be held despite my efforts, and that failure along with those paintings left unfinished would provide an object lesson for the heedless, and an assurance that failure is not only possible, it was inevitable. The face of failure would be drawn large as a warning to all future generations. With a sigh of relief I decided I need not capitulate to old age, merely to ignorance and decay and oblivion.

Perhaps if I had fallen asleep I might have ignored the ringing of the telephone. Or if I had remained instead beside the pool, or perhaps had gone with Marla for a drive, I would not have known that the telephone rang. But from my bed its sound stung my ears, attacked my throbbing head while I could neither ignore that beast nor destroy it. With my head throbbing, I stood and lifted the receiver. The voice began to speak before I could offer a greeting.

"I understand Don spoke to you before he left the campus." John's voice was calm and dry, as if he was speaking to a confidant with whom he spoke every day.

"Yes," I said, "he visited me here. We drank coffee. He was very upset, very disturbed."

"Have you heard anything more from him?"

"What do you know about all of this?"

"No more than you. He's an honest, hard-working fellow. I expect he means well, but he has serious obligations, particularly to you. I sympathize with his unhappiness but there is a limit."

I said, "There is also a young woman who is pregnant with his child. He insisted he plans to marry her. Perhaps his sense of responsibility has expanded beyond the confines of our little universe."

"The dean of women students is trying to contact the girl's parents. Don's very talented, very capable. With his abilities he could have a fine career."

"Perhaps his flight is as much away from the burden of this sparkling career. Perhaps this woman is just the person he needs most. She might save him from a life as a desk-bound bureaucrat driven by self-doubt and frustration." I had become physically tired and now I discovered I was tired of John as well. I wanted to hang up the telephone and go back to sleep. Instead I asked, "Why did you call me about April?"

With convincing confusion John said, "Who?"

"Several nights ago you called me very late making some obscure accusation concerning my relationship with a woman who I hope will model for me. And you even knew her name."

John hesitated. "I have heard a rumor that you intend to employ April Sommerville as a model for your painting. And I know of this woman. She's an average student of no distinction who has been in and out of our department over her lengthened and checkered academic career. But I know nothing more about her. And I certainly have never called you about her."

"You sounded drunk on the telephone," I said. "Perhaps you simply cannot remember."

John hesitated again. "If this is some sort of joke, it is in very bad taste. And if you hope to use this fabrication to intimidate me or influence my decision regarding the activities of the department, you should give it up." John's anger sounded barely restrained.

"The caller did not identify himself," I said. "Perhaps I mistook your voice for that of one of her jealous lovers. The resemblance was remarkable, I promise you, but it was very late at night. I suppose it is possible I made a mistake."

"There's something else we need to talk about." John cleared his throat as if relieved this issue had been settled, another agenda item disposed of. I prepared myself for something officious. He said, "Most of our department meeting yesterday was spent discussing your need for assistance. With Don's departure our first concern is to replace him as quickly as possible. You need help, and several candidates were put forward. It will take a few more days to interview candidates, but I've called to tell you that we're working on it."

"I appreciate your concern, but this is not the reason you have called."

John cleared his throat again. "There were additional expressions of concern about your painting. The department wants to make certain your progress continues. But with Don gone, work on your paintings may come to an end. So, in order to protect the department and the University and the investment that has been made, it was agreed that we would proceed with our plans for your retrospective exhibition." He paused to give me an opportunity to interrupt, but I did not. So he continued.

"Many of us sympathize with your dilemma, but there's the department and the University to consider. Just as it was wrong for Don to abandon you, so it would be wrong for us to risk the reputation of our department. Our first responsibility is to protect it as best we can." He paused again. "Matthews from Archives is ready to consult with you about the choice of works to be put on display and help document those works until we find someone to continue your catalog. If you already have someone in mind we'd be happy to consider him."

The suddenly silent telephone clutched by my hand became fearsome and terrible. John and I sat as if at opposite sides of a long table, but separated by a thick, black curtain. We each waited for some sign from the other. Finally John said, "Hello? Still there?"

I took a deep breath before I spoke. "Do you take me for a complete fool? You hand me your decision and then ask if everything is all right. You place the investment of the University above my work as a painter and then ask if everything is satisfactory. You assure me that everything has been decided so that there is nothing to argue over. Without doubt you may have your will of students like Donald or April, but remember that I am not one of your students. Nor am I one of your miserable, intimidated, careerists lodged precariously in your faculty bird-nest, fearful that every act or decision is a threat which might force me out."

It was John's turn to hesitate, and he did. "When matters become complicated, solutions are rarely simple. I had hoped you would extend us a bit of patience and understanding and perhaps even some cooperation."

"These complications you speak of do not concern me, and patience and understanding will yield me nothing. But your words remind me that there are individuals in this world who are frightened by someone with talent and imagination and the courage of them both."

John quietly laughed, and this added to my fury. "Somehow I suspected this might be your response." Had I not been so angry I might have heard the tremor at the back of his throat. Old as I am, I might still have learned one more thing from one more miserable fatality in this miserable and stupid life.

I said, "I am not afraid of you, nor am I helpless without Donald. I will complete these paintings. And you will fail in your aspiration because I will make certain there is be no retrospective. I am unimpressed by your authority, or that of anyone else. I will not cease working. Because there is only struggle, and the struggle to continue to struggle." With that gloriously arrogant fillip I hung up the telephone.

My hand trembled as it rested on the receiver. My heart pounded and I was breathing hard, as if I had run up a high hill. Of course I did not understand what I had just said and done, and I fought against any realization that I did not understand. I certainly considered the possibility that I might now be dismissed from the University since I had given John both the justification and the opportunity to do so. My understanding of the hierarchy above John was confused and incomplete, but I was certain that as defiant as I might pretend, he need only call the right person and I would be ordered to pack my bag and leave. And where, in that case, would I go?

But my head no longer hurt, at least that one pain had passed. I felt desperate, yet calm. Suddenly each of those paintings, though mildly obscene in their impoverished vision, offered its incompleteness without shame, as if dancing naked under a small bright light. Tiny minds, trivial obsessions, but I convinced myself that in the end John would accomplish nothing.

Even in their incompleteness there was more beauty in one of those canvases than in all of John's file cabinets. In my moment of fury and desperation and fear I was filled with a sudden thirst to complete each of those paintings, immediately, instantly. So I stood.

When I reached up with the charcoal the dull ache in my shoulder began to glow. Scratch a line, and then another, and then an arc to connect them. Another short line, rub a shadow where the color should be dark. But the pain continued to grow, a flower of pain, ultramarine, dark and beautiful, opening slowly, blooming. Where arm and shoulder met, a cobalt chrysanthemum of ache spread upward toward my neck. I studied its progression with an aesthete's curiosity. That pain spread like a vine's tendrils as I scratched one line after another. Reaching to mark a line at the very top of the canvas, the sudden throb of pain filled my eyes with tears. John could never have accomplished anything whose effort was so filled with pain.

The pain in my shoulder sank its teeth deep; it moved and grew until I could taste it on my lips, steely like that copper taste of blood. I became delirious with that taste, felt it break over me as a cresting wave, as if for a moment I might drown.

Outside my window a dog began to bark, then a child's voice cried out, "Shut up!" Suddenly all became quiet.

I lifted my arm once more to try again to make another mark, and instantly discovered that my arm had stiffened and had become impossible to move.

I stepped back away from the painting filled with the insane desire to laugh. What that little bit of sketching had accomplished was even more ugly than the pain itself. Had the heart from which that foul image sprung become gruesome as well? The world would be so much more beautiful if these paintings remained incomplete; and even more beautiful if they were destroyed. But perhaps most beautiful of all if they had never existed. It had all finally come to just these pieces of small disgrace.

Perhaps John had been right all along. And perhaps Donald and Martin as well. I had attempted to live in an impossible fantasy of energy and courage and youth which was as silly and vacuous as it was delusional. So perhaps in fact I really was fit only for a retrospective after all.

CHAPTER TWENTY–EIGHT

GRADUALLY I CAME to realize that Vincent was avoiding me. Perhaps he
had already spoken with John. Or perhaps he knew of John's plan and was
simply embarassed. But I admit I was surprised. I never thought he might
shun me so thoroughly. Yes, I was more than surprised, I was hurt. But
unquestionably I was also still alone.

When my supply of food was finally gone I forced myself to hobble to a
store; nearly two hours walking under that terrible sun and I could only return
with the most necessary things. But something had happened. A low-pitched
hum from deep within my chest was suddenly remarkable by its silence.
After that excursion I did not leave the apartment. I do not know why this
happened; I did not even go out to sit beside the pool.

I remained confined to the apartment as if there was some urgent reason to
sit beside my failed and humiliating canvases. Perhaps I suspected they might
suddenly begin to paint themselves. As if brushes laden with paint might fly
up and begin daubing at the canvas. And as I stared at those frames, images
within unfolded themselves like flowers exposing opportunities, variations,
changes of color and line. Fragments like fallen leaves fluttered past my eyes
as if driven before the wind. But this profligacy of images with their lavish
dissipation of color and line, itself gradually became urgent and demanded to
be resolved. So I felt compelled to return to those paintings, to take up a brush

and try once again. But with each attempt I was driven away and back to my pencils and my fury and despair. Thus, those paintings merely grew more ugly in their feverish confusion.

I slept only three or four hours each night. When I was not asleep or staring at the paintings, I drew with pencil and paper. Sketches continued to accumulate. The sight of that stack of drawings gave me some small bit of relief. John's deadline to choose canvases for the exhibition drew near. And with its approach I became desperate to get on with the painting, even at the risk of creating ugliness, and even without the presence of April.

But without the assistance of Marla, as well?

As with Vincent, I had not heard from Marla since we had had our talk about April. My attempts to contact her failed and she had not called me. This I found even more unsettling. I had believed it would have been otherwise. I was convinced she had heard about Donald's flight, yet she had not called me. And so, abandoned in this way, days passed when I could not face even the necessity to find her. Yet in the end I discovered I had no choice but to continue to try.

When I picked up the telephone, afternoon sunlight had begun to slide through the parting of the draperies to cast a strip of wet yellow light across the brown rug. I listened to the inflection of the buzzing as the telephone rang in her room. And I listened even to the hissing, crackling silence between each chirping buzz. So her sudden voice startled me.

I stumbled about the point. "You have heard about Donald. You know he is no longer helping me. I am embarrassed to ask this, but I need your help; I need an errand."

To my surprise I discovered relief in her voice, or was that simply a quality of the device? "What's been going on?" she asked. "How are you making out?"

"I need a few things, just a few. I will be happy to pay you for them when you arrive." Filled with my own relief I did not ask her any questions, about anything. And by her response she seemed genuinely embarrassed, and this left me touched. Her apologies for having failed to have called sooner embarrassed me, and then I could ask no questions.

I asked her to bring a few simple things. She promised to bring all of it; I thanked her repeatedly before I replaced the receiver. Probably I smiled. Had I genuinely feared she might refuse my request? But I was chastened, reminded again how tenuous my existence had become and how dependent on others I remained.

Waiting for Marla's arrival I gathered together the most recent sketches, selected those I still found most satisfying. Was I once again foolishly optimistic? She and I might at least decide when she would resume work, if she still wished to work with me at all. But simply the arrival of those groceries would earn my gratitude.

I surveyed again those feeble canvases, and their tremulous lines and colors suddenly left me with a mild sense of vertigo. Some ordered shapeliness I had been certain they embodied suddenly evaporated. What remained was a disturbing luminosity; a conflict of colors and antagonisms of lines, contrasts and repulsions which denied every harmony. But I had experienced such confusion before, and I assumed would experience it again.

Among the few satisfactions suitable for an old man is to remember clearly what has been successfully survived and fortunately avoided. There had been times when I lived less comfortably, my reserve of perishables smaller, my energies pressed by more urgent demands. Time, in fact, when all seemed to hang as if by a thread. That entire year after Dedo's death. And then Berlin. And Paris during those months immediately before the Occupation. And of course those first two years living in New York.

New York: a series of lectures I delivered at the invitation of a friend to teach a night-class at one of the schools in Manhattan which enabled me to live in a cramped little below-ground apartment. About a dozen faces over three evenings each week. I had been invited to lead a class in Art History titled The Artist as Citizen of the World. I had already decided to return to Paris at the earliest opportunity and try to make a new start. I had accomplished so little there that it no longer mattered to me whether I stayed or left that city since we were finished with each other. I came to the conclusion that only by returning to Paris could I recover whatever my work seemed to have lost. And so, the words I spoke in those lectures were simply those arguments that rattled through my head. Considering that their explication demanded so many evenings to explore, there must have been a great amount of noise to all of it. But somehow I managed to pique the interest of at least one student.

The student's name was Allen. He was a dancer with a face as unremarkable as the others and who worked during the day as a waiter. Thin and young, a crop of unruly dark hair and with eyes so darkly circled he appeared ill. Hands as wide as dinner plates with long, tapered fingers, his hands would forever prevent him from dancing professionally. This he understood very well, and had resigned himself to. He introduced himself midway through the course and invited me to a restaurant nearby for coffee. He was eager to speak to me, he said, yet the timbre of his voice suggested I should have nothing to do with him. So, I went.

Through the window by our table I watched a November rain begin in a heavy mist, then thicken, quietly glazing cars and trash cans and the sidewalk beyond. He spoke slowly for a New Yorker, about himself and his aspirations and his difficulties as well. I listened to him as I watched men and women scurry, black-coated and glistening, across the hissing bright street. Suddenly he said, "I feel sorry for you."

I looked directly into his eyes, where I found a vicious sort of innocence, like a mildly-intended brutality. He was young, after all, and so deserved my patience. At his words I simply shrugged and looked away.

Large hands with folded fingers locked before him on the table, he leaned forward. In a whisper he said, "You really don't like it here. You really would rather be over there."

Again I could only shrug. He knew nothing, and I could not help him understand.

With a smile he continued, "You're really crazy. You're a famous painter, after all, and you could be making a lot of money. That isn't an option for the rest of us."

I did not resist the impulse to laugh. "I do not know who you have been speaking with, but obviously you have not spoken to my agent."

He leaned back with a bemused expression. Our shadowy restaurant was nearly empty. A short, balding waiter with a heavy black moustache sat several tables away smoking a cigarette, the evening newspaper spread on the table before him and a cup of coffee by his right hand. Allen waved his wide hand between us and said, "Don't kid me. So maybe you aren't as famous as Picasso or Matisse, but people buy your stuff just on your reputation. Sounds like a full bank account to me."

Should I have become angry? But that was impossible. I could only marvel at his ignorance; his impertinence must pass without comment. I simply laughed again.

"Don't laugh at me, I'm serious. What do you bother with giving speeches when you could be sitting in the sunshine in California or Florida. So maybe you have to paint once in a while; big deal." He sighed, lost for a moment in thought. Shaking his head in mild disbelief he said, "You just don't understand."

"And what is keeping you from going away to some place warm, where food grows on trees and everyone is young forever?"

"Don't worry," he said and smiled smugly. "I've got plans. I've been thinking a lot about going to LA to find some work in the movies." Then it was his turn to laugh with embarrassment. "But who am I kidding? That would take some dough. And connections never hurt nobody, ever." He leaned forward then, eyes suddenly bright. "But you've got some dough, or you could get it quick enough. Just sell a few paintings. And you know the right people. This is a free country. Anybody can go anywhere they want. So why not go someplace where it's warm?" He shivered then, his look darkened and he glanced out our window to the street.

The rain continued to fall in a kind of monotony that is reassuring and even comforting in the proper frame of mind. It was a kind of rain I felt comfortable with, though it brought to mind the anguish of Berlin. People walked quickly along the sidewalk and crossed streets leaning forward in that street-lighted darkness with their shoulders hunched, as if burdened with precious secrets. I found myself in the wrong frame of mind to find that rain comforting. At the end of the lunch-counter of our restaurant, a burly man in work clothes stared off into space as he stirred his coffee, his spoon pinged brightly with each turn in the cup. Perhaps he too was thinking of another land warm and sunny and younger than this, and he a younger person within it.

I asked Allen, "So that is your dream? Because it has nothing to do with dancing or acting or art. There is only money to be made while you have nothing you feel compelled to say. You do not need to dance or to perform for others. Perhaps your deepest need is merely to go somewhere warm and sunny and accumulate a pile of money." I smiled though my own question left me feeling suddenly empty and sad.

I expected Allen to become angry, but instead he leaned back and laughed. "That trick is too old to be any good. We were talking about you, never mind what I want. You poured out all that horse manure in class about what it had been like back in the Old Country as if you thought we would take all of it seriously. Now let's talk real serious. You've got enough to go anywhere you want. So what's the scoop? You want to make a big splash? Go back there, back to that Old Country, and you'll just get swallowed up and disappear, and you know it. But if you stay here, or you go south or out west, maybe you don't fall off the face of the earth to disappear into the void. You see what I'm saying?"

"And perhaps a big splash is exactly what I wish to avoid. Perhaps what I want is to fall off the face of the earth and disappear into the void. Simply walk away and never be missed."

His eyes narrowed. "And all that stuff about the world and the artist, that's all just hokum for the locals? Something for the old ladies on their weekly outings?"

"You mean that I am merely a hypocrite, as opposed to being a fool. You believe I say things I do not mean, and mean what I do not say."

Embarrassment reddened his face. "I never said that, and I never would. Somebody who misunderstands their own motives isn't necessarily a hypocrite."

"No," I said, "he is worse; he is a fool."

Again Allen laughed. "For an old guy you're pretty tricky. So let me put it another way. You won't be starting over by going back there. You could start over from a million places, but not by going back to where you started. If you wanted to start over, the place you left is the last place you should go."

He paused. Caught by his suggestion I said nothing. He shrugged, animation left his face. I said, "There is a great secret you have not heard, which is that no one is permitted to start over. Life is not a musical score where one can repeat a difficult cadenza and then continue. Only Americans believe in renewal. At best, one can attempt to remember what has been forgotten. For me that might prove useful, and perhaps even valuable. But to remember that which has been forgotten demands a return to the site which has been forgotten."

Allen made a sour face. "Forgetfulness is a blessing and don't kid yourself. What you need is to remember less. Go someplace where everything is new and you'll recognize what you need to do. Memory is more than just a trap, it's a cage. Go someplace where you can paint without memory, someplace where you can paint without fear of remembering."

"Like Gauguin in Tahiti?" I laughed.

Allen's eyes darkened. "Go ahead and laugh, but the joke's on you. You need a place where your memories can't get at you. Go back to Europe, and the best you can hope for you'll start painting just like you used to. So you paint for a couple of years and finish a few canvases, but eventually you'll remember what you ought to forget, and then you'll discover you've become sick of yourself."

I leaned forward, brought my face to within inches of his. "And you will promise me that if I do not go back there, if I go somewhere else, I need never fear becoming sick to death of myself. You can promise me this?"

He studied me for a time, and we stared into each other's eyes. Finally he leaned forward until our chins nearly touched, and he smiled. "You have my promise," he said quietly. "I guarantee it." We studied each other a moment and then I smiled because at that moment I very nearly believed him.

Sudden knocking at my apartment door startled me awake. My head was thick and caught between moments. I stood, tottered unsteadily against the end of the couch and eventually made my way to the door. The rapping repeated impatiently.

Through the open door sunlight exploded piercing my eyes. Surrounded by that sunlight a blue-black shadow stepped into my doorway, an instant of darkness, and then the sunlight returned. Marla appeared beside me, arms overflowing with brown paper bags.

"Were you asleep?" she asked with bright humor. "I knocked. I wasn't sure you were even still home." She laughed, delighted to be the source of my confusion. "Really; you look like you just woke up. You look really terrible."

She shifted from side to side, a slithering figure in the half-light, sniffing the air with disapproval. She struggled to balance the grocery bags in her arms. I reached out to take one from her. Her eyes narrowed on my hand and she turned away. "I can handle this," she said moving unsteadily toward my table. I turned to follow. Suddenly from behind us came another voice. "Where do want the rest of these?"

She was a black silhouette with a single grocery bag balanced on one cocked hip. My eyes were still useless against all of that blinding light and found only a black oval where her face would be. But the shape of her leg, the squareness of that shoulder leaning against my door frame, the hip rolling out from under the bag.

"Over here," Marla called out, "by the refrigerator. Did you bring the keys from the truck?"

April stepped across my threshold and into my apartment without turning to look at me. To Marla she said, "Sure," while she changed the bag awkwardly to her other arm, her free hand digging into her hip pocket. The bag shifted suddenly, tipped away from her hip. A cascade of red and white cans, shinny bags, boxes in yellow and pink, and a big blue can of coffee; all of it tumbled from the top of the bag and scattered across the brown rug. Marla leaned down and began to gather the things muttering while April laughed with short, bright whoops. She said, "I can't believe I'm so clumsy."

"Don't just stand there laughing," Marla said, but she had already gathered nearly all of the objects and set them on my counter. When I mentioned that nothing appeared to be broken, Marla shivered me with a glance. After a moment she made the formal introductions. She concluded by saying, "And April has some modeling experience."

"Yes," April said, "I've posed a lot."

Masking a trembling in my chest I said, "And I am pleased to hear this."

"I studied ballet when I was a little kid," she said. Then in rapid succession she assumed badly the first four positions. "Kept at it until high school. Mom wanted me to go to Hollywood. She says I look just like Gene Tierney." She looked at me with great seriousness, her large eyes so deeply brown I might have fallen forward. "Do you think I should have stayed with it?"

"Take any cooking lessons?" Marla asked. April turned to answer, but then Marla asked me, "How are you feeling? It's just so weird about Donald. Heard anything more from him?"

I shook my head. "I hoped you might know something. He was here such a short time that morning."

Marla's eyes widened. "So you haven't heard the latest?"

Returned by the closed door to its twilight the room gradually returned to focus. I sat down in a chair beside the table. April walked about the room ignoring us and instead peered intently at each painting, as if recognizing that there was something in each which needed to be deciphered or unraveled. She moved with confidence and self-assurance, with an unshielded curiosity, a woman of evident intentions. Was I already in love, or had I always been? To Marla I said, "Tell me what you've heard."

"Before we do that, you should have one good meal. When was the last time you ate something hot beside a cup of coffee?" With an annoyed look at April she continued, "The painting can wait one more day. We all could use a good meal." Her display of competent hospitality surprised me; a combination of the proprietary and the common-sensical. Was she just a bit afraid of April? Because now, sitting so close to her as she prowled around the room, there was something fearsome about her. Long firm legs moving fluidly, graceful variations of the tempo of her steps, her shoulders and hips moving in some liquid harmony. Yes, she had most certainly been a dancer. And she might well have gone on to Hollywood. Or so I believed that afternoon, within that soothing twilight.

From behind me Marla said, "And she agrees with you, too. April's sure she'll be a perfect model for you."

At the mention of her name the muscles in April's calves and thighs flexed, tightened and rose to the surface of her skin in beautiful striations, but she said nothing.

To April I said, "You make a very kind offer. But it is difficult work, as you already well know. It would demand a considerable amount of your time."

She continued to roam among the canvases offering no sign she had heard me. But suddenly she announced, "I see exactly what you want here. It's pretty clear where these are going." She turned to me then, a glistening watery smile. "Honestly, I'm sure I can help."

Marla sighed loudly. "While you're at it, I could use a hand here, too."

"Jesus, Marla, you're just such a drip." April shook her head and set her long hair swaying.

"She's right," I said to Marla. "Just when my work is being so sensitively understood, you intrude with a mundane question about food." I could not keep the pleasure from my voice. I wanted to sit back and enjoy their raillery, their camaraderie, an empty-headed pleasure, along with the unlikely possibility that something useful eventually might be accomplished. "Forget about dinner for the moment. Just a little painting; the canvas of the swimming pool."

April's grinning approval seemed to ignite Marla's fury. To me she said, "Do whatever you like, but I'm making dinner and then I'm going to eat it. And then I'm going home to do my own work. But first I'm going to eat because I'm hungry. Besides," she said turning suddenly to me, "you might want to think about this just a little more."

Suddenly my anxiety turned to annoyance. "For eight months I have thought of nothing except this." My anger rose as gracelessly as a bubble. "And now Donald is gone. What else is there for me to think about?"

Marla studied my face, her eyes racked mine, and then she turned back to the counter, more womanly than I had ever seen her. With a flurry of noisy activity she began opening packages and taking down pots.

April watched us with undisguised amusement. I turned to her and asked, "What more has been heard concerning Donald?"

April began to laugh, but Marla spoke first. "Don't listen to her." She then made even more noise preparing our meal. "Other people's problems just make her laugh."

Glancing at the counter and its clutter, April said, "All this talk and none of these have been opened yet." She lifted one of the bottles of wine from the paper bag.

Taking her suggestion I told her where the glasses were kept. She brought three down and I took the bottle and the cork-screw from the table. I said, "This is something I still can do myself." Marla smirked.

With glasses full I turned to Marla. "Now tell me what you have heard about Donald."

She laid small steaks in a frying pan. Fork poised at near eye-level as she watched them she said, "John just about exploded when he found out. He called the girlfriend a fool, told Vince she was likely pregnant by somebody else anyway, and was just blaming it on Donald. Then he threatened to sue Donald for the money he'd already been paid for his fellowship; something to do with breach of contract."

April laughed. "I should feel sorry for him."

I glanced at Marla and she shrugged. I could only sigh and shake my head. I endured a sudden sympathy for both of these men over their peculiar delusions. "Things like this sometimes work out; blessings in disguise so to speak. With a wife and child, perhaps Donald will finally discover himself. Such responsibilities sometimes quicken our maturity."

Forking the steaks over, Marla laughed mirthlessly. "Sounds like something my stupid father would say." Before I could add more to my own embarrassment we sat down to the meal she had prepared.

As we ate together I thought more about Donald, but our meal passed without further mention of him. Later over coffee Marla and I discussed how best to complete the paintings. April seemed to take no interest, and only looked up when her name was mentioned and her role was discussed.

As we spoke I wondered if April recognized her importance to these projects. I watched her secretly, the way she held her shoulders poised over her coffee cup, the way her fingers curled gracefully around her cup's handle while her free hand rested carelessly on the table beside her wine glass. Eventually, perhaps from boredom, April stood and wandered about the room again. With furtive glances I studied the profile of her body. Watching her now, I doubted that Marla had explained to her how eager I was that she model. But finally April and I had met, and I would not part from her, not from frustration, nor anger, nor even boredom. I asked if she thought there would be time for her to sit every day.

"Well," she said, "maybe not every day." She turned to Marla then as if hoping for help. Marla said nothing, and this seemed to confuse April.

After another moment of baffled silence Marla stood. "I should start these dishes." But here I stopped her. Offering multiple and infinite gratitudes, I thanked her for bringing the food and preparing our meal, and most emphatically for having finally introduced me to April.

April stood with Marla and reminded her that she needed a ride home. I said, "You lived so long on the other side of our swimming pool, yet I had to wait until you moved away before meeting you." April responded with a flattered smile and offered her hand. I leaned forward gallantly and kissed it. Watching us, Marla laughed. I walked with them to my door, my body feeling suddenly twenty pounds heavier and yet stronger. And then I discovered myself grateful that they had decided to leave. It seemed as if I had not slept in days, and only their presence and my hospitality toward them had prevented me from falling asleep instantly.

When they were gone and I closed my door, I went to the sink and began the wash-up I had denied Marla. The hot water running over my fingers soothed their sore joints and loosened my hands. But before I had finished half of the dishes I put it aside and began to draw.

These sketches came quickly, drawings of April's face and head from memory, and I could have continued for the rest of the night.

There are still times when certain images come so smoothly and with so little effort, I begin to believe that every reflex has prepared for precisely their lines. I no longer remember how long I drew that night, since each line seemed to demand another. I drew until the heaviness in my head, from wine and food and perhaps the surprise of April's appearance too, slowly drew a veil over the paper. My body felt slack, a sack of something with a weak heartbeat. The rest, I decided, would wait because tomorrow would be there for everything unfinished today.

CHAPTER TWENTY–NINE

. . . AN OCEAN OF BROKEN GLASS, sky raining needles, raining diamonds, come out monsters, out serpents, out dragons, my blade is sharp, my bow stout, my arrows true, come out where I can see you, come out where we may converse, come and test my heart, my dry weary heart, come out and raise my lust, flex your hoary spines, clasp me in you talons, sink your teeth into my withered scrawny neck, come bathe my face with your acid breath, test my sad arms, my wheezing chest, that I may thrust, thus and thus and here again, that I may cut and slash there and there, spilling your thick red blood, your yellow and green bile, come to me snarling with rage, bellow and shake these mountains, weaken my heart with your fury, flush with despair, snarling, snarling, come test my shield and my will, come and shake this earth, change the course of rivers, raise mountains, churn even the deep cold sea, see my blade, see the firelight glint from my cold steel, and this groaning earth, watch these blue devils leap from cliff to cliff and spout red as blood to sheath these my tired shriveled arms, my veins rising like the ropes of a billowing sail, roar behemoth, shake the sky into the sea, shake the trees from the hillside, shake the mountains and watch them tumble down, for I fear nothing, my arrows fly more swiftly than you can see, my bow hurls them uncountable to the heavens, my blade cuts what it tastes, I fear neither you nor your demons, those minions, your servants, your henchmen, though they roar like ten thousand winds my shield shines bright and huge, it frightens the sun, serpents swift as death, my arrows fly more swiftly, your devils and dragons groan, bellow, rage, while my saber singing, singing, singing through your black thick air and sulphur heat, blazing heat and burning light, and my arrows singing across chasms, across oceans, across worlds, singing their song to entice you out, come out, come out where I can see you, show yourself, face my withered chest, my fading heart, my tottering knees, my bleary eyes, test these my dry and brittle fingers and spindly arms, can they hold this shield against your mighty blasts, come out where I shall tempt you, come out, I am here where you have wished so long and at your mercy with only my mighty sword, my terrible shield, my vicious arrows, come and look, this miserable mortal awaits you, has awaited you all eternity, waiting for your ivory fangs and steely claws to pierce my chest, to rip out this feeble heart and devour every bit, lap every drop of this thin tepid blood, crush each bone, tear every wiry sinew, I am here and I am unafraid, my arrows tremble like stallions at the course, like dogs at the scent of the deer, my blade leaps to my hand, monsters come out, I am prepared, I await you, come out demons black as night, come out serpents green vicious and wise, you will never see my back, I await you without fear, I am here and I am waiting and I will not flee, I will not move from this spot, come out and we will play, come out bullying coward that we may play, you will be my plaything and we will play, come out, come out, come out . . .

I awoke to what seemed a single sound that then became two.

Someone pounded noisily at my front door, while my telephone rang with the insistent regularity of a pulse.

My head felt twice its normal size and several times its normal weight, too large and too heavy for my skinny, sore neck. When I flexed my legs determined to stand they seemed thicker and even heavier than my head, and wished to move less than I did. I pulled on a shirt and trousers, nearly stumbled picking up the angry telephone. I lifted the receiver saying, "Wait a moment," and then set it on the floor.

When I opened my door, Marla and April stood side by side, not quite blocking the sunlight. I motioned them inside and returned to the telephone on the floor.

Vincent's voice was hushed and for a moment I did not recognize it. "Listen carefully, it's about John. His wife Janet just called from the hospital. He's had a heart attack and they don't know how bad yet. She says he's resting now but they won't know how much damage for a few days." He paused before he added, "His heart stopped twice during the night."

April wandered idly through the apartment, but Marla watched my silent attention with curious eyes.

"I need your help," Vincent continued. "At least until we know how serious his condition is."

"Have you called anyone else?" I suppose it was the tone of my voice that caused April to turn to look at me. Marla moved her lips as if to ask, "What is it?" I ignored them both.

Vincent continued, "Call the others in the department and let them know what's happened. I'm going to the hospital, probably will stay until noon. I'll find out what I can." April sat down on the couch beside Marla and they watched me.

I said, "Of course. Call me when you have more news."

"That'll be fine," Vincent said. His voice was empty and dry as if his message had demanded all of the strength he possessed.

"And tell Janet we are thinking of her. Do that for me, please."

"Of course I will. She'll appreciate that from you."

The telephone clicked and then I replaced the receiver. From the couch, four eyes like hands reached out to touch my face. "John's in the hospital. A heart attack last night."

April's eyes filled suddenly with tears, and she began to tremble. Marla reached her arm around her shoulders. April sobbed, and then she stood. Marla reached for her arm but April brushed her hand away, rushed through my door slamming it behind her. Marla's eyes rested on the closed door and she sighed.

Suddenly she turned to me, eyes bright with tears, and glared angrily at me. I was startled. She looked about the apartment as if words might be painted on the walls or scattered across the floor, or perhaps under something, hidden and just waiting. "This is just terrible," she said while her fingers clawed at the knees of her jeans.

Silence filled my apartment and thickened around us. Even our breathing became measured and constricted. I watched Marla while I thought about April and that look in their eyes of shock and pain.

Marla sighed as if emptied of every breath and looked away. "For a while I thought there might be something between them. But she doesn't talk about those things." She smiled weakly. "Does that surprise you?"

It was my turn to shrug. "Discretion is a virtue and precious to every friend."

She shook her head. "I was with them a couple of times, watched them talking or standing near each other. They just acted like interested strangers; no sixth sense about the other's thoughts." Her voice trailed off smothered by other thoughts.

"Would it make sense to you if they had been lovers?"

After a long pause Marla smiled. "Why should it?" She looked up, eyes larger, sharper. A wicked smile appeared. "I guess they'll have to suspend plans for your exhibition. I'd be relieved right now if I was in your shoes."

Cut by Marla's suggestion I said, "I wanted the man to stop the exhibition, but I never wished him harm." Her smile faded and she looked away.

"This is terrible," she muttered. "I'd better go after her." She stood. "I can't leave her wander around, she'll need a ride home." At the door she stopped but did not turn. "Call if you need anything. I'll stop by tomorrow." She closed the door then, without slamming.

There was coffee and bread, and for these at least I was relieved. And now there were things to do, phone calls to make, arrangements. And another large cup of coffee. Contemplating all of this, my hands lay in my lap like dead fish, as if they knew the day would not end until very late, and nothing would be accomplished except the reminder that nothing is ever truly accomplished and only dissolution is delayed.

I sat for a time expecting the telephone to ring again and wondered whose voice I would hear through it. And I imagined John lying under a plastic tent of oxygen at the center of the turmoil of the critically ill, while Janet and Vincent hovered nearby. And I wondered about Janet and Vincent, their bedside vigil in that sparkling white room. Did sunlight filter through thin white draperies? Did that sunlight touch John's hands as they lay motionless and half-uncovered like small sleeping animals?

The most difficult telephone calls were to those who had already heard the news. They needed to talk about John so that they could demonstrate how badly they felt. They demanded I reassure then that I felt as they did. As thought we needed to affirm how important he was to us, and how terrible all of this was. As if any of us has ever been exempt from sudden extinction.

With all of these calls finally made I waited for Vincent's call. Gradually I detected an odd sensation; I began to envy John. I came to wonder if perhaps there was an unlikely pleasure to an illness such as his. A forced confinement that absolved one of every effort. But news of his illness had reminded me how small my own life was and how trivial my designs. All of the dead I have come to know, killed in battles or automobiles, dying in hospitals or alleyways, and all of those funerals hardly anyone alive still remembered. And I was reminded as well that even in death we remain disguised even to those forces which bind our misery. Affirmation of death's inevitability is impossible to sustain; it fades under the eradicating sunshine of daily events. The inevitability of death is something one must sink one's teeth into if one wishes to derive its value. After all, what might happen if we forgot that inevitability? Imagine any of us capable of forgetting death. Who knows what we might become capable of doing?

When finally the telephone rang, my arm shot out for it as if it was dancing about. "Ah," the voice said, "and I was afraid you would not be at home." Hearing Martin's voice provided an oddly comforting relief.

I said, "You call at a terrible time. Our department chairman has fallen seriously ill. Just last night. He is now in hospital."

Martin remained silent while I told him what had happened. Finally he said, "And this man is so young."

"Compared to antiques such as we." Embarrassed silence bloomed between us and I waited for him to ring off. But suddenly he said, "I will be in San Francisco tomorrow. I had hoped to visit. See how you are getting along. It has been such a long time."

"Affairs are in such turmoil I cannot predict when I will be free. You see my position."

Martin's silence was sentimental and oppressive, like a quiet but continuous moan. I was about to remind him that I was waiting for Vincent's call when Martin suddenly asked, "Do you remember Ralph Millar's funeral?"

"Of course," I answered, saddened and furious that Martin would remind me.

After a long pause he added, "It was a lovely funeral. I know that it has become a cliché, but Catholic funerals always are. When I am buried I want a Catholic funeral; incense, chanting Latin, all of it." I could add nothing. I have never attended a beautiful funeral. He said, "Just you and I were there, you remember? In the cold rain, just you and I and the fat priest."

"Yes," I said, remembering Ralph's many relatives and friends as well. But that was not the funeral Martin wished to remember.

"I paid for his funeral out of my own pocket. No one else had the money, I suppose. Those were very hard times. So I paid for his funeral."

"Yes," I said, because that part was true, but for the wrong reasons.

"People say I was unkind to Ralph. Do you remember?"

"People are often wrong."

"I did everything I could for the man, so ungrateful. He was a fine painter, and I recognized that. No one else would touch him, such a madman he was. But I handled his work and I did well for him."

"You are right, Martin."

"Tessman threw him out of his gallery. You were there, you know what kind of man he was. No one would touch him, but I took him in."

"People forget these things. Time does that to people."

Martin paused, and I wondered if he might be drunk. "It was cold and the rain would not stop. You and I beside the black mud of his grave. And the fat little priest chanting Latin."

"In the face of death, all life is bleak." In our deepening silence I heard Martin sigh several times.

"Do not die, my friend; make me this promise. I dislike funerals on the whole."

"Only if you will make the same promise to me."

Thus we sat, two old men thousands of miles apart feeling sorry for ourselves but not for each other.

Finally in a brighter voice Martin said, "Remember, when you wish to dispel the gloom, call me." Then he added, "I know I should drive out to see you, to see how you are getting along. An obligation to an old friend."

When I did not respond he sighed. "Ah well, perhaps next time."

I replaced the receiver feeling as if my fingers had stiffened around it. And still I had not heard from Vincent. I stood to pour another cup of coffee. But before I reached the refrigerator, the telephone rang.

"Any news?" the voice asked. I did not immediately recognize it. "April," she said. "Have you heard anything more?"

"Where are you? Give me your number and I'll call when there is news."

She hesitated. "I'll call later," she said and hung up.

In the early afternoon Vincent finally called. "He's been moved to intensive care, but it's still touch and go. The doctor says the attack was massive but he thinks John'll pull through."

The relief I felt was genuine.

Vincent continued, "I've talked with the vice-provost. John's going to be out for a while. He suggested I prepare to take over the chairman's duties temporarily for the next semester."

I was only surprised by the casual tone of Vincent's voice. "Very prudent," I said. "You will need some time to put things in order."

"It's the least I can do, and John seems to be out of trouble for the moment."

"I will pass along the information about John's condition. It is probably best if you wait to announce your temporary appointment."

"After a week," Vincent added, "we'll have a better idea how long he'll be away."

"Precisely what I was thinking. No point spreading confusion about a complicated situation."

Contacting the others was simple, as if each waited beside their telephone. Relief over John's condition seemed to erase curiosity. With that chore complete I tried to call Marla but had no response. I was eager to speak to her, to discuss plans for continuing the painting, and also to learn more about April.

Late afternoon sunlight cut past the living room curtains, and I heard no sounds from beside the pool. But by then I was exhausted. For a moment I was tempted to take my glass of wine and my cane out beside the pool to watch the changing sky as sunset approached. My years have assured me the sun sets on long, complicated days, just as it does on short simple ones. But I looked around the apartment at those paintings unmoved, unmarked and unattended. They leaned against the walls, mute and incomplete designs in an ancient tomb, a tomb with shattered walls and hieroglyphs never to be deciphered. What would have happened to those canvases if I myself had suddenly died? Ridiculous question; I have seen, I have been a witness. The unfinished canvas is simply another piece of trash. An incomplete thought, disemboweled, entrails dragging and displayed for all to see. What is missing is more important than what is accomplished. Some friend may cherish one for sentimental reasons. But those canvases leaning against the walls of my apartment, by their size alone, would have made such a gesture of remembrance impossible. Unfinished, those canvases were merely trash.

If they were to endure, my paintings must earn their right not to be destroyed. Not to have their stretchers broken, and then broken again, their canvas rolled and folded haphazardly, rolled a final time and then tied with thick twine into some ugly lump, the whole merely a pile of sticks and paint-spattered white cloth. If that was not to be their future, then those paintings had to be completed.

I poured a glass of wine. With that glass in hand I could do anything. I could even imagine myself still alive when those canvases were finished. A glass of wine beside an abandoned swimming pool in the soft and thick last light of day is a profound thing; a thing not to be ignored. I bathed myself in the certainty that something was about to happen. And that night, once again, I realized I would not die. Not yet, and perhaps not ever. Because if ever, then too soon.

The last light of that day was warm and thick, and I drank all of it.

CHAPTER THIRTY

LIGHT SHIMMERED above me as if I lay at the bottom of a pool of dark water. My body began to rise and the light ceased to shimmer. And then, after a time, I thought I might move about.

It had not been very good wine. Something cheap, no doubt fit only for derelicts. But with this pain I discovered humility. This pain made me wish to be a better person. With both hands anchored firmly to the nearest piece of heavy furniture, I stood. As I took my first step forward, my head was flooded with humility. I lifted the receiver from the telephone and dropped it to the floor. My only source of hope was the knowledge that soon there would be coffee. Moving a sufficient number of times over a short interval, eventually there would be coffee.

Gradually I rediscovered the existence of walls and floors. The floor stopped moving and for this I was grateful. Along the walls my canvases lurked vicious and bitter demanding human sacrifice, human blood, the screams and curses and tears of human victims. I must prepare myself to battle with demons today. Just as soon as there was another cup of coffee.

I had slept until very late and I had not dreamed of John.

When the knock came at my door I stood to answer. The door opened before I reached it and Marla let herself in. She peered around the room, morning light behind her bright and dry. "Don't you lock your door?"

"And would you have waited for an answer?"

"Sorry." She remained in the doorway. "Am I interrupting anything?"

"Yes, my hangover. Come in and shut the door."

"I thought you liked the sunlight." Her voice hinted at smiling malice.

"Your amusement is not shared. Come in or get out, but shut the door."

The door closed and the room went blessedly dark. She approached the table. I said, "Something has put you in a playful mood."

"I tried a couple of times to call you but the line was busy. I came to see if you had heard anything." She stood beside my chair unbending, one hand rested easily on the edge of the table. I felt a space in my chest like a bubble the size of a loaf of bread.

"He is resting comfortably," I said. "Vincent spoke to me briefly late last night." The pain in my head glowed. I rubbed the muscles of my bony skull trying to erase it. "I have left the telephone off the hook all morning. Today John must live or die without me."

She walked to the telephone, leaned down and replaced the receiver in its cradle. When she sat down in the chair at my table I offered her coffee. She shook her head. "Already had too much." I smiled remembering Donald using the same words. I sipped from my cup. Marla reached into her bag saying, "Do you have an ashtray?" She brought out a package of cigarettes. I had never seen her smoke before. I reached to the counter, brought over a small saucer. She lit the cigarette and began to smoke as her eyes traveled everywhere about the apartment except at me. Whatever compelled her thoughts remained her secret. I sipped my coffee watching her. When finally she stubbed the cigarette out she said, "April's pretty upset. Isn't there anything I can tell her?"

My address book was on a small table near the telephone. I opened it to Vincent's home number and handed it to her. "Call him," I said. "He should still be at home. Unless he's been called again to the hospital."

To her look of confusion I said, "Just tell him who you are and that you are calling for me."

She dialed carefully, as a child might, and I had never seen her so uncertain. The pain in my head moved back to the top of my skull. She spoke quietly and then listened. She repeated her telephone number, assured him she would be grateful to be kept informed.

When she had hung up I asked, "Would Vincent know anything about a relationship between April and John?"

Marla returned to the table with a curious and devious expression. "The oddest people know about the oddest things, but no one's called her to give her news."

I said, "Which proves nothing except that he is capable of discretion." Her eyes locked onto mine and would not leave. Our jousting had brought back my headache. I yawned and stretched trying to force the light-headedness away. I asked, "Have you gotten work done on your own canvases recently?"

She shook her head. "April's had me running in circles." She smiled unpleasantly. "I can guess what you old guys find so attractive about her."

"Such a thing should not be difficult to understand." I laughed and immediately regretted it. Marla's weak smile was not reassuring. "But tell me what it is that keeps old men like me chasing at this woman's heels."

She stood. "Look, I'm sorry. It's all my fault we've gotten off on the wrong foot here. I'm just so tired. I didn't come here to argue. I came to find out about John and how you are. When you're ready to go back to work let me know."

I said, "My intentions never change."

With her arms folded she paced the room. Her eyes moved over the canvases one after the other, and then returned to the table. "This will be a lousy day to try to work. How about tomorrow around eleven? Okay?"

"That will be fine," I said. She picked up her bag and walked to the door. I said, "Do you think April will help us tomorrow."

She turned on me suddenly. "How should I know? I'll see what she says. But what if she can't make it? Suppose she never comes back? What if she decides you're a creepy old man and your paintings stink?"

Half furious Marla watched me as I shook my head. "Impossible. In any case, no one is so precious to my art that the work would crumble without their assistance. No one is so important. And that is how it should be. Do you agree?"

After a pause she smiled briefly, a flash of her lips, and then she opened the door. A shaft of white light slashed through the apartment, Marla hesitated at the doorway. Without turning she said, "Tomorrow at eleven. And please don't be hung-over."

When she was gone I felt a vast relief, something I had never felt about her departure before. As the sound of her retreating footsteps died, an ugly lump of remorse filled my throat. Again I felt the void of Donald's absence. I wondered if anyone had contacted him about John's condition. The telephone sat bleakly across from me. Its simple miserable desolation appalled me.

Black is the only appropriate color for all telephones. A telephone of any other color is merely disguised to make its monstrosity more appealing, to disguise its viscous hostility and allow it into the center of family life. A telephone should not be made in any other color except black, unless it is made transparent so that each of its tiny mechanical devices appears naked and exposed. By this we would at least be assured that our loved ones are not locked inside, not its captive, and that they remain just as distant and just as untouchable. A telephone is a toad-like horror and it is appropriate that it remain forever black.

As I stood and went to the canvases I lifted the receiver again from its cradle and dropped it to the floor. In this way I hoped that its fangs had been removed and that it would remain tomb-like in its silence.

CHAPTER THIRTY–ONE

MARLA DID NOT RETURN that next day. Two more days passed and then Vincent called to say that John remained in serious condition but that he had stabilized. "I've spent a lot of time with Janet," he said, and I heard a dazed exhaustion in his voice. And something else as well that made me stare at the wall and imagine his eyes. "I don't know how she does it. John squeezed her hand this morning. Her eyes filled with tears." Vincent paused. "He'll need a lot of rest so Waterson has asked me to take over administrative details at the office. Projects are being delayed, including your show." With another pause he chuckled. "I'm sure you won't complain about that."

His voice trailed off then as if by these words he and I had entered into a conspiracy. As usual my embarrassment was overwhelmed by my clumsy stupidity. I asked what chance there was for the retrospective to be cancelled.

He sighed loudly into the telephone. "Maybe fifty-fifty? Even after John gets back he might be tired of fighting that fight. On the other hand, the University might decide not to continue him as chairman. After all, he might have another attack? The University's spent a lot of money already on your retrospective. Arrangements have been made."

"Perhaps the administration could be convinced to support the display of new work instead."

"Who knows?" he said. Anger swelled in my throat. He continued, "If they decide there's no alternative, it would be better to risk a show of new work, rather than offer no show at all. Besides, if the money's already been spent, how else could they get it back? So maybe that's your best chance. John might decide to show your new paintings just to save his reputation with the University." Vincent's voice drifted off, empty and hollow.

I said, "You have heard that I have hired April to model."

His sigh was filled with impatient annoyance. He lowered his voice. "That's up to you. I'll tell you that others insist she's unreliable. So you only need to answer a single question. Are you sure you're ready to depend on her?"

"Is that also John's opinion?"

"These paintings mean a lot to you, so I'd expect you to take special care that they're completed." He paused. "I promised Janet I'd meet her at the hospital in twenty minutes. If anything develops I'll call you."

When I put the receiver down I felt as if I stood at the top of a mountain and filled my lungs with fresh air to their capacity, almost to the point of pain. Open the windows, pour a glass of wine and spend the day sitting beside the pool. Like a schoolboy whose headmaster has suddenly been taken ill, I reveled in an unexpected holiday and its serendipitous delight. If Marla had called just then I would have told her there would be no work today. Even if April had appeared beside her, I would have sent them both home. Fold the umbrella today and let the beautiful sun burn; I would enjoy a delightful fit of sunstroke. Blinded by sunlight and with my brain thoroughly baked, I would finally have been rendered unfit; incapable of any more art and teetering like John on the threshold of life itself. Perhaps among those sturdy-muscled young men beside our swimming pool there might be one so kind as to toss me into it. Allow me to drown, let all of that pale blue water close over my head, let that bitter chlorinated water rush into my throat, into my lungs until it has filled my chest. Just two or three quick breaths of that sparkling, acrid water and watch as the world turns from green to pale blue to blue and then black.

There were few people surrounding our swimming pool, and none of them looked at me with enough interest to rescue me from that life I found myself encased within and burdened by.

I found a table where the umbrella had not been put up, sat down in a chair that faced the sun and allowed that sun to shine down upon me full and hot. Its light burned through my sunglasses, through my closed eyes and glowed red against the insides of my eyelids, soothing me while it exhausted me. Pearls of perspiration scalded my upper lip, a single drop from my scalp raced past my ear and down to my chest.

There would be enough time. Finally I was certain the time available to me would be sufficient. Soon there would be April. Though I had not heard from Marla and had no idea when April might return to help us, there still would be time. Work would continue and advance, but finally those paintings and their images would reach completion. And for hours and hours, standing motionless and calmly beautiful, there would be April.

I opened my eyes and looked around our patio to recognize that without my realizing it, I had been abandoned. The patio was now populated only by unoccupied furniture. Fragments of sunlight glittered across the surface of the water chased by a warm, dry breeze.

Suffused with an oddly satisfied contentment, I stood and walked to the edge of the pool. This act demanded some complicated effort, but eventually I maneuvered myself to sit down on the edge of the pool, and there let down my old, ugly legs into its cool, blue water. From the water's surface a face shimmered back at me, twisted by the rippling water, an old turtle-headed face, drawn and hairless, undulating between knees as knobby as worn rocks. They looked so odd, those knees and their legs. I had known them so long, yet hanging there and the light working so wondrously, one could hardly have guessed how useless they were. Then I allowed myself to imagine I had no legs at all. Two stumps cut off below the knee just where that cool bright water was lapping. Like that match-seller of Montmartre who I would see on sunny afternoons fishing from the quay below Pont Neuf, sitting in the sunshine with his fishing pole and his pipe, and to one side his false legs removed. Legs lost at Ypres, or so I had been told, but he remained very jolly all the same.

The water felt good against my skin and surrounding those withered muscles. The sunlight and the warm dry air and the silence and all that cool water lapping just below my knees. This was something to enjoy alone and by itself, just this.

CHAPTER THIRTY–TWO

"VINCE HAS pretty much taken over the department," Marla said, but with such amused annoyance I turned to look at her. "He's practically moved his easel into John's office. Even the department's secretary types the notes for his class."

April had just gone but Marla had remained to revise the triptych of the swimming pool while I supervised. April's presence had left the air in my apartment charged and in motion, as if a beautiful trout had swum past just below the still surface of a pond. April and Marla had bickered and then argued, or at least It appeared to be an argument, and now I realized I was utterly confused by what I had witnessed. But for nearly two hours April had been there, and I had drawn her form. Rapid and unhesitating, my thin black lines had caressed her flesh again and again.

Earlier while I had awaited their arrival, I had paced the apartment, sharpened pencils, placed and then moved a large bowl of fruit, set out materials on my table, and otherwise behaved like a nervous teenager on a first date. I had moved the posing stool, arranged curtains searching for the direction of the light, looking constantly for what my eyes might see. I skittered from corner to corner, moving close to the walls, then to the center of the room, looking everywhere, a spider tending the threads of his web.

And then the knock at my door, and then they had arrived. No small talk, no idle chatter, Marla began immediately to set herself up. April turned to me unexcited and asked where she might undress. I pointed toward the bathroom and offered her a white dressing gown. As April closed the door I felt my hand begin to tremble, a tightness in my chest, a touch of vertigo as when one boards an airplane bound for some unknown country.

I gave Marla directions about the placement of the canvas, the selection of sketches to work from, a sequence of tasks as if I had already thought our session through. But it all amounted to just so much stalling. Had there been a plan, what difference could it have made? I prattled on with an anxiety-ridden chatter so that my mind would not go numb, and that my hand would follow my eye.

Soundlessly, white dressing gown slung indifferently from her shoulder, April strode across the room. She walked aware she was without covering, without disguise and as if she knew that no matter her nakedness, she could not offend the eye. Her step was determined, yet the movement of her hips and the way she held her shoulders betrayed an awareness of universal approval. Her movement was studied, the pace of her steps even, like a dancer moving across a stage, acknowledging her dominance of our space as a personal environment.

Was there a pleasure for her in this; some subtle enjoyment? As a dancer within her dance, had she discovered a more complete existence undisguised and fully conscious of her body? And as well, conscious of my desire for her. Just as much desire as is possible to desire.

At the posing stand she shrugged the robe off and laid it across a nearby chair.

She had said nothing, nor looked directly at me since she emerged from the bathroom. When she had perched herself on the stool she watched Marla move the canvas into position. April watched the canvas billow and shuddered at each of Marla's efforts without curiosity. Only after Marla and I had adjusted to her presence did April turn to look at us, her eyes met our eyes assured of our complete attention and approval, and my utter capitulation as well. She turned then to face me directly and smiled.

Marla sat to one side as I began to draw. Both the effort and its result were terrible. Suddenly I recognized I was no longer the observer, aloof, studying and judging. Marla and April now studied my movements, watched my hand as it trembled. My reaction so surprised me and was so unexpected I became discouraged and nearly frightened. With little of the sketch complete I was compelled to stop. I could no longer see.

I walked to the other side of the room. I described to April the posture I wanted, the placement of her right hand, her left foot, her left shoulder. She tried. I described it again, and then again. Several minutes went by and yet still I could not see it. Finally I stepped to her side. With these bony hands I took her flesh, molded her shoulder, her arm, the top of her hip, the back of her thigh; turned them and moved them until my eyes recognized the sensation of her flesh. Marla watched us with nervous suspicion. The moment my fingertips touched April, her body became rigid, her joints inflexible. But lightly with my fingertips I traced along her side. After that everything was all right, everything proceeded smoothly.

Bright highlights from the crests of her hip and shoulder glared under the near-bright sunlight, intensifying the contrast between tanned, frequently-exposed areas of legs, arms, most of her back, and the milky paleness of her breasts and pubis. I stared until my eyes ached, determined to force that contrast away, and to fix her form in my mind's eye. To intensify the continuity of her shape bathed in that thick light in order to burn her form directly onto the back of my eye, to fill my eye with her shape, and then to shift my eye to the blank, white canvas, and see glowing just perceptible on that white surface her body's blue outline perfectly proportioned and glowing just beneath my sense of sight. My hand then moved along that faintly blue line, followed that slightest tint of blue beneath the point of my pencil.

With each glance I took her body into my eye like a child takes a candy into its mouth, letting the tongue wrap around it, and then withdraw to savor, and then repeat to enjoy again. My chest trembled, as if I had not truly drawn in ages, as if until that moment my hand had been locked in ice. I tasted again the pleasure of merely drawing the line, violating the emptiness of the page to inscribe precisely what was there for me to see.

I did not notice the passage of time, or Marla's brooding silence. I simply turned to a fresh sheet of paper and drew again. When finally I suggested we rest, Marla stood and held April's robe for her. Marla then watched with dispassionate curiosity as April leaned and stretched her body dramatically, moaning over her purported stiffness and discomfort. Marla stared at April's body as if it might be made of more than clay and by other hands with unwise designs.

In the midst of our relaxation and adjustment, Marla suddenly announced, "Somebody has heard from Donald." I looked about, obviously confused. Seeing my confusion April smirked while she shook herself into the robe and then tied it tightly at her waist. To Marla she said, "Tell him what Vincent said."

The mention of Donald's name had startled me and caught me by surprise. Marla said, "Vince told me yesterday that one of his students had told him he'd seen Donald two weeks ago on a street in Pocatello."

April giggled unpleasantly. Marla repressed her smile and turned to glance at her. "He was with Barbara," Marla continued, "and this student of Vince's stopped them to say hello. He said that Donald seemed happy, but Barbara had said nothing. Then Barbara took a few steps ahead, and for some reason Donald took this guy aside and told him there had been no baby and that Barbara had never been pregnant." I watched Marla and April exchange smiles.

I said, "It seems odd to acknowledge something like that to a near-stranger on the street. Why would he confide something like that to anyone except a close friend?" I was so confused by what she said that I was compelled to stop drawing. I asked, "You say Vincent told you he heard this from one of his students?" Marla nodded, but my confusion was not eased. Something seemed wrong. I took up the pencil again and returned to my drawing.

In a mocking tone April said, "Maybe Donald's more desperate than you think. Maybe he's so unhappy he's ready to tell anyone. Maybe he's so sorry he left that he'll even talk about it to somebody he doesn't know." Her suggestion made as little sense as any other.

I continued to draw, improving the finish of a sketch I particularly liked, so that I had a reason not to look at either of them. I asked, "And why would this student communicate all of this to Vincent? And why would Vincent tell all of this to you, but not contact me?"

Marla said, "Vince knew I'd come here today. Maybe he figured it would be just as easy for me to tell you." Marla spoke without conviction, as if she might be repeating someone else's lie. But Vincent had decided not to tell me himself, and for a reason I could not guess.

I asked, "Do you think Donald knew all along that she was not pregnant, or do you think he has just discovered this?"

Marla spoke immediately. "He couldn't have known. And hadn't she insisted she didn't want him to follow her? So why would he do that if he knew she wasn't pregnant?"

I said, "If she did not want him to follow her she should never have told him she was pregnant. After all, that would be exactly the thing that would compel him to follow her."

April said, "I think she was pretending all the time because she expected that if he thought she was pregnant, he'd run away. Like any other man." She finished her remark with a sarcastic smile.

I said, "Perhaps she hoped he would follow her, and this was her way of testing him. If she told him she was pregnant and he followed her, then she would know what kind of man he was and whether she really wanted to have a child by him." I believed none of my words, but our speculation clearly captured Marla and April.

Then Marla laughed. "That's too clever for either of them. In any case it doesn't make much difference now. But if any of that was true, Donald's a bigger fool that even I thought."

"The difference is," I said, "if he did not know the truth, then he is one kind of person. But suppose he did know the truth, knew there was no pregnancy. Then we have another sort of question. Whether there was love or not, there was also Donald's sense of duty. Or worse, some sense of doomed inevitability. As if something had been written in the stars."

April stood and began to pace the room as she laughed softly.

I said, "He followed this woman because he loved her, of this I have no doubt. He sat at this table as we sit now, and he confessed all of this to me. And I continue to believe what he said. What difference could those reasons which we invent amount to so long as they enable us to do what we know needs to be done? True or not, he did what he did because he loved her. None of this seems complicated to me."

After a long silence Marla sighed loudly. "If it's true she isn't pregnant, I'll bet we see him soon enough."

I could only shake my head. "It was never the child he pursued, but the woman who would bear it and that life they all would share. Donald once assured me that Barbara could never willingly return to the place where she was born, but that is precisely where they are now. If she would not return to campus with him, what would Donald have returned to? Beyond his painting and his studies, Barbara and that child were to be his life. But John has already turned against him and now there is no child."

Marla shrugged. "His argument with John had nothing to do with Barbara or that baby. John turned on him because Donald would not agree to talk you into doing the show."

My surprise was genuine and complete. "Could John have believed Donald might convince me to agree?"

"What's the difference?" April barked suddenly. "Donald's gone. Besides, sooner or later he'd have gotten her in trouble. Men do that." April smiled bitterly. Marla stood from her chair without looking at her and walked to the window. My skin suddenly felt dry, the nerves beneath the surface as tender as if they had been burned. The vicious dismissal of Donald in April's voice surprised me and made me uneasy, as though I had heard something in her voice that was irreparably broken. It occurred to me then that we had rested too long, and now our rest had become unhealthy.

At my request Marla readjusted the canvas. April stretched cat-like, allowed the robe to slide from her shoulders and slip down her back to puddle about her ankles. She arched her arms as she turned from side to side, the muscles along her side rippled to her buttock. She began to laugh self-consciously, thoroughly amused by this role, her magnetism and her spell.

Marla again avoided looking directly at her. She moved the canvas, moved tubes of paint and rags and brushes. But April now watched her. She spied on Marla waiting to catch her looking. Perhaps she wanted to see what it was that Marla could not look at. That certainly was my curiosity.

I asked April to resume her earlier position. She pushed out her chest and angled her buttocks out, a silly parody of the position I had requested. We all laughed as I stepped to her side.

"Let me have your hand," I asked, then raised that hand high over her head. With my other hand lightly I caressed her breast, allowed my fingers to rest just beneath testing its weight. Marla looked at that hand in horror, as though it might have been a tarantula. April smiled with vague, confused amusement. When I released her arm, removed my hands from her flesh, she resumed the position I requested. Now Marla would not look at me, but turned back to the canvas instead.

As in the drawings, the most difficult problem was to bring her figure into proportion; to adjust the planes of color and leave a slight distortion to provide tension. With the charcoal I worked directly on the canvas, from light, tentative lines graduating to shapes that became firm. But even here, eventually I needed to ask Marla's help. Something continued to elude me; a shape that was there which I could not quite join. So I suggested that Marla try, in the hope she might catch that shape and fall into it. I watched her wondering if she really had drawn April before as she had claimed, or had her story been just that. And suddenly I recognized my own treason, my own disbelief and mistrust. But I had to acknowledge that I had tasted a new and revivified life in April's presence. But would Marla reach for her figure with assurance, and in one gesture capture it?

If Marla had reached for her figure she did not find it. The way she rendered April's form showed no skill or insight. Thus, my confusion only grew.

I asked for the charcoal and I resumed. Certain elements of her figure allowed me to work with some freedom. The other figures of the painting had been brought into a dispersion that only needed April's figure to be set into motion. I was tempted to simplify the volumes of April's back since they possessed their own seduction, a seduction I struggled against. Under that light her body possessed so much intimacy, and so much anticipation. What color was her smell, what texture could simulate her tender flesh. As if a pale yellow cloud of sweet incense arose where she stood. And that tremulous light caressed her, played over her contours and hollows to give her stillness a terrible motion.

Even with frequent periods of rest, after two hours April's fatigue became obvious, and my patience with her had evaporated. Twice I shouted at her, surprising us all. Marla had remained aloof, participating with her brush precisely and only as requested. But April had become tired and childish, whining alternated with foolish clowning. I had not expected her endurance to be infinite, but my thirst for her had not yet been satisfied. If we had continued, would April eventually have learned the art of patience?

When I announced that we had finished for the day April seemed to leap for her robe. Turning from side to side, she flexed her calves and thighs as she stepped. With the robe thrown over her arm she walked to the canvas, paced staring as though she was on the verge of understanding. Marla filled in around the figures, slowly building layers of color, working particularly around April's figure. April strode back and forth until I could no longer restrain myself from asking what the matter could be.

"What's this one supposed to be?" she asked without turning to look at either of us.

Smirking Marla said, "I thought you understood all of this. Didn't you tell me he's your favorite painter?" She laughed.

"And I suppose you understand it all." April attempted to hide her anger with a smile, but she had been stung. Marla had dug into her with some purpose in mind. Was it merely all fatigue? My painting had provided the arrows to carry forward an assault by my assistant upon my model. An attack launched over the question of whether there might be some secret hidden within the painting.

I said, "It is simply an image that has no story to tell, nor wisdom to impart. What more does it need to be?"

April laughed. "You expect me to believe that? You're serious about that? There's no story at all?"

"It isn't important, April," Marla said, no longer amused.

April was suddenly angry. "Wait!" she said. "This isn't just for very smart people. This isn't just for people who've been to college." She slipped her arms into the robe, drew it over her shoulders and tied it tightly about her waist. "Why insist it's all so mysterious?"

I was startled. I said, "But that is precisely what I want you to understand."

"Never mind." April remained annoyed and unappeased. "I don't care. Just forget it."

But now, I too was suddenly tired. Two hours of effort caught up with me in a moment and time had taken its toll. "Here," I said pointing impatiently to the canvas, "is the old but famous painter. And that is the chairman of the painter's academic department. And between them is the wild and beautiful model. It is she who attempts to thwart the schemes of the chairman to humiliate the painter. And that is the old but famous painter kneeling in gratitude to the wild and beautiful model after their victory. It is not much of a story, but it might make a very fine painting."

April looked over to Marla with sudden surprise, her surprise then melting into humor. She turned away and quietly began to laugh. Still laughing she walked to the bathroom. Even with the bathroom's door closed we could hear her quiet laughter, a series of eager, bright sighs, as if her laughter was a sort of breathing ailment, a sound that teetered between bitterness and charm. When finally she emerged fully dressed she had gained control of her breathing and was now clear-eyed with resolve. An edge had appeared around her mouth. She recognized finally that she did not know what she did not know, and that she no longer cared.

April walked up to me looking hard into my eyes. Nodding toward Marla she said, "She's been mad about John and me, even when there wasn't any reason to think badly of him. But she still says he's a bad guy."

"He is adulterous with his student," I said. "Whatever his charm, he is hardly virtuous."

April's eyes widened as if seeing me for the first time. Something I said had offended her. "This has to do with truth, you know," she insisted quietly.

"And what she's been saying just isn't true. She doesn't understand, not at all. I thought you would understand." She shook her head, and the disappointment in her gesture was heart-breaking. "I thought someone with your experience would understand."

"And do you understand?" I asked. "Or are you simply the catalyst for the self-knowledge of others; a being who brings others to wisdom about themselves?"

She turned to Marla, and for a moment Marla appeared about to speak. But she hesitated, her hand moved but she could only look distressed and struggling. April finally turned away, walked quickly to the front door and left without turning to look at either of us.

I was still fascinated then, still certain there was something that would reward careful attention to those confounding interactions between human beings. As if we all lived within classical tragedies; settings where actions and outcomes were somehow still mutually dependent. The door had closed behind April for some minutes before the room was completely without her. As if with her departure, all color had suddenly been withdrawn.

I asked Marla, "Do you think she will return?" My voice seemed to echo in my ears. "So much still needs to be done." I was still hopeful then that with time our efforts would improve, that eventually we would begin to work harmoniously, but only if April could be convinced to return and continue.

After a pause she shrugged and turned back to the canvas. I said, "Perhaps my words were too harsh. She seemed to want sympathy. Can I ask you to go to her for me and extend my apologies?"

With an oddly grim determination, Marla resumed careful work at the canvas. Her hand moved smoothly, a kind of persistent caress as if color flowed from her fingers. Her hand dipped and moved, her shoulders swayed, and slowly the light returned to the room while colors gradually warmed. It was at this moment, after a long silence, that Marla announced, "Vince has just about taken over the department."

Beside my chair stood a tidy stack of fresh drawings, a reservoir of images available to paint from. Although I could not know it at the time, eventually we would nearly finish all of that work before those paintings were destroyed, murdered, and their paint and wood and canvas became a conflagration of pain and chaos and fire.

All that I have ever wished for was simply the opportunity to draw and paint, to complete what was before me and then move on to the next. So despite Marla's announcement I did not question her about Vincent or his intentions in the department. The truth of her report was of no concern to me since it could not help me paint better. What difference could it make to me that Vincent had become enamored with his new bureaucratic power? To the degree he enjoyed his official position, just so he failed as a painter. And I would not concern myself with one more failed painter, the world is too full of them. I could only paint, determined simply to paint well.

So I would not allow myself to become concerned since such interest would merely distract. Vincent had expressed enthusiasm concerning my paintings and their completion and had resisted the temptation to interfere in their creation. But at that moment I still assumed he was prepared to resist those gutless bureaucrats on my behalf and against their exhibition. So for the moment the real question was whether or not April would continue to help me.

By this time Marla had nearly finished the central figure in the swimming pool triptych. April's fiery shape appeared as a flame of gold and red with highlights of blue and green. I looked proudly around the room at my eight canvases, my equivalent to fist-shaking defiance against universal and inevitable mortality. And I believed that we had begun well. By working together those canvases would achieve completion.

"Poor Donald!" That phrase, April's words, still rang in my ears. Even as we engaged in that work, I regretted his absence. Perhaps I even missed him. In any case, I am certain he would have written a very good catalog.

I watched Marla's fluid gestures around April's shape and a kind of enchantment fell upon me, as if her strokes caressed April's flesh in a cool yet brilliant light. One line after the other, each pushing away the acknowledgement that the future remained undecided, and that all of the things I had hoped to avoid had not yet been avoided.

CHAPTER THIRTY–THREE

IN PARIS I WAS OFTEN POOR, when months would pass between sales
of paintings. Then, day after day I would walk past Monsieur Cartier the
landlord, a stupid old man with stupid concerns and stupid complaints, and
each day he would ask when he would see his rent. My sixth floor apartment
was just below the garret of Monsieur Gallette, Biblical scholar, bearded
mutterer in Greek and Hebrew, and inadvertent breeder of cockroaches.
Although my room was dismal in many ways, it had three beautiful windows
which filled its narrow space with light, and so was precious no matter how
cold it became in winter, or how hot in summer.

Sustaining myself daily with bread and soup and hot coffee and wine, I
had painted furiously and brilliantly, and despite the fact that for some time I
had not sold a single painting, I found myself happy. But then the chill winds
of the fall of 1919 arrived, and those dead leaves piled on the ground acquired
ominous shadows. And then, like so many others, I became ill.

At first it seemed merely one of those sicknesses which follow the change of
seasons. But gradually it became worse. My throat and chest became raw until
I was breathless and even my bones ached. With so little food and no medicine
my illness remained even after cool weather turned to cold. In an effort simply
to remain warm I spent evenings in the cafes, devoting entire hours to the
consumption of a single cup of coffee.

One evening, as hungry as usual but thoroughly dazed with the fever that
had captured me, I wandered through the wet November wind into La Rotonde.
The café's windows were opaque with a steamy fog and inside its atmosphere was
another fog of tobacco smoke. Close to the door and beside a wall-mirror, Dedo
sat sketching. More feverish and pink than the last time I had seen him, he
appeared still worse for the fact that it was cold and raining. Across from him sat
Maurice Utrillo, arm flung across the table providing his pillow. Dedo sketched
an English woman who possessed a long nose, too-sharp cheekbones, and large,
pale-gray eyes, sitting beside a man I assumed was her companion. Dedo drew
slowly but certainly, one unique line at its turn.

When I sat down, Maurice raised his head pretending to be awake, but he
was too drunk and immediately returned his head to the cradle of his arm. Dedo
coughed frequently because that winter rain was terrible for him, too, but he
drew slowly, methodically and so beautifully.

I had not eaten since the previous day, and devoured by a constant hunger
my illness deepened and now exhausted and confused me. The gnawing in
my stomach had taken possession of the rhythms of my body while deflecting
the proper operation of my mind, and that gnawing seemed to blossom with
every heartbeat. Jean, one of the regular waiters, placed a glass of red wine
beside my hand, saucer beneath, and stupidly I drank it down in one swallow.
People averted their eyes from our table, except to see Dedo's god-like profile,
even more beautiful in the mirror and a beauty made even more urgent by his
gasping breath.

The wine worked at my mind quickly, and soon that English woman's face
contorted while it lengthened. Dedo's balletic hand and the woman's ghastly face
and the entire café doubled in the mirrors surrounding us. From time to time
Dedo paused from his drawing to bring out a soiled handkerchief with which
he wiped his brow glistening with perspiration despite the cold. Beyond our
window the sharply sparkling lights of the boulevard fractured by the rain and
blurred by the fogged glass turned the color of wet ash in blue-black night.

The English woman's male companion turned and spoke a few words to me
in his language which I could neither understand nor answer. But by then I no
longer saw clearly; everywhere I turned appeared a single and unified smear of
colors, each element around me ran together as if seen though a rain-spattered
pane of glass and illuminated by yellow lights glittering from the raindrops of the
street. I no longer heard the sounds of traffic passing on the other side of that

glass, but only the clash and chatter and cacophony of voices of the café around me, its volume swelling and falling like the roar of a far-off surf. I recognized myself as profoundly ill, my vision shifting and swaying as if I was in a small boat. My body became flushed as that fever I carried expanded when it found fuel within the wine and then increased to a roaring fire.

The woman's companion appeared to recede suddenly very far away, as if our table had grown many meters across. Maurice, who also now seemed far away, lifted his head and turned to Dedo. "Damn you! Where's my glass of wine?"

Dedo looked up and nodded toward Jean. But before the glass of wine could arrive, Maurice's head returned to his arms and then he began to snore quietly. The horse-faced English woman found all of this amusing and laughed. She muttered something to her companion in English. He responded with a whispered scold, but then he too laughed.

Fever crashed over me, a mass of fetid air seemed to rise up around my chair and then our table began to shrink. It became so narrow that my face seemed inches from the face of that English woman. The red wine had soured in my stomach, and as her face seemed to flatten against my own, nausea engorged my throat.

Just then, with a waving flourish of his hand Dedo stopped drawing. He tore the sheet from his sketchbook and handed it to the woman. And just that quickly, my face and her face withdrew and the café's proportions of perspective returned.

The English woman made a great fuss showing the drawing to her companion. Dedo in his chair retreated into some private place where he drank his wine at a haughty disdain for us all. As if all of us had ceased to exist and he sat alone at the peak of a mountain. He had done his work, the angle of his chin seemed to announce; he had made an undeniably beautiful drawing.

Again Maurice lifted his head, but this time as if he already knew what was about to happen. He licked his thick, sleepy lips and then drained the glass of wine that had been left before him. The couple continued to speak to each other in English. As the man spoke, he reached into his pocket and then slowly, too slowly it seemed to me, he brought out a ten-franc note. He passed it along the table to the English woman. She then slid the note across the pale marble tabletop until it was beside Dedo's hand.

Moments ticked by until Dedo agreed to notice the banknote. He took it up as if it was a used napkin and unfolded it, then flattened it with the side of his hand against the table. Then he lifted it by one corner, studied it closely and turned it toward the light, then turned it over and inspected its back. Back and forth he turned it, nodding toward me and then toward Maurice as if curious what we thought.

My ears had begun to buzz. My head seemed to inflate and then retreat, a sort of monstrous pulse which coursed through my brain. By then the fever held me in a furious grip, and I could only wish to curl up under the table and die.

Maurice watched Dedo with sour eyes while he continued to toy with the banknote, then dropped his head to the table again muttering. But finally the English woman and her companion had become impatient. She stood stiffly, the rolled drawing still clutched in her hand and a dark look passed over her face. Her companion stood beside her and muttered a word into her ear. She smiled and then quietly laughed. With a grinning adieu to Dedo she turned, and arm-in-arm with her companion, passed through the door and out into the violet Paris night.

Imprisoned within some fever-driven delirium, to me it seemed suddenly monstrous that Dedo had accepted this pittance in exchange for an example of his genius. Those two had walked away certain that all one needed was a fist-full of peanuts to entice the monkeys to dance. There had been times I had seen Dedo displeased enough to tear up a drawing he recognized as unworthy, regardless of ten-franc notes. But we were there, all three of us, and not one of us had the money to say no to money.

By now my head was swimming, my body was immersed in some warm, yellow and sticky fluid, and I was sweating. The breeze each time the open door suddenly chilled me while I wallowed half-conscious with fever. Images slid from one end of my vision to the other. Dedo, the street lights, people moving along the sidewalk, Maurice, the two women at the table beside ours, everything moved, and then again, and then a third time.

I could endure it no longer and I stood. Dedo and Maurice looked up at me with surprise. "Ten francs," I said. "Where are my ten francs? Paris in a bottle for ten francs. Hand about ten-franc notes. Give away ten-franc notes, and love and beauty will be yours." Face wet with perspiration I reached down to the table as I felt myself sway.

"Quiet," Dedo said, his voice so soft with disdain I could not be certain he was speaking to me. "What difference can it make? My friend, you take these things far too seriously." I sat down again as a smile slowly formed over his lips. He leaned back in his chair, glanced at the street, at Maurice, and then at his own magnificent hands. "You are a serious man, and so you take many things too seriously. This I admire deeply. So much unlike this talentless tramp beside us." Affectionately he proded Maurice's shoulder. "But in the end, what difference can any of it make? Ten francs or ten thousand." He began to laugh.

In my fever-addled delusion I hated him for what suddenly seemed his hypocrisy and his condescension and his collaboration with a dispicable enemy. But he continued to smile. And despite my fury I was as charmed by his smile as I always had been.

"You do me a disservice," he said as if disappointed by my thoughts. "Can you believe that I sold that drawing to them?" A look of subtle disgust replaced his smile. "My friend, you misunderstand completely. I gave that drawing to her, and I did so because I was finished with it and so had lost all interest in it. That bit of money was her stupid gesture, appropriate for one like her and unworthy of the thing she has received. Such a ludicrous bourgeoise notion. After all, money can only buy things. Nothing of real value, nothing truly precious, can be bought or sold."

At some moment Maurice must have awakened. He stood slowly beside me. To Dedo he muttered, "Leave him alone. Stupidity is incurable, don't waste your time. We should pay our respects at La Dome. Cherie will be there by now and maybe she brings her girlfriend. Now we have just enough to buy drinks for them."

As he studied my face Dedo's glance turned to sympathy. He seemed to recognize how ill I was, an illness perhaps that ran deeper even than fever and delirium. In my eyes, the city that towered around us began to sway. Dedo refolded the note and then slide it across the table to me. "Get some food," he said quietly. "And some medicine. And find a girl who will look after you. How can you continue to paint unless you become healthy again?"

Maurice watched Dedo pass the note to me and his expression turned to horror. He screamed, "What are you doing? You stupid oaf! How will we get drinks? How will we get Cherie?" He stumbled around the table to grab Dedo's hand. But Maurice was very drunk.

With an easy gesture Dedo pushed his hand away. "You and I will go to visit your mother," Dedo said. "She always has a few francs lying about."

"Ah, her boyfriend will be there," Maurice said with discouraged annoyance. A sudden gust of exhaustion and defeat swept over his face. "He is certain I will spend all her money before he does. That greasy bastard." Maurice staggered backward into his chair, eyes staring unfocused into space. He sat down heavily. Half into the table-top he muttered, "We should kill him." He propped his elbow onto the table and rested his chin in his hand. "You and me," he said to Dedo. "We should go there now and kill him. I know a man who would get us a gun. With a gun we could kill him." His eyes closed then as if he was about to go back to sleep.

To me Dedo said, "Get yourself some food and some medicine. You will live a long time and you will have years to paint. Do not smile; this is no easy thing to live a long time. It is more than just breathing. Those of us who will die young have the easy part. We need be fine only a short while. But you will need to be good for a long time. Or be crushed, castrated and turned into the grease that lubricates, that allows everything else to be valued and exchanged for money. I wish you good luck, but good luck will not keep you from being devoured."

"Will you ever shut up?" Maurice suddenly slammed his hand on the table. "These eternal sermons. As though you knew anything of any importance to anyone. No wonder no one likes your work." He slammed his hand on the table again. "I am thirsty and it is a long walk to my mother's." The saucers spilled onto the floor with a clatter and Jean appeared suddenly in response.

To Maurice, Dedo said, "We will take the Metro. Our trip will not take long."

"You have the money for the Metro?" Maurice smiled.

"Of course," Dedo said.

"Good. Then buy me another drink and we will walk." Maurice leaned back in his chair, arms crossed behind his head.

"Your mother will care for you," Dedo said to him. "You will be cared for."

"Farmer!" Maurice snarled. "A pimp for pigs. Your own mother slaving in that God-forsaken village in heathen Italy, while you throw away your health whoring and drinking. And still, after all of this time, you have yet to learn to paint. You will never learn to paint. Italians are too stupid to paint. Each and every one of you blind with hard heads."

To me Dedo said, "Work hard and never be afraid. Never envy and never hate. But most of all, never be afraid. Take this money, go home, rest. We will see each other soon." He sighed then and began to cough. He brought out his handkerchief and mopped his brow. Suddenly he smiled. "We should go back to Montpellier. That was a fine holiday. We should make plans. We should leave Maurice and Harricot Rouge behind. Go back to Montpellier and live with the gypsies." And then he began to laugh, his large blackened and rotted teeth yellow under the café lights. Yet so beautiful; his strong face, intelligence, patience and nobility. Who could have helped but love him.

Maurice stood. "If we do not leave soon, mother will be gone and she will leave nothing for us."

Neither of them waved as they passed through the door and followed the sidewalk away from the cafe. Beyond a few steps Maurice shoved Dedo and then fell down himself. Above the noise of the traffic and the noise in my head I heard Dedo still laughing, and then laughing harder, as he watched Maurice struggle to regain his feet. The lights of on-coming cars blinded me, while the two men's silhouettes shrank and then disappeared as each car passed. After each moment of blindness their silhouettes reappeared, but smaller and farther away. For a time I thought I could still see them, though eventually they must have gone out of sight. But I sat as the lights of oncoming cars burned my eyes, the air becoming still colder and the sidewalk more crowded.

And then I found it, soft as a linen handkerchief, in my sweaty hand. The note was worn nearly white, a piece of soft paper with creases blackened by the hands of others.

After a time Jean tapped my shoulder. My eyes would no longer focus, his long dour face and lank greasy black hair insisted on becoming two. My head rolled as I tried to stand. Jean steadied my arm whispering, "Look out," as I made my way to the street.

I prefer to believe that I frightened half of Paris with my ghastly face and my blazing, delirious eyes as I staggered back to my apartment, but I can not recall any of it. A blur of color, faces and streetlights. The ten-franc note melted between my sweaty fingers as gradually I collected a bag of groceries. With that bag full and a tin of heating oil in my other hand, I did not care if old Cartier saw me. But I did not see him or anyone else, and then finally I stood inside my apartment.

Days of sweating and eating soup and sleeping and sweating and eating more soup. Three days, perhaps four, I no longer recall. And then I was merely exhausted. The pain and the fever had gone, but I slept more than ever.

I am not certain how long I remained in that slimy bed within that gray-yellow air that smelled of wet leather and burned cooking grease and heating oil. I only know I remained until I was healthy enough to find further confinement intolerable. My first thought was somehow to get money to Dedo. This demanded several weeks, so at first I could not face him, at least until I had a little something to pay him back.

So I did not try to find him at La Dome, or Rotonde, or any of the other cafes. And I did not go to Brancusi or the Arab, or Kisling or Zoborowski. Day after day, when I was not painting, I looked for paying work, or attempted to sell a painting. And thus I put off seeing Dedo.

And in the end I waited too long. I did not see him again until immediately before he took to his bed for that final time, already fading, drifting away from all of us, from this world of beauty and illusion. And by then that little bit of money I had managed to scrape together was of no value.

It sometimes happens that money has no value.

CHAPTER THIRTY-FOUR

FOR SEVERAL WEEKS Marla and April worked with me nearly every day until finally we had finished the swimming pool triptych. Certainly within two months we would have finished all of the other paintings. The work progressed so that I came to believe that eventually all would be completed, because every obstacle finally had been overcome.

And then one afternoon Marla arrived very late. I had called her apartment several times without a response. When finally she arrived it was already approaching evening and she arrived without April.

"I don't know what could have happened to her." Marla put a large brown bag of groceries on the counter in my kitchen. She sat down on the couch, more fatigue around her eyes and her mouth than I had remembered seeing. She kicked off her shoes. "Last night she said she'd be ready to go." She glanced at the clock. "It's already so late. I feel like the day's been totally wasted."

I agreed with that thought, although I was determined to conceal my disappointment. But I was disappointed; foremost because the painting had progressed so well, but nearly as much because the day would pass and I would not see April.

I looked around the studio to consider those paintings that did not demand April's presence. But Marla's expression told me how thoroughly discouraged she was. I suppose I should not have been surprised by this. Nor should I have been surprised that April had failed to join us. We had worked very hard, and such efforts are not easily sustained, even by those most eager to complete the work. But more, and perhaps worse; something had begun to drain away from each of us. Marla's exhaustion embarrassed me, so I asked if she had been keeping up with her own painting.

She tossed back her head, rolled her eyes to the ceiling, the white of her eyes bold as lights, and she groaned. "Not much." She turned to me with a wry smile. "But if you twisted my arm I might admit I've learned a couple of things from working with you." I detected no irony or sarcasm; she seemed to speak honestly and even with some gratitude. Then her eyes darkened and she shook her head. "But it's cost me. I get to thinking sometimes. I look at these paintings and I wonder, is that really mine? That part right there? Is there a part of me there after all? I know what that must sound like. But every time I come here, almost the first thing I do is look at the paintings to see if you've made changes." She laughed. "When I see something you've worked on and I don't know what to think, you know, whether or not it fits with the rest of the canvas, then I wonder, 'What the hell has he done now? Is he trying to ruin it?'" As we laughed together her cheeks mottled pink with embarrassment. She stood then, asked if I wanted anything from the refrigerator. I asked her for a glass of wine. She poured two glasses and brought them back to the couch.

When she was seated again I asked, "When you feel these tremors of mistrust, what troubles you most? The additions I make, or the fact that they are made without consulting you?" The wine went down quickly, cooling my tight, angry throat. I do not know what made me more furious; the impertinence of her attitude, or the justice of her suspicion. My glass emptied too quickly. I stood and brought the bottle to the couch. Marla would not hold my eyes.

I said, "I apologize, because that is an unfair question. Without your help none of these would exist. I know precisely how hard you have worked to make them possible. But please make no mistake; either all of this is entirely my own work, or none of it is mine."

Without looking up she said, "Maybe there's nothing that's truly your own in any of this. Or in anything you've ever done. Nor is there anything of my own in it, either. Think about it. Maybe nothing in any of it makes it uniquely the product of one person's mind. I had an art history professor who claimed that all works of art are the products of whole armies of people; entire groups of like-minded artisans, members of a particular economic class, a nation sharing a common language and iconography." When she finally looked up there was pity and a disturbing tolerance in her eyes. "Don't misunderstand; I'm not looking for a fight. I don't really know how this will make sense to you, but now that you've agreed to go along with the retrospective, I wonder sometimes about those other paintings, and the other people who've helped you along the way."

But there I had to stop her. I could not believe my ears. As if I might be suffering from some hallucination of the hearing. "What did you say? When did I change my mind? Who told you this?"

Marla's eyes widened, her hands dropped back into her lap as if frightened and hiding. "I heard Vince talking to your agent in New York. I thought you had more confidence in me. And then I heard him arraigning with your agent to have him ship those paintings for the retrospective. So I assumed we were trying so hard to finish these so they'd be included in the exhibition. That's what I told April. This was weeks ago." She watched my face, and gradually her voice changed. "She got real excited about working with you once I told her how big the exhibition would be. That's why I'm surprised she isn't here." She stopped speaking then, as if whatever more she had to say would wait.

I found myself literally speechless. I could only look at her bewildered with astonishment. I asked when she had overheard Vincent talking to Martin.

She shrugged. "Had to be a month ago, maybe more. I never spoke to Vince about it. I just took it for granted the two of you arranged things and that you'd tell us about it when everything was ready."

"And you are certain you heard Vincent was speaking with my agent?"

Marla waved her hand impatiently. "They were making plans to ship your canvases, I heard that much." Suddenly I felt as if I had begun to drown and black waters were closing over my head.

Marla studied me, watched my face, until she said, "You never agreed to any such thing, did you?" When I did not answer, her eyes became large and then she shook her head. "This is crazy! You mean Vince intends to hold this show without your agreement? Is that what you're saying?"

But I could not answer. As I stood, Marla stood up with me. "Are you going to call Vince?"

Words piled inside my head as if they could not find my mouth, but finally

I said, "This is more amazing than anything I have ever heard of. In all my cursed and miserable years I have never heard of anything like it. To have one's colleague and one's agent conspire behind one's back. Like thieves they have decided the old fool needs to be led by the hand. They have convinced themselves that their plans are for my own good, but their intentions are completely self-serving. So they conspire behind my back, because they believe I can have no idea what is in my best interest!"

She stood to block my way to the telephone, as though she had already guessed my intention. "You should think about this. You don't know what's really going on here and you should think about this." She studied my face, her own mouth hard-set and determined, but then she stepped aside. I dialed Vincent's number carefully while questions blossomed and multiplied.

I listened to his telephone ring again and again. Unanswered, I replaced the receiver and swore to Marla that I would hound him until he collapsed. And then I would call Martin.

But Marla placed her hand lightly on my arm. "Hear me out. Just listen to me for a minute."

She spoke quietly, her dark eyes were large with emotion. She returned to the couch. "I never understood why you refused the retrospective. You probably think that's to be expected. I'm young, I'm a woman and American."

Her condescension made me furious. I said, "Am I so blind and indifferent that you believe I do not value you as a colleague?"

For a moment I thought she might begin to weep. "You don't realize how important that show would be for all of us."

"I realize that very clearly."

"I've worked hard to help you, but I want that work to help Vince as well. You owe me that. I've worked to help you, and now there's this chance my work can help Vince. And all you need to do is authorize the exhibition, and let Vince share the credit. It couldn't be more simple."

"He helps himself to my work behind my back to advance his career, without even the courtesy of asking my permission. He leaps upon my back and beats me with his riding crop."

"And you'd rather let us all down." Marla's dark eyes were suddenly brilliant, as if they were seeing me for the first time.

"What do you mean?"

"You'll walk away with your precious pride in tact, and leave the rest of us here. John won't return as department head, no matter how healthy he becomes. Here's a chance to support the depatment and help all of us out. If Vince managed this exhibition when John couldn't get it off the ground, that would change everything. Otherwise, the administration might bring in a new chairman from somewhere else. Suppose that new chairman turned out to be another John, except one who didn't like you very much?"

But I had already heard more than enough. "Tell me just why I should I care for the fate of someone who is prepared to steal my work? Or for a department that regards me as some sort of trophy, a token, a card to be played in some grand card game? What is wrong with me that I am so blind? I am a painter. I live by my eyes. You tell me something without telling me anything. Am I blind?"

She looked at me a long time but said nothing. I said, "And you? What difference could it possibly make to you if Vincent receives this position or not?"

Marla leaned back into the couch and sighed. "If I told you it's very important to me that you help Vince, would you just leave it at that?" I watched her knowing I would discover what I did not wish to think about. She sighed and closed her eyes. "If I told you I was in love with him, would that make any difference?" She paused as if waiting for the earth to open beneath her feet. "Suppose I told you that it was as much a surprise to me because I never really even liked him. Don't make me explain this part. It would take too long and it's too complicated."

I could find nothing to say. The words that had piled in my head suddenly disappeared. My surprise was complete and my shock left me speechless. "All right," she continued, "forget I said anything about Vince and me, and just think about this. If you help him and he gets this position, you'll help all of us. Is that simple enough?" She turned to me and the color and shape of her eyes seemed to fill with appeal. But when I did not respond they hardened. "You won't help him, will you. Or me. Or April. Not even April." This time her sigh was filled with disgust. "Just like you wouldn't help Donald."

Once again the power of speech abandoned me. I watched waiting for her to shed even a single tear. Because at the first glimmer I would have thrown her out.

"Vince is an artist," she said with a dry and certain face. "John's a bureaucrat. Painters who might do new things are too risky, and that's why you're here; and that's what makes him uncomfortable about these new paintings of yours. But

Vince is still young enough to get excited about new work. And he isn't afraid to find good painters to add to the faculty. And that would be good for all of us. Art is always changing, and Vince is eager to change with it."

"You show remarkable faith in a scoundrel." My head was pounding, thick and unwieldy. "You should reconsider such trust." I stood, pained by my own disgust. "You are certain that deceit and duplicity will improve your department." I began to pace despite the pain in my leg because I could no longer sit quietly. The world had moved beneath my feet and I had felt its motion as a tremor, as if an engine had started. I stopped finally and stood directly in front of her. "Did Vincent ask you to work your way into my trust this way, to seduce my acquiescence? Did he decide you could do what he could not? Or was it April instead?"

A throb of panic entered Marla's voice. "It wouldn't have made any difference. I'd have worked with you, anyway. Want to know why? Because I knew I'd learn from you while I helped you. All of this isn't just for Vince or for the others; it's for me, too." Pale suddenly with anger she stood. "And for you. This exhibition would help you, too."

"Please do not tell me what is good for me. Do not dare to tell me that. Because you can not know any more than Vincent or Martin. They have no better idea what would benefit me than you do. So I will tell you because you cannot know. You are doing harm. And Vincent is doing harm. There is no more to be said about this, because you know nothing about what I need."

"I know Vince better than you do," she said and her voice trembled with supressed rage. "Whatever he did was for you and for the department. He'd never have done anything to damage your work or threaten your career. Believe it or not, he doesn't envy you. He understands."

"He does not understand! He could not possibly understand. Neither he nor you understand. But still you both must meddle. So listen to me now; you must stop. You both have gone too far and you do not understand."

"And you?" Marla spoke through clenched teeth. "You understand everything! So simple to understand others, what they want, what they need. I bet you think you're the only person who understands completely. Isn't that true?"

My voice became lost and my mouth would no longer move. I could only look, there was nothing more to say. Marla stepped back. "Vince has signed a contract with your agent, the agreement's been made, the paintings are on their way. Your only choice is to go along."

"I am surrounded by vultures! Pimps and whores who lack the decency to carry yellow cards. And Martin! You use even Martin's delusions for your own advantage. Such diabolical simplicity. Vincent can insist that everyone will benefit, but his benefit is assured. Even more than Martin's."

Marla turned to look out the window as if considering her next words carefully. She held her head beautifully. The light from the window passing into my apartment washed over her forehead and the upper part of her face, while a shadow beginning just below her lips cloaked her mouth, her neck, her lower throat. Why had I never mistrusted such beauty? And why had its recognition come to me suddenly and at just that moment? But now I could no longer enjoy it and found no pleasure in it. Quietly she said, "Do us all one favor. Think all of this through." She waited as if offering me an opportunity to ask her to remain. I said nothing.

"I'll call you tomorrow," she said, "to see if you want to work. No reason to stop, don't you think?"

As she stepped past me I reached out, took her arm, turned her, and by this action startled us both. A monster had taken over my hands. In a whisper I asked, "And what about April?"

Her eyes widened and a hint of humor appeared. "If you expect her to work with us you need to agree to this show. She wants it as much as anybody." She stared at me as if I had become utterly stupid. "But maybe you'd better forget about her, too."

Suddenly recognizing the taste of defeat I asked, "Do I have a choice?"

"After I tell her what you've decided? And remember, there's nothing you can threaten her with. She isn't that sincere." She spoke thought tight lips. "And she won't be impressed by your whining desperation." She wrenched her arm free of my grasp. "Take my advice and forget her." She stepped quickly to the door. As she opened it she said, "April agrees with Vince that you're very talented, but she thinks you're creepy." Her lips parted in a bitterly angry yet sad smile. I had committed some disgraceful transgression and she was merely noting the justice of my chastisement. For an instant her hard eyes seemed to absorb all of the light in the room. "When you change your mind, don't forget to call."

Marla closed the door and I stared at it as if I had never seen one before. Then I picked up the telephone and tried again to call Vincent. His telephone rang dumbly, a voiceless calling across empty space and the hissing of empty wires. I had begun to sweat and my hand trembled. Did I believe any of this could be undone? Marla was Vincent's lover? Perhaps it was this thought that triggered the tremors of my hand. She and this man, together and bound by some feeble emotion. As if all should be forgiven of someone in love. And to honor this love I must yield. I must allow them to dance upon my chest, smile as they step on my face. Vincent's telephone continued to ring in my ear. The silence between its rings angered and frightened me, until finally I replaced the receiver.

To try again; this thought exhausted me and turned my limbs to wet clay. And now Vincent and Marla laughing as they watched the old man, like a turtle turned upon its back under the hot sun struggling, its legs waving uselessly in the air attempting to right itself. And April. Such a distinguished audience awaiting the final act of my pathetic comedy. And Martin, too; could I possibly forget my dear friend Martin?

What had he expected to accomplish? But of course, I already knew. Put aside our long friendship; obviously that must be no impediment to betrayal. And my threats, like bites of a toothless dog, more hilarious the more seriously intended. Just so much fierce noise and saliva. So I needed to speak to him as well.

I called his gallery in New York before realizing it was well-past his office hours. Eventually his answering service cut in to take my name and number. I must wait until Martin returned my call.

I brought the bottle of wine to the table and began that vigil. Once again my life was reduced to waiting for Martin to return my telephone call. As the bottle drained I convinced myself that in those years of my impatient, arrogant, but uncomplicated obscurity I had painted and drawn without conflict or worry. While my hands had worked, time had been suspended, wrapped and contained safely in a thin gray but comforting blanket of ignorance. But my ignorance, though enormous, was no longer profound. It had become compromised and was no longer even beautiful.

When the telephone finally rang I studied it, suddenly amused by its malevolence as it squatted as elegant as the Lucifer of the Dore etchings. I watched while it rang, as mystified as a dog.

"Ah, my friend." Martin's voice was remarkably bright. "I am returning your telephone call at my first opportunity." In the emptiness of Martin's jolly greeting I could hear each of the intervening miles separating us, each of his breaths a sigh from a storming cosmos.

"I have heard a disturbing rumor, Martin, which I am certain you will reassure me is not true. But it has unsettled me."

Martin said nothing. The crackle and hiss of the wires were like the voices of the dead all speaking at once in all of the tongues of history, a babble of groans among the roar of their flames, and their pain.

"I have been told by someone who claims to be well-informed that you have signed a contract to ship my paintings to the University. I assured this person that what they had heard could not possibly be true, that it could only be a fabrication, the product of an evil and jealous mind, a mind jealous particularly of your loyalty. That is what I told this person. That is what we both know to be true, is it not?"

Martin's silence continued, lengthened, grew to proportions that could hardly be contained within the telephone. In my apartment the shadows deepened while monstrous claws reached for my heart as my eyesight faded with the weakening light. My glass of wine shimmered in the approaching darkness. The bottle of wine sat loyally on the floor beside my chair while my heart beat thickly, and then I despaired.

With a sigh Martin said, "You are my oldest and most cherished friend. And you have called me with a heart filled with an anger which I do not deserve."

"So you deny this allegation," I said, not allowing him to continue. "I knew that some mistake had been made. You have relieved my mind of a great weight."

Martin sighed again into the telephone, a gust of air that broke my heart. "If I have sinned, my friend, I have sinned in my determination to help you." Martin whispered hoarsely. The blood in my limbs drained at his words, and my throat tightened as if an assassin had reached thick fingers around it and begun to squeeze. "You must be my confessor, because only you can decide whether I have sinned. Your man Vincent threatened that you would lose your position at the University if I did not send those paintings."

"When you go to the confessional you must open your heart and you must speak only the truth."

"But that is the truth. He said your contract would be terminated. And you and I understand how you depend on this position."

"At worst, my contract would simply not have been renewed. You already understood this. Besides, when was the last time you allowed yourself to be bullied by a school-teacher? In any case, you and I made our own agreement. You would offer certain paintings for sale in your gallery. All of this we agreed long ago."

After another silent pause Martin said, "Calm yourself and let me remind you of something. You remember Van Gogh? So I do not need to explain that during his brief and unhappy life he sold only one single canvas. And now you have an opportunity for a great exhibition, an outpouring of interest and appreciation. Tell me now, since we are in the confessional, do you believe yourself an artist superior to Van Gogh? Because certainly you have sold more paintings than he. And now suddenly there is great interest in your past work. Have you become so ungrateful?"

"Where was your tale of Van Gogh when we made our agreement? Admit that you have behaved like a scoundrel. But since we are about the business of rewriting history, tell me, would you have remained Van Gogh's agent if you had only sold one painting? Can you make a living on the earnings of one sold painting?"

"As your agent I have done what I believe would most help your career. When I help you I also help myself, and we both understand this. Must you insist that I starve beside you?"

"We have sold quite a few canvases together over the years. So let me remind you to consider the future. I told you before that I am working on new paintings. I cannot spare time or thought for anything else. What I expect of you is simple; allow these new paintings to appear first. Permit these paintings to appear alone; allow them stand on their own feet. Can this be so difficult for you to understand? These paintings are different from the others. And perhaps for once you will like them."

I waited, only to hear Martin clear his throat. I said, "You insist I have nothing to lose from this retrospective. But you are wrong, and you know this. Do not deny it. Let these paintings stand alone at your gallery, away from this retrospective. This seems so little to ask of a friend. You must not doubt how important this is to me."

Suddenly there was a thud against my front door, as if something had fallen or was dropped against it.

"Martin," I continued, "I ask only that you allow these pieces to stand alone for one year. After that, if it is still your wish to become involved in a retrospective, I will offer no objections, and even agree to provide assistance."

A thick silence fell around me like a draft of cold air. I was frightened in my own darkening living room, in my own presence. Still gripping the receiver I stood and switched on all of the lights I could reach.

Very quietly Martin said, "Those paintings were shipped two days ago. There is nothing left to do for several more days. But listen to me; if the University signs the bill-of-lading for their safe arrival, it will have possession of the paintings, and I will have no power to demand their return. You see my position? I could perhaps request their return, but the decision would be entirely in their hands."

"Make sure those paintings are returned. I know what a lawyer can do."

Martin suddenly burst into loud laughter. "And the Devil's curse upon your very soul. You dare threaten me with lawyers. Conveniently you forget the show in Munich is barely breaking even, while you have already received advances on several of the canvases hanging there though they remain unsold. Please, we should resist becoming vulgar. In any case, what could a lawyer say to either of us?" After a long pause he sighed. "You are a terrible old man. To force everyone around you to such humiliation, as though they must be tested for their purity. Pure stupidity, most likely. What you do to yourself is your own affair. But to coerce and harass those around you, people who regard themselves as your friends, into collaborating with your insanity. You demand so much, and you demand it all indiscriminately. As if you possessed no good sense. Sometimes it seems you have become too old to be any longer amusing."

He left me with nothing to say, and I did not attempt otherwise.

After another long pause Martin again cleared his throat. "There is for you only one alternative. You must convince the University authorities to refuse delivery of those paintings. Of course, you yourself will bear all of the cost for their return shipping and their insurance. But money means nothing to a man of large spirit such as yourself." He paused again, as if perhaps waiting for my expression of gratitude. I did not give it.

I listened as Martin quietly yawned. "Another day will soon begin here in New York, my friend. The sky will pale to blue, and the stars will wink out. Curse you, old man, for having destroyed one more night of my sleep. But tell me one thing before we end. Does the sky turn blue-grey at dawn there as it does here in Manhattan? In another moment I will begin to hear birds, except that my windows are closed for the air-conditioning. Ah well, I would not have slept anyway. And now this conversation has completely upset me. Does that make you feel better? You have deprived another old man his well-earned rest. Such a selfish creature you have become. Or perhaps you have always been this way."

"And it has taken you all of this time to recognize that? Not very observant of you."

He laughed quietly. "Listen to my advice and consider it carefully. If you must insist on this monomania, this conscience-less egotism, you will need above all to change the minds of your keepers at your University."

"So you will not help me." My hand trembled, a sob escaped my lips. One of us had become a withered and doddering fool.

Martin said, "My friend, if we talk much longer I will see the dawn. Give my words some thought and only call when you have come to your senses." The telephone line went dead before I could wish Martin into hell.

The second bottle of wine stood bright green and still corked on the floor beside the stove. Now past midnight, the air had turned cool. I closed several windows and returned to my chair carrying the uncorked bottle. With a refilled glass in hand I brooded over the wonders of misery, and the delusions of the betrayed. I decided I must settle accounts with Vincent.

Perhaps finally he and I would come to understand each other and come to some agreement. Vincent would understand what needed to be done and he would agree to cancel the show. Because finally he would recognize the truth. Vincent would resolve my crisis, and between us we would determine a way for me to continue to paint that helped secure his cherished position as department head. With these convictions I hypnotized myself into believing that all I needed to do was pick up the telephone and dial his number.

Had I drunk heavily? I suppose so. Had I recognized myself drinking heavily? But I was simply thirsty, merely possessed of a mighty and unquenchable thirst. And what did I regret most of all? Those afternoons with April now lost, of course. Those afternoons which had passed and would never pass again, but even more sadly, afternoons that would never be. I studied those canvases, finished and unfinished, ranged around me like the bars of a cage and the pain of that loss pierced more sharply than any betrayal. But I was not conscious of drinking heavily, only of drinking frequently, filling and re-filling my glass, and that for some reason I remained thirsty.

Once again there was a thump against my door, though I ignored it the moment I heard it. I badly needed to speak with Vincent. I dialed the telephone and heard the ringing from the other end. In a moment the room before my eyes melted, walls merged, divided, fell and reappeared in flashes of yellow and red and bright green, like the flicker of a candle. For a moment the world seemed to turn inside out.

Again there was that thump against my door, but after it I heard voices. Neighbors, perhaps there was a party. If there was a party I was suddenly tempted to go over and introduce myself as the world-famous dead painter. Everyone of course would recognize me and a cry would go up, a cheer. And there would be free drinks pouring from spigots in the walls. Someone would bring out paper and pencil and I would be invited to draw. Immediately the room would fill with bodies disrobing, and I would draw and draw and draw. Each drawing completed would ignite a roar of applause. Frantic hands would snatch at each drawing and then the next, so eagerly taken from my fingers, while instantly another sheet of paper, bright, hopeless and blank, would appear before me, until sheets of blank paper seemed to fall from the ceiling, from the roof, from the sky.

A whining sound blasted from my lap. The receiver lay where it had fallen from my hand and that sound poured visible from it. When had I dropped it? I replaced the receiver and suddenly the walls stopped breathing, the floor no longer undulated, silence kept the furniture from swaying, stopped the electric lights from shimmering. That sudden silence sobered me. I returned to the chair and dialed again. And just as suddenly, Vincent's voice muttered a greeting.

I said, "I apologize for the late hour, but something has come up which needs your immediate attention."

Without waiting for me to finish he said, "You want to talk about the exhibit, and about those paintings coming from New York." When I said nothing he continued, "Marla's here. She told me about your little talk. It's very late and we're all very tired. Let's make this quick."

For one dizzy second Vincent frightened me. His bluntness silenced me, and my heart froze in my chest. For one passing moment Vincent intimidated me.

I said, "What, if it could be given to you, would dissuade you from this exhibition? More money? The department chair? Greater prestige among your colleagues? All of these? So tell me then; are any of these worth your dishonor? What could possibly be so valuable?" The receiver became slippery in my sweaty hand and I gripped it until my hand trembled.

Vincent's voice was dry. "You're right, I'll admit it. I need to justify what I've done for you. But I'd have talked to you eventually." He laughed nervously. "Still, I confess right now that I'm certain nothing I say will change your mind. So I'll tell you this. If I only convince you that I'm working hard for your benefit, and that this show will honor your work, then I'll be satisfied."

"Is that all the justification you need to abuse the trust of a colleague and friend?"

"All right, then, understand this," he said with sudden anger. "Your show will earn you some money. You understand? I'm giving you a chance to earn some money. Tell me what's wrong with that? I want to see you get some of all that money other people have been getting from your work for years. So tell me, how does that make me a bad guy?"

"What am I to think? That you do not understand what this show will mean to me? What can you possibly be thinking?"

"Just because you're old, you think you understand." Vincent's voice became calm, or perhaps merely tired. He sighed heavily. Dampness began to seep into my room like ectoplasm, my shoulders and leg bloomed with pain. "But you understand nothing."

"You have already insulted me. Do you think it is not possible to compound that crime?"

With flat conviction Vincent said, "That other world is dead. You think you can bring it back? If you could, I expect you'd screw that up, too. You're hopeless, because you don't know when people are trying to help you. You want to live in that other world you keep dragging around behind you. But that world's gone, buddy, gone for good and all. And I'm just trying to push you into the new one. And that's what's pissing you off. But I can't force you to join. I can't even make you see yourself in it."

"So modest! But I do not need your instruction. As if you could understand my affairs. You believe there is something you might teach me. Perhaps you are right. But certainly you should begin by telling me how to rid myself of colleagues like you."

"You're afraid, aren't you!" The smile in Vincent's voice chilled me. "You never understood the notion of fair value, so you can't understand the idea of even exchange. Because you believe in grace. You believe in the profligacy of divine love, and so you're afraid because I might be right."

I laughed. "Oh, yes, I am cowering with fear. And driven by this fear I have run to beg you to relent." I laughed without humor, a relief of tension and anger.

"You're afraid because you're certain there's something weird about the buying and selling, the setting of prices, haggling, all of that. And you can't believe anybody would shell out good money to pay your agent's prices. Middle-class philistine to the end, you love those paintings but you can't understand why anyone should pay good money for them." I could say nothing. Vincent continued, "Even John thinks better of your work than you do. He never thought much of your stuff but at least he recognized its dollar-value. If it had been up to him he would have bought your paintings outright and held the exhibition without even inviting you."

"And what about you?" My throat finally found my voice. Suddenly I could laugh. "Since you have taken this temporary position you have come to sound a great deal like John." I waited as Vincent remained silent. "But perhaps I am no longer a colleague, more a subordinate. And tell me, do you see Marla this way as well? You have become a different person, even she agrees. Otherwise you could not have said any of this, and certainly never agreed to what is about to happen."

Refusing my bait Vincent simply laughed. In a suddenly harsh whisper he said, "I'm not about to battle with you. You're like a child who refuses to take unpleasant medicine even though it will make you healthy. Some idiot has offered to build a small gallery to display your work permanently, did you know that? Right here at the University. Bet you think that's stupid, too. You're pig-headed, ungrateful and as dumb as a goddamn peasant. But I grew up with peasants. So I know you weren't beaten enough. Your folks didn't beat you enough. They should have taken a big stick and beaten you hard every day of your damn life." He chuckled, a sound of ancient malevolence.

I gasped unable to catch my breath. "And you must exorcize ghosts! How many souls will be released into heaven? And if I agree to this artistic suicide, will my soul rise with the others? You will have acquired your position of power here. Will you use your power for good? Just do this one bad thing and you will have the power and you will use it to perform good deeds. And you will make a special effort to save the ancient heroes from their self-destructive inclinations. You will give special attention to those old and talented but no longer annoying. And you will pursue more power and save a great number of them, and saving them will redeem a great number of ghosts." I made a last effort to respond to derision with derision.

Vincent was silent so long I wondered if he remained on the line. But finally he said, "What makes it tough is that you're sure you're better than the rest of us. And know what; maybe you're right. Maybe you're a better man even than my father. But I'll tell you; what I think about all the time is my Dad's box. All that music he never heard except inside his head; that whole pile of sounds, those little black marks that never came off the page. I'll tell you this; he worked just as hard over that stuff as you do with you paint and canvas. Just as hard, and just as careful, and sincere, and loving as you. And he made just as many sacrifices, and suffered just as much misery as you. You think your work deserves more attention than his? Fair enough. But do you think he'd have refused if somebody had wanted to play his music? He knew the value of appreciation. At least he'd have been grateful for something he never even had a chance at. He wouldn't have been weird about it, not like you. So you know what I think? The department should give you a medical leave and check if you haven't gone senile." Again he began his low rumbling chuckle.

"And you are crazy too, if you think I will sit by while all of this goes on."

With slow emphasis he said, "Nothing you can do will stop this show." His voice was deep with sincerity. "You can only hurt it, turn it into a zoo without shutting it down. Is that what you want?"

"Do not attempt to tell me what I can and cannot do. I will go to the newspapers. I will expose you and the entire University to ridicule."

"Go to the newspapers, go to the magazines, too." Vincent sounded almost bored. "They'll figure you're just kidding, just trying to juice things up. Make a big noise to get cheap publicity."

Gasping again for air I could only mutter, "I have friends and several of them are lawyers. This is about to become very unpleasant, and thoroughly embarrassing."

Vincent laughed but with more warmth than I expected. "Whenever I hear one painter tell another he's going to get a lawyer, it just tickles me."

"I am not without resources. And I am just enough the bourgeois to resent your theft. As if I owe you or anyone else an explanation for why this show should not continue. You have only one choice to avoid this unpleasantness."

Vincent interrupted. "Martin has already explained that to me. He called saying it wasn't too late, he was ready to accept the return of the paintings. We spent an hour on the telephone talking about you, what you might do. He told me things. Another sentimental old man. He forced me to convince him, time after time, that we were doing the right thing for you and your future." He paused. "You might be good as a painter, but you're no-good as a human being. And I'll bet you think old Martin is just a pile of shit right now." His laughter unnerved me. "You don't care how hard he works for you, how careful he is about you. It's just too bad you're too old to be kicked in the head a few times."

"Spare me your condescension. As if you knew precisely what was best for me. And then to proceed without my permission or even knowledge. Badger my agent as if he was your subordinate. And all of this for my own good, or so you say. You insist, but you cannot know this. You cannot know."

"You're right," he said, and the sudden exhaustion in his voice came from deep within the night, "I don't know everything, but I know enough. I know what I'm doing. This show will happen despite whatever you might try."

"You do not need to explain yourself to me, but you should be prepared to explain yourself to my lawyers."

Again Vincent began to laugh. "Give up on the threats. You won't do it because you detest lawyers, I know this too. And because doing it would leave you feeling more foolish and abused and absurd than you do now. I'll tell you exactly what you're going to do. You're going to hang up that telephone, get very drunk and then go to bed. Because tomorrow you'll understand exactly why all of this must be. Just don't do something foolish. I wouldn't have gone to all this trouble if I'd thought you'd do otherwise."

"You take a great deal for granted."

"Stupid me, I'm counting on your common sense, so maybe you're right. Maybe that's a bad idea because maybe you don't have any. But I'm sure when you've thought this all over, you'll go along. And by the way, I won't hold my breath waiting for you to thank me." His exhaustion sounded like pain.

"You are jealous of my work. You envy my art and you wish to destroy me. You want to hold me up to ridicule, and I will not allow it."

Vincent yawned loudly. "We'll continue this discussion tomorrow. I'm amazed you aren't dead-tired." He stifled another yawn. "Please don't call too early." And then he laughed and said, "Or is it already too early?" And he laughed and laughed until I threw the telephone to the floor.

When I picked it up again there was only the dial tone.

My hands were hot and sore and my head felt filled with concrete. The wine bottle stood nearly drained. And now all of this was worse than embarrassing.

I stood as sore as if I had spent hours digging graves after a battle. My arms and shoulders and back had become twisted and stretched from burying those dead.

Under the counter beside the refrigerator I found it; the last bottle of wine. A large bottle, admittedly enough for the rest of the evening, or had it already become morning. Perhaps enough for the rest of my life. But even that question no longer seemed to matter.

I decided to remain awake, a death-watch of sorts. I recognized it as the last night of something. A death-watch for myself? Had I died and simply not realized that I ought to fall over? Because something was gone. Something had escaped or been realized which could never be called back, like a word or a breath or a sigh.

Those paintings. Betrayed by canvas and wood and oil and pigment; they surrounded me propped against each wall, each beside the next like soldiers awaiting execution. A war had been lost and the rest of my army had been captured by Vincent through the treachery of Martin. With those others held hostage, Vincent did not need even to offer a truce. He had neutralized my army and my power was gone. And now these canvases, the best I had to offer, had failed to hold the ramparts. The walls had been breached and the castle keep had been destroyed. Those soldiers had failed to stop Martin's greed or Vincent's lust for power. Failure, misery and utter shame. Were my paintings ashamed? As I sipped from my glass I thought I saw them turn away, humiliated, unable to face me and incapable of enduring my disgust. Their beauty had been shattered and shredded. The ghost of that beauty faded, their pale, threadbare delight reduced to a mockery of beauty and pleasure. Nothing is saved from the past. Nothing of that work, or of the others, could be salvaged from their impossible completion and inevitable dissolution. Every plane, every effort of design and color had come finally to nothing. No thickness of paint would cleanse them, no addition could purify them. They had accepted their dishonor without a murmur, and quietly they had endured their ravishment. The life-blood had been drained from them, crimson streams puddled together in the center of my floor.

So, to the executioner's block? I could never repaint them, nor could I ignore what they had been, or what I had hoped they would become. The canvases themselves stood saturated with my false hope, with the terror of long and desperate work, and faith and fear. They had become soaked with my love, even the stretchers, the braces of wood and the nails of steel had lost their value, their openness to fresh impressions of the world, of that life they might have possessed. There was no decision necessary, no other choice needed to be made.

I have never enjoyed working with a palette knife. I had once tried impasto, using the knife as a scoop to lift paint, applying it in layers, spreading it. But nothing I have ever done with it has pleased me. As if everything done with that knife is indirect, displaced, a secondary effect, a half-step removed from the paint itself. I do not like that little knife with its tasteful and cunning little angle just at the base of its blade.

The tip of the knife dug through the paint to the threads of the canvas. With a twist of the knife those layers of paint peeled away like an orange's rind and they came away in slivers, like slices. And as the knife dug deeper, the canvas groaned. Or was it my own ribs resounding with their howl? Was it my own throat that had become constricted? Were my own eyes blurred by all that wine, or perhaps by something else? Did I see blood or red paint, or was there something more? Could I have stopped that bleeding if I had wanted to?

And when I lifted that terrible knife, did the canvas turn to shield itself as I scraped away all of the paint still soft and clinging to the canvas, paint so think it was like mud or clay? And was that clay so truly beautiful, so multi-colored and brilliant, like pieces of an abandoned rainbow fallen from the sky?

Or was the paint gray as mud, brown as muck, the color of the primordial soup, a gray-brown-green color unseen by human eyes for a billion years?

The canvases with images of April I scraped clean with long broad strokes, and those horrifying groans continued. With more long and sweeping strokes the entire swimming pool triptych disappeared, evaporated, removed and cleaned, stroke after stroke, like a motion picture run in reverse. The strokes of the knife canceled each stroke of the paint brush. That contemptible little knife spread a terrible destruction.

When, despite being stripped of their paint, those canvases continued to groan I could not resist the impulse, the compulsion. I stabbed at the canvas to cut out its heart, to sever its entrails, to finish the misery it struggled to resist. Weak and tiny screams rang in my ears. The paint ran off my hands warm and wet. My hands were thick with it, sticky with it. I wiped my hands on the white apartment walls, my hands so thick with the blood and the color and all of that breathing. The canvas sighed and undulated. I scraped and scraped their paint away, and I threw its piles against walls. Wherever my feeble arm found the strength for all of this I cannot say, but I threw load after load of that rainbow. I threw it and I did not care where it landed, there was so much of it. Pieces of that perverted rainbow, shafts and strips, strands of light that landed everywhere, even on the ceiling. There were piles on the rug that resembled excrement. They could have been excreted by the canvases, those canvases might have relieved themselves on the rug.

Onward my massacre went. I was in such a fury that my arm moved with impossible ease, as if it was not my personal arm, or in fact as if I had no arm at all. As if I could simply wish the paint away, nothing else mattered. Wherever I looked, that paint fell away to become piles of brown muck. And my arm moved.

But when I finished scraping every one of those paintings, I could still see the lines on the canvas, the faint pale colors that had soaked into the gesso, like ghosts of ghosts. I scraped again and again but those ghosts remained. The ghosts were there to haunt me, and I could do nothing about them. The canvases refused to surrender their images. I could not pull those images entirely off, I could not scrape them completely away. They existed as a result of my actions, and no effort I made would blot them entirely out. Testimony to my own arrogance, or ignorance, or the vanity to believe I would do what must not be done. They were undeniable evidence of my crimes.

I scraped until eventually my shoulder began to hurt and my fingers curled. At that moment I realized I could do nothing more. The images continued to mock me, and their amusement was so vast they could only remain silent.

To eliminate their evidence, I needed to erase the crime. The accusation of those silent canvases had to be destroyed. Yet their images remained, mocking me, proof of my incompetence, my vanity, my foolishness. They remained, and by enduring they would prevail.

And then I saw it, glinting like old silver in the weak light. It lay with its black handle like a threat. The curve of a scimitar blade, the blade of the avenging angel, the blade that had swept across Europe hacking to pieces all of the miserable holiness, the smug contempt, the useless growths of the failed past. Its crescent shape like the quarter-moon, harbinger of fullness, and also emptiness, the on-coming new moon of blackness, but also the full moon of plenty, light at the beginning of the night, or the end of the day. By some providential movement, the Universe had tossed that knife beside my hand at precisely the moment it was most needed. It lay on the table so seductive. Taken up by my hand it expanded, it lengthened and became razor-sharp. It moved in my hand like a fish; it needed neither help from me nor direction. It understood what needed to be done, as if it had discovered its purpose at precisely the same moment as I had discovered it.

And then those canvases truly screamed. They screamed in a chorus of terror the moment that knife was in my hand. Because they realized there was no hope and that it was too late. The knife pierced the gessoed canvas, cut through the tough cloth, sank deep into the heart of the first canvas. And at that moment all of the canvases groaned. The room shook, a great light flashed before my eyes, I felt the very ground shake. Even as the canvases screamed and cursed, the faces of those dead among the living appeared on their surfaces, their ghosts writhed and howled. But somehow my arm had become huge, the arm of Hercules, and the scimitar blade ripped at the painting's entrails.

I repeated each stroke in the bitter, brassy light of the infinite night. I repeated that movement again and again to slash at the canvas. Their screams grew louder, the earth again shook and trembled. I dragged the blade from one end of the canvas to the other, again and again, while those screams grew to a crescendo. I tore at those canvases and slashed them into strips, watched as those strips fell one after the other onto the hard dark floor. Again and again my huge arm moved. The canvas screamed, and somehow those screams filled my arm with unearthly power.

On I went, from one canvas to the next, the screams roaring in my ears, their flesh dripping over my hand, my beautiful, strong, terrible hand, the hand that knew without thought what next needed to be done. Like sickly, over-rip fruit those canvases spilled their seed onto the rug. Until finally the strips of canvas hung from the stretchers like sinews covered in blood. My hand flew to the next, reduced it to its undisguised self, to its final unalterable shape, reduced and therefore completed, completion identical with destruction and transfiguration, a metamorphosis.

And then finally there was nothing except the tatters, those shreds of canvas pendant like thickly-painted intestines from their wooden stretchers, those bones. So finally there was nearly nothing left except the stretchers, those bones.

I stood for a time, the knife still gripped so tightly, my fingers so fiercely cramped around it that I could not open them. To release the knife I needed to use my free hand to peel back my fingers from its handle. And then the knife laid quiet on the floor, surrounded by the fruit of its work. Bathed with sweat, my arms, my hands and shoulders ached. I had wrestled with Satan himself, and I had won. I had destroyed all that was ugly, all that was hideous and disgusting. And then I discovered my face wet with tears while my mouth was dry. To slack my thirst I reached for the glass of wine and it slipped from that hand which would no longer entirely close, and so it spilled to the floor. I took the bottle by the neck and brought it to my lips, spilled it down my chest, poured it over my head. As it had so many times before, the wine soothed me.

But those canvases finally were dead and I had become relieved of their burden. All was over, I could lay myself down, and perhaps I would even sleep.

Yet how could I sleep? The stretchers still leaned against my walls like a collection of so many skeletons and I found I could not ignore them. Somehow they continued to accuse me, to threaten me and I could not look away. I drank more wine, panting so exhausted I thought I might fall down. It occurred to me that I might still sleep, I might rest, and that I could save the decision of what to do with those stretchers for the next day. And then I realized they must be burned.

I wished to burn them but in the end I conceded it was just as well simply to throw them out. They could no longer harm me so I did not need to do anything more. And after all, I might even save a few fragments, mementos, reminders of the price of folly and the cost of vanity.

My sight began to fade, as if my body had worn down. I looked to recognize there was still something left undone and untouched. And at the sight of it my heart weakened. Could so much be left unmolested? Could all of it be allowed to survive? Or might someone come the next day and collect all that was left? I needed to destroy every shred.

But there was so much. Could I ever destroy all of it? I had done the best part, the part that might be most likely to betray until all that was left was scraps. And could I sleep, and wait until the next day, finish all of it then? I felt suddenly so terribly tired.

But then there was a thud against my front door, followed by a slow, heavy-fisted pounding. I tried to ignore it because it could only announce trouble. But curiousity is a powerful weakness. And then I heard the voice.

"What's going on in there? Don't you want to talk to me?"

And I recognized that voice. When I opened the door Donald filled its frame bleary-eyed and swaying slightly from side to side. Or perhaps we both did.

Donald's crooked smile was almost charming. "I must have come by a half-dozen times, you wouldn't open up. Bang on your door and you wouldn't open up. Bang and no answer. You used to treat your guests better than that." He staggered past me into the apartment. "You're going to tell me I told you so, but I don't care. You're going to love this story."

His face appeared bruised as if someone had hit it several times recently. I said, "I have no fatted calf to offer you, unfortunately." I held out what remained of my bottle of wine. His eyes refused to focus, as if the bottle might be floating in the air. He reached awkwardly but finally grabbed it.

"This is more like it," he said and he took a long drink. When he took the bottle away from his lips his eyes had grown brighter and he looked around. And then he saw them.

He stepped past me and went to the stretchers. I said, "You say you have a story to tell. Well, I have one of my own." And suddenly I could laugh out loud.

Vaguely astonished Donald fingered the strands of canvas that still clung to the stretchers. "This place is a mess." He looked around at the walls, the floor, the stacks of sketchbooks piled, all the remnants of my disaster. As I watched him look about in his amazement, my body began to tremble. My head was clear, yet my hands shook like a palsy victim until I could hardly hold the glass.

As I watched him, fatigue forced me to sit in a chair beside the table. I explained what had happened. I recounted everything, indifferent to whether he approved of what I had done or believed that I had been right. It was all too late for that anyway.

He listened without looking at me. Twice he asked about Vincent's actions and what I told him did not seem to surprise him. And this surprised me. After a long silence he sat down on the floor and stared up at the stretchers. "So, what now? What do you figure you'll do with all this?"

"Burn it!" I said. "All of it. Burn the lot. Every stick and page." Suddenly I felt a tremendous relief. Something had been removed from my eyes and once again I could see.

Donald laughed drunkenly. "Wouldn't that piss off Vince?"

"What difference could that make now? The paintings are gone yet the scraps that remain are still mine. And they appear perfect for burning."

He shook his head with a smile. "Can't blame you. Pissed off and everything. Makes a lot of sense. But how you going to do it?"

I ignored his question and asked how he had gotten beaten up.

"Barbara's brothers have big hands." Donald laughed. "They could've done a lot worse. Big boys, it could've been a lot worse. But I was so mad."

"And you still want her. You told me that you loved her."

He waved his hand over his face and shrugged, but he did not look at me. "For a long time that's what I wanted. That seems a long time ago." He stood slowly and moved until he leaned against the wall at a space between stretchers. "But not that way. Some other way, but she was yes and then no and then yes and then no. If there was any love there I didn't understand it. She was sure she was pregnant and she ran right back to Idaho. She did just what she said she'd never do. She never asked what I wanted or even bothered to pretend to care. Like she always knew I would just pack everything and follow her. That's when I came to see you. Stupid thing to do, but I'd become enchanted by stupid ideas. I was dumb enough or desperate enough to think you could tell me what I should do."

His confession astonished me. Nothing more seemed worth saying.

"When I got to Idaho she seemed relieved to see me, to see that she meant that much to me. Something got through to her, so for a while she convinced herself I was good enough, that I would do. We went to see her family, and I can tell you they weren't glad to see me. I was there three days before I was asked what kind of job I'd get. And of course promising that we'd all be seeing each other often because Barbara and I would live right around the corner from them, which around there was anywhere in a radius of fifty miles. And they were very tolerant of the fact that I have a college degree."

"I have lived among farmers," I said. "It is a narrow world."

"You can say that again. But I decided I'd stick with it a couple of years and when things finally got going good I'd pack Barb and the kid and then we'd come back here. So I spent a lot of time arm-wrestling at the bar, got a job at the sawmill and even went to church on Sundays. And I spent every day refusing to ask myself why. Besides, as stupid as all of this was, their town itself is beautiful. Like nothing you've ever seen. New to me and so beautiful I ended up getting some pencils and a pad, started climbing around in the hills. Made a pile of drawings. But honestly, that's probably all that place is good for. It all looks like God made it just to keep people out. Like it was one place God didn't care if a human ever saw, but He was going to make it a place even He would love."

For a moment his eyes shone brightly, as if seeing and again possessed by that vision.

"There was one place; I'd been wandering in the hills one day, and I crossed a ridge. On the other side the slope descended toward a river three or four miles away. Everywhere ahead of me and all around as far as I could see had been burned out. A few months before there'd been a fire. I walked over the most beautifully terrible place I'd ever seen. I couldn't even describe it to myself, couldn't think of the words for it. But I drew. I drew things I hadn't ever imagined. Some of the best things I've done; thick black lines, hard-edged, and a descending scale of gray tones. Really, I amazed myself. And I kept those sketchbooks. I was going to bring them with me tonight." His eyes gleamed with surprise. "Even now when I look at some of those drawings I'm surprised. Walking out in that forest became a lesson in seeing, as if a layer of something had got peeled off my eyes. After that first day I went out there whenever I got a chance. I spent whole days stumbling over black, burnt-out trees and boulders the size of cars. Maybe it all seemed to mirror my experiences, and life out there managed to imitate art. Or maybe some other thing was going on I didn't understand. All I could do was just stare at it. Just a place to walk over and admire and then move on."

Donald laughed and his grin was painful to look at. The red and blue bruises around his left eye stretched and moved. He touched the cut beside his right eye gingerly.

"Barb's Mom was very happy when she heard that Barb wasn't pregnant. Barb's mother celebrated this news at the bar as if she'd just won the lottery. You can imagine attitudes of the rest of the family changed in other ways."

"And Barbara?"

Donald paused, looked around at the floor and then at his hands. "Put it this way. Barb disappeared into the huddle of her family and friends and that town. Regardless of what she'd said, she'd never really abandoned that life. And I should have realized that. I got one chance to talk to her after the news came out that her pregnancy was a phantom. But we failed even then. She'd never really cared much about the University, or this town, or anything except Idaho. That caught me by surprise. I figured there was a chance she might take off after the baby came, with or without me. But I never figured she'd settle back there. She just faded into the twilight, and then I was left pretty much on my own. At first I decided to stick around to see if she'd change her mind. She still mattered to me, you see? That went on a few weeks, and then a couple of nights ago I was at the bar drinking with her brothers and her father." He pointed to the bruises on his face. "Don't ask how it started because even I can't believe it. Anyway, the next day the father must have had something like an attack of conscience. Maybe it was because of the way my face looked. So the old man stuffed a bunch of bills and a bus ticket into my pocket and drove me to the bus station. He never apologized, and nobody saw me off at the bus."

Donald's eyes moved about the room large and confused.

I said, "You have every right to feel bitter toward those people."

He shrugged. "So what. Who the hell cares? I don't understand anything any more."

Small bright gems appeared at the corners of his eyes. They glistened, but did not fall. As drunk as I was, he managed to surprise me. As if all that he had described had not purged him of his feelings for that woman. I would not have thought he was capable. But who among us can ever know such things?

After a moment he added, "But even with the stupid job at the sawmill I had a lot of time on my hands. And now I've got a sketchbook full of nice drawings. Pretty good for five months work." He paused then turned to study the stretchers again.

He did not turn to look at me when he said, "I came by to see if I could sort of, you know, work on those drawings with you. Maybe even do a little painting. With you, I mean. I came by to tell you about what I've been working on. I thought you might like to know." He grinned. He wanted my approval. And I suppose I wanted to shake his hand, pat him on the back. I wanted to tell him that he had made the right choice and it was a wonderful thing. Yet, in the face of all that had happened to both of us, how could I assure him of anything?

I asked, "Have you decided to throw the rest of your life away? You are unhappy with this woman, I understand this. But is this your justification? Whatever you decide, do not put the responsibility for that on me. What you hope for is a difficult thing, but you take its decision lightly. You take up painting because a woman has made you unhappy. I am not impressed."

His head wobbled drunkenly and his smile grew. "You're so full of shit!"

"And do you now understand everything? If that is the case, why have you come to me? How do you expect me to help you? Because if you ask, I have no help to offer you. This should be obvious, just look around you. There is nothing I can do for you or for anyone, even myself."

With a look of injured feeling he said, "You could start by taking a look at my stuff." His expression darkened, eyes narrowed, he was completely earnest. "Tell me what you think of it. Not like those other times, feeding me all that bullshit. This time at least you could be honest. You could do that. Or tell me I've just wasted my time."

The clouds in my head had thickened, like a soup left too long on the fire. My mind had dulled and become heavy, as if it would no longer move. It struggled against some constraint. I thrashed and pulled, but the grip of those clouds only tightened. Somehow I had become bound down with my arms and legs trussed by something inexplicable.

Donald asked, "You want me to make a deal with you? Is that it? I'm supposed to agree to something, and then you'll look at my stuff?"

I shrugged. "My request is not large, and I promise it will not prove onerous to someone as strong as you are. A simple request and it will demand only a little of your time or your strength."

He studied me as if considering whether to hear me out so I decided to explain further. "You have helped me for a long time. Believe me when I tell you that I remain grateful for all of your help. But in your absence I have found myself even more grateful. Your excursion, in fact, has only increased my gratitude and respect for what you have done. So I promise to look at your drawings because I want to see them. And because I have never been able to look away."

His face smoothed and he grinned, and then his grin widened.

"All I ask in return," I continued, "is that you just get these dead stretchers out of here. Take them out along with the sketchbooks and paints and brushes."

His grin disappeared, replaced by something bewildered. He turned and paced slowly before the wrecked stretchers. "So this is what it's all about, right? Death and truth and some kind of purified weirdness. Have I got it right yet?" He turned away shaking his head. "You must be really pissed off with Vince."

"He believes I am too weak to resist. What else can I do?"

"You call this resistance? Looks more like suicide to me. Or is that word too informal?"

"We are wasting words, and time. I need to know if you will help me. Get on with it or step aside, because I still have much to do."

He shrugged. "You really have gone crazy."

"Tell me just one thing. Had you been in Vincent's position, would you have done what he did?"

He hesitated and then looked away. "Maybe I would have. But what does that matter? You don't have any choice now. You could've avoided all this if you'd just gone along with the show in the first place. That's something I'll never understand. In a million years I'll never understand."

"At least," I said with a gust of relief, "you are capable of admitting you do not understand. You have sufficient depth of spirit to make such an admission. If only Vincent had been so capable, or so courageous."

Donald came to stand in front of me. His eyes were bloodshot red; how did he manage to keep them open? Those cuts and bruises, his drunkenness, his entire life was etched there on his face. Quietly he said, "So just tell me one more thing. What happens after all of this? What happens when we've dumped everything and it's all gone? Just tell me where you expect we'll go from here."

I had to turn away. Something inside me began to struggle. Something crawled up into my throat and into my chest and face. I felt my face twist to push it away, but it would not go. There was nothing to do but surrender. So I began to laugh.

"You know, I am flattered that you use that word 'we'." He stared at me as I continued to laugh. I gasped for breath, became dizzy from the effort. "But honestly, I have no answer to that." He became preoccupied with his confusion. I waited as long as I could. "In any case, no matter what the future holds, I have no more time. Leave me alone and allow me to finish what I have started."

His look darkened as if he suspected he was being mocked. "You've really gone crazy. But do whatever you want, because I don't care any more."

Hearing this I laughed even more. "And there you are wrong, my friend. What I need now is exactly a man who no longer cares. But that man is not you. You are still committed to something. Something prevents you from helping me by doing what I ask. Very well, clear out and leave me alone." From my chair I looked up suddenly light-headed and reached for my glass of wine. He remained standing before me surrounded by those desecrated stretchers now watching us.

He said, "At least let me stay and watch. It'll make a good story someday."

"There will be nothing to watch." I refilled my glass. "With these hands, it will all demand rather a long time. To break those stretchers, I mean. And those stretchers need to be broken." When the wine reached my stomach a wave of something warm washed over me clouding my eyes.

Hands in pockets, Donald turned to wander among the stretchers, toed each with his shoe. To his back I said, "A fire, after all, needs firewood."

Donald shook his head; a slow, half-annoyed movement, like a man awakening from a long confused sleep. "Stretchers," he muttered, "all broken up. That's all you want me to do." He lifted one with his hand and held it, a tattered and shredded sail. At that moment I recalled watching him assemble them so long ago, both of us then bright with promise. With his sleepy look of disinterest he flexed the piece of wood, moved its ends back and forth easily. "You know, they put sick people on stretchers, too." With a quick movement he slapped it against his upraised knee. The wood snapped loudly, its broken ends showing jagged and raw yellow.

He turned to me with a smile. "Like that?" He took up another side of the stretcher and with the same quick motion broke it into two pieces. Like matchsticks, with impassive industry he proceeded to break one after another until he had done the same to every one. And with each of those pieces of wood festooned with shreds of pale and soiled canvas, something burdensome and confining fell away from me. As if a great thick chain was dropping from my arms and legs, link by link.

When finally all lay broken in a pile on the floor he and I gathered them up, along with the drawings, the stacks of sketchbooks, the tubes of paint, jars and cans filled with turpentine and spirits, paint brushes and rags. Armload after armload, slowly we carried all of it to a wide and empty area of the patio beside our swimming pool.

We worked together in silence in that open space of concrete, the scene of so many hours of pleasure. The air had become fresh and cool and it awakened me. I shivered as I walked, the hour was very late. The sky above us was black and silver-starred, but the deepest blue nimbus began to edge the eastern horizon that announced the coming of dawn. When we had brought all of it down from my apartment I took a great and vivifying breath. For a moment my head emerged from its opaque fog. For a moment everything that had confused me suddenly became clear and bright and perfect. Even Vincent's activities acquired a crystalline clarity.

Donald laid the pieces of stretchers across each other, and then he laid the sketchbooks over the pieces of canvas. On top of these he stacked tubes of paint, brushes, everything else. When he finished making this tall pile I emptied the cans and jars of turpentine, paint-remover and spirits over all of it. A soft breeze sprang up and its lightly moving breath of air flowed past us. Above the odor of those chemical fluids and paints I detected the combined scent of horse manure, thick honeysuckle, and brine.

From my pocket I brought out a packet of paper matches. I tore off one, tried to strike it, but suddenly a hand emerged from the darkness. That hand engulfed my own. "You really mean to burn all of this?" Donald was all but invisible except for his hand in our darkness.

I pulled my hand from his. "Of course!" But he gripped harder, twisted my fingers into each other, crushed them together until I felt pain.

"Are you really sure you want to do this?" I could not make out his face clearly, the upper half of his body was wrapped entirely in black shadow. I laughed.

"Release my hand," I said, "and see what I do." His grip relaxed slightly but there was still no way I could wrestle free of him. We waited, and then I could see his eyes; light from somewhere glinted and his eyes emerged from the darkness. He released my hands, stepped back and his shadow shrank to human size.

Still, it was difficult to start that fire. The first match blew out in the breeze, as did the next. And even when finally the stack began to burn I had to touch it off at several places. Small, weak, almost pitiful flames trembled still vulnerable to a sudden gust. I stood trembling as well from an unaccountable chill and watched as those tiny flames begin to lick timidly. For a moment I feared that even at this endeavor I would miserably fail.

Then, as if the Devil himself had suddenly stood up, a tremendous and furious flame leaped reaching high as it pierced the black sky. Everything around us became bathed in orange and gold and red. Thick black smoke billowed but then flattened before the wind. The flames reached higher, surging, growing larger until the fire became enormous, roaring as its heat washed over us like a wind from Hell.

The brassy flame reached higher while the entire pile began to burn. The flames broadened, their heat covered us splashing against my face and over my body. Perhaps because of its source, that heat soothed me as it began to sear closed my many scars. Even my leg began to feel more limber. Those flames burned suddenly brighter, as if they had discovered a fuel even more to their liking. Heat broke over us in waves. It blew against my chest as if the flames wanted to lap at my heart. In that heat the muscles of my body became stronger. Even my hands. I held them up before that light, watched them thicken until their tendons were firm, and then all pain disappeared as if the fire was washing them clean of pain, washing away even the memory of pain. Flames licked between my fingers until their pain disappeared.

I stared at my fingers and at the red and yellow tongues that licked between them. I watched mystified and delighted, amused beyond my expectation. This was all going very well and I was delighted.

Then, at the very heart of this conflagration, I saw it. Round and small as a bird's egg, I saw the purest white light I have ever imagined. That sphere of white light in the center of the orange and red and gold, began to grow. From an egg shape it gradually became perfectly round. And it continued to grow until it was the size of a peach, and then the size of a small melon. As it grew its roundness became more perfect. The whiteness of the light was brilliant. And then it grew still larger. That pure white light took on a silver sheen, as if it might be cooler than the fire around it; as if the fire purified it, taking away whatever was gross and incomplete, leaving only that whiteness of perfect contemplation. The white light flared suddenly, became even larger and its brilliance hurt my eyes. So I closed my eyes in order to continue to study that gorgeous light, to contemplate and admire it. Through my closed eyes I studied its harmony, its subtle self-consistency, its perfection of purity. Finally, a kind of perfection had been achieved, just that perfection for which I had struggled.

At that moment I discovered an overwhelming need to possess utterly and completely that pure light. Only its perfection and nothing more. As if the shimmering perfection of this light could annul or erase or expunge every other imperfection, complete every incompletion. The whiteness of that light contained every color it is possible to desire, every shade and each nuance, each reflection and every refraction of every light from every source or substance. That sphere of pure light hovered coolly over the heart of the flames. And the flames began to speak. In a language I had never heard before, nor was I even certain I was hearing then, that light spoke to me. And the light spoke approvingly. It approved of what I had done and congratulated me on my decision. And then the light invited me to possess it. The light invited me to take it up and carry it away to a place where it would teach me and comfort me and delight me. The light spoke to me with complete confidence. I would begin again, it said, as if until now I had known nothing. With the help of the light all would be made clear. I need simply reach out for this sphere of perfect beauty. It promised that by intense and subtle contemplation I would unlock every secret. All of this was offered to me by that light, that terrifying, perfect light. All I need do was take it up.

So I reached. I reached slowly forward, fearful of the heat. But the voice calmed my fear. The heat would do no harm. The fire could only purify. What remained would be itself perfect; a perfection which I would eventually comprehend through its contemplation. I reached further. As they moved forward, my hands and fingers became supple. They grew long and muscled and alert. All apprehension dropped away from me. I need only reach further and further toward that light even as it grew toward me.

Suddenly a voice that was not the voice of the flames said, "Wait!"

I reached still further as the light grew softer and cooler, and that other voice, cried, "Wait!"

The light's coolness kissed my fingertips. For one moment my hands reached around the perfect, bright sphere and then grasped it. For one moment my hands closed over that sphere of cool and perfect light. For one moment my fingers embraced its perfection. For one moment my closed eyes were blinded, and for one dying moment that perfect light belonged to me alone. I held it in my hands as carefully and joyfully as if it was my child.

The other voice, that other voice, again cried, "Wait!" Suddenly the light shriveled and then withdrew its perfect whiteness, retreated, dying, fading into perfect blackness, dying into that other absolute purity, the purity of black.

CHAPTER THIRTY–FIVE

FROM THE WINDOW before my desk I look down on the roof of the venerable Academy of Music. The roof is covered in black. I do not know what material it is, although if I asked Howard, our building superintendent, he would tell me. Despite the pimples on his face, the narrowness of his forehead, and his knobby, long-fingered hands, Howard knows about many things.

The roof of the Academy is oddly-angled. There is a cupola at its peak around which flocks of gray, diseased pigeons swoop and soar. The roof falls away in asymmetrical planes, each a different size and tipped at a different angle. I like that roof most when it rains. It glitters a gleaming black and it becomes a beautiful object of contemplation.

My view beyond the roof of the Academy of Music is of the city's skyline toward the west and the setting sun. Before me and reaching almost to the horizon I see low, flat roofs of the same black, interrupted by the broad green crowns of the trees of a small park, followed beyond by more flat black roofs, while scattered like exclamation points I see the pale steeples of churches. Much to my surprise, there appear to be many churches here.

To my right and half-hidden behind several office buildings and therefore only partially visible to me, is City Hall, a most impressive and depressing structure. For its partial-visibility I am quite grateful, since it is a grotesquely ornate confection of a building. At the peak of its tallest tower stands a Calder statue of a man wearing a hat and holding a scroll of paper in his hand. Beneath him is the huge, round yellow face of a clock. Although half-visible from my apartment, the drone of its tolling bells is an insistent reminder of the passage of time, a most deplorable effect that is also reassuring. If I forget that time continues to pass, those bells ringing at the hour and then the half-hour drone even into the walls and floor of my apartment.

Below me at my feet is a broad boulevard, an artery of travel that could just as appropriately be called Busy Street, because even at midnight, pedestrians and automobiles pass along it with a conspicuous sense of purpose. But I am contentedly situated. With a glance through my window I am reassured; this world has not died, life continues, hard-working men walk home, climb slow stairs with newspapers tucked under arms, or women amble with children, or young couples stroll out for an evening's entertainment. And on various evenings, crowds gather on the steps of the Academy bathed by bright lights, lights of this city, lights that dance exuberant as children. Occasionally there are sirens of officials racing to murders and fires which shatter the background drone and at every hour. These sounds provide a kind of fluid, another sort of medium for life, yet life none the less. As for the weather, the winter here is very cold, and the summer is distressingly hot and humid. Yet it remains true, physical discomfort is another sort of reassurance.

Martin arranged a teaching position for me at the College of Art only a few blocks away in a building easily seen from my window. Two old friends from Manhattan are also members of its faculty, and I suspect they were also at least partly responsible for the invitation to join the College. They visit me now and again, their concern is unambiguous, and they ask questions to which I can reply honestly. To be honest, I am relieved to be at this College.

As a result of the fire I spent three months in the University's hospital recovering, at least as much as was possible. Those were days and nights bathed in blissful helplessness, a sort of coma of the spirit. And then Martin visited. I had been found guilty of committing an unpardonable sin, and the University's administration had been scandalized. Martin informed me that I would not be invited to return to their faculty. No one else from the University called me. No one. Disillusionment is a costly exercise.

So now I conduct two classes each week at the Art College; one, a lecture on art history, and the other a lecture on art theory and criticism. Just imagine. Thirty or so bright young minds busily becoming perverted by my lies,

my postures and my prejudices, as if any of these might be of any value or
significance. But I give these out freely, since they are of no interest to me.

But my hands. Three months in hospital, the doctors performed four
operations, or so I was told. Why they waited until they had tried four times
before telling me I would never draw or paint again I do not understand. I
could have told them this at the start. But they tried very hard, really, and I
suppose I should be grateful. Indeed, I suppose I am grateful.

And then there is Donald. Surprisingly he decided to follow me here.
I fear sometimes that he is here out of guilt, as if he should have prevented
what happened but had not. After being arrested for starting the fire, he was
expelled from the University. The administrators consider him persona non
grata; the fact that the University insists he no longer exists is of considerable
interest to us both. Although he is now enrolled at the Art College, wisely he
attends none of my lectures. That, after all, is course material he has already
covered. He takes classes in painting and drawing, and he lives very close by.
From time to time he stops here to rest and talk and see how I am getting
along. I believe he has a girlfriend somewhere nearby as well. I have not yet
been introduced to her, but I feel quite certain of her existence. He claims his
work continues to progress, occasionally he even shows it to me. In any case he
appears nearly satisfied, if not quite happy.

And my hands. When the doctors finally admitted that they would be
forever nearly useless, they provided me a pair of beautiful black leather gloves.
To cover the scares, they said. But such a shame to hide them, those scares are
really quite amazing. My fingers are pink as fresh shrimp, and the pale veins
of scar tissue are as intricate as fine lace. I wear the gloves only as a courtesy
to others. Because they do not need to see the scars, they are of no value to
anyone except me. And really, I am the only person who might benefit from
them. Greetings Herr Markel; you have won after all.

I received a letter from Marla some months ago, her only communication
and undoubtedly her last. After the conventional pieties and expressions of
sympathy she mentioned that Vincent planned an exhibition of her work.
This tells me something. She is very excited by this prospect, she said,
and then she was prolific in her expressions of gratitude for my help and
encouragement, etc. She ended her letter by suggesting she might come here
to visit. Her threat casts no fear in my heart. I expect never to see her again.
And that fact gives me no pleasure either, only a false sense of security. As a

postscript, she mentioned that April had become engaged to be married. A young photographer from Los Angeles has discovered her. April anticipates a successful career. A pleasant irony, since I have become something of a photographer. In any case, I will not wish all of them success, only sanctuary from despair.

Sometime between the second and third operations on my hands, Martin came to see me at the University's hospital. His face was gray and he did not look at all well. I said, "What is wrong with you? Would you like to move in here next to me? Or are you disappointed that you will not witness my last rites?" He did not smile. Though as is usual for Martin he was perfectly attired, but with his hat in his hand and that expression on his face he looked very much like any other tired old man. In that clean precise white hospital room, an old man stood by the door gloomily regarding an old man in the bed. Pathetic.

"My friend," Martin said, "I hope that you are happy." I said nothing, waiting for Martin and the words that would follow. "Your exhibition has been a great success. If it had not been for the fire, I cannot imagine what would have happened. But every day people come to see your work. And when I tell you how many paintings you have sold, you will call me a liar."

"That was my secret plan all along," I said. "And my calculations have proved correct. It has all happened just as I expected." I smiled, or attempted to smile. Behind my bandages I do not know if Martin saw my smile, or perhaps only heard it in my voice.

"Laugh if you wish," Martin said, "but I have already sold all of the paintings which you had authorized for sale. You may guess how much money that amounts to. I hope you are proud of yourself. And I hope your disaster is somewhat compensated."

"Do not toy with me. My attempt to stop that exhibition was a failure. My work has been stolen and I have become an art-world freak, a novelty of one more circus. Your stack of money does not cheer me."

"Bah!" Martin said waving his hand as he dragged a chair to my bedside. "You talk as usual, and as usual you make no sense. Have they given you any drugs for the pain?"

I nodded. "But not enough. Certainly not enough to heal my heart. Do me a favor and speak to the doctors about that."

Again Martin shook his head. "There are not enough drugs for that. Now listen to me, my friend, for I have come on a mission of business. I want your permission to sell the others. Those paintings you wished held aside; I want your permission to sell those as well."

"Permission granted," I said. "Is there anything else on your mind?"

Martin's eyes grew large, flooded by a bit of fear perhaps. He had anticipated a battle, and I had failed him. After a long pause he said, "I do not expect to sell them all. So tell me now, which of them would you like held aside for you?"

"You ask a difficult question. To be honest, none of them." I paused to assure him I was serious. "Yes, that is my honest answer. Sell them all."

Again Martin waved his hand. This gesture annoyed me. "Believe me; sulking will not improve your situation. You will not heal any faster by being petulant. I have asked a civilized question, and I expect your civilized answer."

"Sell them all. That is my civilized answer."

Martin stood from his chair then. His hat still hanging from his hand he walked slowly to my window and looked out. "The sun shines very nicely today. Perhaps with the money you have earned from these sales you might take up permanent residence, despite the University. It might be possible to arrange a teaching position at another institution nearby." Still without turning he continued, "I know several people, and there are phone calls I could make." I said nothing. Finally he turned to face me. "Ah well, just a thought. In any case, I have much better connections back east. We'll find you something, old man, one way or the other. You must not concern yourself about that." He returned to his chair, placed his hat on the bed and sat down. "Now I will ask you once more. Which of the paintings would you like kept aside for you?"

"Please avoid being tedious, Martin. I am in no condition to spar with you. Sell them all, or any that you wish. Just spare me the details."

Gradually a kind of pain crept over Martin's face. Something that resembled a tortured grimace which I could not quite decipher moved from the edges of his face to his eyes and then to his mouth. "If you wish to punish me for my indiscretion, you have already succeeded admirably. I recognize that I cannot restore what you have lost, and you must recognize this as well. But at some point our war must end. Each side must tally its losses and bury its dead. No more daydreams, my friend. Help me to know how I can help you." He paused again and looked away. "I intend to put aside five canvases for you. So now you must tell me which they should be."

I did not know whether to be flattered or annoyed. "Any which you cannot sell."

"Basta!" he shouted. "In another moment I will forget that you are wrapped in bandages gravely ill, and I will beat you senseless. You are not satisfied that I admit my guilt, my terrible sorrow. You are not satisfied with anything I say or do. You wish to punish me further, am I correct? Perhaps I should set myself on fire, too? Would that please you? Would you finally be happy?"

Suddenly he snatched his hat from my bed, took several steps toward the door. "The drugs, it can only be the drugs. You talk out of your head and I can make no sense of it." He stopped and then shook his head. "Listen to me. What if I gave all of the money back to all of the people who have bought your work? Would that satisfy you? Is that what you want? I will get back all of the canvases and give all of the money back. Will that be sufficient? Because all I have ever done is try to sell your paintings for you, so that you might have a little money. Obviously I have been wrong. Obviously that is not what you want. Well and good, I will do as you wish. You remain poor but pure. Does that please you? I am sorry I ever sold even a single one of your works. I should have kept them all in a box. I should have bought a warehouse and kept them all there. That would have pleased you, am I right? Such a fool I have been, how hard I have worked to see money for your work. Yes, you are right and I have been a fool. There is nothing more to do except demand that your paintings be returned and the money given back to their owners." He remained with one hand on the door handle staring, nose flared and breathing hard.

I said nothing. It was as if my mouth had ceased to operate. There seemed nothing more for me to say. There was a hollowness in my chest which I would not release but I clung to it like a life rope. Martin turned then and studied me from the door as if waiting for me to speak. And I did not.

He took his hand from the door, slowly he returned bent nearly double as he walked, feet dragging, to the chair beside my bed. Poor Martin looked suddenly so tired. He sat down and sighed.

After a pause he said, "My friend, we have grown old, you and I, but we have not grown sentimental enough. We have forgotten many things that are not important, but we have failed to learn those things that matter. I say we have grown old and soft in the head, but we have not grown soft in the heart. No, we have not learned such a thing. More's the pity for all of that."

He looked at me as if waiting for me to speak. When I still said nothing he stood again. "Think about what I have told you. I will hold out five canvases. If you do not decide which they should be, I will make that decision. We cannot turn back the clock, not on anything, not for any reason. This much I, at least, have learned. And if you have learned anything at your age, you should have learned this, too."

He stood and walked again to the door. When he reached it he turned. "I will return tomorrow. Perhaps when you have had the chance to think about these things we can talk together seriously."

Was it the shape of his back as he walked to the door? Perhaps it was the way his thin yellow hand rested lightly on the chrome door handle. Or perhaps it was the way he held his hat, four fingers within the crown, thumb curling the brim back, hat and hand hanging together from a straight arm by his side.

I said, "You need only hold out three canvases. There are only three that still have any value to me."

He stood for a moment, hand still on the door handle, and now looking at the door. "I will hold five for you, my friend."

"I ask that three be held for me. I have no use for the others. Sell the others, but hold three for me," and then I named them. I did not need to describe those paintings, Martin knew which I meant. "Just those and sell the others, and then there will be that much more money. You are right, as usual. I will need all of that money, too. Although for a man such as yourself, with such enormous wealth at your disposal, what could you do with even more money?"

Martin turned and looked up at me with narrowed eyes, perhaps to see through my bandages, to see my face, to see me smiling. And then he too smiled. With a flick of his wrist he sailed his hat toward me. It landed on my chest. "You are no-good. You are a bad man, fortunate to have reached your present age without someone having already killed you. But there is always tomorrow. But beware, because no matter how old, there is always tomorrow." He opened the door saying, "In any case, if no one kills you I will be back tomorrow. To fetch my hat." And then he was gone.

Those three canvases now hang in this apartment. I am not certain this is so very good, but I enjoy an odd reassurance that they are here. And they make very quiet companions.

Since I moved here, Martin has come down from Manhattan about once every two months. We have opportunities to talk and I find his interest in my well-being curiously reassuring as well. Perhaps he is right that I have grown old without understanding.

While in hospital I lost a great deal of weight. Skin now hangs in folds from my arms, my chest and stomach. And there are the scars; a part of my face, my neck and my arms. And of course there are the scars on my hands. I undress before my mirror with electric lights burning brightly. Perhaps this bent and scared body might be of some interest to a circus.

On the window-sill beside the commode in my bathroom I keep a small camera. Each time I excrete I take a photograph of what I have created. They float primly in their white porcelain bowl, perfect subjects for photographic reproduction. I also keep a notebook in which I note down dates, times of day, approximate times of duration, and then some general comments, speculations about meaning and significance. This, at least, is something these crippled fingers do not prevent me from doing.

About every two weeks I bring the completed roll of film to the drugstore across the street. When I leave the film for processing I purchase a fresh roll, and always from the same clerk. A tall thin man of some indeterminate middle-age, he wears a thin black moustache and a false hair piece that is the wrong color. When I had left film with him several times he found the temerity to ask what my photographs were of.

"Grandchildren," I said. He has asked nothing more since.

But I am certain he knows. I am certain he has looked inside my envelope of processed photographs, and he knows. He gives me mistrustful looks whenever I go there. He does not like me, of this I am certain. For a time I thought to take my film to another store, but I decided that no matter where I might bring it, sooner or later another clerk would become curious, and that clerk would become displeased with me as well, while the clerk across the street is already disgusted with me. Why upset another clerk somewhere else? I do not like this man any more than he likes me. Earnestly, I hope he becomes nauseous each time he looks into my envelope of photographs. Besides, he has abysmal taste in clothing.

After more than a year I have accumulated several boxes of photographs and a very thick journal. Appropriate for someone who teaches art history and theory. The research I have begun will continue for years more and already I find its documentation formidable. Classification and cross-indexing alone could consume the rest of my days. No doubt I have begun a project which will need the rest of my life to complete.

Unfortunately, the most difficult and painful part of this project is the effort needed to get onto my knees in order to take these photographs.

I have a theory.

A.W. DEANNUNTIS lives in Philadelphia, Pennsylvania and has published fiction in periodicals that include *Philadelphia Short Stories, Silent Voices, The Armchair Aesthete, Timber Creek Review, Lynx Eye, Los Angeles Review, Yemassee, First Class, Pacific Coast Journal, Short Stories Bimonthly, Luna Negra, CrossConnect, Spout, The Iconoclast, North Atlantic Review, Nite-Writer's International, Onionhead, Nuthouse, Mind in Motion* (Pushcart Prize nomination), *Kiosk, Cimarron Review, California Quarterly, Dog River Review* and *Coe Review*, as well as the novel *Master Siger's Dream* (2011) with What Books Press. A video of the author reading at the Philadelphia Free Library Book Festival, 2011 can be found on the YouTube website.

www.ingramcontent.com/pod-product-compliance
Lightning Source LLC
Chambersburg PA
CBHW031951120726
47898CB00002BA/332